K'S E
1220
Roc
853-

D0283944

WORDS FROM THE HEART

Matt shut Maggie up then, not with words, but with his mouth, all but smothering her with a kiss that seared right through to her soul. She understood somehow that Matt's passion came from within himself. Then again, maybe she just wanted to believe his kiss and the flames that it touched off were ignited by a mutual desire, not by sheer physical need that could have been sated anywhere, by anyone. Not that allowing herself to believe Matt actually desired her made a lot of sense to Maggie—he could just as easily been driven by a sense of guilt or pity, and not the genuine lust she herself felt.

She knew but one thing for sure at the moment—the sudden awakening of her desire had a single source; the man himself. The very fever of being near Matt threatened to consume her, and had done so, she realized, since the moment she'd first looked at him as a man, and not simply the means to an end. The thought shocked, terrified and confused her so, she pushed away from him, robbing herself of what she desperately needed.

The moment her lips left his, Matt came after her again, this time assaulting her senses with his words.

"Just in case you're wondering, Maggie," he said, "make no mistake about what just happened here. That was no accident, my kissing you. I've wanted to do that since before you sent me after Rafe Hollister."

BOOK YOUR PLACE ON OUR WEBSITE
AND MAKE THE
READING CONNECTION!

We've created a customized website just for our very special readers, where you can get the inside scoop on everything that's going on with Zebra, Pinnacle and Kensington books.

When you come online, you'll have the exciting opportunity to:

- View covers of upcoming books
- Read sample chapters
- Learn about our future publishing schedule (listed by publication month *and author*)
- Find out when your favorite authors will be visiting a city near you
- Search for and order backlist books from our online catalog
- Check out author bios and background information
- Send e-mail to your favorite authors
- Meet the Kensington staff online
- Join us in weekly chats with authors, readers and other guests
- Get writing guidelines
- AND MUCH MORE!

Visit our website at
http://www.zebrabooks.com

MAGGIE'S WISH

Sharon Ihle

Zebra Books
Kensington Publishing Corp.
http://www.zebrabooks.com

For my favorite "Zonies"—Don and Leona Flowers.
And for Cecil and Arlis Crews—because I'd never
hear the end of it if they weren't mentioned, too.

ZEBRA BOOKS are published by

Kensington Publishing Corp.
850 Third Avenue
New York, NY 10022

Copyright © 1998 by Sharon Ihle

All rights reserved. No part of this book may be reproduced
in any form or by any means without the prior written consent
of the Publisher, excepting brief quotes used in reviews.

If you purchased this book without a cover you should be
aware that this book is stolen property. It was reported as "un-
sold and destroyed" to the Publisher and neither the Author
nor the Publisher has received any payment for this "stripped
book."

Zebra and the Z logo Reg. U.S. Pat. & TM Off.

First Printing: December, 1998
10 9 8 7 6 5 4 3 2 1

Printed in the United States of America

Special thanks to Alicia K. Fribert, my scaly critter expert, and the wonderful, warm, and very informed folks at the Sharlot Hall Museum and Visitor's Center in Prescott, AZ.

One

If ever a woman was born to spinsterhood, it was Maggie Hollister.

She was as plain as a buttermilk biscuit, tall enough to know that a man was going bald before he did, and just a few months shy of her thirtieth birthday. Even if she wasn't known around town as the wronged wife of a chronically truant husband—and therefore unavailable—Maggie had no doubt she'd be facing her personal crucible the same way she had for the last seven years. Alone. She didn't quite possess the attributes most men looked for in a woman. Not if he intended to have more than a passing interest, anyway.

Luckily for Maggie, the last thing she wanted these days was another man. In fact she wasn't even sure she wanted the one she could rightfully claim. What she wanted—*needed*—was someone to help ease the burden of raising a fatherless child.

The load began to pile up a few weeks back the way it always did this time of year, about the time fall was mixing the paint to wash the leaves in shades of rust and vibrant yellow. Maggie had been helping her young daughter to hoe her little pumpkin patch, a simple gardening task that turned into such a heart-wrenching spectacle, she had to run and hide in the kitchen to keep Holly from seeing her tears. What Maggie had begun so long ago as a ritual hope, had evolved into a cruel reminder of the inevitable anguish to come—Halloween was just around the corner, which meant "the season of sorrow" was hot on its heels.

Maggie vowed that day to do something this year to turn things around, to make the holidays right for little Holly before they were ruined forever. This Christmas would be different from all the others, the best ever, God willing. Never again would she watch helplessly as her daughter's tears fell on Christmas morning. Nevermore would she endure the agony of explaining the virtually unexplainable—why Santa Claus continued to refuse Holly the only gift she'd ever wished for. Her very own daddy.

As she pondered these things and her ideas for setting them right, Maggie cleaned up after the breakfast crowd and set each of the eight yellow and white tablecloths with clean napkins and forks. Diners at Gus's Squat and Gobble Cafe had to ask for a knife if they wanted one, but only got it if they could prove to Gus that he'd cooked them up something too tough to cut with the edge of a fork.

Maggie's duties at the restaurant included baking the breads, cakes, and pies that accompanied each meal, but she also stocked and oversaw the small bakery set up near the front door of the restaurant. In addition to those chores, she was the only waitress in the place except on the rare occasions her aunt came by to help out. Normally Hattie, who was raising the turkeys Gus fed his customers, was too busy to be bothered with serving them, too.

Maggie was just filling a ceramic salt shaker shaped like a turkey when the door opened behind her, setting off the "new customer" bell. She turned to see Sheriff Ben Sloan standing there, hat in hand. His eyes were twinkling, secretive.

"Morning, Maggie girl," he said with a wink.

"Morning, Ben. Be right with you."

He knew something. Maggie would have bet a month's wages on it. Something good. Her hands began to shake so badly as she tried to finish filling the salt shaker, she got more salt on the table than she did in the ceramic bird. In all of Prescott, Sheriff Sloan was the person she most trusted outside of her own family. And in some ways, even more. Maggie had enough faith in Ben to ask for his help, and he'd promised to solve the problem, if possible. Now every nerve in her body screamed that he'd done just that.

When she approached him, she couldn't help but ask, "Is it good news, Ben? Did you find someone?"

He took a fast glance around the cafe. "Let's go sit a spell before we get to talking about my news. Won't do to have Gus popping up unexpected-like."

Maggie knew that the kitchen door was closed tight and that Gus, who was busy filling a huge kettle for the supper crowd with his famous son-of-a-gun stew, couldn't overhear what they had to say to one another. Still, Ben had a very good point.

Taking the extra precaution of keeping her voice low, she said, "We can use the corner table by the window. Would you like some coffee and an apple dumpling or something?"

"Martha just stuffed me from here to New Year's with a pile of her acorn slapjacks," he said with a groan. "I ain't got room for another bite."

"Well, then . . ." Maggie's hands were suddenly damp. She wiped her palms against her soiled apron. "Let's sit down."

Once they were settled at the table, she didn't waste any more time. "So how is . . . everything?"

"Like I said, Martha is still feeding me up like I was a starving kid—hey, don't you want to hear about my news?"

Maggie loved the man like a father, but at times, Ben Sloan could be thicker than pancake batter. "Why else would I be sitting here staring at you like a hound on a jackrabbit?" she said impatiently. "Did you find a tracker for me or not?"

He colored a little, making her feel guilty, but Maggie wasn't about to take eight steps backwards by apologizing for her sharp tongue. Making amends would only set Ben off on a whole other subject.

"I rounded up something better than a tracker," he boasted with a thorny smugness. "In fact, this particular fella's so good, he could hunt down a whisper in a thunderstorm."

He *had* done it! Ben had actually made enough progress to set her plan in motion at last. Maggie wasn't at all sure how she would feel when it came time to put wheels on the second part of her scheme, but for now, the fact that she actually had a tracker was good enough.

"This fella," she said. "He isn't some kind of gunfighter, is he? I won't do business with a criminal type."

"Not to worry, gal. I rangered with this fella's father back during the Comanche wars, and he followed in his father's footsteps. For you," he said proudly, "I rounded up nothing less than a Texas Ranger, a captain recently retired from service."

"Retired?" Suddenly, Maggie was less than impressed with Ben's work. Her shoulders slumped right along with her spirits as she said, "You know that my husband isn't much older than I am, Ben, and that he'll probably give anyone who comes after him a hard time. I thought for sure you'd find someone a little younger than . . ." Too late, Maggie realized where her thoughts and words were headed.

"Younger than me, is that what you meant to say?"

"Oh, Ben, I didn't mean that at all."

She did of course, and they both knew it. If he hadn't been so instrumental in civilizing Prescott to its present peaceful state, Ben Sloan would have been put out to pasture years ago. As it was, Territorial Marshal Dake, and Ben's two young deputies handled the tougher jobs, leaving the easier tasks for him, duties like keeping peace between the drunkards who frequented Whisky Row. Not that keeping an unfit lawman like

Ben in office ever stirred up debates among the townsfolk. They all considered Sheriff Sloan to be as much a landmark in Prescott as Thumb Butte, a rock-ribbed monolith just west of town.

At the moment, the living landmark with the thinning gray hair and weather-carved features was silently forgiving Maggie her unintended slight. Ben smiled. Both understanding and deep affection were shining in his aging blue eyes. Then he cleared his throat and gruffly explained his choice of tracker.

"You ought to be happy to know, Mrs. Finicky, that the word *retired* in the case of this ranger don't mean old. He gave up the badge and hard chases because of a bum leg, shotgun to the hip, if I recollect."

Maggie didn't see how a crippled lawman could be appreciatively better than an old one, but she withheld her opinion and urged Ben to continue. "If he's gunshot, how can you be sure he's up to the job?"

"I wrote Marshal Stoudenmire down in El Paso, a friend of mine who knows this fella like his own son. He swears that Matt Weston is perfect for the job you got in mind, and that he's good—extra *special* good at finding people who don't even know they went and got lost."

Ben wasn't given to exaggeration as a rule, which gave Maggie reason to rejoice. Suddenly, a truly merry Christmas seemed tantalizingly close to reality. Leaning forward, she swept the clean napkins and utensils aside.

"Did you contact Weston yet?" she asked, questions popping like corn, one after the other. "Will he do it? What about money? Did you make sure to let him know that I can't pay much?"

"Oh, Maggie, girl, you got to go easier on an old man like me." Ben leaned back in his chair and cut loose with his unique titter, a laugh that jiggled the belly that had earned him the role of Prescott's Santa Claus for the last eight years. "You're gonna wear me out before I ever get the chance to tell you everything."

"Sorry, Ben." Maggie was so desperate and eager to have Holly's dreams come true, she could hardly slow down, even then. "It's just that suddenly this whole plan seems real, like it might even stand a good chance of working."

"I understand that, and the fact you got your mind set on this scheme and mean to ride it like a wild bronco, but odds are you're gonna get bucked off a time or two before it's over." He sighed heavily. "I'm mighty fond of you, Maggie. I hate to think of you getting all bruised up again."

She wanted to hug the man, at the least, give him a little peck on the cheek, but she knew neither option was open. Ben would have died of mortification on the spot. She reassured him instead, the next best thing.

"I appreciate your concern and all the help, more than you'll ever know, but please don't worry about me. I've been so badly bruised by Rafe Hollister's indifference to me and Holly over the years, my heart has calluses thick enough to brand. He can't hurt me anymore, honest. Not ever again."

Ben didn't look particularly convinced, but then neither was Maggie. He gave a half-nod, reluctantly sealing their pact, and finally said what she'd been waiting to hear.

"Captain Weston already knows about your finances and that you can't pay much toward his expenses. He agreed to sign up for the job anyway."

"Oh, thank the Lord." After the brief prayer came more questions. "What do I do now? How do I contact Mr. Weston? Did you tell him everything he needs to know about Rafe and all?"

"If you'll hush up a minute, I'll be getting to that." Ben glanced out the window where Gurley Street separated the courthouse and his office from the cafe. "On second thought, I believe I'll just let the captain fill you in on all the details. After he stabled his horse, he stopped off at the bath house to clean himself up from his long ride. The man didn't want to meet you all dirty and stinking of the trail."

"Weston's *here* . . . in Prescott?"

Again he lit up with a smug grin. "That's your man outside in the big white hat."

Maggie tore open the yellow and white checkerboard curtains that matched the tablecloths, and peered out at the street. It was an unusually quiet morning in the sleepy little town, sunny and almost too warm, as the final dog days of summer burned themselves out. She saw that Homer Ludlow, who owned the barbershop adjacent to the restaurant, was sitting in a rocker outside his establishment as usual. Instead of whittling a nickel to add to his collection of wooden coins, Homer's hands were still and his mouth was hanging open like a hollowed-out feed bag. Maggie could almost hear him snoring.

The only movement other than the rise and fall of Homer's chest came from a team of mules slowly dragging a double wagonload of supplies up the street. Waiting for the dozen mules to pass by him stood a man who bore absolutely no resemblance to the crippled old man Maggie had pictured. When the ranger resumed his journey to the boardwalk in front of the cafe, Maggie glimpsed enough of the face beneath the wide-brimmed hat to know that the captain was even closer to her own age than she could have hoped for. He walked with the expected limp, but it wasn't much worse than the hobbling gaits of half the men who lived and ranched in Prescott. The captain was also a big man, tall and solid, as formidable a sight as the nickel-plated Colt .45 he wore strapped to his right hip. When and if Weston found Rafe, Maggie had no doubt the irresponsible rat would think twice before trying to escape such a man as this ranger.

She didn't get a chance beyond that to contemplate the tracker or his chances of success. Before she knew it, he was inside the cafe and Ben was making the introductions.

"This here's Maggie Hollister," he said, leaping out of his chair. "The woman I've been telling you about."

Captain Weston removed his white hat and snagged it on the brass rack before acknowledging Maggie. With a short nod and an even more clipped tone, he said, "A pleasure, ma'am."

"Maggie?" said Ben, backing away from her. "This here's Matt Weston. No sense me hanging around any longer. You got plenty to discuss that don't need a third pair of ears. I'll just go see if I can't round up a cabin for you, Captain. And remember—in the meantime, you're welcome to bunk with me and the missus."

The ranger nodded his dark head. "Thanks, Ben, but I'd just as soon get settled into my own place tonight, if possible."

"Then I'd best get to it."

With that, Ben was gone, leaving Maggie to face yet another awkward conversation with no clear beginning. It didn't take long for her to discover that Matt Weston was direct and intense, a man who didn't waste time with preliminaries or his words. And that he expected the same in return.

He'd barely accommodated himself in the chair across the table from her before Weston said, "Tell me about your husband."

He spoke in a soft drawl, yet the words were harsh somehow, more like an order than a request. Feeling as if he were interrogating her the way he would a criminal, Maggie let her hackles rise a little as she coolly replied.

"I understood that Sheriff Sloan told you most of what you need to know about Rafe. If you want more information, I'll be happy to supply what I can, but first, why don't we make ourselves a little more comfortable?" She pushed her chair away from the table. "Wouldn't you like some refreshments, coffee perhaps and an assortment of cakes? The apple crop this year has been absolutely outstan—"

"Thanks, ma'am." He cut her off without so much as an

excuse me. "I don't need a thing except answers when I ask a question. Understood?"

Maggie was so taken back by the man's abrupt, if not down-right rude way of doing business, she couldn't think how to answer or even find her tongue. Not that it mattered to this Texas Ranger. He had tongue enough for the both of them.

"I want you to forget that Ben ever mentioned your husband's name to me. I need to hear about him from you, not second-hand."

His brash gray eyes openly measured her, checking her un-doubtedly, for signs of intelligence so he could decide if she was capable of comprehending his simple words. Maggie told herself that she didn't have to like the man for him to do his job well. She calmed down even more as she realized how Weston's aggressive way of doing business might even be an asset when it came time to convince Rafe that he ought to face up to his responsibilities.

"I understand." Maggie didn't bother to soften the brisk edge to her voice. "What exactly do you need to know?"

"Everything, leave nothing out." He still hadn't taken his eyes off of her, not even to blink. "Tell it like I don't know you or a thing about your troubles. Most important of all, be sure to tell it true."

Maggie flinched from somewhere deep inside, an instant fin-ger-pointing kind of response she couldn't have stopped if she'd had the chance. She hoped her reaction hadn't rippled to the surface. The ranger's intense impersonal gaze would never miss such an obvious admission of guilt. Not that Maggie considered herself a dishonest woman.

"What's the trouble, ma'am?" asked Weston impatiently. "Are you having a problem with your memory or with telling the truth?"

Maggie's mouth fell open in shock. "Captain Weston! I must

inform you that I resent both your tone and the implications that my standards are less than high."

He regarded her a long moment, longer than it had taken him to insult her, but at least there was no amusement or even censure in his expression. When Weston spoke again, the words came slowly, more carefully than before.

"I apologize if I've offended you, ma'am. I'm just trying to do this job as quickly and painlessly as I can."

"Painlessly, hmmm?" She paused to make sure any guilt he might be feeling had a chance to jab him good and hard. "You might try a little harder, and while you're at it, please stop calling me ma'am. I believe Ben introduced us properly."

Weston nodded curtly. "That, he did. Again I apologize, Mrs. Hollister. I thought I'd learned long ago never to spur a willing horse—so to speak."

Maggie smiled. "Maybe you just need to learn how to be a little more patient. Given enough time, even an egg will get up and walk if you want it to." She couldn't resist adding, "Understand?"

The captain's expression remained unchanged. From the moment they met, Weston had been steady, stoical almost to the point of indifference. The man didn't seem to know how to smile. It occurred to Maggie then, and on the late side, that the ranger might not be so willing to overlook a certain insolence she'd come to embrace as part of her personality since coming to Prescott. A woman in these parts with an absentee husband and no chance of getting a new one, got away with a lot—a sassy tongue, for one thing. Obviously this man wasn't used to such boldness.

Maggie was just thinking of apologizing when Weston slowly raised his left eyebrow, a shift that made him look less edgy and explosive. His teeth were still clenched and his mouth was closed, but his lips twitched a little, then spread ever so slightly. She chose to accept the new expression as his idea of a smile.

The captain's tone, however, remained flat and businesslike as he said, "Maybe we ought to start over. Why don't you tell me exactly what it is you want me to do."

Simple enough. That information lived in Maggie's heart and soul, not in the back of her mind where the pieces of the past and thoughts of her lost love were tangled into painful knots.

Forcing herself to be as direct and detached as the ranger, she said, "I'm hiring you to locate Rafe Hollister, to make sure that the man is capable of behaving himself around decent folks and young children, and to bring him to Prescott."

She paused, trying to think of a delicate way to word the rest, then settled on the captain's preference for honesty.

"If it turns out that Rafe is dead or even in prison, I need proof so I can close the matter once and for all. If he's alive, I want you to make the man understand that he has a daughter who desperately needs him. If he lies and says he doesn't have a wife or a child, rope him as if he were a maverick calf and drag him back to town."

Her cards pretty much on the table, Maggie looked Weston in the eye and issued her final words on the subject. "Do whatever you have to short of murder, but bring him to me before Christmas. Is that clear enough?"

After that startlingly candid admission, Maggie expected a few words of censure, or at the least, the expression of a man who'd begun to wonder if he hadn't gone into cahoots with Calamity Jane. All she got back from Weston was the same intense scrutiny and his usual blunt tone.

"You can be sure that I'll do my part. Let's move on to your husband now. How soon after you were married did he run off?"

Lord, but Maggie hated the thought of answering such personal questions. Unable to face the captain's intuitive gaze any longer, Maggie dropped her chin and lowered her eyes.

"Rafe left shortly after I told him that Holly was on the way." That was truthful enough.

"Were you here in Prescott at the time?"

She shook her head. "We were still in Utah with my family."

Shades of the truth about a time Maggie would never, ever forget. Winter had been particularly hard that year, bringing with it the kind of cold that bites hollows in the chubbiest cheeks and that was if a body stayed indoors. She and Rafe hadn't exactly lived together on the Thorne farm—not so the rest of the family was aware of it anyway. As a wounded outlaw on the run, Rafe happened to choose their barn as a hideout. Maggie, fool that she was, took pity on the man and secretly nursed him back to health.

"Mrs. Hollister."

Maggie glanced up in surprise, her thoughts clouded with the past.

"When did your husband leave you and why?"

"Oh, ah . . ." She lowered her head again and went on with the story she'd told a thousand times. "Rafe didn't want us to have to depend on my family, so we ran off together to get married. We found out about Holly shortly after that, and he went in search of gold to support us. I went on ahead to Prescott, where I had kin, Gus and Hattie, who own this restaurant. Rafe was supposed to meet me here before Holly was born, which turned out to be Christmas Day."

"I assume he didn't make it."

"You assume correctly."

"And that's it, the whole story?"

It was if she could get away with it. She said with a shrug, "Pretty much all you need to know."

Weston shoved his chair back and climbed out of it. When Maggie started to do likewise, he gestured for her to stay put.

"Don't bother, Mrs. Hollister. I can see my way out." He adjusted his belt so the holster containing his revolver ran dead parallel to his outer thigh. "I'm going to have a look around town. I'll be back in an hour for that coffee you offered earlier, and one other thing—the truth."

"But I told you the truth."

He frowned, looking even more dour than he had when he walked into the cafe.

"What's wrong?" she asked. "Is hunting down a petty thief like Rafe Hollister too big a job for you?"

That little bit of sass finally got a genuine smile out of the man, making him show, of all things, a hint of dimples.

Somehow Maggie preferred the scowl, especially as he went on to say, "I expect that finding Rafe Hollister will be about the easiest job I ever had."

Weston looked so pleased with himself, Maggie wanted to kick him.

"Getting the truth out of you," he went on, "looks like it's going to be a touch harder. I'm not one for wasting time, ma'am. If you don't think you can manage the truth by the time I get back, then don't trouble yourself on my account."

He reached for his hat and started for the door. "If I can't get a clear picture of what I'm heading into, I won't be taking that easy job or staying in Prescott long enough to bother with coffee."

Two

The kitchen at the Squat and Gobble Cafe took up the same amount of space that Maggie and Holly's bedrooms occupied in the apartment directly above the restaurant. Though it was small, the working area was efficiently organized—with a restaurant-sized stove featuring two huge ovens and a newfangled floor made of cork linoleum, which made clean-up something akin to child's play. It was only when she and her Uncle Gus, who did most of the cooking, were whipping up culinary delights at the same time that they got to banging elbows.

Gus had already staked out most of the counter spaces before Maggie came into the kitchen, cluttering them up with loaves of wheat bread she'd baked that morning, thick slabs of onion, and of course the main ingredients of his most requested noontime item, fried oyster and turkey sandwiches. Gus loved oysters and thought they belonged in *everything*. He even tried to convince Maggie to put them in a batch of corn muffins once, a thought that gagged her. She'd never been to the seashore, but she thought she had a pretty good idea what one smelled like.

To stay clear of the odor and out of Gus's way, she took her production to a corner where the fruit and vegetable bins were located, then sat down on a milking stool to finish coring and peeling the last of three bushels of apples. It was tedious work, but mindless, too, a good thing considering the fact that Maggie couldn't concentrate on anything except Matt Weston's ultimatum.

Exactly what part of the truth was the man looking for or even entitled to? How much of the past did he honestly expect her to share? Surely not everything. Maggie wished she had someone to confide in, a sage and ethical person she could trust with her secrets. Uncle Gus, who was her mother's brother, wouldn't do—even though he was the most honest and God-fearing man in Prescott. For one thing, he wasn't at all interested in "women's" troubles and would probably tell her to go see his wife if she needed advice. For another, he too would demand the whole truth—something she could never give him.

As for confiding in Gus's wife—that possibility was completely out of the question. While Maggie adored Aunt Hattie and her funny little ways, the woman simply couldn't be trusted. Oh, she meant well and never intended to harm anyone, but Hattie's mouth was like a creek at spring thaw, always flooding the banks of discretion and surging far ahead of her brain. She never quite understood why folks were sometimes offended by her remarks.

In this case, it really didn't matter. Neither Gus nor Hattie could ever know the truth about why Maggie had come to Prescott and stayed on. Gus for sure would never look at her again without censure and disappointment in his eyes—assuming he glanced her way at all. And one or both of them would take it as their solemn duty to inform Maggie's family back in Utah as to what her exact circumstances were. As much as that would have destroyed her, it wasn't on her own behalf that Maggie worried about revealing the truth. Her main concern was the possibility of a loose tongue where Holly might overhear. If she got wind of the fact that Maggie was trying to bring Rafe Hollister to town in time for Christmas, and then he failed to put in an appearance for one reason or another, it would break what was left of poor Holly's already fragile heart. The plan had to remain a secret, which meant there was no way to seek anyone's advice.

"Maggie, girl," said Gus, startling her. "You sure you know what you're doing down there?"

She glanced up to see him peering over the work table where he was wrapping sandwiches for delivery to gold and copper mines. Bald as a peeled egg, Gus's head reflected a perfect circle of light from the lamp above, making him look as if he were wearing a halo. Fitting, she thought, since Gus considered himself more pious than most ordained preachers.

"I'm making apple butter," she replied. "Of course I know what I'm doing."

"Since when are taters a part of the recipe?"

Maggie looked down to see that she'd peeled and quartered at least three potatoes, then tossed them into the kettle with the apples and cooked-down cider. "Heavens above," she said with a shake of her head. "I didn't realize I was so distracted."

"Something wrong?"

"Well . . . yes." She figured that even general advice would help at this point. "I was wondering how much truth a body's expected to tell when dealing in business matters."

Gus had a long handlebar mustache and a prominent ridge above his eyes that ran from temple to temple, a feature he shared with Maggie's mother. It made them look like hell's fire and damnation when they were smiling—and mean enough to wrestle grizzlies when they were not.

Gus's expression was somewhere in between, as he thumped the counter and declared, "An honest man is God's noblest work, and that goes for women, too. I'm surprised at you for even wondering if there's a time to be less than truthful."

It occurred to Maggie that the only advice she'd needed, but chose not to heed, was her own when she'd made up her mind not to seek counsel. With a sigh, she said, "I didn't mean to suggest that dishonesty should ever be condoned. I was wondering if it'd be permissible to omit part of the truth, not if lying was all right."

The ridge supporting his eyebrows swelled as Gus-the-bear-wrestler proclaimed, "Apparently you didn't hear me, girl. The truth might be blamed now and again, but it can never be shamed. Understand? There is no shame in what's true."

Obviously Gus hadn't considered the kind of truth that could cost a woman her own family. Sorry she'd ever opened her mouth, Maggie went back to her apples. "Thank you, Uncle Gus. You've been a lot of help."

Since customers were few and far between except for early morning, noon dinner, and supper hour, Gus had tied a pair of long-handled spoons to the cord connected to the bell at the front door. That way when a stray customer came in, he'd know it without having to listen too hard. Those spoons *jangled* now, launching Maggie to her feet so quickly, she kicked the milking stool over.

"I'll go see who that is," she said a little too anxiously. She did *not* want to explain Matt Weston to Gus—not yet anyway. "It's probably just Mary Jane picking up pies for her daddy's hotel."

Thankfully, Gus didn't give her an argument or even seem to realize that she'd left the kitchen.

On the other hand, once Maggie stepped into the cafe and closed the kitchen door behind her, Matt Weston noticed her enough for two men. He was standing by the bakery nook, a mountain of a man himself, yet he dared to look at her the way he might have observed Thumb Butte; awestruck, and wondering who in tarnation might be fool enough to tackle the climb.

Maggie had seen this sort of reaction before, whenever a stranger got his first good look at her, especially if he was the sort who had to borrow a ladder to kick a gnat in the knee. Since Weston looked to be at least as tall as Maggie, she hadn't expected the former ranger to be so surprised now that she wasn't all folded up in a chair. At five feet nine inches in her stocking feet, nobody, least of all this ranger, had to remind Maggie that she had a better view of the countryside than all of the women and just about every man in town.

Both her ire and her hems were raised, as she marched across the room to where Weston stood and drew up to her full height. She fell a good three or four inches below the top of his head.

"Nice of you to come back," she said without apology. "Are you planning to stay long enough to hear me out this time?"

Although he wasn't a man easily amused, Matt almost laughed. The woman had come at him like a gamecock, all spurs, ruffled feathers, and flashing eyes. Maggie Hollister was furious, no doubt about it, but even Matt, who'd made a career out of knowing what went on inside other folks' heads, didn't know why. Maybe she was still smoldering over the terms he'd set down earlier.

"I'll stay as long as you like," he promised, adding a reminder of those terms. "Or as long as you stick to the truth. It's up to you."

"Fair enough, I suppose." She glanced out the window. "Any time now a few regular customers might start trickling into the cafe. Please keep in mind that the business between us has to stay right there—between us. You still want that coffee?"

Since he'd just wet his whistle with a beer at Brow's Palace Bar Matt refused the offer. Besides, he wasn't so sure he wanted a woman this easily riled, to hover over him with a pot of scalding liquid.

"Forget the coffee," he said. "Where do you want to talk?"

Maggie led him back to the same table they'd shared before, then settled in across from him. Her hands were clasped together tightly, barely resting against the edge of the table, and her head was bowed so low, she had to look up and through her lashes just to catch a glimpse of him. If ever a woman had something to hide, she was one.

Matt figured nothing less than the direct route would do. "If you want to hire me," he began, watching her closely for signs of deceit, "nothing less than the absolute truth will do. If you can't give me that, then I can't take the job. It's just that simple."

She raised her head enough for him to see the sincerity she tried to convey by fluttering her long brown lashes.

"I understand completely," she said softly, "but there's one thing we need to settle on my behalf before we go any further. I have to be absolutely certain the information we discuss will be kept completely confidential. Can you assure me of that?"

"I don't think so."

"What?" She reared back in her chair like a green-broke filly, all female pretensions aside. "Then how on earth can you possibly make any demands on me?"

It suddenly seemed like a good idea to ease up some. With very little apology in his tone, Matt said, "I should have explained myself a little better. I can and do give my word that whatever you say will go no further, and also guarantee that I never break my word. That's the best I can offer, if it's of any assurance to you."

The expression she tossed back at Matt was speculative, long and hard, with eyes narrow and suspicious, maybe even a little bit resentful. It surprised him when she agreed to his terms, but even more when she made a surrender of their agreement.

"All right, you win. We'll do it your way." With a heavy sigh, she asked, "What part of the truth do you need so badly?"

Matt fought off a rare attack of what his father used to call "the feel-sorries." After all, he didn't know this woman any better than she knew him. He leaned back in his chair and propped his elbows on the arms. Maybe if he looked relaxed, she would be more inclined to loosen her stiff spine.

"Let's start at the beginning again," he suggested. "How did you meet Hollister and where?"

"I already told you. I found Rafe in the barn one winter

morning when I was doing my chores. He was on the run from the law, shot-up and half frozen to death. He begged me not to tell my father that he was there, and well . . . I didn't."

"You must have said something sooner or later."

She shook her head vehemently. "Never. As far as I know, my family doesn't even remember Rafe's name. They only know that I ran off and married some drifter, that I bore him a daughter, and that he deserted us both." Maggie raised her chin, looking both proud and vulnerable. "No one knows anything beyond that except me and Rafe."

They'd reached a point where a lady like Maggie Hollister wouldn't normally be expected to continue such a personal discussion, least of all with a stranger. Matt was none too keen about the idea either. Since he'd turned fifteen around seventeen years ago, he'd been a lawman of some kind or a Texas Ranger. That made it easy for him to avoid entanglements with the opposite sex and the perils of getting too cozy with altar-bound females. Now that he was retired from active duty, desk-bound far more often than he liked, he got cornered frequently by the single ladies of El Paso. Matt didn't particularly mind the attention, but even with recent experience, he still didn't know enough about women and their ways to fill a rifle shell. Picking up the thread of this conversation with Maggie struck him as more threatening than showing up empty-handed at a gunfight.

"Why don't you just go on as things happened," he said, making it easy on himself. "If I have questions, I'll interrupt."

Maggie frowned and again lowered her chin, but she did as he asked. "Utah had a tough winter that year so Rafe stayed on till spring thaw. I was quite in love with him by then, and thought maybe . . ." She paused for a breath, then closed her eyes and admitted, "And knew for sure there was a baby on the way."

It wasn't that Matt hadn't been expecting something like that, but to hear it in such a painful whisper from such an obviously proud woman, made him distinctly uncomfortable. He shifted in the chair, crossing his left boot over the top of his right knee. When that didn't help, he reversed the position, then linked his fingers across his belt buckle and cleared his throat.

"When you told Hollister about the, ah, that you were in a family way, is that when the two of you got married?"

Her cheeks aflame, Maggie slowly shook her head. "Rafe wasn't too happy about the baby. He insisted that he hadn't done a blasted thing wrong, but that he was still wanted by the law and had to clear his name before he settled down and raised a family."

She looked up at Matt expectantly, as if waiting for him to comment or question her more deeply about the time she spent with Rafe. He'd just as soon have taken a bath in a barrel of kerosene. He gestured for her to continue.

As before, Maggie closed her eyes, offering the pain of the past to Matt through a voice tight with emotion. "When Rafe refused to take me with him, I just about went crazy because I knew I could never stay behind. If my family found out about the trouble I was in, my father would have hanged me and Mother would have tightened the knot."

Maggie paused for a breath and perhaps to swallow the tears Matt thought he heard boiling up in her throat. More composed, she went on to explain, "I threatened Rafe, saying that I'd wake up the whole family and tell them what he'd done to me if he didn't take me with him, so he did. We went to Salt Lake City to get married, then he put me on a stagecoach heading south with just enough money to reach Prescott. He said that after he straightened things out with the law, he'd join me here and build us a home."

Thinking like a ranger again instead of like a man poking his nose where it had no right to be, Matt asked, "What made him decide on Prescott? Is he from this area?"

"No. In fact, he said he was from Fort Worth. I don't think

he lied about that either because he spoke in a drawl something like yours, but it was more exaggerated. He couldn't say two words without tossing in a y'all."

Matt wasn't ashamed of his roots or the colorful way many Texans had of expressing themselves, but he winced at the comparison.

"Anyway," she went on. "I picked Prescott because my Uncle Gus, who owns this cafe, had just set up shop here. He and his wife took me in, thinking my husband would be joining me soon. That was six long years ago. In the meantime, Gus and Hattie built their own home at the edge of town, and turned the apartment upstairs over to me and Holly."

The revelation that Hollister had gone ahead and married Maggie came as a surprise, even a bit of a disappointment. The fact that he'd never bothered to join her didn't make a whole lot of sense to Matt either—unless the man had been detained in some unavoidable way, such as prison or an unexpected journey to boot hill.

"Is there anything else?"

"Not that I can think of," said Maggie, her eyes as slick as a moonlit pond. "All you really need to know is that I'm doing all this for Holly, not myself. I'm hiring you for her and in secret so her little heart won't be broken any more than it already has been. I hope you can understand that and take pity on the child."

Far from condemning her, Matt admired what he'd seen and learned of Maggie so far. In fact, he'd never met a woman with such admirable reasons for putting a price on a man's head. He did have to wonder, however, if she'd considered all the things that could go wrong with her little plan.

"Your secret is safe, as I promised, but there are a few things you ought to think about," he warned. "After what you've just told me, I have to make sure you realize that it's more than possible I'll find your husband in jail. Or worse."

"I'm aware that Rafe may be dead. Sometimes I think that's the only way I can forgive him for abandoning us this way."

Maggie leaned forward, throwing herself across the table, on his mercy. The longing in her expression, the naked desperation, was as hard to watch as it was inspiring.

"But again, it isn't on my behalf that I want him back. At each of the last four Christmases, Holly has had to face the fact that no matter how much she begs God or Santa Claus, her daddy won't be coming to see her. This year I'm counting on you to make things different." She put her palms together, then drew the tips of her fingers to her lips as if praying. "Just this once, Holly's wish simply *has* to come true. If Rafe is alive, you're the one who can make that happen. I beg of you, please do everything you can to find him and bring him back."

Something twisted in Matt's gut, something sharp like the tip of his Bowie knife, but warm too, reminiscent of a shot of fine whisky, a languid and potent taste of fire. He glanced at Maggie and saw in her lovely face the utter honesty of a saint shaded with the courage of a warrior. Although something in his gut told him he probably should have, Matt suddenly didn't have it in himself to deny her anything.

"I'll bring Hollister back to you or die trying," he promised. "You've got my word on that as a Texas Ranger, Maggie. May I call you Maggie?"

She nodded, tears still glistening in her eyes.

"After I find that husband of yours and have a word or two with him, I guarantee he'll be more than happy to ride into Prescott and make your daughter's wish come true."

The collection of tears finally tumbled over the edge and began rolling down Maggie's cheeks. Matt wanted nothing more at that moment than to run out the door and keep on running until he hit Texas. Anything but tears.

Looking for another subject, something to divert the flood,

he asked, "Er, what about you? Any wishes I can fulfill on your behalf while I'm at it?"

She laughed a little, sounding almost as relieved as Matt felt. With a tentative smile and a short little nod, more a curtsy of the chin than anything, she said, "I already told you. I have just one wish—to see my daughter wake up on Christmas morning with a smile on her face for a change."

The door to the cafe opened then, setting off an irritating, high-pitched bell. Maggie grabbed a napkin off the table and tended her nose as she jumped up from her chair. In a hurried whisper she said, "I've got customers now, but before I go, I want to thank you for everything."

"I haven't done anything yet, and actually, we haven't finished talking either. I've got a lot more questions, but they can wait a while. You've given me enough information to get started."

"Well, thanks anyway for taking the job."

Matt watched as Maggie turned and walked away, then kept on watching, drawn to the seductive way her hips rolled beneath the slick black fabric of her skirt. Her stride was strong and purposeful, powered by legs long enough to grip a man good and tight, yet distinctly and utterly feminine.

Jesus, what a woman, he thought, amazed to find his mind traveling down that road. He was supposed to be tracking her husband, hauling him in by whatever means necessary and making sure that the man was worthy of Maggie and her daughter. What the hell was *he* doing thinking about this woman on his own behalf?

It didn't matter that she struck Matt as more than woman enough to fill his hungry arms, or that she was a sturdy, unpretentious female, one he wouldn't worry about being fragile as a teacup whenever he came to her. Maggie Hollister was spoken for, married even if her husband was missing, the bastard. There had to be other women capable of talking to him in that same straight-on way, the kind who wouldn't mind showing a spark or two of intelligence in their vibrant brown eyes, or even flashes of anger when he got out of line—and he had. There were others like Maggie, Matt convinced himself. He simply hadn't been looking hard enough. In fact, he hadn't been looking at all.

The job was all that mattered anyway, all that could matter. Matt only hoped that for Maggie's sake, he'd find Hollister alive. And that when he finally met up with him, the son of a bitch wouldn't do anything stupid enough to rile Matt or force him into a situation where he might even have to kill him.

Of course, none of his sudden anger or thoughts of violence made much sense, considering the fact that he'd never met Rafe Hollister or even heard his name before today.

But already Matt hated the bastard's guts.

Three

The second Sunday of October had been selected by the citizens of Prescott for the Fall Festival, a community picnic intended to celebrate the harvest. Most came to sample the vast array of edibles, an ongoing activity as they argued over which farmer reaped the most bushels per acre of corn, produced the juiciest apples, or grew the biggest pumpkin.

Matt came to the festival for only one reason—to pick up where he left off with Maggie Hollister almost a week ago. He'd seen her since then, of course, mostly because he'd made a daily habit of stopping by the cafe for breakfast and supper. Not only did regular visits to the restaurant give him the chance to learn more about Maggie, and therefore do his job better, she also made the best damned bread and biscuits he'd ever tasted in his life. The fact that he enjoyed watching Maggie as she moved from table to table was an extra bonus.

Mealtimes at the Squat and Gobble Cafe were hectic. Her neighbors were constantly coming and going. No place in which to finish their discussion about Rafe Hollister, a matter that needed tending to soon. It wouldn't be easy to have a moment alone with her here either, considering the fact that the entire town and then some had congregated on the large park-like expanse of grass that surrounded the courthouse. Not that space was tight. A small herd of longhorns could have joined the crowd milling around the rows and rows of tables displaying fall's bounty, and Matt doubted that anyone would take notice.

Since he was uncomfortable in crowded situations, he stayed on the sidelines to look for Maggie and observe the festivities, propping one boot against a low whitewashed fence that set the boundaries of the charming plaza. In addition to the grass, the grounds also supported a community watermelon patch and a bandstand that doubled as a gazebo. That little open-air meeting spot was now filled with musicians of every kind, from banjo players to fiddlers, and even one fellow who was blowing on a crude wooden harmonica. Surprisingly enough, the performers were all on the same key, playing as one, and doing a mighty fine job of entertaining the townsfolk.

As for the job Matt had been hired to do, there wasn't much left now but to get a few more answers from Maggie and wait for a lead on his man. With the help of Sheriff Sloan, Matt had already sent several wires to lawmen throughout the Southwest, concentrating on the Texas area, Fort Worth in particular. Outlaws, in Matt's estimation, weren't much different from homing pigeons—most of them couldn't resist the lure of their roosts even if they had to fly through a firestorm of buckshot to get there.

Sloan also located an abandoned cabin for Matt to use indefinitely as his own. Set off to itself at the southwest edge of town, the place was a perfect one-room dwelling that not only suited his sense of privacy, but would do nicely when he returned to Prescott with Hollister in tow. Over the last couple of days Matt made a few alterations to the door, security measures that could turn the cabin into a jailhouse should such an arrangement became necessary.

"Weston!" shouted a familiar voice from somewhere off to Matt's left. "I've been looking all over for you."

Matt turned to see Sheriff Sloan approaching.

"Got an answer to one of your inquiries," said the lawman,

waving a telegram under his nose. "Bet you can't guess where from."

Kicking away from the fence, Matt went for the obvious. "Fort Worth?"

"Nope, better yet. It come from the town you just left—El Paso." Sloan gave him the wire. "Kinda funny, huh?"

Matt failed to see the humor in the fact that he and the Texan he was tracking had practically been sharing the same boarding house back home. Ignoring the man he now knew to be more of a figurehead than a genuine lawman, Matt quickly read the missive:

> *Weston: Had some trouble two nights back with a man*
> *called Hollister and a whore he says is his sister. Stop.*
> *Did not have cause to arrest either. Stop. Do you? Stop.*
> *Advise. Stop.*

The telegram had been sent by Marshal Dallas Stoudenmire himself, a famed lawman from New Mexico who had recently been hired by El Paso's frazzled citizens to clean up their town. This particular marshal, an old family friend, wasn't given to making careless decisions or reckless identifications. Odds were, he'd located Rafe Hollister.

Matt's blood roared as he thought ahead to the chase. He glanced at Sloan. "Can you send an immediate reply?"

"You betcha." Sloan puffed out his chest and curled his thumbs under his suspenders, like an aging stag snorting hollow challenges as his final winter approached. "Exactly what do you think we ought to say? We don't want to be giving away too much of what you're up to, do we?"

Taking a little pity on the man, Matt went along with the notion that they were working together on the case. "Maybe we ought to ask the marshal to keep a close watch on Hollister," he said, "but not to alert or arrest him. What do you think?"

"That sounds about right." The old man hitched up his pants and curled his lip, blood in his eye. "I expect I also ought to mention that you'll be back in El Paso soon?"

"I'll leave first thing in the morning." Matt tested his bad hip and gritted his teeth against the pain. There was no way he could make the ride to Maricopa in less than five days, not if he wanted to board the train to El Paso on foot instead of laid out on a stretcher. Grumbling to himself, he muttered, "Tell Stoudenmire I'll be there in about a week, give or take."

Sloan didn't even take the time to confirm. He spun around in his excitement and damn near fell over a small child who had come up on his blind side.

"God in heaven, girl!" Sloan caught himself just short of smashing her head against the fence. "I pretty near laid you out. Don't you know better than to go sneaking up on a fella?"

She completely ignored the warning and the question, choosing instead to show off the big paper star she carried. "Look what I got, Sheriff Ben!"

"I see you got yourself a kite, young lady."

"Uh-huh!" Squealing with enthusiasm, she hopped in place like a rabbit caught in a bog, her pale blond curls springing right along with her. She wore a pair of spectacles mounted on nickel-plated wires, making her eyes appear unusually large and luminous. The glasses were bouncing, too.

"Where'd you get that kite, Holly?" Sloan frowned into the face of all that girlish enthusiasm, dampening it a little. "You didn't take it away from Jethro or Billy, did you?"

"It's mine and nobody else's." Her tiny voice squeaked with indignation. "Mama said I could fly it if I got someone to help."

"Oh, honey, kite flying's for boys." Sloan glanced at Matt, chuckling as if they shared some private joke. Then he turned back to the girl. "Run along now and give it to one of the little fellas who don't have a kite."

"No!" She stamped her foot. "It's mine and I want to fly it. Will you help me please?"

Patting his soufflé of a belly, Sloan shook his head. "Better look somewheres else, little gal, like Captain Weston here." He glanced at Matt, who quickly shook his head—but not fast enough. "This is Maggie's girl, Matt. Help her out a little while I tend to that business we got at the office."

With a wave of the yellow paper, Sloan was off, leaving Matt alone with the youngster. A girl, he discovered, who didn't take no for an answer or have a shy bone in her body. Just like her mother.

"Can you help me right now, mister?" She looked up through her lenses with Maggie's mink brown eyes. "I can't make it go up in the sky."

As a male raised mostly by his father in the company of other adult men, Matt didn't know the first thing about children or kites. Moreover, he didn't want to know.

"Sorry, kid, but you'll have to find someone else to help you out."

"But mister," said the persistent child as she tugged on his pants leg, "Sheriff Ben said you would help, so you have to. Do you got any string?"

"No, I don't."

Matt scanned the fringes of the crowd hoping to spot Maggie's honey-colored hair, but there was no sign of her. He glanced down, preparing to send Holly on her way, and found her staring back at him with eyes far older than her years. He didn't know if the spectacles made her look that way or if it was something in her nature, but the child was definitely sizing him up, the way a full grown woman might—and finding him lacking.

It was an eerie sensation considering the girl's age and her almost comical appearance. Holly's glasses were askew after bouncing down to the middle of her nose and her pearly white hair was in shambles, the mass of ringlets both kinked and cottony except for one perfect coil arching down over her forehead. Longfellow's poem immediately came to Matt's mind—*There was a little girl who had a little curl* . . .

"Let's go get some string," Holly demanded, kicking the toe of his boot. "Right now."

. . . *but when she was bad she was horrid.* Suddenly, there wasn't enough room at the festival for both Matt and this child. "Go ask your mother to help you. I don't have the time."

Holly pushed out an exaggerated sigh, blowing that perfect curl all to hell in the process. "Mama can't help 'cause she already has a job doing apple dumpys and Uncle Gus has a job, too. He has a whole big turkey in a pot. I brought my punkins to the festible, but they're really for Halloween."

"Good for you," he said absently, still hoping to catch a glimpse of Maggie.

"Mama is making a costume for me to wear at Halloween that has a big tall hat and my very own broom. I'm gonna be a witch."

Matt regarded the gabby child with quiet amusement. "I'm sure you'll be a very good one, too. Now run along."

"You got to go with me, mister. Ben said so."

Without further discussion, Holly stuck her slightly damaged kite into one of Matt's hands, then grabbed hold of the other and tugged. "Come on. Mama can tell us where to get string."

If not for the fact that he needed to talk to Maggie before leaving town, Matt might have resisted the tenacious little whelp's attempts to drag him into the crowd. As it was, he let her pull him along behind her as if he were a wagonload of toys. They wandered past tables weighed down with baskets of shiny red apples, bright orange carrots as thick as a man's wrist, and every shape and color of squash imaginable. Casseroles, hams, and great clods of roast beef and venison filled the air with their mouth-watering aromas, and reminded Matt that he was long overdue for a good meal.

He might have stopped to sample the fare if Holly hadn't been so damn noisy as she maneuvered through the crowd. She shouted "Mama!" every few feet, drawing inquiries from her neighbors and precisely the kind of attention Matt avoided at all costs.

"Morning, Holly," several different women said, most of them adding, "Who's your new friend?"

The townsmen were a little more direct. "Hey there, sweetheart," they'd say. "Your mama know this fella?"

Intent on her mission, Holly pretty much ignored the inquiries, continuing on her way with brief explanations about how Matt was going to teach her how to fly a kite. In spite of her sketchy answers—maybe because of them—suspicious eyes followed them every step of the way, making Matt feel like some kind of miscreant.

When at last they arrived at the table laden with cakes, pies, and other baked goods from Maggie's kitchen, Matt couldn't extract his hand from the child's fast enough or get rid of the blasted kite any too soon. He propped it against the table as Holly called to her mother.

"I found a helper, Mama!"

Maggie was sitting on the other side of the table using an inverted pickle barrel for a chair, and stirring what looked like the ass end of a whole turkey in a large cauldron of boiling oil. The pot hung down from a length of pipe over a deep fire pit.

After giving the bird one more turn with a long-handled spoon, Maggie glanced over her shoulder to where her daughter stood. "What did you say, sugar?"

"I got a new friend, mister, uh . . ." She looked up at Matt with a frown. "I forgot your name."

"It's Matt Weston, but don't bother to introduce me. Your mother and I have already met."

Maggie craned her neck until she saw him, then pushed a

few damp strands of hair away from her face. "Oh, hello, Matt. Be right with you."

A moment later when she eased herself off the barrel and started toward him, Matt could see that Maggie's cheeks were flushed from the fire, her skin glistening with perspiration and something else; a certain radiance that hadn't been there before. Gone was the tension he'd noticed the first time they met, the rigid mask she wore to hide her little secrets. In place of that edgy lady came an earthy, seductive woman, the lusty sort lionized through the ages as the ideal female.

When she reached the edge of the table, the perfect woman gave Matt a direct look with just the hint of a frown. "Why are you here with my daughter? Is *everything* all right?"

It took a full minute for his befuddled brain to understand that Maggie was inquiring about her secrets and his vow of silence in regards to them. After that, Matt's tongue practically tied itself in knots as he worked at reassuring her.

"Oh, hell yes, Maggie, everything is fine, don't worry about that. Ben Sloan asked me to help Holly with her kite and I said that I would."

The sound of an irritating, squeaky voice cleared the last of Matt's cobwebs.

"He said hell, Mama." Holly looked up at her mother. "Isn't that a bad word?"

Maggie narrowed her gaze and fired both barrels at Matt. "Yes, darling, it certainly is. I'm afraid Mr. Weston forgot his manners."

"Sorry," he muttered, canting his head toward Holly. It was bad enough being chastised by a child—did Maggie have to treat him as if he were one, too? Matt couldn't keep the sarcasm out of his tone as he added, "I'll try not to forget my manners again."

"I'm sure you won't." Her words were clipped until she turned to her daughter, then it was all sugar and spice, just the way Maggie smelled. "So what's all this about Captain Weston helping you with your kite, Holly? Did he fly it for you?"

"Not yet 'cause we need string. Can I have some?"

"I already told you that I don't have any, sweetheart. Maybe if you ask Mr. Goldwater nicely, he might find that he has an extra spool to loan you."

Without another word, the girl darted under the table and disappeared into the crowd. Once that consarned child with the babbling, accusing tongue wasn't there to distract her, Matt was pleased to see that Maggie had relaxed again. She even produced a smile that could only have been meant for one person—him.

"I really appreciate your kindness," she said, looking undeniably sincere. "Holly doesn't always understand that not every man she meets wants to become her father for a while. I hope she didn't badger you into agreeing to fly her kite."

"Uh, well actually, I don't intend to help her at all. That was Ben Sloan's idea, not mine. I don't have time for that kind of nonsense."

Matt knew the minute the words left his lips that he'd made a terrible mistake. Maggie's sudden scowl and blazing eyes merely substantiated his belated good judgment.

"I stood here not five minutes ago and heard you announce that you'd promised to help Holly with her kite, and that you did so in the presence of our sheriff, no less." Long slender fingers splayed, she slapped her hands against her curvaceous hips. "Earlier this week you assured me that you were a man of your word, Captain Weston. If I'm to trust you, how can you possibly break the promise you made to Ben and my daughter?"

He should never have discussed the wire with Ben Sloan. Matt understood that now, even though it was too late to undo the damage. He should also have marched over to the telegraph office and sent the reply to El Paso himself. Then he should have gone to the stable to get his horse, Louie, saddled the gelding up, and ridden out of Prescott without so much as a look back. But no, Matt grumbled to himself—he had to go and look at Maggie as something other than a simple assignment, to let himself see her with less than the calculating eyes and indifferent mind that had kept him alive and alert during his years as an active ranger.

There could be only one reason for this uncharacteristic lapse. He'd gone soft in retirement. How else could he have been turned into such a damn fool, and so easily? Two years ago Matt probably wouldn't have noticed Maggie's soft brown eyes or her luscious figure, even though she had a body capable of launching a thousand and one ships. As it was, Maggie Hollister turned his head so often of late, Matt figured it was sheer luck that he hadn't managed to wring his own neck by now.

He may have gone soft, but he figured he was still man enough to admit when he was wrong. Removing his hat, Matt pressed it against his chest and murmured, "You're absolutely right, Maggie. I did promise to help your girl and I never break my word. I was thinking of the long ride ahead of me, I guess, without realizing that I'd be breaking my promise."

She cocked her head. "You're leaving?"

"At dawn," he confirmed. "Don't get your hopes up too high, but I received a reply from one of my inquiries." He glanced over each of his shoulders, ensuring privacy, then lowered his voice. "The man we're looking for may have been spotted recently in El Paso."

Maggie's hands flew to her mouth, but her gasp was still audible, filled with both surprise and joy. "You've *found* him—and so soon?"

"Careful now," Matt cautioned. "You don't want the entire town in on this do you? Besides, while there may be cause for hope, his identity isn't confirmed and won't be until I get some more information from you. I don't even know what the man looks like. That's one reason I said I didn't have time to mess with your daughter's kite. You and I have to have a little talk in private before I can head out."

"Yes, yes, of course." Maggie paused long enough to think up a plan. "Since you're leaving so soon, you're going to need a good meal and a decent store for the road. I'd like to fix you up, if you don't mind."

Matt's stomach wasn't about to let his brain turn her down. "If things taste as good as they smell around here, I'd be a fool not to accept the offer."

"Good. That's settled. Now there's just one other problem for us to—"

"String, Mama! I got lots of string!"

Maggie turned toward the sound of her daughter's voice, then smiled back at Matt. "And here comes that little problem now. Why don't you and Holly take her kite and ride on out by Clough's Ranch? Just follow Granite Creek out of town. Holly knows the way. You two can work on her kite there while I get your store ready for the trail. I'll join you shortly after that with a picnic supper for us all."

Matt shook his head. "I don't see how that gives us time to talk."

"Holly doesn't sit still for long, even when she's eating. We'll have plenty of opportunities to talk in private. Any other problems?"

Plenty of them, but they weren't the sort Matt could argue with any conviction. He'd already lost the war anyway, which left him in no position to dictate the terms of his surrender—especially since his own mouth had gotten him into this predicament in the first place.

Resigned to his fate, Matt slid his hat in place, reshaped the brim into a perfect funnel at the tip, and said, "I think you've pretty much got things under control. See you down the creek a ways."

Something tugged on his pants leg. He glanced down to see Holly's nearly toothless grin smiling up at him.

"Do you got your own horse, mister? We can borrow Billy's if you don't got one."

"Have one, Holly," said Maggie. "And yes, Captain Weston does have a horse."

"Does it got a name?"

Before her mother could correct her again, Matt said, "Yes, he does *have* a name. It's Louie."

"Louie?" She giggled. "That's a funny name for a horse. Let's go get him!"

Matt wondered if all children sounded like a rusty gate hinge when they spoke, or just this one. He also wondered how much string she'd managed to bamboozle out of the shopkeeper. And if it was strong enough to lash a towheaded magpie to a flimsy paper kite.

It took Maggie better than an hour to pack up Matt's saddle-bags and fill the picnic basket with their supper. After the long hours she'd spent baking for the festival, not to mention all the work she'd done during the affair, she was almost too tired to hitch Hattie's horse to the buggy. Once she was on the road, however, it wasn't long before Maggie got her second wind.

Although it was still unseasonably warm for mid-October, a cool breeze caressed her flushed skin as the rig left the main road and started up the slight incline which led to the picnic area. Maggie finally began to wake up a little. A few puffy clouds had mushroomed out of nowhere, most of them snowy white, but there were also a few sooty streaks among them, the kind that could wreak havoc with the supper she'd packed.

Inhaling deeply, she detected the promise of rain, and thought perhaps they were in for at least a few sprinkles or even her favorite, a rip-roaring thunderstorm. Cloudy days and blustery weather had long fascinated her, and this purple-mottled sky captured her completely. Maggie was so distracted, in fact, that she nearly tumbled over the side of the buggy when the little bay mare suddenly shied and swerved to the road's edge.

After taking a few moments to calm both herself and the horse, Maggie glanced back at the road to see what had upset the animal so much. There in the dust, its frame battered and bent at impossible angles, lay Holly's kite, reduced now to a tangle of butcher's paper, wood splinters, and string. She looked around, assuming her daughter and Matt were close by, and picked up the sound of voices filtering through the fragrant pines.

". . . and besides all that," said Matt. "I warned you from the start that I didn't know how to fly a kite, didn't I?" A long silence followed. "Well, didn't I?"

"Yeth!"

Things between the two were not going well, if Holly's attitude was any indication. She was sometimes difficult to understand—so far, only half of a tooth had grown back to replace the two she'd lost—but her stubborn I'm-right-and-you're-wrong-no-matter-what tone left no question about her mood.

"Boys fly kites all the time," Holly griped. "Sheriff Ben said so. Boys are s'posed to know how to fly kites, not looth them!"

"I didn't lose the damn thing, it just got away from me. Hang onto your woollies a while longer and we're bound to come across it."

"You said a bad word, and what's woollies? I don't have any woollies."

"Oh, for the love of . . . has anyone ever told you that you talk too much?" Another long pause followed. "Well it's true, you're a regular magpie. Why don't you do us both a favor and give that poor tongue of yours a rest before it falls right out of your mouth."

"You're mean! I don't like you."

"Yeah, well, you're no bargain yourself. Hey—Louie, you son of a bitch! Get up here."

"You said more bad words. I'm telling Mama."

About the time Maggie decided it would be a good idea to break up their quarrel, she saw her daughter's little blond head cresting the knoll, with the crown of Matt Weston's white hat not far behind. A big black horse—Louie, she assumed—dragged along behind them, his head hanging down as if he were ashamed to be in the company of two such obnoxious scrappers.

Holly looked up and spotted the kite on the ground. But she didn't see Maggie sitting at the side of the road. Holly raced with arms outstretched to her wounded toy.

"It's broke!" she cried, dropping to her knees and gathering the remains. She struggled to her feet, the mangled kite clutched to her breast, then turned to hurl accusations at her "helper." "You killed it! You didn't want to fly it, so you killed it!"

"I did not. I'm sure there's a way to fix it up again."

Matt's feeble assurances came to an end when he saw Maggie and the buggy. He tipped his hat her way, shrugged, then reached out to Holly.

"Why don't you give it to me? Maybe I can fix it good enough to fly again."

She stamped her foot and probably would have refused the offer, but Maggie chose that moment to intervene and come to Matt's rescue.

"Thank you for the offer, Captain Weston," she called. "That sounds like a good idea."

At the sound of her mother's voice, Holly whirled around, dropped the kite and ran to the buggy. "Mama!" she cried, pointing behind her. "He—"

"I know what happened, sweetheart. Captain Weston will do what he can to put your kite back together again."

Out of the corner of her eye, Maggie saw Matt scoop the paper and bits of wood off the ground, then turn and disappear over the rise. As before, Louie dragged along behind him, looking as if he'd rather be anywhere than chasing kites with his master.

Once Matt was out of earshot, Maggie let her young, impulsive daughter know in no uncertain terms that she owed the ranger an apology for her insolence and lack of respect. Holly agreed to the terms, then quietly went in search of Matt Weston.

After that was settled, Maggie found a grassy spot on a knoll overlooking Granite Creek and the rugged granite formations known as Point of Rocks, then quickly spread a blanket near a stand of cottonwood trees and set out the picnic food. In the distance she could see Holly and Matt hunched over their work, which gave her a few minutes to safely indulge her passion for cloud-watching.

Maggie stretched out on the blanket, listening to the sound of Holly's high-pitched squeals and giggles, expressions of delight that would soon fade if Matt wasn't successful in his mission. Suddenly overwhelmed by the sense of desperation that usually swept over her at this time of year, Maggie closed her eyes against the silvery allure of the skies and prayed that days like this could be the norm from now on, not the exception. And that little Holly would finally have the kind of family she'd wished for and deserved. Then, feeling drowsy, she gave herself up to a little cat nap.

Matt, on the other hand, found himself wishing this day were at an end. The minute he finally got the resurrected kite aloft, he tied the string to Holly's wrist, leaving her alone to fly what he'd turned into a soaring crazy quilt. Not that she wanted him to stick around. Hell, Matt felt the same way. He couldn't wait to get out of Prescott and away from Hollister's demanding, screeching daughter. Even after he spotted the edge of the picnic blanket, Matt was prepared to leave town hungry to avoid further contact with the sassy little imp.

But then as he drew near, he saw Maggie lying there like some pagan goddess, loaves of crusty bread, slices of crispy turkey, and mounds of fresh apple dumplings all around her. Suddenly it seemed like a really good idea to stay and enjoy himself for a while. He stood there quietly, studying the array of delectable morsels, but his eyes kept going back to what tempted him the most—the lovely, kind, and very married, Maggie Hollister. Forbidden fruit.

Resisting the urge to run like hell and forget that he'd ever ridden into the town of Prescott, Matt cleared his throat and said, "Hey, there—are you sleeping?"

Maggie's eyes popped open and she jerked herself to a sitting position. "My heavens—I guess so. I was up baking half the night for the festival." She patted the blanket beside her. "Come, sit down and help me get rid of some of this food. I think I packed enough to feed every last soldier at Fort Whipple."

Matt sank onto the blanket cross-legged as directed, but didn't even glance at the fare. "I don't know how long that kite's going to stay in the air, so we'd better get our business out of the way before we eat."

"You got it to fly?"

Maggie shaded her eyes and looked out on the horizon, her smile bright enough to light the increasingly dark skies. Almost afraid of what he might see, Matt followed her gaze. Amazingly enough, the strange kite was mastering the wind gusts quite handily, as was its captain, Holly-the-magpie. Even more curious, a warm sense of satisfaction ran through him as he watched the girl skipping along with the breeze, happy in spite of the mess he'd made out of her kite.

"Matt?"

He turned to see Maggie staring at his throat with open admiration.

"Did you make the kite's tail out of your own kerchief?"

He had, and suddenly, Matt was at a loss to explain why he'd made the sacrifice. He couldn't even explain it to himself. Avoiding the subject entirely, he said, "As I mentioned, I don't think that thing's going to fly for long. We really need to talk about your husband."

"Of course, but first, let me thank you for being so kind to Holly. I can't tell you how happy it makes me to hear her laugh like that, especially since I suspect that none of this has been easy for you."

It had been nothing short of a pain, but Matt couldn't imagine that Maggie had drawn the same conclusion. "Why do you say that?"

"I somehow got the impression that you aren't used to being around children, and probably don't have any of your own. You don't, do you?"

"Uh, no, I surely do not. That's probably for the best."

Maggie laughed softly. "What about a wife? Have you ever been married?"

Why was she asking such personal questions? They were supposed to be talking about her missing husband, not his own empty life. Besides, Matt was used to being the interrogator, not the other way around—and he didn't care for the reversal one damn bit.

"No kids, no wife," he said abruptly before moving onto new territory. "What I need from you is the most detailed description you can give to help identify your husband, everything right down to his mannerisms."

Maggie sighed heavily. "It's been a long time since I last saw Rafe, but I'll do the best I can." She stared off toward the creek, her expression pensive, cast in shadows of the past. When she was ready to go on, her voice wasn't much more than a whisper.

"I remember his big calf eyes the best. They're brown, but much darker than mine, and fringed with thick lashes that curled back to his lids. I doubt there's a woman alive who wouldn't trade her best dress for those eyelashes. I know I would."

Matt couldn't imagine why. Maggie's lashes were black as pitch and long enough to sweep her cheeks each time she took a sidelong glance. True, they weren't particularly curly, but the way they arched up into a graceful curve gave her a kind of dreamy look, the suggestion of an inner, smoldering passion.

"Rafe's hair, on the other hand," said Maggie, tossing cold water on Matt's increasingly improper thoughts. "Resembled a hailed-out wheat crop, if you know what I mean. It stuck up in uneven tufts, falling every whichway whenever he moved his head. The man definitely had more than his share of cowlicks."

"Is he blond?" asked Matt, regretting that he had to have this conversation at all. "Like Holly?"

Maggie shrugged. "I suppose he was when he was her age. I'd say the color is more a dirty or sandy blond, maybe even darker by now."

Matt thought dirty ought to do it. "What about his height and build? Can you remember how tall he is, say in relation to me?"

Again she laughed. "I never have a problem with my memory when it comes to height, no matter who you're talking about. When you're as tall a woman as I am, you tend to measure both men and women against the yardstick of your own body—and not necessarily so you can describe that person years later."

This comment threw Matt at first, leading him into another subject that would have been better left alone. "I'm not sure I know what you're talking about."

"You don't?" She actually looked surprised. "You should. I clearly remember your reaction the first time you saw me standing instead of sitting."

He gulped. Had he really been so obvious in his undisguised appreciation of Maggie as a woman?

"Let me help your memory along," she continued. "Your

mouth dropped open and you looked as if you'd just crossed paths with Goliath's big sister."

That wasn't at all the way Matt remembered it, but there wasn't a lot he could do to set Maggie straight. Not if he wanted to come out of this conversation with his honor, and possibly his manhood, intact. Left with virtually no option, Matt had to let her go on thinking that he considered her a little too big to be attractive, but the idea didn't set well.

Ashamed of himself on too many levels to count, he forged ahead with his questions. "Measuring your husband any way you like, can you give me some idea of Hollister's general build and height?"

Maggie took a long time answering, too long for Matt's liking as she was undoubtedly remembering the hours she'd spent in the bastard's arms.

"Rafe was almost as tall as I am," she finally said. "About an inch shorter I think, and very thin back then, skinny as a snake on stilts." She glanced at Matt, scanning his shoulders and chest. "He may have gotten some meat on his bones by now, but even if he filled out good, he wouldn't be as big or as muscular as you are."

Matt didn't even get a chance to enjoy the comparison before the sound of a small screechy voice singing in rhyme reached his ears. Worse than her shrill soprano, the sound was definitely growing louder with each note. He glanced at the sky, and as he feared, could find no signs of the kite.

"Quickly, Maggie," Matt urged, moving closer to her. "Holly will be here soon. Tell me about the way Rafe walked and talked, anything that might help me to make a positive identification."

She furrowed her brow, taking up far too many of their precious few seconds, then finally she shrugged and said, "I already told you about his Texas accent. He walked like anyone else, I suppose. I don't know if this will be of any help, but when he set his mind to it, Rafe could really be charming. He wasn't exactly what you'd call handsome at first glance, but he was awfully good at tricking a lady into *thinking* he's handsome. Do you know what I mean?"

He did, and it irritated the bloody blue hell out of him. "I think so. You've been very helpful."

"Oh." Maggie snapped her fingers. "There is one more thing that might help. Rafe used to bite his fingernails something awful, chewed them down to the quick until they bled."

Matt had never personally known a nail-biting man. "That might just make the difference right there. If you think of anything else before I leave town, do whatever you have to in order to get me aside and tell me about it. Agreed?"

"Agreed," she said, an odd secretive gleam in her eye. "In fact I've already thought of a couple more things I should tell you before Holly gets back."

She surprised Matt by leaning into him then, almost, but not quite touching shoulders. She smelled a little like orange blossoms and something else, dried currants perhaps, perfume enough to get him thinking forbidden thoughts again.

If her scent wasn't hard enough for him to ignore, Maggie's mouth was but a whisper away from his, too damn close when she finally said, "First, I want to wish you good luck and God bless on your journey."

Her warm breath feathered those sentiments across Matt's cheek, drawing a response from each of his vital organs that staggered him. She then compounded the torment by pressing her petal-soft lips a mere inch from the corner of his mouth. When Matt thought he might drown in the turmoil boiling up inside him, or maybe just curl up and die from the want of touching her, Maggie took her sweet lips away and settled back into her former spot on the blanket.

Her smile innocent and unashamed, the expression of a woman who had no idea of her power over men, she warned, "Please remember this above all as you go about your business—whatever else my husband may be when you find him, he's bound to be the same liar he always was, the kind of man who could give false oath in church, then curse at the Lord on his way out the door."

Maggie had wasted her sweet breath on that little caution, thought Matt. He knew exactly what her truant husband was, even if the man was too damn dumb to know it for himself.

Rafe Hollister was the luckiest son of a bitch on the face of the earth.

Four

El Paso, Texas

It took him ten full days and almost as many shots of whisky to dull the pain in his hip, but Matt finally stumbled across the luckiest son of a bitch on the face of the earth at the Holy Moses Saloon and Dancing Palace.

He'd stopped by Marshal Stoudenmire's office the minute he hit town, matched the lawman's description to the one Maggie had provided, then went straight to the saloons spilling onto the boardwalks of San Antonio Street. Matt expected to find his quarry begging for drinks or cheating other gamblers out of what was theirs; at the least, charming hurdy-gurdy gals into thinking that he was the best-looking man in all of Texas.

Instead Matt stumbled across Rafe Hollister as he lay face-down on the dirt floor near the saloon's entrance. Out cold, Hollister had unwittingly become a human threshold and boot scraper, an irksome lump for some customers to trip over, a convenient spot to clean the horse dung off the shoes of others. Matt favored the idea of wiping his boots on Hollister's scrawny ass if for no other reason than to help purge the unreasonable rage that tore through him at the thought of this filthy bastard touching Maggie. He didn't, but Matt did savor a moment's pleasure just thinking about it.

After his eyes adjusted to the murky lighting, Matt hunkered down beside Hollister and checked to make sure the man was still alive. One side of his dirty blond head was ground into the dirt, animal droppings, tobacco juice, and whatever else had collected or been spit onto the floor, but his nose was clear of the filth.

Unfortunately, Hollister was still breathing.

A quick scan of the man's body showed narrow hips that barely filled his jeans and shoulder blades jutting up from the back of his shirt. If Maggie's husband had put any meat on his body over the past seven years, it couldn't have amounted to more than a pan or two of hardtack.

Dropping to one knee in order to rouse the man from his drunken slumber, Matt got an abrupt awakening himself. Even here in the stifling atmosphere of one of El Paso's cheapest dives, a room featuring air contaminated by stale urine, unwashed humanity, and tobacco smoke among other things, the gut-churning stench of this fool's clothing was the most noxious odor of all.

Turning his nose aside, Matt shouted, "Hollister!"

When that got no response, he grabbed a fistful of spiky hair and raised him up from the floor. Shaking him like the dog that he was, Matt barked into the man's ear. "I mean business, *compadre*. If I have to, I'll put a few holes in you to get you moving, starting at your feet."

Rafe opened his mouth as if to speak, but burped up a putrid bubble of gas instead. Another odor that made the air seem fresh as a bouquet of flowers by comparison. Matt released the clump of hair. Hollister hit the dirt with a soft thump and a profound groan.

Leaving the sot to himself for a moment, Matt glanced around the saloon. Damned if he would spend any more time than absolutely necessary in such a stinking hell-hole. The only light in the place came from a trio of candles lashed to a jerry-built chandelier swinging down from the ceiling. Two small panes of glass above the doorway should have served as windows, but both were so fogged over with grime and smoke, they barely emitted a ribbon of sunlight.

Matt wanted out of the place, and now. Enlisting the aid of the other patrons didn't seem likely, even though the lowly watering hole was packed with revelers. Most of them were Mexican laborers in various stages of intoxication. All of them seemed hell-bent on turning over their meager wages to sharpers who lured them with games of monte, roulette, chuck-a-luck and poker. None of them would be interested in helping a Texas Ranger, retired or not, to bring one of their compadres to justice. They might wipe their boots on Rafe Hollister's ass, but that's where they'd draw the line. If Hollister had been drinking here long enough to pass out, they undoubtedly thought of him as one of their own. Hell, they hadn't even bothered to steal the man's boots.

Accepting the fact that he was on his own, Matt considered ways of getting Hollister out of the saloon without bringing too much attention to himself. Two years ago or under different circumstances, he would simply have slung the unconscious man over his shoulder and walked out the door. Now, thanks to his injury and the ride between Phoenix and Maricopa, his damaged hip and left leg could barely support his own weight.

Deciding to hurry the sobering process along, Matt hobbled over to the bar, ordered an extra large mug of beer, and limped back to where Hollister snored face down in the dirt. Then he dumped the entire brew over his head.

Sputtering, coughing and gasping, Hollister finally raised his chin. "Wha—wha're?"

Matt leaned in as close as he could without gagging. "Hey— did you hear? Free drinks! Get up before the place runs dry."

That got Hollister's attention, blurry-eyed as it may have been. With a little help from Matt and a few failed attempts, the drunken man finally got his wobbly legs under him well

enough to stand up. With a firm grasp on Hollister's collar and
the seat of his pants, Matt steered Maggie's errant husband toward the doorway, pushing him the way he would a wheelbar-
row.

About the time Matt thought they were in the clear, the sot
suddenly locked his knees.

"Hey!" Hollister shouted, sounding surprisingly sober. "This
ain't the bar. S'over there."

He then swung his arm around in an awkward circle, nearly
skimming the hat from Matt's head.

"Don't worry, *amigo*," he said, forcing a gentle tone. "This
isn't the saloon serving the free drinks. The Road to Hell Cantina across the street is giving them away."

"No foolin'?"

"Would I fool you?"

Since Hollister couldn't think of a response, in fact, couldn't
think at all, Matt had no trouble easing him closer to the doorway. They'd gotten as far as the threshold before the fool balked
again.

"Wait, dammee," he slurred. "Wait one!"

Heels dug into the dirt, his bony back leaning against Matt's
chest, Hollister twisted his head around and looked over both
their shoulders.

"Peggy!" he shouted, damn near rupturing Matt's eardrum.
"Get to hopping, gal, we're a-movin' on! Y'all hear me,
woman?"

"Forget her," said Matt as he spun Hollister around in his
arms and propped him against the door jamb. "There's plenty
of female companionship across the street and they're a lot better looking than anything you can find here."

Hollister's eyes rolled, then closed. Assuming he'd passed out
again, Matt slid his hands under the man's arms and prepared
to heave the bastard over his shoulder, bad leg be damned.
About that time an airy female voice filled his right ear.

"Hey, mister—what're ya doin' to Rafy?"

Matt turned to find a pudgy little saloon gal standing behind him, hands on hips. Peggy, he assumed, with breasts exploding over the top of her dress like a pair of new feather pillows. She also had a shock of flamboyantly red hair and a cute little up-turned nose, now wrinkled with suspicion.

"Rafe and I have a little business to tend to," Matt explained with a friendly wink. "It's kind of private."

"Can't be too private," she challenged. "Seems to me that Rafy just hollered I should come join him."

The sound of the woman's voice brought Hollister around a little. His head rolled between his shoulder blades as if it were on a swivel and his eyeballs rolled right along with it as he mumbled, "Free drinks, Peggy, acrosh . . . at Hell."

"That'll be the day." The saloon gal shot a skeptical glance at Matt. "Who're you, anyways? Ain't seen you around here before."

Matt forced a bigger grin, one that showed plenty of teeth and popped a cursedly boyish, but occasionally useful pair of dimples into place. "Then you haven't been looking too hard, little darlin'," he murmured. "'Cause I've sure seen you."

"I ain't so hard to find," she cooed, batting her lashes. Her expression was shy, giggly, but just hesitant enough for Matt to realize that she hadn't entirely bought his act.

"I'm new in town," he replied, making up his story as he went along. "I've looked around some, but so far, I haven't come across anything quite like you."

"You won't neither." She raised her shoulders then pushed them back, jiggling her puffy breasts. "I ought to warn you now that I ain't cheap like some of the others 'round here. I never get less than a dollar a throw, two if you just got to have me by your side all night long."

Matt nodded, trying to look impressed. "Sounds like that's what I'd be interested in, but we have to wait for our business

until later. My business with Rafe can't wait another minute. If
all goes well at the cantina, we'll both be rich men the next
time you see us—so rich in fact, I might just feel like keeping
you with me for a whole week."

That final remark got a bright smile out of the hollow-eyed
whore, smoothing a few of the wrinkles that had aged her before
her time.

"Well, all right," she muttered. "But take it easy on the tan-
glefoot, would ya? Poor Rafy's already got hisself a snoot-full,
in case you ain't noticed."

"I noticed, darlin', and will proceed with caution."

She offered a tired smile by way of thanks, prompting Matt
to tip his hat. Without waiting to make sure she went on about
her business, he turned to Hollister, who was losing the battle
to remain conscious, wrapped his right arm around his waist,
then half-walked and half-dragged his ass out the door.

As they made their way toward Rosa's Boarding House under
the blaze of the setting sun, the toes of "Rafy's" boots plowed
a trail of neat little corn rows in their wake, furrows even a
blind tracker could have followed. Matt didn't worry about that
or the possibility that anyone might take a notion to follow him
home.

He was too busy thinking about Maggie to concern himself
with anything else. Too caught up wondering what she would
think of her husband if she could see him now. And if she could,
whether she'd still be in such a damn hurry to get him home
and back into her arms.

An hour later Matt passed Rafe's stinking clothing to Rosa,
who was standing just outside his room at her boarding house.

"Madre de Dios!" she cried, pinching her nostrils shut with
her free hand as she accepted the garments. "Has your *amigo*
been lying with the hogs, Señor Weston?"

"Something like that." He dropped a few coins into her apron. "I'll pay you double that if you can get the stink out and have them ready to wear again in the next two or three days."

Rosa raised her chin, turning her nose as far away from the offending odor as possible. "I can do it, but I think it will cost you more than a few extra pesos. Perhaps a sweet would make the job easier?"

Since boarding with Rosa almost two years ago, Matt had learned how to cajole or tempt the woman into doing just about every chore he loathed, including his laundry. Though feisty, tough, and intractable with her other boarders, Rosa became a kind of second mother to Matt once he'd learned that she would march through the fires of hell for a taste of chocolate. Since then Matt had never failed to bring the spirited *señora* a special treat after he returned from an assignment.

"Now that I think of it," he teased. "I do believe that I might have ordered two pounds of Hazel's pecan fudge this morning—it ought to be delivered to your door sometime this afternoon."

Rosa sighed and licked her lips. "It is a sin against my *Umberto,* the way you make me feel, Señor Weston. Maybe I should go to confession."

"Be sure to leave my name out of it when you do." Matt pinched her chubby cheek. "In the meantime, you'd better get started on that laundry. I think the stink is beginning to grow on you."

With a muted shriek of horror, Rosa whirled around in the narrow hallway, all hips and flashes of crimson petticoats, then waddled out of sight. Laughing to himself, Matt bolted the door and went back to work.

Rafe Hollister had been drifting in and out of consciousness ever since Matt had hauled him up to his second-floor room and stripped him naked. He almost came around once and even put up a feeble argument when Matt buried him up to his neck in the barrel of hot water Rosa had sent up. Since then he'd just sat there, his chin bobbing against his bony chest every time he snored.

Matt, usually patient, couldn't seem to spare so much as a drop of tolerance for this man. Exhausted from the journey to El Paso, physically spent after hauling the fool across town, Matt was in no mood or condition to wait for Nature to take its course. Driven by the pain in his hip along with an unusual sense of impatience, he stalked over to the barrel, pushed Hollister's head underwater, then held it there until the bastard's struggles were truly attentive.

Only then did Matt release him and step away from the tub.

The baffled sot looked up with surprisingly clear eyes and sputtered, "W-what're y'all tryin to do? Drown me?"

"That's a very tempting idea, Hollister, but no."

After dragging the chair out from under his desk, Matt spun it around in front of the barrel, then straddled it so he could look the drunken bastard in the eye.

"I was only trying to get you awake enough to take a bath," he explained. "You're stinking up my room."

Hollister's suddenly fearful gaze swept the four walls, skimming but not lingering on the spartan furnishings; a single bed, narrow dresser, and writing desk complete with gas lamp.

"But why am I in y'all's room?" he asked. "We ain't never met . . . have we?"

"Not yet, but you'll make my acquaintance—and soon. Real soon." Matt reached down to the floor to collect the towel, scrub brush and bar of lye soap Rosa had supplied. "Before we make our introductions, partner, you're gonna have to scrub that stench from your body, even if it means losing a little skin in the bargain."

Hollister eyed the soap with an almost comical bewilderment, then raised his hands out of the water to take it from Matt.

That's when he realized that he was wearing handcuffs. "Uh, why, uh . . . y'all the law?"

"You might say that."

Hollister gulped, rattling a scrawny and rather prominent Adam's apple. "What kind a trouble did I get into?"

Matt could have and probably should have listed Hollister's offenses then and there, starting with the way he'd ruined the life of a decent, honest woman, but he was just too damn tired to explain. Even worse, Matt wasn't sure he could keep his temper in check once Maggie's name entered the discussion. If Hollister wanted to go on living and Matt wanted to stay out of jail, the bastard would have to stay ignorant of the "charges" against him until they'd both had a good night's sleep.

"Just take your bath and shut up, Hollister. You'll get your answers when I'm good and ready to give them."

"That ain't fair. Y'all can't keep me trussed up like this without telling me why. 'Sides, if I done wrong, why ain't I in jail? And where in tarnation is the marshal?"

Fatigue catching up with him, Matt raised a clenched fist and buried it in the scraggly mustache beneath Hollister's nose. "I'm the law, you idiot, and as a Texas Ranger, I make the demands and the rules around here, not the likes of you. Do you have a problem with that?"

Now that Matt had identified himself as a ranger, even if it wasn't quite true anymore, Hollister cowered in the barrel. "No, sir."

"Good. You've got exactly ten minutes to clean yourself up and get into that dry bedroll on the floor, and do it with your mouth shut. If you can't meet those terms, I'll gag you and let you to sleep in that water barrel for the rest of the night. *Comprende?*"

Hollister shivered violently, but nodded in mute surrender, pleasing Matt in a such a savage way that it made him feel a little crazed. To calm himself, he backed away from the tub and headed for the basin to wash up.

As he splashed cold water on his face, Matt found himself doing something he hadn't done since he was a young boy, not since the day his mother ran off with the man cutting her portrait—praying. The pleas were not for himself, but for Hollister, not for anything so righteous as the man's soul, but simply for his miserable life.

Somehow he had to find it in himself to grant Maggie's husband a little mercy, to think of the man as an assignment, not a personal insult. But damn, it wasn't going to be easy. Matt just hoped that if there was a God, He might help him to find his usual sense of honor and commitment to fair play—and that they showed up again sometime before dawn.

During his years as a fully functional Texas Ranger, Matt tracked and battled scores of Indian raiding parties, recovered thousands of stolen horses and cattle, and even rescued a couple of citizens who'd been carried off by Apaches. In regard to performance of duty, patriotic devotion, and courage, he excelled beyond the high standards the Rangers demanded of those who wore the *cinco peso* in lieu of a badge. Among his exceptional talents was an inborn instinct that warned him when danger was near, even in a dead sleep. Matt was known on both sides of the law as a man who could hear the footfalls of a flea on his pillow or feel the vibrations of cat paws if a cougar was stalking prey nearby.

So far, those keen instincts hadn't faded much in Matt's softer life as a retired ranger. Although deep into some much-needed sleep during the wee hours of the next morning, he heard the scrapes and faint scratches of someone slipping into his room through the open window. As he caught a whiff of rancid perfume, then picked up the distinct rustle of petticoats, the gun

Matt kept beneath his pillow was in his hand and cocked before those none-too-dainty feet could hit the floor.

At the expected feminine gasp, he said, "That's right. You just heard me chambering one of six bullets. With very little effort, I'm sure it can find a new home in one or the both of you. Any questions?"

"Ah, no sir," came Hollister's weak reply.

"Good. Tell the lady to light the lamp. She'll find it on the desk by the window she used to get into my room."

The next voice was airy, feminine, and all too familiar. The saloon whore muttered, "Keep your pants on, mister, I'm going."

After she lit the wick, illuminating features that were even more haggard than they'd been back at the saloon, Matt waved the gun the woman's way and said, "Good morning, Peggy. Would you mind putting your hands up where I can keep an eye on them, darlin'?"

"No need for the gun, mister," she complained as she slowly raised her arms. "I was just checking up on my brother here, seeing if he was all right since you brung him to your room and never let him back out again."

Her brother? This was a surprise. Matt's gut also told him it was probably a lie. He eased the gun's hammer back in place, then aimed the barrel and his next question at Hollister.

"Is this charming little saloon *entertainer* really your sister?"

"That's what she said, ain't it?" Somehow during the night, the man had dredged up a little courage, foolish bravado. "And mind what you say about her," he went on to demand.

It was then Matt realized that his prayers had indeed been answered. Otherwise Rafe Hollister and his smart mouth would have been staring at him through a third eye, the one drilled directly between the other two by a .45 caliber bullet.

Instead Matt was able to smile at the man, moderately amused by the sight of the scrawny bastard as he stood in the middle of the mussed bedroll trying to defend his sister, the saloon whore. Shackled hand and foot, Hollister was also trembling from head to toe and hanging on for dear life to the bunched-up waist of the long underwear Matt had been kind enough to loan him. Only a white-tailed deer trying out the coat of a bull elk could have looked more ridiculous.

"Have you always been a slow learner, Hollister?" Matt asked drolly. "Or are you only stupid enough to let your tongue do your thinking after you've drank yourself into the shakes? I asked you a civil question and I expect a civil answer in return."

"Didn't mean no disrespect, Ranger." At least he had the good sense to look slightly contrite and ashamed. "It's just that Peggy's my sis and I don't cotton to folks making fun of her. She's a good little gal, a regular angel."

"Never mind about me," said Rafy's sister, the saloon angel. Dark smudges deepened the hollows beneath her pale eyes and her lip rouge was smeared into the cracks above her mouth. And yet she demanded of Matt, "I wanna know why you got my brother chained up like a common horse thief. You said you was gonna make him rich, not arrest him. What's he done?"

Naked beneath the sheet, Matt swung his legs over the edge of the mattress, careful to keep a wide strip of cotton in place from his upper thighs to his navel. Waving the Colt between the siblings, either of which could have been hiding a weapon the woman brought with her, Matt gave Hollister a chance to conduct their business in private.

"What your brother has done and what he must do to set things right are topics best discussed between the two of us." He glanced at Hollister. "Our business is extremely private, but I'll leave the decision about whether she stays or goes, up to you."

After a moment of none-too-deliberate consideration, Rafe shrugged and said, "Don't make no nevermind to me if Peggy stays. I ain't done nothing she don't or cain't know about."

"In that case, Peggy," said Matt. "I'm going to have to ask you to turn your back for a minute."

She did so grudgingly, her hands still raised in the air. Matt quickly tugged on his drawers and jeans, but left the rest for later in favor of searching the Hollisters for weapons. Once he was satisfied that both were unarmed, as much as he could be without stripping the woman down to her stockings anyway, Matt offered his chair to Peggy, directed Rafe to sit down on the bedroll, then propped himself against the sturdy little desk.

"I've been hired to find you, Hollister," he began, "clean you up, and take you back to Arizona Territory, to the town of Prescott to be precise. Sound familiar?"

If he knew where this conversation was going, the man didn't show it. He shrugged and shook his head.

"Maybe this will jog your memory. I was hired for this job by your wife, Maggie Hollister."

This got the reaction Matt was looking for. And then some.

"His *wife?*" cried Peggy, her eyes both wide and accusing as she turned an incredulous gaze on her brother. "What wife?"

"Hell, I dunno. I ain't never been married." He looked over at Matt with all the outrage of an innocent man. "Y'all chasing down the wrong dog, mister. That pup won't suck."

"There's no question I've got the right mongrel, Hollister, and by the way, I'm Captain Matt Weston. Call me by name from now on."

"Yessir, Captain Weston."

Although he normally would never have approached a prisoner without his gun drawn, Matt wasn't one hundred percent sure he could trust his suddenly itchy trigger finger around this bastard. Leaving the Colt behind on the desk and with only his bare hands as weapons—almost as deadly as the gun—he stalked over to where Hollister sat on his blanket.

"I suppose a man could forget his wedding day if he wanted to," Matt said, fighting the hatred simmering in his gut. "But there's no way you could possibly forget an entire winter, especially the one you spent hidden in a Utah barn with Maggie tending to your every need."

Sitting there with knees folded like a frog on a lily pad, Hollister paled so rapidly it was as if someone had pulled the cork on his blood supply, draining him dry. He swallowed, gulping audibly, then brought his cuffed hands to his mouth. Without sparing a word or a glance to either Matt or his sister, he jammed the tip of his thumb between his tight-set lips and began gnawing on what was left of the nail.

"Surely you recall the following spring," Matt went on to say, cutting short the occasional attempts by Peggy to interrupt him. "That's when you and Maggie left the farm for Salt Lake City, remember? And you couldn't possibly have forgotten the scandalous reason she was forced to leave her family and run off with you in the first place. Could you?"

Hollister was nibbling on the nail of his left index finger, his right hand flopping about in the cuff as he maneuvered the finger back and forth between his teeth. As Matt's words sank in, all movement suddenly ceased. With a graphic display of increasing awareness, the kind of tattletale expression that only the guilty can provide, Hollister slowly raised his chin until he was trapped in Matt's critical gaze. The bastard didn't speak or even try to respond to the query, but the sudden look in his eyes, an undeniable recognition of the fact that he'd been cornered was eloquent enough for an entire courtroom of lawyers.

"In case you're interested," Matt snarled softly, "Maggie had a little girl. You're the father of a six-year-old daughter named Holly."

"Daughter!" Peggy tried desperately to insinuate herself between Matt and her brother, but Matt held her back.

"What's he talking about, Rafy?" she cried, almost in tears. "You ain't got no wife and kid, do you?" She glanced at Matt, accusing him as if he were the guilty party. "Doncha think I'd know about it if my own brother had a wife and kid?"

"Peggy's got a point there," said Hollister, who'd finally found his tongue. "And b'sides, it's like I told y'all before—I ain't never been dumb enough to get married to no one. If'n I ever got a hankering to do something so stupid, I sure wouldn't be getting hitched to no lying, horse-faced old maid like Maggie Thorne."

Matt's response was swift and impulsive, a gut reaction that didn't give him so much as a second to consider alternatives. He dropped to one knee and delivered a vicious uppercut to the soft underside of Hollister's chin, raising the bastard off the bedroll and smashing him against the wall.

"Oh, glory!" cried Peggy, rushing to her brother's aid.

Blood trickled over Hollister's bottom lip, his eyeballs had rolled back in his head, and his chin was resting awkwardly on his right shoulder.

"You've gone and kilt him!" Peggy accused, sparing Matt a scalding glare. "Oh, Rafy, speak to me, honey boy, say something. Are you dead?"

The thought that he might have hit the man a little too hard was enough to bring Matt to his senses. He went to the crumpled heap that was Maggie's husband, nudged Peggy aside, and quickly examined him.

"Your brother's just fine," he assured the weeping woman after a quick look. "He has a split lip, nothing to worry about, and he'll be out cold for a minute or two. I'm sure it's not the first time."

"But his eyes!" she wailed, not at all reassured. "Look at them eyes!"

Matt couldn't deny that they were a sight to behold. Rafe Hollister may have had enviable lashes that curled up damn near to his hairline, but the twitching whites of his eyes pretty much canceled out the appeal of those lush lashes. Matt slapped the man's cheeks, drawing protests from his sister, but finally managed to bring Hollister around.

After giving the man a few minutes to focus—long enough anyway to realize that he was face to face with the ranger who'd just scrambled his brains, Matt laid down the law.

"I just gave you what I call a gentle warning," he said. "The next time you open that filthy mouth of yours and even think of spitting out lies or disrespectful words where your wife is concerned, will be the last time you say anything at all. To anyone. *Comprende?"*

For a crazy moment, Matt thought he saw an argument building up in Hollister's expression. But then his breath wheezed out, his shoulders bowed in toward his breastbone, and Rafe agreed to the terms with a short, painful nod.

Sick of the entire business, Matt climbed to his feet and explained what would come next. "As soon as I can get you cleaned up a little better, you and I are going to take a little trip to Prescott."

"But what for?" asked Peggy. "Rafy said that he don't got no—"

"Don't matter what I said before," muttered Hollister. "So don't be getting all riled up over nothing. I'll be back 'fore y'all know I even left."

Matt couldn't imagine that Peggy didn't realize what a liar her brother was, but he thought it a kindness to make sure she understood. "I wouldn't count on Rafy coming back to El Paso, sweetheart. He's got a lot to keep him busy in Prescott for a good long time."

Surprising him, she burst into tears.

Hollister looked from Matt to his sister, then scowled. "Shut yur damn mouth, woman, and I don't mean maybe. If I should commence to setting up stakes in Prescott, I'll send for y'all first chance I get. I promise."

Matt nearly laughed out loud, and would have, if Peggy hadn't looked so completely shattered. Instead, he gave in to a burst of compassion. "Tell you what, darlin'. As soon as we hit Prescott, I'll send you a wire letting you know how things are going. I'll also make sure that Rafe writes you a letter every week thereafter for as long as I'm in town. Would that set your mind at ease?"

She looked past Matt to the man on the floor and began to sob. Her eyes were red and puffy by now, and her nose was dripping, unchecked, into the canyon of cleavage below.

"Rafy?" she begged through her tears. "Cain't I please go with you? I ain't no trouble. You know that."

"I don't got no choice in the matter, dammit." He glared at Matt but continued talking to his sister. "Y'all heard the captain, woman. I got to go and y'all got to stay. That's it."

Sobbing wildly now, Peggy made a pathetic dash for the door and flung it open. As she took off down the hallway, Matt noticed that her gait was awkward, beyond his own relatively simple limp, and noisy, too, leaving a distinct *thump-bump* echo behind as she ran.

After closing the door, Matt turned to Hollister and asked, "Did Peggy hurt herself climbing in my window just now?"

Hollister shrugged. "Dunno. Why?"

"She was limping pretty badly as she left."

He snorted a laugh. "She always walks like that 'cause a' her legs." Again he laughed, more of a hoot. "Just the one troubles her actually—it got blowed off during a train robbery. That's why most everyone but me calls her Peg. Y'all get it? Like in peg leg. Her real name's something like Sally or Tilly."

Matt had come across a few one-legged men in his time, and held a certain sympathy for each one of them, but never had he come in contact with a woman in the same condition. It troubled him as he thought back to the way he'd spoken to her and especially as he recalled the way he'd pushed her around a little. But then he remembered how, crippled or not, she'd been tough enough to make the climb to his second-floor room and crawl through the window, with or without two good legs.

Able to ease past his own guilt after that, Matt concentrated instead on an inconsistency he thought he'd heard in Hollister's statement. Cocking his head as he sifted through the previous conversation, he stared down at the bastard with a renewed loathing.

"You just said that Peggy's real name is Sally or Tilly, didn't you?"

Dumb as he looked, Hollister admitted, "Yep, but hell, it could just as easy be Mabel or Pearl. I don't rightly recall."

"Is that so?" Matt advanced on the man. "I find it curious, in fact downright unbelievable, that any man could forget his own sister's name."

Hollister gulped and Matt rolled up his sleeves. "Then again, some men only tell the truth when it's beaten out of them. What are your thoughts on the subject, Rafy?"

Five

Maggie adjusted the chair by her apartment window until it was angled to take full advantage of the late afternoon sunlight. The room she laughingly referred to as her parlor was situated at the front of the building, but didn't feature much of a view unless she happened to be sitting in exactly this spot. To attract attention to his business, Gus had built a huge sign above the restaurant's entrance one floor below, all but hiding Maggie's window. She supposed she ought to be happy that he hadn't decided on an oyster. At least she could see through the tail feathers of the wooden turkey he settled on, an elaborately carved and painted false front above an equally colorful sign bearing the name of the eatery, the Squat and Gobble Cafe.

Those standards looked out from the corner of Gurley and Montezuma Streets, two of four wide thoroughfares that surrounded the courthouse and the charming little plaza. Between the location on the busy street corner, Gus's realistic depiction of a nice fat tom, and banners proclaiming kettle-fried turkey as the chef's specialty, new customers flocked to the cafe whenever a stagecoach or freight wagon rolled into town.

Unfortunately, part of the view when she looked out the window through Gus's wooden turkey feathers included some of the thirty-plus saloons that made up a stretch known as Whisky

Row. The area, which filled most of Montezuma Street, never failed to exhibit the many drunkards and sinners who frequented those establishments.

What Maggie's parlor lacked in atmosphere, however, was more than made up for by the southwestern exposure and its extra moments of daylight, which meant a tidy savings on candles and lamp oil. Another plus, the view southwest of Whisky Row bordered on spectacular, featuring the meandering waters of Granite Creek and pine-topped forests beyond. Almost dead west sat the imposing rock-ribbed crest of Thumb Butte, a friendly beacon of sorts that guided weary travelers into the town of Prescott.

Today Maggie didn't have time to concern herself about the reprobates milling around the Quartz Rock Saloon or to enjoy the view beyond Granite Creek. She was busy putting the finishing touches on Holly's Halloween costume, a plain black dress she'd emblazoned with shiny purple sateen cut into shapes that resembled bats, ghosts, and jack-o'-lanterns. As she fastened the last hook and eye to the back of the collar, Maggie found herself wondering, as she had several times each day over the past two weeks, if Matt had come across Rafe. And if so, whether he'd found him alive and well or six feet under—the way she'd pictured the coward on several occasions over the last seven years.

Maggie knew, of course, that thoughts of Rafe and Matt's tracking abilities were a waste of her time, but she couldn't seem to stop her mind from wandering in that direction. Mental images were all she had to keep her hopes alive until Matt rode back into town again. No telegram would be forthcoming. No messenger would be sent. She and Matt had agreed to those rules the night he left for Texas, basing that understanding on Maggie's hopes of keeping her plans for a reunion between father and daughter a secret.

"Mama?" called Holly, startling Maggie as she bounded into

the room. "Do I *have* to wear these?" She held up a pair of woollen drawers and matching undershirt.

"I'm afraid so, little miss. Even witches can take a chill and come down sick."

"But I hate them! They itch."

Holly jutted out her bottom lip and moaned loudly, but Maggie wouldn't be dissuaded on this issue. Although there was still plenty of sunshine to be had in Prescott, the daytime temperatures were getting crisp and the nights were dropping to near freezing, occasionally below.

"Please, Mama?" Holly sidled up to Maggie's cane-backed rocker. "Becka doesn't got to wear scratchy drawers, and she's gonna be a angel."

"An angel," corrected Maggie as she bit off the thread, finishing her task. "I don't care what Becka does or doesn't do. You're wearing your woollen underwear or you're not going to the town party with me."

Holly kept the pout, but sat down on the floor and began tugging on the hated drawers. As she struggled with the garment, she suddenly froze and asked, "Are these woollies, Mama?"

Listening with one ear now, Maggie shrugged as she said, "Some people call them that, I suppose."

"Matt told me to hang onto mine." With a burst of sudden enthusiasm, Holly tugged on her drawers. "Does Matt wear woollies, too?"

"Holly!" Maggie jabbed herself with the needle, but didn't even slow down long enough to see if the finger was bleeding. "It's Captain Weston to you, young lady, and what he wears under his clothing is not a fitting subject for either one of us to be discussing."

She pouted, but only for a moment. "When is Captain Weston coming back?"

"I don't know for sure." This wasn't the first time Holly had inquired about the ranger, but she was easily put off the subject. As a rule.

"Does Captain Weston got a wife?"

"Does he *have* a wife, and no, sweetheart, he doesn't."

That should have been the end of Holly's curiosity, especially if the past was any indication, but questions continued to tumble out of her like tailings from the Tip Top Mine.

"If he doesn't have a wife, he can marry me—right?"

Maggie dropped the costume into her lap. "What did you say?"

"I want to marry with Captain Weston when I get big like you."

Their earlier conversations regarding the ranger had never gone on this long *or* touched on such a surprising and baffling subject. Trying to understand what had prompted those thoughts in Holly, Maggie argued, "But I thought you didn't like the captain. Why would you want to marry someone you don't like?"

"But I do like him," she insisted. "And I want to marry with him."

Beyond baffled, Maggie shook her head. "But sweetheart, I heard the way you talked to the captain the day of the picnic. You were yelling and shouting at him, and he was hollering back at you and using bad words. Remember?"

Holly nodded vigorously as she pulled the woollen undershirt over her head, knocking her glasses askew.

"Then how can you possibly like him?"

She struggled to her feet. "'Cause he's hansum and smart and he fixed my kite. When's he coming back?"

Maggie held off with her answer. She wanted to compliment Holly's taste in men, to let her know that she at least stood a chance of finding some happiness in the future. If men like Matt Weston turned her head already, maybe Maggie wouldn't have to worry about her daughter turning out like she had—unloved and alone.

Then again, the last thing she needed to do was encourage her daughter to get too attached to Matt, even in his absence. There was always that danger whenever a strong, authoritative man stepped into Holly's life, no matter how briefly. It didn't take but one afternoon of admiring a near-stranger for Holly to begin calling him Daddy, a fact that irritated Maggie almost as much as it broke her heart.

After all, it wasn't as if she hadn't tried to provide her daughter with some kind of father figure. Gus, God love him, who knew nothing of little girls and their needs, worked hard at being both uncle and father to Holly, and had since the day she was born. Unfortunately, Gus and Hattie had no children of their own, and tended to treated Holly as if she were a fragile princess, a dandelion figurine apt to blow away if they dared to stir up her little world. Gus tiptoed around the princess, always willing to do things her way, and generally let Holly do pretty much what she pleased. It had been a very long time, if ever, that a man like Matt Weston had taken the time to notice Holly, much less went to the trouble of giving her the devil when she got a little too big for her britches. Apparently Holly took to that kind of notice like whitewash on a picket fence.

"When, Mama, when?"

Maggie had forgotten the question. "Soon, sweetheart," she murmured absently. Thinking back through Holly's brief contact with Matt, Maggie asked, "What did Captain Weston have to say when you apologized for yelling at him?"

She shrugged. "I don't member exactly, but he did told me that I'd grow up to be a bitch if I—"

"Holly!" Maggie clutched her throat, partly to keep from clutching her daughter's. "You know better than to use that kind of language. What's gotten into you?"

"Nuthin', Mama—I was just telling you what he said." She

stamped her foot and went on as if that closed the subject. "He told me that if I didn't want to be a bitch no man would marry, I'd best learn to mind my tongue."

That statement scored a direct hit on Maggie's funnybone, curseword and all. She turned to look out the window so Holly wouldn't see her trembling lips as she said, "Captain Weston *may* have a point about that, and I'm not saying that he does, but even if he's wrong, I still don't want to hear such words coming out of your mouth ever again. Understand?"

"Yes, Mama." Holly nodded violently, blond curls quaking like aspen leaves. "How long do I have to wait till I'm big enough to marry with him?"

The urge to laugh evaporated as Maggie thought ahead to Holly's disappointment. "Sweetheart, please listen to me and try to understand. Captain Weston is much too old to marry you, and even if he wasn't, when he gets back to town, he won't be staying long."

"Why not?"

"He lives in Texas and only came here to help Sheriff Ben with some important work. The captain has to go back home when his job is finished."

Holly had no comment for that. Instead she twisted her body from side to side, swinging her arms along with her hips, then fixed her gaze on a pile of Maggie's mending and changed the subject; her way of handling topics she couldn't or wouldn't face.

"I told Matt that I want a horse of my very own like Louie, or maybe a lamb to play with. He said a puppy was best. Can I have a puppy, Mama?"

"It's Captain Weston, sweetheart." Maggie hesitated after that, searching for a gentle way of denying the request and silently cursing Matt Weston with a few unladylike words of her own. "Let me think about that puppy a little, all right?"

"Think about it," echoed Holly in a grumble. She grabbed the costume out of Maggie's lap, picked her witch's hat up off the floor and smashed it onto her head. Then she marched toward her bedroom door muttering, "Think about it means, no, I can't have a puppy. Think about it always means no."

Maggie bit her tongue and watched as Holly left the room, afraid if she spoke, she'd give into her daughter's latest demands. If she did, Maggie had a notion that she'd spend more time racing up and down the stairs at the whims of a whining, piddling, puppy than she would rolling out pie dough, the main source of her meager income. She just wished that Matt could walk through the door this minute, with or without Rafe. Let him, the man with the great ideas and none of the responsibilities, tell Holly that getting a puppy would be a mistake. How easy would it be for him to shut his eyes and heart to her tears and forlorn expressions?

Maggie finally found a reason to laugh as she imagined a great burst of cursing and complaining from the big ranger, guessing that in the end, Matt would give up and find a puppy for Holly if he had to ride from one end of the territory to the other. If for no other reason than simply to shut her up.

As she visualized Matt in that light, taking on the responsibilities of a family, it occurred to Maggie that he would probably make a great husband and father for some lucky woman. True, he was afflicted with a tendency to curse, a little too mysterious even when dealing with him from a business standpoint, and a hard man to fit into just anyone's boots, but she also sensed that Matt Weston was a decent and honorable man, the sort that should have been swept up by a quick-thinking female long ago.

Trying to think of all the reasons Matt might have avoided marriage so far, Maggie suddenly found herself thinking about Rafe again. How much could she dare to hope that he'd changed over the years? Enough that he'd grown into a man who shared at least a few of Matt Weston's attributes? Or would he still be the same, selfish Rafe Hollister who'd walked out on her seven long years ago?

* * *

As it turned out, Matt didn't have to beat Hollister to get him to admit that Peggy wasn't his sister. In fact he'd been a little too damn eager to explain that the saloon whore was just a one-legged gal he'd taken on as his partner shortly after his arrival in El Paso. He then went on to boast that the two of them had passed themselves off as siblings simply because it suited their penny-ante operation.

Matt didn't believe either yarn for a minute.

The second tale sounded as much a lie to his ear as the brother/sister act they'd performed in his room back in El Paso. What Matt didn't know was why the man would continue to lie about his companion. Who was he protecting—her or himself? His sister or his partner? In either case, Matt had to consider the possibility that Peggy might actually take it in her head to follow them and somehow ruin the assignment.

The inconsistencies and possible repercussions of Hollister's wild tales stuck in Matt's throat all the way to Phoenix. Yet in spite of his misgivings and gut-level loathing for the man, he decided to take it upon himself to clean the miserable bastard up a little before they got to Prescott. For Maggie's sake, of course, not Hollister's. Instead of starting what would be the long and painful ride between Phoenix and Prescott the minute they got off the train, Matt's generosity had him standing in Goldwater's Mercantile thumbing the lapel of a blue flannel sack suit. He couldn't decide whether to buy it, or the cheaper seersucker, a suit done up in god-awful shades of apricot and straw-colored plaid.

"Hey, what about this'un?" asked Rafe, pointing toward an expensive suit of striped broadcloth. "I ain't likely to disgrace Maggie's sensitivities in a getup like that."

"Probably not," grumbled Matt. "But you'd sure as hell disgrace what's left of my poke."

"Didn't reckon y'all'd be so stingy. I thought I was s'posed to look right spiffy for Maggie." Again he pointed out the striped broadcloth. "Why if I was to turn up in that there fancy suit of clothes, I bet the minute that Maggie laid eyes on me, she'd up and roll over backwards into a sweaty faint."

Matt wrapped the long fingers of his right hand around Hollister's stringy upper arm, raised him to his tiptoes, then grated his teeth loud enough for him and half the other customers to hear.

"You don't have much of a memory do you?" he growled under his breath. "I recall you talking your way into coming here with me even though my better judgment said I ought to cuff you to a tree and leave you at the edge of town. Do you remember what made me change my mind, Rafy boy?"

He gulped almost as loudly as Matt had ground his molars. "Uh, 'cause I promised to keep my mouth shut and stay right b'side y'all?"

"Precisely." He got right in Hollister's face. "When a fella breaks his promise to me, I get pretty mad. I expect by now you have some idea of just how mad I can get—don't you?"

"Yessir."

"Then why don't you do yourself a favor and keep that promise in mind from here on out. Speak only if I ask you a question—got it?"

Hollister agreed with a short nod and Matt released his arm. His mood in charge of the selections now, he picked up the ugly seersucker suit, which would offer Hollister little protection against the winter months ahead, and moved onto the counter featuring toiletries.

On the rare occasions that Matt had allowed Hollister the privilege of speaking to him, he'd noticed that the man's teeth were badly in need of tending. The enamel had been stained to a kind of jaundiced chestnut—too much chewing tobacco and coffee, Matt assumed—and he seemed to have twice as many teeth as places to put them. When Hollister grinned, he looked as if he'd tried to swallow a well-used, badly shuffled deck of cards.

Matt selected a wooden toothbrush with dark bristles, then waved it beneath Hollister's nose. "Ever seen one of these before?"

Rafe hesitated a moment, undoubtedly weighing the sentence to make sure it was phrased as a question. "Yessir, that's for cleaning the teeth."

"You and this toothbrush are going to become very good friends before we reach Prescott." Matt handed the device to him along with a cake of Thompson's Tooth Soap. Then he scrutinized Hollister's hat.

It was mountaineer-style, tall of crown and floppy-brimmed, but too far gone to save. Not only was the doeskin greasy with stains, but the edges were raggedy, beyond repair. Matt resigned himself to the fact that he would also have to invest in a new hat if he intended to make the man completely presentable by the time they hit Prescott. But at this rate, he grumbled to himself, the job Ben Sloan had lined up for him as a favor, was looking like it might cost him a whole lot more than he'd been paid.

After stopping by the millinery department for a straw derby, Matt impulsively picked out a pair of roller skates for Holly. Next time the little hoyden wanted to fly that damned kite, he meant to be prepared with an irresistible distraction.

Hedging the bet, he also added a deck of good bristle-board playing cards to his bill. That way if Holly failed to master the art of skating or, heaven forbid, broke an arm or a leg, he'd have some kind of back-up to keep her mind off that wretched kite.

At least with a deck of cards, Matt was in familiar territory. Hell, he might even stand a chance of keeping the kid's mouth shut long enough to show her how to play.

Six

With less than two weeks to go before the Thanksgiving holiday, a ritual that turned the Squat and Gobble Cafe into a madhouse and depleted Hattie's charming turkey ranch of a good portion of its stock, Maggie began to have serious doubts about whether she would ever see Holly's Christmas wish fulfilled. Matt had been gone for over a month now, not a particularly ominous sign on its own, but worrisome enough to give her a case of the dithers. When Homer Ludlow came into the cafe this morning for his usual plate of biscuits and gravy, she all but grabbed him by the throat and shook him when he suggested that his coffee could be a little hotter!

After that, Maggie calmed herself by clinging to as many positive thoughts as she could think of. Four weeks plus, for example, wasn't an exorbitant amount of time for a tracker to locate Rafe and bring him back to Prescott, especially considering the ranger's troubles with his bad hip. Matt explained the night he left that there would be many days on the trail he couldn't sit his horse for more than an hour without climbing down from the saddle and resting up for at least as long as he'd ridden. Tying Louie behind a concord stage and riding inside it, cushioned seat or not, was an even less appealing choice given the rutted trails and rocky roads the coach had to traverse. He'd also made it a point to explain that while he might no longer be the fastest tracker in all the territories, he was still better than most—good enough to dog a bear through running water, in fact, if she didn't mind him saying so.

Maggie hadn't minded a bit. She only wished he could have offered a few guarantees along with his claims. As it was, she only knew that with or without Rafe, Matt could ride into town as early as next week, as late as next month, or never be heard from again. Just thinking about the latter possibility was enough to dampen her spirits, a thought that turned the dithers into a case of the quivering all-overs.

Tucking her legs tight under the moss green afghan Hattie had knitted for her last Christmas, Maggie glanced out at the night through the wooden turkey feathers and saw that a light mist had settled over her window. Bordered with a sparkling layer of sugary dew drops, the glass attracted the light from her candle, turning the endless gloom beyond into a field of tiny stars—into glimmers of what felt like hope.

Until then, Maggie hadn't realized how long it had been since something so vital as hope had been a part of her life. She wondered exactly when she'd lost the ability to believe in miracles, or even wishes, as Holly still did. She couldn't remember. The girlish enthusiasm began to fade shortly after she bore her child into a fatherless world. Perhaps that was the beginning of her inner despair, thought Maggie. The freeze that took the very last leaf from her tree of hope. Shivering both inside and outside now, Maggie burrowed even further into the afghan and made herself return to the book she'd been reading.

She figured she'd studied the same passage of Jules Verne's *Around the World in 80 Days* at least three times so far and still couldn't make sense of what she'd read. Small wonder considering the direction her thoughts had taken, not to mention it was well past her bedtime. She was exhausted, gritty-eyed from lack of sleep, and yet for some reason, Maggie couldn't seem to make herself head for her cold, lonely bed. She yawned instead, refreshing herself a little, then rubbed her tired eyes and focused once again on the novel.

She'd just found her place, a passage featuring Phineas Fogg and a very smart monkey, when Maggie thought she heard birds pecking on her window. Her spine stiff, her mind suddenly clear and alert, she lowered the novel to her lap and listened intently. Again came the pecks, noises she recognized this time as someone throwing pebbles at the wooden turkey, occasionally hitting the glass. Either a drunk from Whisky Row had lost his way, or someone was trying to get her attention.

Her heart in her throat, Maggie didn't even stop to consider her apparel, a plain muslin nightgown and matching robe that only reached her to mid-calf. She threw off the afghan, pushed out of the rocker, then flung open the window and poked her head out between two wooden tail feathers.

"Hello?" she called, peering over the giant tom and into the street below. "Is someone there?"

Her visitor backed away from the boardwalk and out from under the balcony. Then he tilted his head back and identified himself in a shouted whisper, an effort wasted on Maggie. She recognized the vague outline of Matt Weston's big white hat before he ever opened his mouth.

"It's me, Matt. I didn't want to alarm you, but I saw your light and thought this might be a good time for us to meet without anyone the wiser. Can I come up?"

"No," she whispered back. "Go around to the back door. I'll be down to let you in shortly."

Her heart leapt into a gallop the moment Maggie realized her visitor was Matt, but now that she was actually going to talk to him, her blood was racing, pumping through her system like a team of runaway horses. Although she realized that she hadn't seen any sign of Rafe, Maggie assured herself as she snatched the candle off the table that he was somewhere close to Matt, hidden in the darkness perhaps, or even down the road a piece, waiting for his signal to approach.

Filled with a peculiar yet pleasurable sense of euphoria, a feeling of excitement she hadn't had since the day Holly was born, Maggie dashed down the stairs and into the kitchen. She struggled with the latch for a moment, then quickly opened the door. Matt's broad shoulders filled the entry, making it impossible to see beyond him.

"Evening," he said, touching the brim of his hat as he crossed the threshold and strode into the kitchen.

"Evening," she murmured, straining her eyes as she searched the darkness for movement or another masculine silhouette. All was as still as her suddenly lifeless pulse. Maggie closed the door and glanced over her shoulder as Matt tossed his big white Stetson on the counter where Gus had been chopping vegetables for his soups and stews.

Fitting the candle into a nearby wall sconce, she swallowed her disappointment and turned to him. "Well?"

"What's wrong?" he asked, studying her intently in the shadowy light.

Maggie realized that she'd been holding her breath since she'd unlatched the door, and was still standing there as rigidly as a flagpole. She eased the air out of her lungs with a soft chuckle and moved along the wall until she was face to face with Matt—so close she could smell the trail on him. No sour-sweat odor, but rather a stimulating blend of horse and leather spiced with a hint of pine, seasonings that complimented the powerful musk of the man himself. The scent was disquieting at the least, making Maggie feel tingly all over and a little light-headed.

"I'm fine," she said, not feeling that way at all. "Just a little tired."

She raised her eyes to meet Matt's unrelenting gaze and something stirred deep inside of her, a fluttering of down-soft flurries that rose up from low in her belly and spread throughout her breasts. She suddenly felt awkward and girlish, as if she might burst out laughing and crying at the same time.

Speaking in his usual slow drawl, but with what sounded like a fair amount of difficulty, Matt declared, "Dammit, I shouldn't have come here tonight."

He shoved his hands into his pockets with the same kind of abruptness she'd heard in his tone. His expression was just short of a frown, and there was an edgy hesitance about him, an impression that something was amiss. With slowly dawning horror, it occurred to Maggie that Matt might have trailed Rafe all the way to his grave, and that he couldn't bring himself to tell her the man was dead. Before she could voice that concern, he sliced through her anxiety with an unrelated, but surprisingly keen-edged remark.

"Maybe this wasn't such a good idea after all." Slowly looking her over from head to toe, Matt's gaze lingered a little too long below the knee. "You should have told me that you were getting ready to turn in for the night."

Maggie glanced down at herself, remembering on the late side that her too-short nightgown exposed the lower part of her legs down to her ankles and woolen slippers. She'd intended to add a few ruffles to the hem as she did to give all her store-bought gowns the proper length, but simply hadn't gotten around to it yet. Other articles of mending took priority over something that exposed Maggie's legs to no one but her daughter—until tonight, anyway.

In addition to her scandalous attire, she'd let down her hair earlier for its nightly brushing, allowing the unbound locks to fall every which way across the front and back of her robe. If Matt's dour expression was any indication, Maggie figured she probably resembled an ungainly, none-too-attractive entertainer from Whisky Row.

Her hackles rising, she snapped, "I'm terribly sorry if my

immodesty makes you uncomfortable, but you're the one who chose the time and place for this little meeting."

Maggie's cheeks were so hot with both shame and hurt pride, she knew they had to be deep crimson, but she'd waited too long for news of Rafe to let her own feelings prolong the agony.

Forcing herself to speak more softly, she said, "The last thing I'm concerned about at this moment is propriety. You're the one who suggested we talk now and I agreed that it was a good idea. Next time we meet, if there is one, I assure you that I'll be properly dressed. If that meets with your approval, can we get on with the reason for your visit?"

Matt reared back a little, looking for a brief moment as if she'd slapped him. Just as quickly he gave a little sideways grin and said, "Sorry if I offended you Maggie. I sure didn't mean to. You're right—I should have mentioned Rafe the minute I walked in here. He's alive and well."

"He is?" His transgressions forgotten, Maggie inched even closer to Matt. "What did he say? Does he want to see me and Holly? Why isn't he with you? Where is he now?"

"Whoa, slow down a minute. I left him . . ." Matt hesitated, half-smiling out one corner of his mouth again. "Let's just say he's *secured* for the night back at my cabin."

"He's here?" She could hardly believe her ears. "In Prescott?"

"Dusty and dirty, but alive," he confirmed. "Just the way you ordered him."

Relief beyond her wildest hopes swept through Maggie as she imagined Holly's delight on Christmas morning, a sensation as intangible as her prayers and at least as compelling. Swamped by a sudden, dizzying array of emotions, she threw herself into Matt's arms in gratitude. And to keep her legs from sliding out from under her. At least, that's what she told herself.

Maggie's ears rustled with scattered thoughts, swirling around in her mind. She thought of Holly, or wanted to keep on thinking of her and her joy at having her wish come true, but suddenly all she could do was feel—Matt's strong arms surrounding her, the welcoming comfort of his muscular body, and her own, reckless desires. Through the din in her head, she thought she heard Matt speak, his voice sounding odd and distant.

"Maggie," he said, groaning. "Christ, Maggie, what are you doing?"

Confused and dazed, not understanding what he meant, she leaned back for a glimpse of Matt's travel-weary face. His jaw was tight, the muscles and skin there, taut. His gray eyes were dark and turbulent, building into a thunderstorm of emotion that frightened her as much as it enticed her. When that tempestuous gaze settled on Maggie's mouth with a determined intensity, she didn't question her automatic response. She rose to meet Matt's parted lips, then kissed him with all the gratitude her woman's heart could supply.

Their embrace was brief, lasting only a few seconds, but in those stolen moments came a lifetime of bottled-up passion, a wellspring of her own femininity and stirrings of a desire that had gone neglected for much too long. She could have stayed in Matt's arms like this forever, thought Maggie, and she even gave frantic consideration to surrendering to the raging emotions he'd unleashed in her for at least this one night. Just as the kiss began to deepen with an intensity neither of them could have corralled, Matt suddenly gripped Maggie's shoulders and roughly set her away from him.

"Christ," he said, his voice oddly distant. "I don't know what I could have been thinking. I'm sorry, Maggie."

Before she could think of what to say or a way to absolve him of at least half of the blame, Matt turned his back to her, collecting his hat, and didn't swing around to face her again after fitting the Stetson to his head.

"We'll talk more in the morning," he said with a coldness

that chilled the remnants of her desire. "We can make arrangements then for you and Rafe to meet. I'll stop by the cafe for breakfast."

Then, before she could catch her breath or find her tongue, he slammed out the door and into the night, letting the darkness swallow him whole.

Even though he knew it was wrong, and knew that nothing good would ever come of it, Matt couldn't seem to stop thinking about Maggie as he made his way back to the cabin at the southern edge of town. He could still smell the faint, unusual bouquet of orange blossoms in her hair, feel the silken strands he'd wound around his fingers while she was in his embrace, and think of the forbidden—of burying himself to the hilt and living inside Maggie Hollister forever.

All that did was make him go weak in the knees, so feeble he could barely walk, and even weaker in the brain. Matt threw open his coat, then peeled it off altogether, welcoming the chill of the night against the heat of a body too long confined to the company of other men. If he couldn't will himself to cool off, maybe the elements would do it for him.

As he walked, he berated himself for having been in such an all-fired rush to get back to Prescott. To Maggie. Cursing as he started up the tree-lined path to the cabin, he damned himself for not staying in El Paso a little longer, for failing to visit eager female admirers he'd discovered since his retirement. He could have done something, anything but lust after the wife of his own captive, a man who didn't deserve to be in the same room with Maggie, much less the same bed.

Just picturing the two of them together got Matt so damn mad, he had to strip down to his jeans and boots to ease the pressure building up inside him and let off a little steam. By the time he reached the cabin, however, he still hadn't cooled off enough to go inside and get the rest he so desperately needed.

So Matt stood outside the door, half-naked and shivering in the frigid November night, and waited for the urge to blow a hole in Rafe Hollister to pass. There was no point in waiting for the urge to bed the man's wife to subside. If he did that, there was a damn good chance that he'd freeze to death first.

He stood outside longer than he cared to know that night, but finally went in and got a little sleep. The following morning Matt finally felt as if most of his senses had returned. It was ass-kicking time, his own, and a long time coming, given the fact that he'd been hunting his own pleasures in another man's backyard—and had been since the day he first rode into Prescott. All that was about to change, and would by God, if he had to cuff himself to a tree. He might never be able to forget the taste of Maggie or the sight of her by candlelight looking so damned vulnerable and desirable in her nightclothes, but Matt vowed that he would never lose control around her again. Nevermore would he let himself forget that she was another man's wife.

After cleaning himself up and squaring Rafe away, Matt headed to town, as promised. When he entered the restaurant, he chose a table near the door out of the other customer's hearing distance, then settled into the chair and waited for Maggie. Within moments, she came through the kitchen door with a steaming mug of coffee in one hand and a small notebook and pencil in the other.

"Good morning, Captain Weston," she said brightly, not quite meeting his gaze. Setting the coffee on the table, she slid it under his nose. "What can I get for you?"

Playing along with her, Matt propped his elbows on the table and leaned forward, using her body as a shield against the prying eyes of two elderly gentlemen who'd suddenly taken an interest in him.

"I'm starved," he said. "Hungry enough for *two* men without time enough to sit. Can you pack me up a double-large order of the biggest breakfast you've got?"

Without writing anything down, she asked, "How does a half dozen flapjacks, a pair of thick venison steaks smothered with oysters and scrambled eggs, and a pan load of buttermilk biscuits sound?"

Matt was salivating as he said, "Just about right, ma'am. Perfect, in fact." Then he added in a whisper, "How soon do you want to see *him?*"

Speaking under her breath, Maggie continually glanced around the room. "As soon as possible, I suppose. I have to know what his thoughts are about us after all this time, and then figure out if seeing him will help or harm, ah, you know who. What are your thoughts on the subject?"

With his own furtive glance at the other customers, Matt took a sip of coffee before he said, "I agree, but I have to warn you that although I've cleaned him up a little, he's still a long way from what you'd call parlor-broke."

"I'll be sure to keep that in mind."

Her voice seemed brittle, the words clipped. Matt couldn't help but wonder if her detached attitude was part of the act or because of his crude behavior the night before. He was pretty sure he knew. Concentrating on the coffee instead of the censure he'd most likely see in her eyes, Matt said, "When can you come by?"

"About an hour, I think. Will that do?"

"An hour sounds about right. Perfect."

Better than an hour later, closer to two, in fact, Matt finally heard the expected knock on the cabin door.

Spearing Rafe with one final pointed glance, he warned, "Remember what I said about behaving yourself. Think twice before you foul the air with that tongue of yours and keep your hands to yourself. If you don't abide by the rules, all future meetings between you and Maggie will be conducted with you in chains from head to foot. *Comprende?*"

"Yeah, Captain, I know what y'all want. Let's git this over with, okay?"

Matt couldn't have agreed more. He went to the door and opened it just enough for him to slip outside with Maggie. She'd changed from the black skirt and starched white blouse she'd worn when working at the cafe. Now she had on a butter yellow dress and matching bonnet. Both the gown and the hat featured golden brown trim in the exact same shade as her hair, a shimmering color somewhere between topaz and chestnut. The next thing he knew, Matt was picturing that lustrous hair the way it fell over her robe last evening, wild and free to follow the soft contours of her body the way he could never do.

"Is something wrong with Rafe?" she asked, obviously alarmed by his pained expression.

"No," he said, mad at himself again. "I just thought we'd better get the rules straight before you two meet. Do you want me to stay in the cabin with you or give the two of you some privacy?"

Maggie didn't answer right away. She was busy looking around Matt's shoulder and into the crack in the door for a glimpse of her long lost love.

Trying to keep the anger out of his tone, Matt called her name. "Maggie? What's it going to be? Do you want me to stay with you or not?"

"Oh, ah . . ." Still she didn't take her eyes off the door, nor did she think about her answer for long—not nearly long enough, in Matt's opinion. "No, I don't think that will be necessary. I can't imagine that Rafe wants to hurt me."

"As you wish, but if anything goes wrong, I'll be right outside the door. Just holler." With one final glare at the luckiest bastard on the face of the earth, Matt allowed Maggie to pass inside the cabin, then closed the door behind her.

Forcing himself away from the tiny windows, he leaned against a scraggly pinion tree nearby and tried not to think about the reunion taking place a few feet away. As he waited, it was Matt's fervent hope that he'd done his job well, good enough anyway to have cleaned Hollister up and tutored him to a level worthy of an audience with Maggie.

It was Matt's most heartfelt wish, however, that he'd failed miserably in those efforts.

Seven

The cabin was a one-room affair built in haste by a miner who had run out of luck before he could put the finishing touches on the place. It had the necessities—such as a fireplace, a cook stove and a pair of small beds—but there were no countertops, shelving or other furnishings. Ten-penny nails served as storage for everything from pots to clothing. The water closet was a falling-down privy out back. Small squares cut into the walls on either side of the front and only door served as windows, and a long narrow gap between logs supplied ventilation from the back of the room. None of the openings sported glass, which meant that freezing air was free to come and go at will unless the shutters were closed. Then the cabin became more of a tomb than a home.

Maggie didn't concern herself with the cold, the lack of furnishings, or the crude dirt floor. Her entire attention was focused on the face of the man she'd once loved. Her first thought was that Rafe hadn't changed much over the years, at least not where outward appearances were concerned. He still had that same unruly mop of wheat-colored hair, long narrow face, and a body so thin a strong breeze could have lifted him off his feet. Her heart lurched, then skipped a beat.

Memories from long ago flooded Maggie, images of those cold winter days she'd spent snuggled in Rafe's arms, of him warming her inside and out. Showing her, ultimately, what it meant to be a woman. For that she supposed she was grateful, especially since their dalliance had led to Holly's birth. Despite the hatred she'd built up for the man over the years, it occurred to Maggie that she might still be harboring some feelings for Rafe. Enough love, perhaps, to think about building a future together, if that's what he had in mind.

Unfortunately, Rafe opened his mouth to speak about then.

"I'm right flattered y'all missed me enough to put a Texas Ranger on my tail, woman, but I got to say it right out—this here kidnapping business has got me plenty pissed."

Taken back for a moment, Maggie responded in kind. "Sorry you feel that way, Rafe, but I've spent a lot more time than you have being, er, *pissed,* as you say, just waiting around for you to show up."

His chin snapped up, giving Maggie the impression that he'd been expecting the timid, insecure girl she'd once been instead of the strong woman she'd grown into. When he answered, it was with much less force.

"Then maybe y'all should have forgot about me and got on with it."

"Believe me," she said from deep in her throat. "I would have if you hadn't left me in a family way."

He shrugged, not really looking all that concerned. "Well, them times aside, yur lookin' a mite better than I remember. Guess y'all didn't get no shorter though, did ya? Musta growed another two hands or so, eh?"

There was something ugly in his grin, something that made her feel even more awkward and ungainly than she'd been as a girl on the cusp of womanhood. Maggie thought she'd come to terms with her size since coming to Prescott, that she'd even grown comfortable in her own skin, no matter how big it was compared to other women. It seemed that all it took to rob her of that confidence was one cruel remark from Rafe. She didn't however, have to stand there and let him know how much power he still held over her.

Turning away from the former love of her life, Maggie strolled idly around the cabin and drifted over by the stove, behaving as if she were completely unconcerned about his opinion. As she hoped, he took her indifference as an insult to his glib tongue.

"Didn't y'all hear me, woman? I'm a-talking to ya."

"I didn't come here to discuss my looks," she said casually, not bothering to look his way at first. "Our business has nothing to do with my height or your appalling taste in clothing."

Now Maggie chose to turn around, pausing briefly and pointedly to look him over again. "Whatever possessed you to buy that suit? You look like a stalk of corn they missed at harvest."

Rafe tried to strike an indignant pose, but only managed to turn himself into a caricature of a scarecrow. "Weren't my idear of a suit. This is the doin's of that ranger y'all sicced on me."

Laughing to herself, Maggie went back to examining the stove, taking note of the grime crusted around the cooking surfaces and in particular, the remnants of the breakfast she'd packed up for Matt and Rafe. There were a few bits of eggs along with some venison scraps and oyster leavings that had bonded themselves to the plates, but not a bite of pancake or crumb from the dozen biscuits she'd sent along could be found.

"Well?" said Rafe, his tone impatient. "Y'all got me here. What do ya want?"

Smiling to herself, Maggie turned back to the man who'd abandoned her so long ago. "Do you have any idea how long it's been since you put me on that stage in Salt Lake City, Rafe?"

He looked down at his hands. The right hand was busy picking at the stubby nails of the left. "I reckon it's been a spell."

"Yes, it certainly has. Better than seven years, in fact. How come you never came after me like you said you would? Lose your sense of direction?"

Rafe's head snapped up again, clearly showing her that he hadn't been expecting to find any grit in her craw, a commodity she'd lacked during their short period together.

Recovering a little, he cocked his head in arrogant denial. "No sense in gitting yur britches in an uproar, is there, woman? I got sidetracked, s'all. Let bygones be bygones."

Maggie had to laugh. "That's easy for you to say, Rafe, considering you're the only one in this room who has any bygones to apologize for."

"Now that ain't quite right." Wagging his index finger at her, Rafe advanced. "If y'all don't call a bygone hiring some crazed Texas Ranger to come drag me off to Arizonie at gunpoint, then sugar, ain't a bygone to be had by anyone in this here room."

He stood but a few feet away now, close enough for Maggie to notice that Rafe still had those beautiful calf eyes complete with enviably thick lashes. She melted a little, allowing a soft spot for the hopelessly-in-love girl she'd once been.

"I hadn't thought of the difficulties you might endure once my tracker got hold of you." She smiled sweetly. "I suppose you think that makes us about even?"

"Damn tootin' it does."

He hitched up his trousers, then squinted Maggie's way, apparently struggling to bring her into focus. Now that she had some idea where Holly's faulty vision had come from, she used that characteristic as a bridge to approach the only thing that mattered here—their daughter.

"I don't remember you squinting so much, Rafe. Are you having a little trouble seeing these days?"

"Not if'n I'm good and close to a subject, woman." Vanity puffed him up to his full height, but he still fell short of Maggie by about two inches. "I kin see just fine when it suits me."

"Whatever you say, Rafe, but if I were you, I'd have my eyes checked." As ready as she'd ever be to broach the reason he'd been tracked in the first place, Maggie swallowed hard and added, "Ever since she turned three, Holly has had to wear glasses just to cross her bedroom. I guess she got her eyesight from your side of the family."

As she hoped, mention of the daughter they shared caught Rafe off guard. He sagged a little, both in girth and height, then went back to studying his hands.

"How is the girl?" he finally asked. "Anything else wrong with her I ought to know about?"

"She's quite healthy, Rafe, and I don't consider a problem with her vision as being 'something wrong with her.' " Did the man have nothing nice to say about anyone? "If you want the chance to meet Holly, you're going to have to promise that you'll have the decency to keep opinions like that to yourself."

"What do y'all mean *if* I git a chance to meet her?" He stood there bandy-legged and a little unsteady, but full up with righteous indignation. "Captain Weston said y'all wanted me brung here cause the kid had a hankerin' to see me."

"That's part of it all right."

He laughed, then jutted out his chest. "I reckon the other part is that y'all been wanting to get an eyeful of me for a while, too, eh?"

In the interests of keeping their discussion as civil as possible, Maggie decided against denying Rafe his moment of self-adoration. Besides, his presumptions weren't entirely without merit.

Still, she couldn't keep a hint of sarcasm out of her tone as she replied, "I can't tell you what a thrill it's been to see you again, Rafe, but then we aren't here to talk about us today, are we?"

Rafe kind of flipped his head, the way a stallion will toss his mane if he senses another stud is too near. "Nope, I guess we didn't. Yur gonna have to wait a spell longer 'fore you try getting

personal with me agin. Right now I just want to see my little
girl."

Again Maggie swallowed the urge to throttle the man. "I
understand that, Rafe, but before I can allow you to approach
Holly, I have to know that her time with you will be of some
benefit and not cause her more problems than she already has
as a fatherless child."

"Well . . . hell."

He stood there scratching his head after that as if actually
pondering some of the things Holly might have endured. Maggie couldn't imagine that he had the first idea of what she'd
been through. Since she had his attention, she decided to go
ahead with the list of conditions she'd drawn up for him.

"I have a few things I want you to keep in mind when you
see her. Has Matt explained that you won't actually have contact
with Holly until Christmas Day?"

"Matt, sugar?" This time when he narrowed one eye, Rafe
wasn't squinting to bring her in focus. He was accusing her.
"Y'all gotten cozy with that there ranger, have ya? Is that why
he's always in such an all-fired hurry to take up the slack in
my noose?"

In light of what had occurred between her and Matt last evening, Maggie had to ball up her fists and plant her feet to keep
from backing away from Rafe. She could barely think about the
shameless way she'd behaved with Matt, much less address the
issue with this man. Given his nature, Rafe might even consider
taking Holly away from her if he found out how wantonly she'd
led the captain astray—and there was no doubt in her mind that
she'd done exactly that. Even with seven years between occasions, Maggie had no trouble recognizing the condition when
a man was fully aroused.

Her cheeks on fire, she fibbed, "I don't know what you're
talking about. Matt Weston is nothing more to me than a tracker
I hired at the suggestion of Sheriff Ben Sloan. If you two had

some difficulties on the trail, I assure you it had nothing to do with me."

"Difficulties, sugar?" Rafe reared back and hooted a laugh, displaying a mouthful of teeth. "I'd call the way he's been chaining me up like I was some kind a' horse thief, a mite tougher than just difficult. Hell, I'druther sleep with a grizzly every night than have that crazy bastard on my tail agin."

"I'm sorry you think you were treated badly by the man I hired." She apologized, but only because she was desperate to move on. Not for a minute did Maggie believe Rafe's wild tales about being chained. "Maybe you ought to remember that none of this would have happened if you'd simply kept your promise and come to Prescott before Holly was born—or even after."

"I told y'all, woman! I got held up with business and such."

She raised a skeptical brow. "Are you saying that you actually meant to join me here someday, that you've even given me or our child a single thought since the day you put me on that stagecoach?"

He shrugged his bony shoulders. "I reckon I give thought to y'all now and then. No call to badger me about it, is there?"

Maggie didn't know whether to laugh or punch Rafe in the nose. She knew which she'd *rather* do, but left it at this. "It doesn't matter what your intentions were then. All I care about is now. Do you want to see your daughter or not?"

"I b'lieve," he muttered with a deliberate and nasty drawl, "that I already done said I'd see the kid. Didn't yur ears git as big as the rest of y'all?"

Finally putting a little space between herself and Rafe, not because he'd intimidated her as before, or even because he'd insulted her yet again, but simply because Maggie suddenly feared something new—herself and the violent tendencies he brought out in her—she chose to ignore Rafe's insults, and ended their meeting.

"I think I'd like to go now," she said, heading toward the

door. "After we've talked a few more times and I'm satisfied that you want to do more than just have a look at the child you created, we'll discuss your plans for taking part in Holly's life from here on out."

His gangly body as agile as ever, Rafe leapt between Maggie and her escape route. "What in tarnation are y'all talking about now, woman? I said I want to see the kid. Bring her to me right now so's I kin get on back to my regular business."

"I won't do anything of the sort. In fact," she said, trying to check herself while she was still able to maintain a slow simmer, "I'm beginning to regret bringing you here at all. Now get out of my way."

Again Rafe puffed himself up and again he fell short. "I ain't done talking yet. I got a right to see that kid whenever I take a mind to."

"You have no rights at all where Holly's concerned, Rafe Hollister." Maggie was rapidly reaching the boiling point and she knew it, but couldn't seem to cool down. "You're lucky you even have a daughter!"

"Hah! That's a laugh." But he wasn't laughing and Maggie couldn't see anything humorous in Rafe's expression. "Yur the lucky one, being the beauticious, bodacious creature y'all growed up to be. Hell woman, you ought to be thanking me for the favor of bedding a big ole homely pup such as yurself instead of—"

The back of Maggie's hand slapped the rest of Rafe's loathsome sentence right out of his mouth. She got to savor the taste of revenge for only a split second before he was all over her again. Grabbing hold of her arm with a surprisingly strong left hand, Rafe folded the right into a fist and waved it under her nose.

"I've had just about all the goddang beatin's I kin take betwixt y'all and that there ranger, woman." His eyes were bulging, ringed with white. "It's about time one of ya commenced to understanding that I ain't gonna take it no more."

From the corner of her eye, Maggie caught a glimpse of a shadow at the one opened window. In the next moment, the door exploded and in came Matt, snorting like an enraged bull.

"Take your filthy hands off of her," he demanded of Rafe in a voice Maggie had never heard Matt use before. Deadly as a rattler, coiled to strike, he kept his lethal gaze on Rafe as he added, "Do it *now,* Hollister."

There must have been some truth to Rafe's description of life on the trail with Matt Weston. His eyes remained huge with plenty of white showing, but they were ringed with fear now, not anger. Turning her loose the way he might have dropped the business end of a hot branding iron, his hands shot straight up in surrender.

Still staring Rafe down, Matt asked Maggie, "Did he hurt you in any way?"

"No, I'm fine. Honest." More than simply embarrassed by the way things had gone between her and Rafe, Maggie also felt as if she'd failed. Not only had she lost control of the situation, she'd lost control of herself. "We're just having a little argument," she added lamely.

"Don't move a muscle," Matt instructed Rafe. Then he took Maggie by the elbow and led her out through the open door.

"Would you mind waiting here a moment?" he asked, settling her beneath the shade of a pinion tree. "I'll be right back."

She agreed with a quiet nod, and after he'd gone, folded her arms and listened to the muffled shouts, thumps, and occasional groans coming from inside the cabin. Just as quickly as the noises began, everything suddenly went quiet. A moment later Matt stepped over the threshold and slammed the door shut behind him.

"I'm sorry about that," he said, joining her by the tree. "I thought I'd civilized the man well enough for a private meeting with you. Are you sure you're all right?"

"Yes, of course I am. And don't worry about the little disagreement we just had."

Simply voicing the thought gave it credence to Maggie, turning the angry exchange and hurtful words into nothing more potent than the first snowflakes of winter, evaporated before they could hit the heart.

Finally much calmer, she went on to say, "Rafe and I had a few things we had to get out in the open, I guess, things we needed to put to rest. Now that we've done that, I think we should be able to move on to Holly and her happiness without further incident between us."

"If you're sure."

Maggie found that she was able to look him in the eye and smile. "I'm quite sure."

Matt took a deep breath then, as if deliberating the correct way to bring up a ponderous subject. For one horrifying moment, she thought he might be working on a way of mentioning last night and their moment of insanity. To her undying relief, Matt's eyes lit up and he grinned, flashing a deep and intriguing pair of dimples.

"I, ah, brought something back for Holly," he explained. "A pet actually, but I thought I'd better make sure it's all right with you before I give it to her."

Oh, Lord, no, thought Maggie, not a puppy! But she said, "That's very thoughtful of you, Matt. What, er, is it?"

"If you don't mind waiting just one more minute, I'll go get it and show you."

"All right."

As he dashed into the cabin, Maggie struggled with polite ways of telling him that Holly simply couldn't accept the responsibilities of a puppy at her young age, that anything less than complete devotion, would be terribly unfair to the animal as well. When Matt returned, careful to slam the cabin door behind him again, she was still looking for the right words to decline the gift.

"Here we go," Matt said, displaying a small bundle of pale blue flannel in his palms. "Go ahead, take it, but be careful. She's a little fragile."

As Maggie reached for the bundle, it moved, kicking up a feeble protest. More certain than ever that a wet nose would soon greet her, Maggie reluctantly removed the last bit of cloth to reveal a wizened old face instead.

She looked up at Matt in shock. "It's a turtle!"

"Actually, it's a tortoise," Matt corrected. "A young desert tortoise around four or five years old, I'd guess. I thought about bringing Holly a puppy, but when I came across this pitiful little thing, I decided it would be less trouble for you than a dog."

Filling the palm of one hand from Maggie's fingertips to her wrist, the reptile sported a wide band of blue flannel around her middle, a girth about the size of an extra large apple. "Why do you have it tied up like this?"

"That's a bandage," he explained. "She has a cracked shell— might have been caught in a landslide or even mistaken as supper by a hungry coyote. I can't find any signs of infection and the edges of the shell seem to be lined up pretty good, so she ought to heal just fine." He looked away from the tortoise and into Maggie's eyes. "I thought a little girl might be just the kind of doctoring this critter needs."

"I think you might be right," said Maggie, touched by his concern for both the turtle and her daughter. "Holly is free to accept your gift, but only if you promise to take the time to explain how to feed and care for an injured tortoise, then make sure she understands."

"That's a promise I can keep. And will."

"Good." Maggie handed the reptile back to Matt. "Just be sure to do all that before you actually agree to let her have it."

Matt glanced down at the tortoise then up at Maggie, solicitous in both gesture and tone. "But I thought you'd give it to her. I'm not much for—"

"Excuse me for interrupting, but I'm not a turtle expert nor am I about to be put in the position of giving Holly a gift that comes with such a responsibility."

He paused long enough to give her the idea that he was considering her predicament, but Maggie sensed that Matt was still going to try and foist the turtle off on her. What was he so afraid of? The gratitude of a six-year-old girl?

Smiling deeply again, charming her, he proved her theory even before he began to speak.

"I see your point," he said. "But as pets go, these little guys are less trouble than most. You don't have to worry. I'm sure that Holly will do just fine with the thing."

"I'm sure she will." Maggie gave him a bright smile. "And it's definitely your job to see that she does. Holly likes to come to the cafe after school to help me set the tables for the supper crowd. Why don't you and your scaly little friend stop by to see her late this afternoon?"

Maggie stepped away from the tree before he could come up with other ways to convince her, then started down the path. Hesitating before she got so far away she'd have to shout to be heard—which meant that Rafe might also overhear her—she turned back to see Matt staring down at the tortoise like a man who'd never seen one before.

After the way she'd behaved around him last night, there was no question she should have continued on her way without another word, especially since what she had in mind might be interpreted as flirtatious. Not that she was fooling herself about their moment of indiscretion. Even though Matt had responded to her, Maggie knew better than to think of his ardor as anything more than the reactions of a man too long on the road. A quick visit to Whisky Row was what he'd been needing and probably where he'd gone after their brief encounter.

The thought of Matt falling into another woman's arms after he left her settled about as well as one of Gus's fried onion and oyster sandwiches, but even that couldn't dull the warm glow in her breast. Unintended or not, it had been a long time since she'd felt like a complete woman; feminine, sensual, and desirable. And for that, she was grateful.

Allowing those feelings to lead her on, she flashed Matt a saucy grin and said, "By the way—you really ought to smile more often. Did you know that when you do, a pair of the most perfectly ad—"

"Don't say it," he warned, looking up from the reptile. "Don't you dare say that you think I have adorable dimples."

Maggie laughed. "Apparently I wouldn't be the first one to do so, but no, I wouldn't say that. What you have are the most unusual, engaging, er . . . in other words, the most *adorable* dimples I've ever seen."

Leaving him to sputter and complain to his tiny elephant-footed friend, Maggie continued on down the path feeling more lighthearted than she had in years.

Close to 400 miles southeast of Prescott, just outside the railroad camp of Willcox, stood a small tent city with no name. Built to serve the appetites of the soldiers at nearby Fort Bowie, the hastily erected establishments offered whisky, women, and gambling, ostensibly to help offset the spartan life the men had to endure at the lonely little outpost. The tent city also provided the entrepreneurial vagabonds who moved it from site to site with plenty of cash to line their pockets.

In that same effort, Mildred Dawson, also known as Peggy Hollister, had just earned herself another three bucks toward her train fare to Phoenix.

When the bulky sergeant gave a final thrust, then groaned, she pushed against his sweaty chest, rolling him onto his back. Within moments the man's snoring filled the tiny space that belonged to Peggy when she was conducting business. Separated from the other makeshift cribs by thin blankets hung on baling wire, each cubicle contained a small cot and a washstand that housed a honey pot below. Peggy kept most of her meager belongings in a grain sack beneath the cot, but hid a gun she'd stolen off a customer back in El Paso behind the washstand.

Kicking away from the soldier with her one good leg, she quietly lifted his cartridge belt off the dirt floor and checked to see if the bullets matched the caliber of her ill-gotten pistol. They did. Quickly stealing as many as she could without his noticing the loss, she dropped them into the cup of her peg leg, then strapped the apparatus to her thigh.

Not all of Peggy's customers asked her to remove the leg, of course, but occasionally a man offered to pay extra like this one had just to have a look at the stump. She didn't mind much unless they grimaced or carried on like they'd just set eyes on a bucket of guts. Rafe had never done anything like that or even made fun of her peg leg. In fact, sometimes when the pain got too bad or the stump ached after too long on her feet, he would lovingly massage the area, telling her how beautiful she was over and over. He was the only man who'd ever treated her decent, and never once called her Peg Leg Millie like some others in the past, or even Peg for short, a name that stuck. Rafe called her Peggy from the start, his very own special way of saying that he loved her. She loved the name, Peggy, and took it from that moment on as her very own. She also loved Rafe Hollister with all her heart, and thought of him the same way.

Of course not everyone felt that way about Rafe, that was for sure. More often than Peggy liked, she'd had to plead for his life when he got too cocky with some half-drunk cowboy or so liquored up himself he forgot that he wasn't the biggest, the meanest, or the fastest gunfighter in the west. Times like that was when their brother/sister act really came in handy. Sure, Rafe was all bluster and show sometimes, a real cocky-boy with a big mouth who used his hurtful tongue the way other men had used their fists on her, but he never meant much by the things he said. And never once in all their four years together had he raised a hand to her in anger. Maybe no one else had noticed, but Peggy knew that deep down Rafe wasn't nothing but a scared little kid, about as tough as a kitten rolling in a bowl of cream. Just like she was.

Although she'd had a hard life most of her twenty-three years, having been dumped at the back door of a bawdy house by her very own pa around the time she turned eight, Peggy was none too proud of her occupation as a whore—especially once she and Rafe threw in together. After that she hadn't once whored herself out unless Rafe personally chose the customer and set the price. Now, thanks to that doodle-headed ranger who run off with her man, it looked as if she was going to have to whore herself all the way to Prescott—which she gladly intended to do if it meant saving Rafe from whatever that woman who claimed to be his wife had in mind.

Rafe would have done the same thing for her, if this business between men and women were reversed.

That was another reason Peggy loved Rafe so much. She knew in the bottom of her heart that he'd do anything for her— just anything. And that was why no one, especially not some female itching to get her hands on him, was going to steal him away. Once she got to Prescott, Peggy was prepared to do whatever it took to get her man back. If she had to lie, steal, or even do murder to get the woman to drop her claim against Rafe, she would do it all in a heartbeat.

She'd never actually had to shoot anyone before, praise Jesus

Eight

Not that he thought he owed the man an apology, but Matt did have a twinge of guilt over the way he'd pasted Hollister after he'd separated him from Maggie. It wasn't like him to have such a hair-trigger on his temper, but he'd just about gone crazy when he looked into the window and saw that bastard shaking her the way he'd beat a rug.

That jab of remorse was a big part of the reason Matt had spent the rest of the day working with Rafe on his manners and just plain talking to him. He figured if he got to know the man better, maybe he could somehow understand why Maggie had ever bothered to look twice at the penny-ante gambler.

"How's that eye doing?" he asked Hollister, who was holding a piece of raw deer liver against that side of his face.

"Better, I think." He tossed the organ onto the dirt floor. "Good 'nuff, anyways. I cain't stand the smell of them animal innards. Never could."

Matt checked the eye, saw that the swelling had gone down enough for Hollister to see clearly again, then scooped the chunk of liver off the floor and hurled it out the window for the scavengers.

Turning back to his captive, he said, "I'm going on over to the cafe pretty soon. Want me to set up another meeting with Maggie? I'll be sure to tell her you're all straightened out on the rules."

Hollister looked up from his seat on the bunk. "Don't see why I cain't go tell her all that myself."

Matt blew out a frustrated sigh, but kept his temper in check. "We've been over that a hundred times, Rafe. You're Holly's Christmas and birthday present, one she's been waiting for close to seven years. If she can wait that long, you can sure as hell sit right here for a few more weeks."

"I expect I kin," he agreed, hanging his head. "But I don't see why I got to wait it out chained up like a circus bear. Cain't y'all see yur way to taking these off?"

He held up his chains, begging like a prisoner only minutes from the hangman's noose. Although Matt had worked hard at tolerating the man over the last few hours, he still didn't trust him beyond the cabin door. Besides, it wasn't as if he hadn't given Hollister a certain amount of freedom. He was cuffed and chained, yes, but that chain stretched to every corner of the cabin, leaving Rafe free to wander around, stoke the fire, or use the slop jar any time he chose.

"Sorry," said Matt, surprised to find that he actually felt that way. "But until you have things worked out a little better with Maggie, I'm afraid I'll have to keep you locked up."

Hollister muttered something under his breath, something Matt obviously was better off not knowing, then quietly said to him, "It ain't like I run out on Maggie 'cause I wanted to, ya know. I had some trouble with the law, and then I just kinda forgot about her. Ain't my fault she didn't stick inside my head, is it?"

Matt couldn't imagine how any man could ever forget Maggie, but then he wasn't exactly an expert on husbands and wives. "What about Holly? Don't tell me that you forgot you were about to become a father that easily."

"Well, now, I sorta did forget that too, but only because I didn't entirely b'lieve Maggie when she told me she was in a family way." He sniffed his liver-stained fingers then wrinkled his nose. "Course, I know'd it was possible, but I also figured she reckoned on using me as a way to git off that farm. Hell, if I hadn't taken her to Salt Lake City and put her on a train, she'd be a dried-up old spinster by now, still milking them stinking cows for her daddy."

"Damn it all, Hollister." Matt struggled with his control. "No matter how hard I try to get it through your thick skull that you've got to stop thinking and talking about Maggie that way, you just keep on doing it. I guess I haven't made a good enough impression on you yet—think that's the problem?" He rolled up his sleeves.

"No, no, no." Hollister hopped off the bunk and dragged himself and his chains to the far corner. "That ain't it, a'tall. I was just speaking the truth the way y'all told me to. I only said what I think, s'all. Didn't mean no disrespect to the lady, no sir."

Matt had learned long ago that when the horse dies, it's time to get off. "All right, Rafe. I'm willing to forget what I just heard, but understand that you've told me and Maggie about all the truth we want to hear. From here on out, you speak to her and of her in a manner befitting the lady that she is, or you won't be speaking to anyone at all. Got it?"

"Yessir, and y'all can be sure that I'll be doing us proud from now on."

Matt nodded, wondering what in the hell this fool could possibly do to make him feel proud. "You do that, Rafe. In the meantime, I'm going to head to the cafe. Anything special you want me to bring back for supper?"

Hollister thought a minute. "Whisky? I been dry a good long spell now."

Just what he needed, thought Matt—not simply a fool but a drunken fool. "I'm going to have to think about that a while. Be back in an hour or so."

As he collected his jacket and hat, Matt glanced at the roller skates hanging above his cot. He thought about taking them along to deliver with the turtle, then decided to save them and the playing cards for later. No sense spoiling the little imp. Besides, the skates would come in handy as his Christmas gift for Holly, the cards, a way to say goodbye the next day.

When Matt walked into the cafe fifteen minutes later, Maggie and her daughter were nowhere to be seen. Except for Gus Townes, a man he'd met briefly, the restaurant was deserted.

"Afternoon," said Gus, wiping his hands on his thoroughly stained apron. Approaching him with his hand outstretched, he asked, "It's Matt, isn't it, Ben Sloan's friend?"

"Matt Weston, and yes, I've been working with Ben." He shook the chef's hand, then looked down to see that his fingers were dusted with flour.

"Sorry about that," laughed Gus. "I was just fixing a little fried asparagus for the supper menu when you rang the bell. At least it wasn't the usual—turkey gizzards and raw oysters! What can I do for you?"

"Well . . ." Matt hesitated, giving his stomach a moment to settle at the thought of Gus's raw oysters. The slimy little ocean delicacies might have been hugely popular with everyone else out West, but as far as he was concerned, he'd just as soon have swallowed a live scorpion.

"You okay, Weston?" asked Gus, his head cocked to one side.

"Just a little indigestion." Not precisely a lie. "I'm supposed to meet your niece and her daughter about now. Are they back in the kitchen?"

"They're not anywhere I know of yet." He stroked one corner of his thick mustache, flouring the few hairs that hadn't already turned gray. "Ought to show up any time now. You got some business with Maggie, do you?"

Matt knew to be cautious with Gus, and that Maggie hadn't taken him into her confidence. "Not business exactly. Just a little present for Holly. It can wait."

Matt was just about to head out the door before he got tripped up in one of his stories, when it suddenly opened and in came Maggie with Holly skipping along behind her. When the youngster saw Matt, she flung the books she'd been carrying into the air and raced toward him, arms outstretched.

"Captain Matt!" she cried, propelling herself into his startled arms. "You came back!"

"Holly, for heaven's sake." Hands on hips, Maggie joined them. "Leave the poor man alone. And what's all this about Matt? He's Captain Weston to you, remember?"

"I remember," she said, clinging to Matt's neck as he adjusted her wriggling body in his arms. "But I also 'membered that if I say sheriff or uncle first, that you said it's okay to say the wrong name. Isn't captain like saying sheriff?"

Maggie rolled her eyes and Gus narrowed his. Both of them were staring at Matt, one seeking approval, the other, answers.

"I don't mind if Holly wants to call me Captain Matt," he said, feeling way too much pressure to say and do the right thing.

"If you're sure you don't mind, I guess it's all right."

Maggie's tone and expression didn't quite agree with her approval, but then it didn't really matter. Holly wasn't paying any attention to her mother anyway. She'd cupped Matt's face between her small hands and was in the midst of rubbing his cheeks, patting him as if he were a dog. Her big brown eyes, magnified by the lenses of her glasses, were sparkling with excitement. If her grin got any wider, Matt figured the corners of her mouth would actually touch the tips of her ears.

He couldn't understand the kid's reactions at all. Last time he'd seen Holly, he'd not only scolded her several times, but turned her new kite into an embarrassing piece of rubbish. Now she was hugging him, and God help him, kissing his cheek. While he'd never been a man given to blushing, Matt was horrified to feel his face growing warm. Leaning over, he tried to set the little troublemaker on her feet, but she clung to him like a baby possum.

"Holly," said Maggie in a firm, no questions asked voice. "I think Captain Weston is trying to show you something. Let go of him."

She obeyed, but stood right up next to his leg. "Did you bring me a present?"

"Ah, it's not exactly, you know, a present, Holly." Matt fumbled around inside his jacket the way he'd just fumbled for the right words, and finally scooped the tortoise out of its warm nest in his pocket. Removing the blanket of flannel as he hunkered down to the child's level he explained, "It's more of a little pet. How do you like it?"

She squealed and clapped her hands, then reached for the reptile.

"Not so fast," warned Matt, holding it out of her reach. "There are lots of things you need to know about this critter before I can just turn it over to you."

"It's a turtle, I know that!"

"Well, I guess you can call it a turtle if you want to, same family I think, but this is a tortoise."

"No matter what you call it," said Gus. "It don't look like it eats too much. I expect it'll be welcome in my kitchen, which is where I've got to get going right now. Coming back for supper, Matt? Besides the usual turkey, tonight we've got pork hocks and beans and Maggie's pumpkin blossom fritters."

His mouth watered at the thought. Best of all, he hadn't made any mention of those damned oysters. "I wouldn't miss it," he said, glancing around the room. "In fact I think I'll stake out a table now."

Chuckling, Gus headed off to the kitchen. Maggie took a chair from a nearby table and sat down to listen to Matt's instructions.

"Is it a girl turtle or a boy?" Holly wanted to know, interested only in her idea of specifics. "I think it's a girl, so I have to get a girl name."

Matt flipped the reptile over, checked its shell, then flipped it upright again. Curious about Holly's judgement, he asked, "What makes you think this is a girl?"

She pointed to the head. "She gots paint on her lips like the bad ladies on Whisky Row."

"Holly!" Maggie clutched her throat in horror. "Where on earth—how did you ever hear about such ladies?"

"Aunt Hattie told me. She said they gots red lips and big hair and ankles mens can see."

"That's enough young lady. We'll discuss this later."

Matt could see that Maggie's cheeks were aflame and she was shrinking inside her dress, but he couldn't help laughing as he did her the favor of changing the subject.

"As it turns out, Holly," he said, still chuckling. "You're right about the tortoise being a girl, but not for the reason you think. Her mouth is red because I've been feeding her prickly pear fruit. She loves it."

Looking up at Maggie, who'd regained most of her composure, he added, "That's all this critter eats, by the way—fruits and vegetables, no meat."

Even with the new subject, Holly still hadn't quite gotten past the reptile's sex. Lightly petting the shell and getting used to the feel of the plates, she asked, "Then how do you know she's a girl and not a boy?"

"Well," he explained easily. "Girl turtles have flat shells on their bellies and the boys look kind of scooped out, like a dip." He maneuvered his hand in the shape.

"Why," she asked, "does the boy turtle got a dip?"

Totally unprepared for the conversation to have gotten to this point, Matt tossed Maggie a wild-eyed plea for help. How was he to explain to a child that the scoop would fit nicely over the female's humped back, allowing the male to mount her when the urge to mate struck?

Thankfully, Maggie was ready with an answer. "That's Nature's way, sweetheart. You must listen to Captain Weston now and stop asking so many questions. This tortoise has been hurt and needs someone to take care of it—do you think you're big enough to do whatever is necessary to make her feel better as well as feed and water her every day? Those are very big jobs."

"I can do it, I can, I can." Her head was nodding up and down like a pony at trot, little blond ringlets bouncing every which way. "Will you let me hold her now, Captain Matt?"

He eased the reptile onto the cushion she'd made by holding her palms together tightly. "Be careful of that bandaged area. That's where her shell is cracked."

Matt went through the procedure for cleaning and binding the wound each day, gave her a clearer idea about what and when to feed the tortoise, and then asked Holly to repeat his instructions; not once, but twice. Satisfied she understood and would take good care of her new pet, he rose and stretched his legs.

Holly looked up to ask, "Can I call her Louie?"

Maggie laughed. "That's a boy's name, honey. Can't you think of something that would sound better for a girl?"

Holly strained, then said, "I know. I'll call her Mattsie 'cause you gave her to me, Captain Matt, okay?"

He looked to Maggie with a helpless shrug. Again she saved his skin.

"That's very thoughtful of you, sweetheart. If you want to name her after Captain Weston, why not call her Matilda? That's a real lady's name."

"Matilda?" Holly raised the tortoise to her face, noses touching, eye to eye. "Yes, Matilda is a good name for you. Let's go find you a bed, Matilda."

"Look in my closet," Maggie suggested. "On the floor there's a sewing box full of buttons. You may empty them onto my bed and use that for Matilda. It's nice and soft inside."

Giggling wildly, Holly scampered off toward the kitchen where the stairs were located, skidded to a halt, then ran back to where Matt stood.

Looking up at him with big round eyes, she said, "Thank you very much, Captain Matt. Matilda is the best present I ever got. Are you going to get married very soon?"

"Holly, for heaven's sake." Maggie shook her head. "Leave the poor man alone."

"It's just one question." She looked back at Matt. "Are you?"

"Ah, I'm not planning to for a good long time." Like a fool, he didn't let it go at that. He had to ask, "Why?"

Holly lit up with one of those ear-to-ear grins. " 'Cause then you can wait for me a good, long time! Mama said you were too old to marry me, but when I'm old enough to be as old as you, then you can marry with me."

After that utterly confusing statement, she took off again, this time disappearing into the kitchen and up the stairs.

"What does that mean, I'm too old to marry?" Matt couldn't believe he'd heard her right. "And what else did she say?"

Instead of answering him, Maggie produced a wobbly smile and began backing toward the kitchen just as Gus pushed open the door and popped his head into the room.

"Maggie?" he said. "You planning to tend that pot on the stove or should I just let it boil down to nothing?"

"Oh, Lord, my blossoms." Turning to Matt only briefly, she quickly added, "I have to go—see you at suppertime?"

Matt eyed the door where Gus still lingered. "See you then, I guess."

She gave a slight nod, that silly grin still in place, then turned and fled into the kitchen.

* * *

After that embarrassing moment, the rest of the afternoon and evening went by in a blur for Maggie. As promised, Matt returned to the cafe for dinner, but the restaurant was so crowded, they didn't get a chance to speak beyond his ordering two meals packed into a box to take back to the cabin. The best he managed was to make an appointment with her in the kitchen for later that evening, around ten. Once the cafe was closed for the night, Holly spent the rest of her evening tending to and playing with her new pet, leaving Maggie free to fret over her upcoming meeting with Matt.

She'd handled the confrontation with Rafe badly, no question there. What concerned her now was whether she'd damaged the chances of Rafe remaining in Prescott long enough to even want to be any kind of father to Holly. She could hardly blame the man if he chose to move on instead of sticking around to face more of the animosity she'd displayed. For all Maggie knew, he'd saddled up and ridden out of town the minute Matt turned his back.

With those thoughts and worse as her only company, the night dragged on. By the time Holly was in bed and sleeping soundly, and ten o'clock finally rolled around, Maggie was as nervous as a lovesick cat. Matt barely got through the kitchen door before she attacked him with her most pressing concerns.

"Where is Rafe?" she wanted to know. "Is he still in town?"

Matt glanced her way, then slowly—much too slowly, in Maggie's opinion—made his way to Gus's counter. After removing his hat and setting it down, he finger-combed his hair and finally addressed the questions.

"Rafe is at the cabin where I left him. Don't worry—he isn't going anywhere."

"But how can you be so sure?" Wringing her hands, Maggie crossed over to where he stood. "We didn't exactly part on friendly terms, if you recall. Maybe he's decided to—"

"At this point, any decisions concerning Rafe, including

whether he stays or goes, are entirely up to you." He smiled but not deeply enough to flash his adorable dimples. Something was troubling him, but what? "Does that make you feel any better?"

"I wish it did," she said, wringing her hands. "But for all you know, he could be riding out of town as we speak."

"It'd take a mighty big horse."

Playing word games was not at all what Maggie had in mind. "What's that supposed to mean? I asked you a simple question."

"Rafe couldn't leave the cabin if he wanted to," he said flatly, completely without emotion. "I thought you knew that I had him chained to the rafters."

"Chained?" Maggie didn't know if the idea horrified or humiliated the most, but it definitely did both. "Are you telling me that Rafe has been chained up since you brought him here?"

"Except for the brief visit with you, yes."

"My God, how barbaric."

He started a little, looking as if she'd slapped him. Then he came back at her, his voice harsh and a little ragged.

"I don't understand why you're so surprised or upset, Maggie. You knew that Hollister wasn't exactly willing to come to Prescott in the first place. How do you think I got him here and still managed to get a little sleep on the way? Your husband is not what you'd call a man of his word, you know."

And just that quickly and cruelly, there it was—the simple fact that the only way Matt could capture and keep hold of the man who once said he loved her, was to chain him up like a wild animal. Swamped by a sudden sense of inadequacy, as if every slight and disappointment she'd ever known as a woman had fused into one huge river of self-doubt, Maggie burst into tears before she even realized the damn had broken. Worse, it happened before she could turn away from Matt. The last thing she wanted was for him to witness this final humiliation, and she certainly didn't expect him to comfort or calm her, but before she could even try to stop him, he took her into his arms.

"Christ, Maggie," he whispered softly. "I guess I should have known how much it would upset you to hear that the man you love is in chains. I'm an idiot. Please forgive me."

She wanted to laugh. In her hysteria and his confusion, she *was* laughing, in fact, but still the sounds came out as the sobs of a shattered woman. Misunderstanding, Matt held her even tighter.

"He's coming around, I swear, he is," said Matt, still whispering against her hair. "Rafe wants to see you again, any time tomorrow morning, whenever you can get away."

"What good is that?"

Suddenly aware that her lips were touching the skin of his throat, Maggie moved back a little, not quite pulling out of the comfort of Matt's arms.

"Can't you see?" she went on. "What good is any of it if you have to chain the man to keep him in the same town with me? Do you know how that makes me feel? Like the most undesirable, unattractive, and hated woman that ever lived."

Matt shut her up then, not with words, but with his mouth, all but smothering her with a kiss that seared right through to Maggie's soul. Until that moment, she assumed he felt much the way she did; that any female who had to hire a tracker to bring her man back, and then had to keep him chained up to make sure he stayed around, couldn't have been much of a woman, in any sense of the word. Now she wasn't so sure.

She understood somehow that Matt's passion came from within himself. Then again, maybe she just wanted to believe that his kiss and the flames that it touched off were ignited by their desire, not by sheer physical need that could have been sated anywhere, by anyone. Not that allowing herself to believe Matt actually desired her made a lot of sense to Maggie—he could just as easily have been driven by a sense of guilt or pity, and not the genuine lust she herself felt.

She knew one thing for sure at the moment—the awakening of her desire had a single source; the man himself. The fever of being near Matt had threatened to consume her, and had done so, she realized, since the moment she'd first looked at him as a man, and not simply the means to an end. The thought shocked, terrified and confused her so, she pushed away from him, robbing herself of what she desperately needed while she still could.

The moment her lips left his, Matt came after her again, this time assaulting her senses with his words.

"Just in case you're wondering, Maggie," he said, a strange rage deepening his lust-choked voice. "Make no mistake about what just happened here. That was no accident, my kissing you. I've wanted to do that since before you sent me after Rafe Hollister, a man who must be deaf and blind as well as dumb."

"Matt, don't." She tried to pull out of his grasp, but he wouldn't let her go. "You don't have to do this, don't have to say these things. I know what I am, and even more, what I'm not. I didn't hire you to make me feel better about myself."

He laughed, sounding hoarse. "You think you know everything, do you? Do you know this? I promised myself that I wouldn't let anything like this happen again, swore that I would keep my hands off of you from now on. I take pride in being a man of my word, Maggie, especially when I make a vow to myself. It took one hell of a woman to make me break it."

She didn't dare try to make sense of his words, not beyond this moment. Stunned by what she'd heard, the best Maggie could manage was a feeble, "I—I don't know what to say, what to think."

"There's still a lot you don't know." He pulled her tight against his body again. "You took my breath away the first time

I saw you walking out of this kitchen. Do you remember what you accused me of that day?"

Her senses on fire, her mind in a whirl, Maggie drifted back to the past, but didn't have to think about it for long. It had been so many years since any man looked at her with anything other than surprise or horror, she'd automatically taken Matt's undisguised appraisal that day as a criticism of her height. As if he'd judged her and found her less than feminine. Had she really been so wrong?

Half afraid to believe him, Maggie glanced up at Matt. She was overflowing with both wonder and gratitude, but couldn't seem to find the words to convey what she felt so strongly in her heart.

"That's right," Matt said for her. "You were wrong. About as wrong as you'll ever be about anything."

He released her and reached for his hat, then strode over to the door, asking from over his shoulder, "Can we expect you at the cabin around mid-morning?"

Out of both words and thoughts, perhaps even her mind, Maggie could barely manage the word, "Yes."

"We'll be waiting for you."

Then he was gone.

Maggie stood rooted to the spot long after the door closed behind him, savoring memories of their embrace and wondering how she would ever be able to go on from here. All of her hopes, her plans, even the hiring of Matt, all had been done for Holly. Everything she'd done over the last seven years from learning how to be a baker in order to earn a living, to taking part in community "Gab and Jab" needlepoint sessions had been for only one person, for only one reason: for Holly and her happiness.

Now at long last it looked as if Maggie's hopes, dreams and plans for her daughter's happy future were about to come to fruition, a time for joy and for celebration.

Why then, she had to wonder, did she suddenly feel so desolate, as if she'd forgotten to add the most important ingredient to her well-thought-out recipe for success?

Nine

Over the next week, Matt put all of his time, energy, and as much concentration as possible on his task. Even as a captain in the Frontier Battalion until his forced retirement, Matt couldn't remember when he'd worked so hard on a single project. Turning Rafe Hollister into something that resembled a gentleman was like breaking a wild mule in a hailstorm.

First, Matt allowed a meeting between Maggie and her husband, a rendezvous that went fairly well—at least this time, there wasn't any violence. The fact that he insisted on staying in the room with them might have had something to do with the genial tone of the meeting. Or maybe it was Matt's new rule. He insisted they not see each other during Rafe's "training period," and set the date of their next meeting for one week down the road.

Initially, this plan met with Rafe's rowdy approval and great relief, although Maggie had been less than convinced that keeping them separated would do anything but make Rafe harder for her to reach. Matt thought the time was just what he needed to make sure Maggie had a husband worthy of her attention. And he was right. By the time six of the seven days had passed, Rafe could hardly wait to see his wife again, as planned.

As for Maggie's state of mind by then, Matt could only guess. While he wasn't the least bit contrite or even apologetic about the way he'd felt about her the last time they'd been together,

Matt made a new promise to himself that night in which he vowed to never put his hands on her again. This time, he meant to honor those good intentions if he had to chain *himself* to the cabin's rafters.

Of course Matt realized that in order to make sure he kept that vow he would have to avoid seeing Maggie whenever possible—and never again, alone in the dark. Unfortunately, that didn't help much when it came to forgetting about her. Hard as he tried, Matt couldn't stop thinking about her, even though he hadn't so much as passed by the cafe in a week. He even stooped to sampling the other restaurants in town during the next six days or stopped by the grocer's and went back to the cabin to cook. After all, even if he wasn't that fond of the company there, Matt was fairly handy with a frying pan and a stove.

Now that the prescribed week had passed and Maggie was expected at any minute, Matt was certain that his efforts with Rafe stood every chance of effecting a reunion between the Hollisters. That in turn would eventually help them become the kind of family they'd set out to be so many years ago. To have her mother and father united again, would surely guarantee the happiest Christmas little Holly had ever known. The fact that it was turning out to be Matt's worst holiday season was insignificant, at least where this job was concerned.

Once Maggie finally arrived at the cabin on the appointed hour, Matt felt his strength and all his good intentions start to dissolve when he opened the door and saw her standing there. She was dressed to suit the weather in a warm dress of rust-colored wool, and her hair was twisted into a fashionable knot at the back of her head. Her eyes were bright with excitement and her lips, a little too eager to smile. He couldn't think of a time that she'd looked more beautiful. Or more desirable.

"Good morning," she said. "Is Rafe ready for our meeting?"

Slapped in the face with that reality, Matt stepped aside and waved her into the cabin. "Morning. Please, come on in."

"Maggie, darlin'," said Rafe, taking her by the hand as he joined them near the door. "Yur looking mighty good today. As pretty as a shined-up penny."

Her eyes went wide and her cheeks flooded with color. "Good to see you again, too, Rafe. What a nice suit. Is it new?"

"Come right out of Goldwater's just yesterday." Still dragging her by the hand, he said, "Come sit a spell on my bunk. We got lots to talk about."

"Oh, well . . . all right."

Arm in arm the two passed by Matt. Maggie paused long enough to say, "By the way—Holly's been wondering why you don't come by anymore. Is something wrong?"

"No, I've just been awfully busy." Matt suddenly wanted out of that cabin more than he wanted anything—including Maggie. Something about witnessing the results of his efforts hit him hard, stung him in places no one had ever reached before. "Tell Holly that I'm sorry, would you? I'll leave you two alone a while now, and check back in what, about a half an hour?"

Rafe's suddenly amorous gaze never left his wife's face as he said, "Make it an hour, would y'all? Me and Maggie got lots of ground to cover."

Sick at heart, Matt said, "That all right with you, Maggie?"

She, too, seemed hypnotized, utterly fascinated by this newly polished Rafe. "It's fine with me."

"As you wish."

Matt grabbed his hat and smashed it onto his head without so much as reshaping the brim. Then he stalked on out of the cabin, slammed the door behind him, and started down the lonely path to nowhere without ever looking back.

For the first few minutes, Maggie didn't say a word. She just sat there staring at Rafe, looking at a man she'd never seen before. His hair was smoothed down, slick with some kind of pomade or oil, and he'd groomed his little mustache, nothing more now than a sparse shadow above his lip that resembled a coffee stain. Even more unusual was his manner as he began to speak, a curious combination of confidence and hesitancy.

"I know I done ya wrong, Maggie girl, especially the way I run out when y'all was in trouble, in a family way and all." He paced the floor in front of her, hands behind his back instead of at his mouth or picking at each other. "It was real cowardly of me to send y'all to Prescott alone, promising the way I did—"

"Rafe," she cut in. "You don't have to do this. I'm not looking for apologies or even excuses for what happened back then. All I want from you is a little of your time, enough anyway for you to have a chance to know and love Holly, and to finally make her wish come true."

He stopped pacing and stood before her. Looking stunned, as if she'd gut-punched him, he asked, "That's it? For honest?"

"That's it," she replied, able at last to offer him a genuine smile.

"But what about us?" Rafe actually sounded hurt, as if she'd disappointed him somehow. "I thought y'all wanted us to be together, like a family."

She shrugged, caught off guard by this Rafe, a man apparently considering the possibility of taking on such a huge responsibility.

Answering carefully, Maggie said, "Being a family would be nice, I suppose, but it's not the reason I sent for you. I didn't put you or myself through all this because I wanted you back, Rafe. You have to believe me. I did it for Holly, and only for Holly."

He seemed to accept this. "Yeah, I reckon I kin understand that, but it's not like y'all would actually *mind* if'n we was to become a family. Ain't that right?"

Maggie hadn't concerned herself with that possibility for so long, she honestly didn't know how to react. Again she chose her words with great care. "I didn't say that I'd mind, Rafe. I just want you to know that I'm not putting any pressure on you to stay in Prescott on my behalf. Holly is—"

"Yeah, yeah, woman, I know all that about the kid, three times over, I know it."

After that outburst from the old Rafe, he dusted off his trousers, a new pair made of black broadcloth with a matching vest and jacket, then ran his hands over his hair to make sure it was still plastered to his head.

Apparently satisfied by his appearance, he dropped onto the bunk beside Maggie and reached for her hand. "I been thinking about us the last few days, recollecting how it used to be betwixt us. Remember?"

Looking so deeply into his calf eyes, while his hand was gently massaging hers, she found it hard not to remember the nights she'd spent in Rafe's arms. Confused enough over her recent feelings for Matt, Maggie wasn't about to risk what was left of her sanity by falling in love with this man again. Not yet anyway. Besides, she had to be certain that Holly's heart was in good hands before she could even think about thawing her own.

She pulled out of Rafe's grip and jumped to her feet. "Don't misunderstand, but I'm not ready to do much talking about us yet, past or present. I came here to discuss Holly. I'd hoped that she was your main concern, too. Was I wrong?"

"No, no." Though he couldn't hide the scowl of a spurned suitor who hadn't gotten his way, he urged Maggie down the path she'd chosen. "I want to know all about the girl, but mostly I'm wondering when I get to see her. Christmas surely does seem a long ways off."

"That's the way it's got to be."

He grumbled a little, but accepted his fate. "All right, but kin you at least tell me a little about her. What's she like?"

Surprised to learn that he even cared, Maggie gave him a

brief overview of Holly's life to date. "Well, as you may know, Aunt Hattie and Uncle Gus took me in when I arrived in Prescott, and were very helpful when Holly was born the following Christmas. They've been wonderful to her, almost like parents, and she loves them a lot."

"So the two of y'all ain't had it so bad then, what with living off yur kin all this time?"

Maggie's lip curled as she cocked her head and stared down at him. Why was it that every time she thought something good about Rafe, he had to show her that she was wrong?

Trying to keep a civil tone, she said, "To spare me, not you, I have no intention of going into the bad times, of which there were plenty, but no, we did not live off anyone else. The minute I arrived in town, I started working at the restaurant and have earned mine and Holly's keep there ever since."

Rafe whistled his appreciation.

"Thank you, but now that I think about it, I have to say that isn't quite the truth." Warmed by motherly pride, Maggie went on to explain. "Hattie and Gus live on a ranch close by where she raises turkeys for the restaurant. Gus runs the cafe by himself, with my help. For the last two years, Holly has been earning her own keep by working with Hattie at the ranch taking care of the hatchlings until they're old enough to join the flock. She has a real affinity for animals, Rafe."

Pondering that statement, he scratched his head and unwittingly freed one of his cowlicks. It went waving back and forth like a single stalk of corn in a high wind. He asked, "She's wanting to be some kind a nun for critters, is that what y'all mean?"

It took Maggie a moment to figure out that Rafe had confused affinity with divinity. Rewording, she had to look away from him as she explained, "I just meant to say that she feels a kinship for most animals, the way you do with horses and even the cows on my pa's farm."

He smoothed the scraggly hairs of his mustache, nodding as sagely as a man of his limited education could. "Guess she's got me to thank for that. What else about her is like me?"

Doing her best to find Rafe's good points, Maggie searched for something to say. "Her eyesight?" was the best she could do.

"That ain't something good. How's she with a deck of cards?"

Maggie frowned. "She only knows how to play old maid, Rafe. I haven't noticed that she's particularly adept at shuffling them or rigging the deck, if that's what you mean."

"Now just a dang minute."

He was up and off the bunk in a flash. About the same time Matt knocked on the door and called in through the window.

"Everything all right in there? I'm back."

Maggie took it upon herself to answer him. "Everything's fine. I'll be right out!"

Rafe took her by the arm when she turned to leave.

"When y'all planning to come visitin' again?" he asked, plainly disappointed to see her go.

"Soon," she promised. "In less than a week, I hope. Next time I come, I'll bring some of Holly's schoolwork and drawings. She's doing quite well, you know."

He seemed delighted by this news. "Cain't say that I did know, but I'm right pleased to hear that y'all put the girl in school. I hardly went past learning how to read my own name."

Maggie hoped to remedy that—if Rafe chose to stick around and become part of Holly's life. In the meantime she said, "Goodbye for now. I'll let myself out."

"S'long."

Rafe looked as if he planned to reach for her after that, possibly to bestow a farewell kiss, but Maggie ducked by him and hurried toward the door.

Outside, Matt stood with his back to the door a few feet away, hands buried in his jacket pockets as he waited for Maggie. When she finally came through the door and closed it behind her, he waited until she'd joined him before so much as turning to look her way.

"In case you're interested," she said, bundling herself against the suddenly chill wind. "You've made quite a lot of progress with Rafe over the past week. I wouldn't have believed it possible."

"Thanks." What else was there to say? He sure as hell didn't want the details of her wifely visit. "When do you want to set up the next meeting?"

"Not before Saturday, I'm afraid, what with Thanksgiving and all." She paused, then tapped his shoulder to make him look at her. "You are planning to come to supper on Thanksgiving, aren't you?"

Her big brown eyes were pleading with him, so lovely, it hurt to look at them. "I don't think that's a very good idea, Maggie, but thanks for asking."

"Look, I know this may be a little awkward for you after the other night, but—"

He reached out and put his finger across her mouth, soft, soft lips he longed to kiss. "Forget about that," he said quietly. "I have."

If those words stunned or angered her, she didn't let it show. Instead, Maggie kept at him about the holiday dinner.

"Please come, Matt. If you don't show up, it will break Holly's heart. She doesn't understand why you haven't come by to see her again now that you're back to town, especially since you left an injured turtle in her care. She's really been working hard with Matilda and needs your approval."

Holly always won out, no matter the insanity of the situation. Resigned to his fate, Matt said, "All right. Tell the little imp I'll be there as long as she promises to save me some pumpkin pie."

"That's a promise I know she'll keep. Until Thursday, then?"

"Until Thursday," he echoed.

"Oh, and Matt, I have one more request of you. Will you please promise me that you'll never use those chains on Rafe again?"

Matt would have done anything she asked. Anything but that. "Sorry, but I don't think that's such a good idea."

"But why not?" Maggie's eyes flared and she held her head high. "Rafe and I have come to a certain understanding. I'm positive that he's not planning to run away from his responsibilities this time."

Although he was dead set against giving the man his freedom, Matt knew this was a battle he was going to lose—and in every way imaginable. With a short nod he agreed. "As you wish."

"Thanks, Matt."

He stood there watching as Maggie started down the path, but didn't stay there until she'd disappeared from view. Suddenly, watching her come or go was too painful a hobby. Instead Matt ducked out of the icy wind and retreated into the relative warmth of the cabin.

"I was wondering what was keeping y'all," said Rafe, as if he cared. "For a minute there I thought you might be outside sparking my woman."

"Shut up, Rafe," he grumbled, otherwise paying him no mind. "And get the hell out of that suit before you ruin it. Cost me a week's pay."

"Don't think I don't appreciate it neither, no sir."

While the man preened, carrying on about what a handsome devil he thought he was in his new suit, Matt went over to the stove and began stuffing more logs into it. The weather had turned as bad as Matt's mood—stormy, dark and cloudy. An early winter was predicted by the old folks in town, and Matt was inclined to believe them. The wind alone with its strong brisk gusts was sharp enough to cut a man in half if he faced it head on.

As he poked and prodded the glowing embers, coaxing them to ignite the new logs, Matt thought he heard what sounded like a light knock on the door.

"I'd best get that," Rafe said, obviously hearing the same knock. "Might be Maggie come back for a little good-night kiss."

Matt was thinking about how much he'd like to take one of the fiery logs out of the stove and beat Rafe over the head with it when a familiar and very squeaky voice blew into the cabin on the chill wind.

"H-hi m-mister. W-who are y-you and w-where is Captain M-matt?"

"That there depends on who wants to know, kid."

Horrified, Matt climbed to his feet, and turned to the door. "Holly? What are you doing here?"

Ducking around her father, she said, "Captain M-matt! It's m-me! A-and I b-brought M-matilda."

"I can see that it's you, Holly," he replied, spearing Rafe with a meaningful glance.

The man was so caught up at the moment by his first glimpse of his progeny, however, he didn't seem to be breathing, much less capable of forming the words that would ruin Maggie's plan.

As Matt drew closer to Holly, he could see that she was trembling from the cold. Taking her by the hand, he pulled her inside the cabin and shut the door against the frigid wind.

Again he asked, "What are you doing here?"

"M-matilda." She reached inside her thin sweater, pulled out a bundle wrapped up in a puffy square of quilting, and opened it. "S-see? S-she's b-better and I-I f-fixed her." Then Holly showed the tortoise to Rafe and again asked, "W-who are y-you, m-mister?"

"Well, ah kid . . ." His voice was choked with the kind of emotion Matt wouldn't have expected to find in the man.

"He lives here with me, Holly," explained Matt, still not trusting Rafe to say the right thing. "He's a . . . friend."

"That's right," Rafe chimed in, himself again. "I'm a Texas Ranger just like the captain here."

Too late to do anything else, Matt narrowed his eyes at the cocky fool, silently promising him that sooner or later he would pay for that remark.

"W-what's y-your n-name, Mister Ranger?" Holly asked.

"Er, well, ah . . ."

Rafe gulped loudly, and for a moment, Matt thought he was going to do the smart thing and let him handle the situation. As usual, the fool opened his mouth without thinking.

Hitching up his trousers, he said, "Most folks in these parts know me as the, ah, El Paso Kid."

Her eyes big and round as the lenses she looked through, Holly turned to Matt in awe. "I-is he f-famous?"

While Matt was plenty irritated by Rafe's high-handed attempts to aggrandize himself, he was more concerned about the fact that Holly was shivering so badly. Hunkering down to the child's level, he noticed that the edges of her lips were blue.

"Holly," he said, setting the tortoise on the floor and rubbing her tiny hands between his. "Does your mother know you're out in this weather, and that you're *here,* of all places?"

She shook her head, her teeth chattering hard enough to crush quartz. Swearing softly under his breath, Matt scooped Holly's freezing body into his arms and headed for the stove.

"Hey!" shouted Rafe behind him, his possessive instincts overriding his newfound fatherly concern. "Where're you going with her?"

"To see if I can't warm her up a little, *Kid.* Do us both a favor—sit down and stay out of my way."

"Don't see why I should. After all, she's my—"

"Shut up, Kid." Matt turned with Holly clutched tightly against his chest, then shot yet another scathing glance Rafe's way. "She doesn't know you, remember? Don't you think we'll have enough trouble on our hands when Maggie finds out that Holly's been here, without your big mouth adding to the problem?"

Rafe turned as white as Holly, save for the blue lips, then slowly sank onto the bunk. "Sorry," he managed to say, sounding numb. "I guess I wasn't thinking."

"No harm done yet. Besides, no one's paying you to think."

Then Matt turned his entire attention on Holly. As he set her on her feet near the hot stove and pulled off her damp sweater, he pieced together the circumstances that brought her to the cabin. "How did you know that I lived here, sweetheart?"

Glad to be out of her frozen sweater and near warmth, she rubbed her hands together as she explained, "I-I f-followed M-mama w-when s-she l-left the c-cafe."

"You mean today, over an hour ago?"

Nodding, Holly began hopping from foot to foot.

Christ, no wonder she was half frozen. Matt left the girl long enough to pull the blankets off his bed, then returned and draped them across the top of the stove.

Again dropping down to her level, he surmised, "You're saying that you followed your mama here, then hid in the trees and waited for her to leave the cabin before you came to the door? You didn't want your mama to know that you'd come here to see me?"

Nodding slowly, she admitted, "I asked M-mama if I c-could c-come to get you, but s-she wouldn't l-let me."

"Then why didn't you come after me once your mother went inside the cabin? I was just down the path looking for signs of deer."

Tears filled Holly's eyes, but hadn't begun to spill. "I s-saw you going away, but I t-thought you were c-coming right back to talk to M-mama. I waited a l-long time for you to c-come b-back."

The tears finally rolled over the rims of her eyes, fogging up her little glasses with the warm moisture. Sliding the spectacles off of her face, Matt folded them and slipped them into his shirt pocket. Then he took one of the heated blankets off the stove and wrapped Holly's trembling body in it, reassuring her as he bundled her into his arms, that everything would be all right.

"There, there, sweetheart. Don't cry. I'm sure we can find a way to fix this with your mother."

Matt had no idea how he would manage that, of course, but he meant to do whatever it took to keep from turning that vow into an empty promise.

"First we've got to get you warm so you don't come down sick. Your mama would never forgive me if I let that happen."

Hell, thought Matt as he wrapped the second hot blanket around her small body. He wouldn't be able to forgive himself. Hugging her even more tightly than he had before, Matt considered his next move.

He could take Holly back to the cafe immediately, make up a story about finding her lost in the woods, and then hope to hell that she never mentioned her visit to the cabin or the fact that she'd met the famous El Paso Kid. Doing that would expose the girl to more freezing temperatures before she'd had time to warm up, thereby increasing her chances of becoming quite ill. That in turn would also earn him more of Maggie's wrath, a commodity in which he figured he was already well-invested by now.

If he kept Holly with him long enough to warm her thoroughly, the extra time away from home might be just enough to send Maggie on a frantic search for her missing daughter. When Matt looked at it that way, it didn't take much more of his imagination to envision the concerned—and armed—citizens who might want to help with the search, neighbors who would undoubtedly go berserk if they came across the missing girl accompanied by two strange men in a remote cabin.

Leaving Holly alone with Rafe while he went to town to inform Maggie of her daughter's whereabouts wasn't much of an option either, given Rafe's penchant for talking without thinking. The reverse—sending Rafe to town with the news—seemed an even less attractive idea for the very same reason.

Racked with indecision, Matt looked down into Holly's tiny face. While most of the blue was gone from her lips, they were swollen and red, still cold to the touch.

"What," he softly asked her, "Am I going to do with you?"

Ten

Maggie knew she had no choice but to wait at the cafe for word of Holly, but that was the hardest job of all. Others, the menfolks and even a few women, were out in the freezing winds scouring the streets and forests for her daughter, who'd been missing over an hour now. Waiting and wondering was a lot harder, on both body and soul. Maggie couldn't make sense of it, not the fact that Holly had disappeared, and not the fact that she hadn't turned up yet. Surely she'd just ventured into some-one's shop looking to earn a little extra money for Christmas presents.

Maggie couldn't even entertain the idea that Holly had wan-dered beyond the perimeters of town. Most of the trouble-mak-ing Indians, Tonto Apache and a few Yavapai, had been hauled off to reservations the year before Maggie came to Prescott. Still there were a few renegades around, enough to cause an occasional skirmish and put the blame on the Indians, rightly or wrongly, whenever anyone went missing. Settlers occasion-ally disappeared in the forests, never to be seen again. Hunters and lumberjacks told tales of slinking shadows among the trees, never quite sure if they'd seen the real thing, or merely ghostly remnants of the great tribes who had once roamed the area.

Maggie shivered and grew ill at the very thought of her daughter so helpless and alone in the forest. Even if there were no Indians lurking in the trees, a copse of thick pines was no place for a young girl to be lost. At this time of year, torrential rains could hit without warning, turning the terrain into a muddy bog capable of trapping a full grown horse. Given the drop in temperature, snow wasn't entirely out of the question either. Between the dampness in the air and the fierce cold, little Holly wouldn't have a chance of surviving if she wasn't found soon.

The kitchen door suddenly opened and closed behind her, and then Maggie heard the timid, anxious voice of her aunt.

"Is my little sugar still out playing?" asked Hattie.

"She's not playing, for God's sake, she's lost!"

At once, Maggie regretted losing her temper with Hattie. The woman could hardly keep track of the days of the week under normal conditions. When she was upset, she barely knew day from night.

Turning to her, Maggie quietly said, "I'm sorry. I didn't mean to shout at you, but I'm terribly worried about Holly."

Worried didn't begin to describe the way she felt. Maggie was hanging by her thumbs at the edge of panic.

"Well, don't you worry, dear," said Hattie as she headed back to the kitchen. "I lost a pearl earring once and it turned up under my bed. I think I'll just go on upstairs and look under your bed. I wouldn't be at all surprised to find Holly there."

As ridiculous as the idea was, it did give Maggie something to think about for a minute or so. Then she turned back to where she'd been standing for what seemed like forever—framed in the front window of the cafe. It was raining now, coming down in soft, but steady sheets. Tears sprang into Maggie's eyes and might have fallen harder than the raindrops had she not spotted Matt Weston striding up the boardwalk about then with a large, navy blue bundle in his arms. When he reached the Squat and Gobble Cafe, he kicked at the door, unable to knock.

It wasn't until Maggie let him into the restaurant that she noticed several corkscrews of flaxen hair. "Holly?" she cried, her heart in her throat.

"Hi, Mama," came her tiny little voice. "I got cold so Captain Matt brung me home."

After that, Maggie wasn't sure if she snatched her daughter out of Matt's arms, or if he made the transfer himself. All she knew was that her baby was safe, alive, well, and back in her arms again. She buried her face against her daughter's sweet hair, breathing deeply of Holly's scent, assuring her mother's heart that this was indeed her very own child, home again. Only then was Maggie able to set Holly away from her long enough to give the child a cursory examination.

"Are you all right?" she asked, dropping beside her to open the blanket. "Are you hurt anywhere? Where on earth have you been?"

"There's really nothing to worry about, Maggie."

Matt's voice startled her. She'd forgotten all about him.

"Holly may have taken a little chill, but she's all right. I promise you."

"Oh, Matt—thank you, thank you, so much." She touched his pant leg in gratitude, but quickly withdrew her fingers. "Where did you find her?"

Before he could get a word out, the kitchen door banged open and in came Hattie, fiddling with her ears. "Stars in heaven, Maggie, if I haven't gone and lost my pearl earrings. Do you suppose they're under my bed?"

"Hattie," she said. "Holly's been found."

The old woman looked up in surprise. "There you are you little dickens! Oh, and that ranger fellow is here, too. Where have you two been keeping yourselves?"

She crossed the room and swept Holly into her embrace. "Are you all right, precious baby? Were you off playing somewhere?"

While Hattie all but smothered Holly with hugs and kisses, Maggie went back to questioning Matt. "Where did you find her? Down by Granite Creek? Gus was planning to cover that area, but he's not as young as he once was. Did you see him? Does he know that you found Holly?"

"Wait a minute," he said, not looking at all happy. "Are you saying that you have folks out looking for her?"

"Of course, I do." What kind of mother did he take her for? "Holly's been missing for almost two hours. Did you think I'd just sit here and hope that she'd turn up again someday?"

"No, dammit."

Matt glanced at Hattie, still hugging her niece, then raised his brows at Maggie, telling her something with his eyes that he couldn't say with words.

"I didn't realize," he went on to say, "that Holly had been missing for so long or I wouldn't have taken the time to warm her up a little before bringing her home. She was mighty cold when she turned up at *my* cabin."

"Your . . . cabin?" Maggie's entire system froze up. "You mean that's where she's been all this time?"

"Part of it. She wanted to show me how nicely Matilda's shell was coming along." Again he glanced toward Hattie, then lowered his voice even more. "She *followed* someone there."

Maggie knew exactly who he was talking about. "Oh, no. My God, she doesn't—"

"Don't worry," he assured her. "Everything is still all right, for now anyway. You mentioned searchers—how many and where are they looking?"

"Oh, I'd forgotten about them." As she thought about it, Maggie suddenly saw the problem for what it was. In a panic of another kind now, she said, "I don't know how many men are involved for sure, but Gus and Homer Ludlow for two, and probably anyone who was in his barbershop. There are bound to be other searchers as well."

"Searchers?" said Hattie, suddenly a part of the conversation. "I helped with that, thank you. Why I'm the one who told the marshal he ought to get off his lazy backside and go join in the search like the others. That's what he's paid all that money for, isn't it?"

Maggie prayed that Hattie had the lawmen's titles mixed up; at least Ben knew about Rafe and most of the circumstances. "You mean you asked Sheriff Ben to help with the search?"

"No," she said in a huff. "I wouldn't send that old fool on such an important mission. I marched down to the Hotel Winsor and grabbed Marshal Dake right out of the lobby, I did. Shamed him into doing his part, don't you know."

Maggie paused just long enough to wish that Hattie's poor memory had been disconnected before she went in search of the Territorial Marshal. Then she exchanged a fast and very concerned glance with Matt.

"This," she said carefully, "could be a problem."

He nodded, agreeing. "Maybe I ought to be getting back to the cabin to make sure everything is all right."

Holly, content to remain silent much longer than usual, squeezed between Maggie and her aunt. "But Captain Matt," she said, "how can anything be wrong at the cabin? The El Paso Kid is there guarding it, isn't he?"

Looking to Matt in confusion, Maggie said, "The El Paso Kid? Who's that?"

He rolled his eyes and loosened his collar, giving her the distinct impression that he'd left out a few parts of the story.

"No," Maggie said, willing with all of her might that it wasn't true. "Oh, no. Please tell me she isn't talking about . . . him."

"It's the El Paso Kid, Mama. Didn't you see him?"

Deftly changing the subject—it could only get worse from here on, especially with Hattie listening in—Maggie took Holly by the shoulders. "It's time I got you into a tub of hot water, little miss. Now please thank the captain for bringing you home. He has to leave."

Obeying without an argument for once in her life, she threw her arms around Matt's waist and gave him a hug. "Thank you for bringing me home, Captain Matt, and thank you for making me warm again."

"You're welcome, Holly. The next time you decide to take a walk, do it in town."

Then, touching the brim of his hat, he bade them all farewell and made tracks out the door.

In the fresh air again, Matt breathed deeply, picking up the scent of pine, sharp and rich upon the cold air, then let it out in a long sigh. In ways it was a sigh of relief, but he knew that was a reprieve until he got back to the cabin and made sure that all was well. For one thing, Rafe was unchained as Maggie wished, and for another, he wasn't sure what the fool would do if Marshal Dake happened upon him and questioned him about Holly.

Matt stepped into the street, determined to make sure that didn't happen. As he glanced up the road toward the southern edge of town, where his cabin was located, he saw that a man wearing a badge was riding toward him and Gurley Street, a lawman who seemed to be sitting exceptionally tall in his saddle. Behind his horse at the end of a length of rope came a gangly figure in handcuffs, a stumble-gaited captive who lunged back and forth across the horse's tracks in a pathetic and awkward attempt to keep up with the slowly moving animal.

Groaning with a hopelessness that went beyond despair, Matt slowly lowered himself to the edge of the boardwalk and planted his boots in the rain-soaked muck. In no hurry to put himself in the middle of yet another impossible situation, he buried his face in his hands and pretended that he hadn't seen the men approaching. If he could have, he would have pretended away the last two months. All too soon came the sound of the grating voice he'd come to hate, and suddenly, Matt was flung back to reality with a jolt.

"Hey, Weston!" Rafe shouted. "Get off yur butt and come tell this damned fool marshal he ain't got no call to rope me and drag me all over the countryside like I'm some kind a criminal! Weston? Dang it, I know y'all can hear me!"

Taking his time to raise his head, Matt turned to look down the rain-soaked street just about the time Rafe fell over his own feet and pitched forward into the mud. He might even have laughed at the spectacle if the dimwit hadn't been wearing the new suit Matt had been stupid enough to pay ten bucks for—not three days ago. How could such a supposedly simple job have turned into such big trouble?

As the lawman rode up, Matt dragged himself to his feet and tried to salvage what was left of his reputation. After tying the marshal's horse to the hitching rail, he waited for him to dismount before greeting him.

"Afternoon, Marshal Dake. I'm Captain Matt Weston of the Texas Rangers. I'm in town working on a special project with Ben Sloan."

After shaking Matt's hand, Dake said, "Heard a little about you from Ben, now that I think on it. So how do you like our little town now that you've been here a while?"

Matt thought that for a Territorial Capital, Prescott wasn't too well located, although plans were in the works to bring the railroad into town in the next few years. He suspected that wasn't the kind of comment the marshal had in mind.

Instead, he honestly said, "I'd have to say that Prescott is one of the cleanest, friendliest places I've ever had the pleasure of visiting."

Still spitting mud, Rafe shouted, "Why don't someone ask me what I think of Prescott? I think this here town stinks, that's what. It purely smells like the back-ass of this here stinking horse, is what I think!"

"Take it easy back there," warned Matt, hoping that gentle threat would be enough to shut Rafe's mouth for a while.

"I hope you ain't acquainted with this fella," Dake groused. "I found him hiding in an abandoned cabin outside of town.

Found this on him, too." He pulled out the square of quilting Holly had used to wrap her tortoise. "I think that filthy animal might have had something to do with a little town girl that's gone missing today."

"I do know that fella, Marshal," Matt hated to admit. "And I also know for a fact that he didn't have anything to do with Holly's disappearance."

A door creaked open behind Matt then followed by a tiny gasp. About the time he thought things couldn't get any worse, a voice snuck over Matt's shoulder from that same direction, a sound that reminded him way too much of a rusty gate hinge.

"See? There he is, Mama. The El Paso Kid!"

"The El Paso Kid?" echoed the marshal. "Who in tarnation is she talking about?"

Out of options, not that he'd ever had any, Matt forced himself to say, "The fella you've got tied to your horse. He's known as the El Paso Kid."

"No kidding?" With only a quick glance at Rafe, Dake turned to Holly and said, "Good to see you're back home where you belong. You all right, child?"

"She's fine, Marshal Dake," said Maggie. "I'm afraid Holly decided to do a little exploring in the woods without bothering to tell any of us where she was going. Captain Weston was kind enough to bring her back home."

"That so?" His attention returning to Matt, Dake said, "I heard you were about the best tracker in all the territories. I guess it's true."

Rafe, pretty much forgotten by everyone, tossed in his opinion. "I'm a damn fine tracker myself. I'm also a damn fine Texas Ranger. If'n one of y'all don't git back here right now and turn me loose, I reckon I might have to show y'all what a damn fine shot I am, too!"

Dake turned an incredulous eye on Matt. "Is that true? Is this fella really a ranger like you?"

As nightmares went, this one had reached a truly lofty status, worthy of everything that had ever gone wrong in Matt's entire life—up to and including the shotgun blast that nearly tore his leg off at the thigh.

Gagging on the thought before he actually put words to it, he heard himself say, "It's true, all right. Next to me, the Kid is one of the best."

The marshal whistled long and low. "Can't say I've ever heard of the El Paso Kid. What's his real name?"

Dodging yet another bullet, Matt explained, "Sorry, but that information is confidential. No one, not even I know his true identity. Security and all, you understand."

Dake's eyes shifted between Matt and Rafe as he spoke. "If you say so, but I am the territorial law around these parts. If there's something going on in Prescott, I damn well better know about it."

Matt shrugged, looking for a way out of the increasingly inane conversation. "It's Texas business, nothing to do with Arizona. All I can say is that it's a highly sensitive case. Now if you'll excuse me, I'd better cut my, er, partner loose."

"Oh, right. I'm afraid I cuffed him, too."

Spinning around, the marshal dogged his steps so closely, there wasn't a moment's privacy for Matt to grab hold of Hollister and try to drag him down a few notches before he got completely out of hand. As Matt feared, once the lunatic was free, he immediately took his fraudulent identity to heart. And to extremes.

Looking Dake up and down, Hollister spat on the lawman's boots as he said, "That's one I owe y'all. From now on, s'long as I'm anywheres in this here stinking territory, anyways, y'all had best stay clear of me."

Dake did not appreciate the reprimand. "Look here, fella. I'm sorry I had to bring you in like that, but you weren't exactly cooperating when I come upon you. Why didn't you just come out and tell me you were a ranger?"

"He was just doing his job, Kid," said Matt, stepping between Rafe and the marshal in hopes of ending the entire charade. "Come on. Let's get on back to the cabin."

"I ain't in no hurry to go back to that jailhouse."

Rafe's breath was even stronger than his protest. Matt didn't have to call on his years of training as a Texas Ranger to figure out that Hollister had found the whisky he'd hidden out back of the cabin.

"Then let's go and have us a little drink instead, Kid." Matt used the absurd nickname simply for Marshal Dake's benefit.

"Y'all go on ahead," said Rafe, stubborn as ever. "I'll be along later."

Tired of listening to the two, Dake mounted up, wheeled his horse around and rode off at last. Matt wasted no time jumping down Rafe's throat. "I ought to take a bullwhip to you. What the hell do you think you're doing?"

"Taking care of myself," he said, avoiding Matt's gaze. "Now if you'll excuse me, I got other business to tend to."

Looking past Matt to where the womenfolk still huddled in front of the cafe, Rafe's lips spread into an idiotic grin as he started for them. "Afternoon, gals. If'n y'all aren't a sight for these lonesome eyeballs, I don't know what is."

"Dammit all, Rafe," Matt threatened under his breath. "Leave them the hell alone."

But, possibly because of a little too much whisky bravado, he ignored the clear order and leapt up instead onto the boardwalk and swaggered toward Holly and her family. Matt bought the damn booze for the bastard out of some misguided sense of empathy, but at least he'd made sure the whisky was out of Hollister's reach—where it would have remained if Maggie hadn't insisted on setting her fool husband free. Watching as the drunken idiot staggered toward her, Matt wondered if she still thought turning him loose was such a great idea.

Joining the group as they moved inside the cafe and out of the cold, Matt strolled into the room as Holly, of all people, made the introductions. "This is my mama, Ranger El Paso, and this is my Aunt Hattie. She's really my mama's aunt first, but then she's mine, so I get to call her Aunt Hattie, too."

"Pleased to make yur acquaintance, ladies."

Rafe, who was hatless, tipped an imaginary derby toward Maggie, then pretended to sweep it off of his head as he focused on Hattie. At some fifteen years older than Maggie and round as a pickle barrel, the lady's youthful sparkle and fetchingly cherubic features preserved her as a still-handsome woman. An opinion Rafe apparently shared.

Incredibly enough, even for Hollister, he suddenly pinched Hattie's cheek and said, "It's easy to see where that little gal Holly gets her good looks—yur a regular beaut, sugar."

Between those impudent remarks and the unforgivably familiar gesture, Matt naturally assumed that Hattie would either haul off and paste Rafe, but good, or at least ask someone like himself to do it for her. Instead she blushed like a schoolgirl and burst into the giggles.

"Oh, you, you kidder you," she said, still cackling like a hen in a barrel of grain. "I'm afraid I'm not much of a stunner these days, but there was a time . . ."

As the two swapped lies, Maggie slowly made her way toward Matt until she was standing within earshot. She glanced at him with horrified eyes, then back to the couple as Rafe started in on Hattie again.

"If that's true, sugar," he said, strategically draping a hand across his chest. "It's a good thing I didn't cross yur path back then. Yur about the best looking piece of dry goods I've seen in a good long spell—and don't furgit—y'all's talking to a Texas Ranger, a man sworn to always tell the truth."

"I don't believe this," Matt muttered under his breath.

"I doubt that He would even want to know what's going on here," Maggie whispered out the side of her mouth. "This simply cannot be happening."

"Well it is, but don't blame me. It wasn't my idea to set the man free, if you'll recall. At least while 'The El Paso Kid' was in chains, I had a little control over his sorry ass—if you'll pardon my tongue."

Maggie scowled in return, but didn't try to defend her actions. "What's done is done," she whispered back. "Now please get him out of here. He'll ruin everything."

"I'll try, but you ought to know that he's been nipping at a bottle of whisky I kept hidden out back of the cabin. I think he's a little drunk. We really shouldn't agitate him in that condition."

Maggie closed her eyes in defeat but they didn't stay that way long. Hattie's garrulous voice rang out with a perfectly asinine suggestion.

"But Mister El Paso—you simply must join us for Thanksgiving supper, and I don't mean when we open the cafe for the townsfolk either. Captain Weston will be joining us later when it's just family, so it only seems right that you should come along with him. I simply won't take no for an answer."

"Yay," cried Holly, clapping her hands. Turning toward her mother, she yelped, "The El Paso Kid is gonna Thanksgivy with us, Mama. Him and Captain Matt, too."

"That's nice, sweetheart," said Maggie, her voice as stiff as her chin. "Why don't you run along upstairs now and pick out some warm clothing. Your bath water ought to be about ready by now."

Holly's ecstatic expression immediately dropped into a pout, but she did as she was told without further argument. Once her daughter left the room, Maggie leaned against Matt's shoulder and shouted a whisper into his ear.

"I don't care if you have to cuff, chain, *and* bull dog that man until the Twelfth Night! Just get him the devil out of here— *now."*

Then she took off after Holly without so much as a glance or a goodbye for her suddenly flamboyant, if none too eloquent, husband.

Thanksgiving was a time at the Squat and Gobble Cafe when Gus and Hattie opened the little eatery to anyone who was alone for the holiday, drifters and townsfolk alike. Inviting others to share in their bounty, free of charge, was their way of giving thanks for all the riches that had come their way over the years. It wasn't until after those citizens were fed that the cafe was closed for the day, leaving the small family of four in private to enjoy their holiday meal. This year and despite Maggie's feeble arguments against it, there were six diners at the Townes' festive table—seven if you counted Matilda, who sat in her box on top of her very own chair.

As much as she'd hated the idea of having to entertain Rafe Hollister under a cloak of lies, not to mention, spend the entire meal worrying that he'd say or do the wrong thing, as the evening progressed, Maggie had to admit that Rafe had done her and himself proud. Oh, he still carried on about Hattie as if she were the apple of his eye, but he was equally attentive to her husband, going on and on about the perfectly roasted turkey and Gus's famous oyster stuffing.

An unexpected bonus was the way Rafe indulged Holly, telling her how pretty she looked in her new pink dress one minute, then insisting on cutting up all of her food himself, even the mashed potatoes. Somewhere in the midst of all that newfound fatherly pride, he also managed to compliment Maggie's holiday dress, a gown of claret velvet and bronze-colored satin that had seen its better days. After making it a point to tell her how nice her hair looked, a gesture that touched her even more, Maggie wasn't sure what to think of this new side of Rafe Hollister.

He was showing some dramatic and definite improvements, no doubt about that, but Maggie was still wary. How could just a few short days have brought about such striking reforms in any man? Though he was as overblown as usual, Rafe carried himself with a new confidence and even spoke in a more dignified manner. She supposed that some of those changes could have been prompted by his fraudulent new identity as a Texas Ranger and feared gunfighter. Either or both titles easily earned most any man a certain amount of respect, something Maggie suspected, that Rafe had rarely, if ever known throughout his life. Still there had to be other reasons for his sudden transformation, changes that turned what could have been a nightmare into a truly wonderful Thanksgiving supper.

Maggie knew without question that Rafe's turnabout had been successful in large to the efforts of Matt Weston. Even if it had been Rafe's idea to make himself more presentable in such a short time, he could not have done it without the ranger's help. Matt had done ever so much more than she'd asked of him when he took on the tracking job, Maggie didn't know how she would ever repay the debt. She owed him a lot, not simply on Holly's behalf, but on her own as well. All the man had to do was walk into the room and look her way, and at once, she was all aglow, an utterly feminine blossom unfolding beneath the warmth of his sunny smile.

When Matt returned to the cafe a few days after Thanksgiving, Maggie decided to make sure he knew how much all of his efforts were appreciated. After he left his coat and hat at what Gus had dubbed "The Hanging Tree," she grabbed a pot of coffee and seated him at a table away from the few lingering diners.

"Morning," she said, rattling off the specials of the day as she filled his mug. "Where's your, ah, partner?"

He glanced at her, sparing a tight smile. "If you're talking about The El Paso Kid, he's back at the cabin, but don't worry—he's not in chains, cuffs or ropes."

Able to see the humor in that situation at last, she laughed. "How many times do I have to say I'm sorry, I was wrong? I promise never to interfere with your job again, all right?"

"That's a promise I intend to hold you to."

Matt smiled, flashing those dimples, and she knew everything was all right between them. Then he said, "I stopped by to let you know that he's ready to meet with you again, privately."

"I appreciate that." Maggie made a quick study of the cafe's occupants. "The place should be pretty well cleared out by the time I bring your breakfast. We can discuss when and where then. In the meantime, what would you like to eat?"

"The pumpkin flapjacks sound pretty good. What are fried apples?"

"Hmmm." Maggie's mouth watered at the thought. "Gus fries slices of sour apple in the pan leavings after cooking up pork strips or steaks. They're really wonderful."

"Better have some, in that case, and I guess you might as well double that order while you're at it. I promised our friend I'd bring something back for him."

Thinking she might as well take the meal back to Rafe herself and have their meeting then, Maggie hurried off to the kitchen.

Coffee mug in hand, Matt stretched his long legs under the table and leaned back in his chair, enjoying not just the solitude, but the view of the picturesque town square across the street. The weather had cleared, allowing a burst of sunshine to flood the little town, and its citizens were bustling about, taking advantage of the respite. Matt knew of at least one temporary citizen who wouldn't be out and about today.

He'd solved the problem of worrying about when and where Rafe Hollister might turn up. He'd rigged a lock to the outside of the cabin door, thereby keeping his "partner" under control without using the chains Maggie so abhorred. She hadn't asked about the new arrangement yet, and Matt sure as hell wasn't going to tell her. For the first time since he'd ridden into town, everything seemed to be on track. And he intended to see that things stayed that way.

Later that afternoon, the stage from Phoenix rolled into Prescott and came to a halt at the freight office. After a family of three, and a trail-weary cowboy climbed out of the coach, Peggy allowed the pair of dandies who'd flanked her during the long ride to help her out of the stage. Then she permitted them to carry her meager belongings as they led the way to Whisky Row.

Both of the gamblers claimed to know Prescott well and promised to put in a good word for her at the highest-paying saloons in town. While Peggy appreciated their efforts on her behalf, she figured they were wasting their time. Once she located Rafe and they were partners again, she wouldn't have to go out whoring for a while. In fact, if she had her way and they got married, she'd never whore again for as long as she lived. Before she could do that, of course, Peggy had a couple of irritating pebbles to dig out of her shoe.

The first was that high-and-mighty Texas Ranger, Matt Weston. He would probably be the most difficult problem, him being a man of the law and all, but she'd figure a way to get him off Rafe's back without putting them both in jeopardy.

Then of course there was the second, even more threatening obstacle blocking her future with the man she loved—the lying, thieving bitch who had enough grit in her craw to call herself Mrs. Rafe Hollister.

Peggy ran her hand over the lump inside her small handbag, reassuring herself—the way she'd done at least once an hour since boarding the stagecoach—that her gun was still there. It

Eleven

When Maggie met with Rafe later that same day, he stunned her by greeting her with a kiss. It was brief, but right on target, a mashing of his lips to hers along with a sudden, unexpected embrace. She hadn't been prepared for the gesture or the rush of emotions it unearthed in her, and so she pretty well stood still for the assault.

"Well," said Matt from somewhere behind her. "I guess that's my signal to go on into town for a while and give you two some privacy."

By the time she'd extracted herself from Rafe's arms, Matt had gone, leaving her to deal with this new Rafe Hollister alone. It was all Maggie could do not to rush out the door behind him.

"Come on over here," said Rafe. "And sit a spell, woman."

She turned to see that he'd smoothed a spot on his bed for her. Between the otherwise rumpled blanket and the narrow, contemplative look Rafe was casting her way, Maggie gave another thought to bolting out the door behind Matt.

"Didn't y'all hear me, sweets? Come on get a little cozier."

"I'd just as soon stand," she said, strolling over by the warmth of the stove. "What do you think of Holly, now that you've gotten a chance to know her?"

"I think she's a right nice young lady. Is that what y'all got to hear me say 'fore yu'll spare me a minute?"

When Maggie turned to look at him, she saw that Rafe was

standing his ground next to the bed. And that he was still pointing down at the smoothed area. "Come on over here, woman.
What do y'all think I'm gonna do? Jump ya?"

Though putting herself in such a vulnerable position was
against her better judgement, Maggie also wanted to keep things
between them as friendly as possible. To accomplish that, she
had to at least look as if she trusted him.

Forcing herself to head for the bunk, she said, "I'm not worried that you won't behave as a gentleman, Rafe. I just think
better on my feet."

He laughed. "I think better sitting down, and it seems to me
that what we got to say ought to be said whilst we're looking
one another in the eye. We cain't hardly do that if'n I'm sitting
and yur standing, now can we?"

It was against her better judgement, and not because she
thought Rafe would actually rape her or do something to compromise her, but still Maggie felt uneasy about the situation. In
spite of all that, she lowered herself onto the spot he'd pointed
out.

After dropping onto the blanket beside her, Rafe took Maggie's hand in his and said, "First off, I want to say that I think
y'all done a right admirable job of raising that gal, especially
since it got done pretty much by yurself, near as I can figure."

"Why thank you, Rafe." Had she been too quick to judge?
He had made an awful lot of changes since coming to Prescott.

"She's also a comely gal," he continued. "Well, except maybe
for them spectacles. Still she might even turn out to be a real
beaut some day. Y'all done good, Maggie girl, real good."

She bit her tongue instead of lashing out at him over his
remark about Holly's glasses. After all, this was Rafe's idea of
a compliment. She did wonder, however, if he had any idea how
perfectly ridiculous he looked sitting there with that scraggly
mustache twitching like a dying centipede.

After he'd grown tired of waiting for Maggie to thank him

for all his wonderful compliments, Rafe finally went on with his idea of a discussion—he talks, she listens.

"I also been thinking about what y'all got in mind for Holly's Christmas present. I weren't too happy about it at first, but now I think that's a right good idea, too—the part about us surprising her with me, and all."

Until then, Maggie had assumed the plan was firm. Giving him a little of what he wanted—her undying gratitude—she said, "I'm so glad you understand how important this is to her. You'll be the best present Holly has ever had."

"Oh, don't think I don't know that," he said with a laugh. "Me and her get on real good. Did you see how she let me feed that turtle of hers at supper the other night? You know I seen that little critter on the road before Weston did, and that's the truth."

"Really?" At his enthusiastic nod, she asked, "Why didn't you pick it up and bring it back for Holly?"

Some of the air went out of his lungs. He kind of shrugged as he said, "Looked pretty sickly to me. I was for pounding it with a rock and putting it out of its misery, but that bull-headed ranger figured it was worth saving. Guess he was right."

"I guess he was."

Rafe looked at her, opened his mouth, but then closed it and looked away. She could see he was struggling to say something, but for the life of her, she couldn't figure out what could possibly be so daunting now that the issue of their daughter's Christmas wish was settled.

"What is it, Rafe?" she said, creating an opening. "I can see that something is troubling you. Is there something more about Holly?"

He shook his greasy head. "No, but yur right. There is something I reckon that we ought to get talking about. Us."

Maggie's neck hairs prickled and she went cold all over. "Us,

Rafe?" she said, hoping he'd move onto another topic. "I don't see that we have much to talk about in that regard."

"That's where yur wrong, woman." He said it softly, then raised his hand and brushed the backs of his fingers across her cheek. "Least ways where I'm concerned. It's come to me that y'all have done a lot of talking around here on the subject of us. I'm thinking it's about my turn."

Goose bumps sprang up along her arms and down her spine. He surely wouldn't ruin everything now, not when Holly's happiness was so close at hand.

"What are you saying?" she asked, getting right to the point. "Are you thinking of blackmailing me in some manner? To what end? I have no money. All you can do is destroy my life here, which would also destroy Holly's. Is that what you want, what you really wanted all along?"

He blinked his eyes several times, fluttering those beautiful lashes, then said, "Huh?"

It occurred to Maggie that maybe she'd overstated her case. Retreating a little, she said, "What's on your mind, Rafe? Something seems to be disturbing you."

"Oh, right." He straightened his collar the way a preacher might just before launching into his sermon. "It's true that I ain't hardly got past the flyleaf of a first-grade primer, but I am smart enough to figure out how you done talked a Texas Ranger into dragging my ass all the way to Arizonie."

Knowing exactly where he was heading now, Maggie tried to rise up off the bunk. In a surprising show of strength, Rafe reached out and held her in place.

"Y'all can go in a minute, if'n yur still sure that's what y'all want, darlin'. First, I think I'd like to hear from these two lips," he touched her mouth with one of his puffy fingertips, "the whopper y'all done told that there captain."

* * *

At the other end of town, Matt was up to his elbows in turkey droppings and feathers.

When he decided to stop by Hattie's ranch to check on Holly, he was only looking for a distraction, anything to keep him from thinking about Maggie and what might be going on between her and Rafe during their private meeting back at the cabin. He hadn't missed the way the bastard kissed her when she arrived or the unmistakable gleam of lust in his eyes. Mostly Matt wished to hell that this entire job was over and that he was back in Texas. Where he belonged.

"Captain Matt," said Holly, her tiny voice full of exasperation. "I told you that my baby turkeys can't go outside yet 'cause they might die."

He'd been helping her to clean out the henhouse that had been sheltering the young birds throughout the winter, and apparently let a couple of the little poopers escape. "Sorry, Holly. I guess I'm just not cut out to be a turkey rancher."

"Don't worry, Captain Matt, maybe you can be something else. I can do it because I'm a good turkey rancher."

Then she proceeded to show him just how good, by rounding up the escapees and locking them up with the rest of the flock for the night.

"See how easy?" she said, joining him outside the fenced area. "Maybe you could try helping Gus at the cafe. He gots lots of potatoes to peel and too many dishes to clean. I can't help do that 'cause I'm too little, even with a chair to stand on."

"Thanks, Holly, but I already have a job. In fact, I should go see about it right now."

Ready to do just that, or at least, to check and see if Maggie had returned to the cafe yet, Matt started down the path that led to town. Holly lingered just long enough to grab the handle of the little wagon that served as Matilda's carriage, and was right on his heels, still talking.

"What kind of job do you got, Captain Matt?"

"Being a Texas Ranger is my job," he explained, hoping that would close the subject.

"But what do you do?"

"These days I mostly look for people that are lost."

A long silence followed this, giving Matt the impression that he'd accomplished the impossible—satisfied her curiosity.

"You mean," she suddenly asked, "that you look for people like my daddy? He's been lost a long, long time."

This wasn't the first time since he'd ridden into Prescott and Maggie and Holly's lives that Matt had started down a path that led to nothing but trouble. He hoped to God that this time would be the last.

"I'm what you might call a detective, Holly. Do you know what that means?"

She shook her blond curls.

"It means that what I do must be kept secret and that I can't talk about my work to you or anyone else. Sorry."

She seemed to accept this, but then asked, "Do people pay you to do your secret work?"

"They sure do." And with the exception of the current case, he usually made a tidy profit.

"How much?"

Relaxed and back to thinking about Maggie again, Matt lost track of the conversation. "How much what, Holly?"

"How much monies do I need for you to find my lost daddy?"

Matt stopped right there at the edge of Gurley Street. Why was it that every time he thought he was in the clear, the kid came up with another impossible question? Hunkering down to her level, Matt took Holly's fragile face between his hands and did his best to close the subject.

"I could never take your money, sweetheart, but I would help you if I could. Thing is, I already have a job right now." Smug with his expert handling of the situation, he finished with risky innuendo. "If you still want me to find your daddy, why don't you ask me to look for him again around the first of the year?"

Tears welled up in Holly's eyes, but she didn't look the least bit sad. "Okay, Captain Matt, I will. I betcha you can find *anyone*. And you know what else? I love you."

"Oh, sweetheart . . ." *Christ*. How was he to respond to that?

She didn't give him a chance. "I love you even if you can't marry with me because you're old like Mama said. Know why?"

Now Matt didn't know whether to laugh or be insulted. Holly quickly pulled yet another emotion out of him, one he wouldn't have expected in a million years. She flung her arms around his neck, then buried her face against his throat, muffling her voice a little, but unfortunately, not enough to block it from his ears.

"I wish you could be my daddy, Captain Matt," she cried. "And then you wouldn't even have to do a job for me. I wish it with all my heart 'cause I love you as big as I can."

She was sobbing into his shirt now, stinging his own eyes with something he didn't even want to think about. He knew what he had to do—if not for himself, for her—but he didn't know how he would ever pull it off.

Taking Holly from around his neck and setting her aside, Matt climbed to his feet and said, "That's just plain ridiculous talk." His voice was gruff, not with the anger he tried to convey, but from something raw that ached deep inside of him. "I don't have the time for a kid or a use for one. You get that crazy thinking out of your head right now."

Hoping that would be the end of it, he started up the street toward the Squat and Gobble Cafe before Holly could launch a protest. It didn't take but two strides for him to realize that she was still one step behind him.

Sobbing intermittently, she said, "P-please don't be m-mad at me, Captain M-matt."

"I'm not mad," he said over his shoulder. "I just don't want to hear any more about me being a daddy, yours or anyone else's, understand?"

"Uh, huh." She hiccuped. "No more daddy talk. C-can I still say that I l-love you?"

"No," he said, surprising even himself with the force he used behind the word. "I don't want to hear any of that kind of talk, either."

Little sniffles and sobs were all he got by way of an answer, but even that tiny reply was enough to break Matt's heart. For the next two blocks, he had to fight the urge to whisk Holly into his arms and dry her tears; to tell her that he'd lied and that he'd give anything to be her father. Most of all he struggled against the need to tell her how happy he would be if she could go on telling him she loved him, even if she did it a thousand times a day. Somehow Matt controlled himself enough to win the battle, but it was a victory that tasted a lot like defeat.

By the time the two reached the restaurant, Holly's sobs had subsided, but it was clear to anyone who looked at her that she'd been crying. Hoping to avoid yet another unpleasant confrontation, this one with Maggie, Matt took her aside.

"I have to go inside to ask your mother a question in private," he said. "Will you please wait out here a few minutes?"

"No! You're gonna tell her I was bad, and I wasn't."

"No, I'm not. What we have to talk about has nothing to do with you."

"I don't care. I don't like you anymore." It wasn't stubbornness Matt heard in her tiny voice, but rage. "I just want my mama."

Snatching Matilda out of the wagon, Holly then brushed past Matt and stormed into the cafe. Coward that he was when it came to emotional displays, especially where women of any age were involved, Matt thought about turning tail and heading back to the cabin. He might have done just that, and probably should have too, but then he caught sight of Maggie waving and urging him inside the cafe.

Caught, as it were, Matt went through the front door and met her halfway across the room.

"Afternoon," he said, removing his hat. "How did things go during your meeting?"

"Fine, and don't worry about being overheard. Gus and Roy from the butchery have gone up to Clough's Ranch to pick up some cattle before the road gets any worse." Her lips weren't soft and full as usual, but taut and thin as she went on. "Holly won't be a problem either—she's upstairs in her room, where she'll probably stay for a week. Exactly what did you say to get her so upset with you?"

Matt didn't have any idea how to go about explaining, especially while Maggie stood there so radiant. She was glowing with anger, irresistibly beautiful, but also in a bit of a mess. Her bun had come loose, allowing several strands of hair to escape. She'd obviously tried to push those locks back in place as she tended to her baking chores. Streaks of flour painted her face and her hair, and a particularly interesting smudge of what looked like chocolate underscored her bottom lip. Thinking he'd like nothing better than the job of licking her clean, Matt made the mistake of looking into Maggie's eyes. Then he felt his own lips slide into what had to be an idiotic grin.

With an expression quite the reverse of his, she said, "I don't see anything funny about my daughter coming home in tears. Now what did you say to her?"

Since he couldn't find a delicate way around the subject, he pretty much told her what happened. "She mentioned a couple of things about me being her daddy, things she ought to be saving for Rafe, so I thought maybe she was getting a little too attached to me. I told her that I didn't much like kids."

"Matt, how could you?"

While he was none too happy to be the object of Maggie's scorn, Matt loved the passion of her mother's heart, the way the sparks in her eyes and honeyed strands of her hair seemed to catch fire right along with the spirited defense of her young daughter.

"Sorry," was all he could think to say. "Holly's comments took me by surprise and I didn't know how to handle the situation. I thought you already knew that I'm not much good around kids."

"Maybe I'm the one who ought to apologize," she said with a weary sigh. "None of this is your fault. Holly has been needing a man to look up to for a long time now. I'm sorry she asked you to be her daddy, but don't feel too bad. She's done that before."

He didn't know why, especially since Maggie had pretty well let him off the hook, but the knowledge stung.

"You're the one who has an apology coming," she added. "I'll see that Holly gives you one when she's feeling a little better."

"No, don't do that. Let's just forget it. It's not a problem."

She agreed, but Matt could see that something was still a problem. There was an exhaustion that went beyond weariness in Maggie, almost hopelessness. It didn't make sense, given the fact that all her dreams for her daughter and herself were about to come true. It made him wonder if things had taken a turn for the worse out at the cabin.

"How did everything go between you and Rafe today?" he asked, still studying her.

"Fine." She seemed startled, as if she'd completely forgotten about the meeting with her husband. "In fact, better than fine. Rafe has agreed to all of my terms and promised to keep himself scarce around Holly until Christmas morning."

She strolled away from him then, pulling soiled linens from the tables and pinching out candles that still burned. Matt followed along behind her, puzzled by the sudden awkwardness between them, the feeling that he'd done something terribly wrong. Or perhaps she simply continued to be upset about the way he'd talked to Holly.

"What is it, Maggie?" He spoke softly, willing and eager to apologize all over again if that's what it would take to make her smile.

She turned abruptly, accidentally knocking a lit candle over onto the back of her hand. "Ouch!"

"Let me see that," said Matt, taking her hand in his. "You're probably burned."

Hot wax had molded itself across the backs of her fingers, but already it had cooled enough to curl at the edges. As gently as possible, Matt peeled the layers of wax away from her skin, then impulsively brought her hand to his mouth. The next thing he knew he was kissing those tender fingers, the skin there made soft and pink by the hot wax, then suddenly he was thinking of other places, of soft, pink skin he couldn't see or touch.

Matt didn't know what the hell had come over him.

Suddenly, giving his word meant nothing, not even if he gave it to himself. He couldn't be trusted by anyone. It didn't make sense. Unlike some other men, Matt had never been attracted to the forbidden, the unattainable. Always before he'd taken his vows, his very life as a Texas Ranger to heart. Honor was more than a word to Matt, never to be bandied about or taken lightly. Honor was a way of life—his way of life. Yet here he was wanting what didn't belong to him, craving another man's wife the way others thirsted for alcohol. He was intoxicated by Maggie's scent, enslaved by the very thought of her, powerless under her touch. Christ, how he wanted her.

Matt lowered his head, daring himself to kiss her right there in broad daylight, where anyone passing by the cafe could look in and observe the utter disintegration of what was left of this former man of honor. Instead of sending him away, Maggie raised her chin, bringing her lips within a bare whisper from his, permission granted. Matt was having trouble breathing, almost as much trouble as Maggie, whose breath was coming in short wispy pants. Her eyes were growing darker by the minute, drugged with unmistakable desire. She wanted him, maybe as much as he wanted her.

Matt could hardly believe he'd brought her to this, and so quickly, but he gave silent thanks that he had. It was seeing her this way, knowing what she would think of her behavior later, that made it possible for him to tear himself away. For her and her marriage, not for himself, he found the strength to do the impossible.

Shoving both of his hands into his pockets, Matt turned to look out the window. "How do your fingers feel now?"

She cleared her throat. "All right."

"They didn't seem to be too badly burned," he said, thinking about how badly he still burned for her. "Maybe you ought to rub a little butter on them."

"Well, yes. I suppose that might help."

Matt caught the little twitter in her voice, knew that she was upset and needed something more from him than his back, but feared if he turned to her now, he might never let her go.

He was trying to think of what to say, how to make things right between them again—when Matt noticed that a pair of dandies were escorting a woman across the street, heading it appeared, for Whisky Row. The female looked vaguely familiar.

Matt stepped right up to the window and pressed his nose against the glass.

Flame-red curls spilled out from beneath the woman's bonnet, a hat nearly obliterated by the mounds of frothy violet and white ostrich feathers that topped it. Her gown was made of shiny purple material trimmed in black, and the bodice was extremely low cut, exposing a scandalous amount of cleavage. As the trio passed by the cafe, Matt could also see that she walked with a decided limp, bouncing those big, pillowy, breasts with each step that she took.

Damned if it wasn't Rafe's little saloon angel!

It occurred to Matt then that he hadn't been back to the cabin since Rafe and Maggie had finished their private meeting. He was also quite certain that Hollister wouldn't have asked Maggie to lock him up again when she left.

"Damn," he said under his breath, horrified by the thought of the havoc Peggy might provoke—especially if she had plans for teaming up with Rafe again.

"Matt, please don't blame yourself," said Maggie in a very small voice. "You've done nothing wrong, but I do think we should talk about this. It's very important to me that we do."

Her voice sounded distant, as if fighting its way through the fog his mind had become, Matt heard Maggie talking but he was so distracted by wild thoughts of Rafe and Peggy, she wasn't making a damn bit of sense to him. All he knew for sure was that he had to do something to prevent the disasters ahead, and do it now.

Without so much as chancing a look Maggie's way, Matt grabbed his hat off the table and started for the door.

Maggie called to him before he could get clear of the cafe. "Matt? Where are you going? We have to talk about this—we have to."

"Thanks anyway, but I've got to get going," he said as he went through the door. "Besides, I couldn't eat another bite."

Twelve

Oddly enough, Matt didn't have to search far to find Rafe Hollister. He was exactly where Maggie had left him, although she undoubtedly had no idea that he was curled up on his bunk with what was left of the bottle of whisky.

The afternoon was cold, gray and dreary. In a lazy effort to keep warm, Rafe had closed the shutters, turning the cabin as dark and murky as the pit of a mine shaft. Matt took it upon himself to stoke the fire and ease the constant chill of the room, then lit a hanging lantern before approaching the bunk. At first Hollister appeared to be sleeping or passed out, but the minute Matt's shadow fell across his face, his eyes popped open.

"Hey, there, if'n it ain't my jailer." Not quite drunk, but close, Rafe propped himself up on his elbows, then collapsed again. "I been wondering when y'all was gonna come back. We got us some business to discuss."

Matt pulled up a chair Maggie had loaned them from the cafe and sat down. "You don't know the half of the business you and I have to discuss. Maybe you'd better go first."

This time when he propped himself up, Hollister stayed put. His greased-up hair stuck out in all directions and his eyes were veined with spidery red lines. The man looked as if he'd been hit by a bolt of lightning.

"I'm a-needing to get my hands on some cash," Rafe said. "If y'all know what I mean. I was hoping y'all might stake me for a couple a games of chuck-a-luck in the saloons around here. Son of a bitch, I swear if'n there's ten there's a hundred of 'em in this little ole town."

"What the hell do you need money for?" Matt slid down in the chair and propped his boots on Rafe's bunk. "You've been spending mine like it's yours since we met."

" 'Tain't my doing." His eyes bulged and he sat up a little straighter, looking even more like he'd been struck by lightening. "Yur the one dragged me off from El Paso without so much as a nickel in my pockets."

Rafe waved the whisky bottle above his head. "This here's one reason I could use a few bucks. I'm about dry agin for one thing, and for another, I'm thinking that it's about time I did a proper job of sparking Maggie. How am I s'pposed to do any of that if'n I cain't even afford to buy her a sarsaparilla?"

Matt could hardly argue those sentiments, even though he had no intention of turning Rafe Hollister loose on Whisky Row. As for making sure that the man had enough money to woo his wife back into his arms—even if it was part of the job, his sworn duty—Matt simply wasn't in the right frame of mind just then to discuss that option. Besides, before he poured any more of his own finances into the assignment, he wanted to make damn sure that Rafe intended to stick around and be a husband and father after Christmas was over.

Hoping it wouldn't turn out to be a promise he regretted, Matt said, "I'll get you another bottle of whisky tonight. As for the rest, I'll have to think about all that a little longer."

"Well don't be dawdling whilst yur thinking. I ain't got a whole lot of time to sweep Maggie off'n her feet and onto her back, ya know."

"Goddammit—I said I'd get to it, didn't I?"

Rafe drew up his knees and shrank back against the cot, terror in his eyes. Matt glanced down at his hand, surprised to see that he'd drawn his gun. Muttering to himself, he holstered the weapon, then addressed the issue he'd come here to settle.

"Do you have any idea who I found strutting around town today as if she thought she was the Queen of the Territories?"

Rafe's eyes were still bugged out, but he was no longer curled up like a newborn kitten.

"H-holly?" he guessed, either too scared to draw a logical conclusion, or just too damn stupid.

"No, not your daughter," said Matt quietly. He was determined to keep his wits about him from here on out, and would have no problem doing so, as long as Hollister didn't bring up his plans for Maggie again. "The little darling I'm talking about is a good bit older than Holly, and she was wearing one of the most indecent dresses I've ever seen on any woman."

"Maggie?"

"Jesus, Rafe . . ." Matt paused, willing himself to calm down. "It was your charming friend, the saloon angel from El Paso. Remember her?"

Although Matt had expected some kind of reaction from the man, Rafe surprised him by bolting off the bunk, an abrupt shift that knocked the bottle of whisky onto the floor. He didn't even seem to notice that his precious alcohol was slowly bleeding into the hard-packed dirt.

"Peggy?" he said at last. "My l'il Peggy is here in Prescott?"

"She most certainly is Rafe. Peggy *and* her glorious bosoms have arrived in town. My question is, what the hell am I supposed to do with her, short of finding another cabin and locking her up just like you?"

"Y'all cain't go locking my Peggy up like she's some kinda thief! She ain't done y'all no harm."

After that impassioned remark, Hollister surprised Matt by lunging for him, ready to do battle.

Matt leaped out of the chair just as Rafe dove at him, which sent the chair and Hollister ass over teakettle across the dirt floor. Taking no chances with the man, Matt straddled him while he was down and drove a forearm against his scrawny throat.

"Take it easy, *amigo*," he said, a gentle warning. "You don't have a hell of a lot to say about what I do or don't do with Peggy. It can go either way depending on your attitude."

"Yeah, well . . ." Cooling off a little, Rafe finally came across an intelligent thought. "I didn't mean to jump y'all, it's just that Peggy don't deserve to be treated like no criminal. She done a little whoring all right, but she ain't bad."

Releasing his hold on Hollister's throat, Matt climbed off of him and then pulled him to his feet. Getting right to the point he said, "The truth, Rafe—what's Peggy to you?"

He hung his head and trudged back to the cot, undoubtedly thinking things over. While staring down at the floor, he finally noticed the bottle of whisky and picked it up.

Cradling the booze in his arms, Rafe finally said, "Peggy is a special kinda partner, and has been for a spell. She don't mean nuthin' to me in a courting way, if'n that's what y'all want to know, but I don't want to see no harm come to her either. Something wrong with that?"

"No, Rafe, there isn't." He almost felt sorry for the pair. Matt rested a moment as Hollister drained what was left in the bottle, then he said, "What is wrong is how your partner's presence might go over with Maggie and Holly. Peggy could ruin everything, you know."

"She wouldn't do nuthin' like that. Peggy ain't the mean sort."

"I'm not saying that she is, Rafe, but she came here for a reason. What do you think that reason might be?"

Matt had a pretty good idea himself—he had an inkling that Peggy had come here as a woman following after her man, and that the business aspect of their relationship was purely incidental, at least to her. It dawned on Matt then that this drunken heap of humanity was the object of two women's affections, one hardly worthy of the other, but both at least as determined to claim Rafe Hollister as their own. What in God's name did this man have that could possibly drive a woman—hell, a fine *lady*—to such extremes?

"Peggy most likely came after me," Hollister finally admitted. "I reckon I kin have a talk with her if'n y'all want me too. I kin let her down real easy-like and make her see that I ain't free for the taking no more. She'll most likely take it hard, but I kin do it, if'n I have to."

Not that Matt hadn't considered insisting that Rafe send the woman away—he had—but now that he was reminded of Hollister's newfound arrogance, not to mention the asinine title he'd assigned himself, The El Paso Kid, it suddenly didn't seem like such a good idea to turn him loose at all.

"Tell you what I'll do," Matt said. "I'll go look Peggy up myself and explain things a little better than I did back in El Paso. If she still thinks sticking around Prescott is what she wants to do, I'll let you take over from there."

Hollister's simple thoughts were so transparent, it was easy to see that he didn't like that proposition one bit. Despite his qualms, something, maybe it was the way Matt was fingering the handle of his gun, suddenly made him agree to those terms.

"All right," he said with a dramatic sigh. "But y'all got to promise to go easy on that gal. I don't want no rough stuff done to her."

"Don't worry about a thing, Rafe. Slapping women around has never interested me in the least." He started for the door, halting a moment as Hollister shouted one last request.

"I expect yur gonna find Peggy in a saloon somewheres. If'n she is and maybe thinking about doing some whoring, would y'all mind doing me a favor?"

Always cautious before he gave his word, especially in light of the way things were going lately in that regard, Matt said, "That depends on the favor. What do you want me to do?"

"Make her stop it—the whoring, that is. 'Tain't right for no crippled-up gal like Peggy to have to do whoring to earn her keep. 'Tain't right a'tall."

Matt searched the establishments along the aptly named Whisky Row without success that night. Although he'd stopped by the Bucket of Blood Saloon for Rafe's whisky a week or so ago, he hadn't really paid much attention to the area or to the surprising number of saloons in the town. Stretched out from one end of the mile-long street to the other, he figured there had to be close to thirty drinking establishments lined up cheek to jowl. And yet the town was surprisingly peaceful, lacking the brawls and gunfights he'd come to expect when liquor flowed freely and gambling was close at hand.

Impressed with the rustic little capital, even if it did lack a railroad, Matt wandered down that same avenue the following evening well after dark, and finally struck gold at the Little Feather Inn. The saloon featured the statue of a wooden Indian out front, as well as hostesses wearing feathered headbands and buckskin dresses with skimpy bodices.

Although she was dressed like all the other gals, Matt spotted Peggy almost immediately. She was leaning against the bar, elbows propped on the railing, and cozied up to a fella in uniform, probably a soldier from nearby Fort Whipple. The man was a regular giraffe; as thin as a bed slat and probably a foot taller than Matt. Peggy's chin barely reached past his belt buckle, and to talk to him, she had to bend her head back at an impossible angle.

Matt figured that getting rid of that customer could be looked at as doing her a favor, even if he hadn't made the promise to Rafe.

Approaching the pair he said, "There you are, my sweet little angel. I was beginning to think that you'd forgotten the deal we made back in El Paso."

She turned to him, eyes and mouth agog, and said, *"You!"*

"That's right, me." Matt laughed wickedly. "You promised to stay right by my side all night long, sweet darlin', remember?"

"Uh, excuse me," said the man in the uniform. "This little gal's with me."

Matt turned to the soldier and shot him a look mean enough to pucker a hog's butt. Then he said, "I hope you find a woman to your liking before the night's over, Private, but it won't be this one. She's taken."

Young and green, the kid did everything but salute Matt. "She's all yours, sir. We were just visiting a little and having us a drink."

Not exactly the bashful type, Peggy rammed her elbow into Matt's ribs and let fly with her own thoughts on the subject.

"Who in hell do you think you are coming in here and talking through both sides of your mouth like that? I decide who I'm gonna go off with, and it definitely ain't gonna be no stinking Texas Ranger."

If she hoped her comments would inflame the soldier into defending his rights, Peggy was sadly mistaken. The minute he heard the words "Texas Ranger," the young man gasped out loud and gripped the bar to keep his legs from buckling out from underneath him. Smiling to himself in spite of his aching ribs, Matt flipped a ten-dollar gold piece onto the bar.

"You were a lot friendlier in El Paso, sugar," he said. "Unless my memory's gone bad, that's the price we agreed on, too. You telling me this fella here offered you more?"

"Oh, no. Not me, mister. I ain't got that kind of money." Backing away, the private grabbed his beer, then took off like his ass was on fire and disappeared into the crowd.

Fast as a stomped-on rattler, Peggy reached out and snatched the gold coin off the bar. Before Matt could stop her, she'd dropped it down inside the bodice of her squaw costume where her enormous bosom immediately swallowed it up.

"If you think for one minute," Matt warned. "That I'd hesitate—here and now—to dive right inside your corset and collect what's mine, you'd best think again. I owe you a bruised rib or two."

Looking a little more subdued, maybe even a touch alarmed, Peggy whittled a considerable chunk off the chip on her shoulder.

"I wasn't planning to cheat you none," she claimed. "Didn't you say that you was a-wanting me for all night long? Well, that's the price."

He laughed. "Sorry, sugar, but it seems to me that the price in Texas was less than five bucks."

"That was back in El Paso. I spent a considerable fortune getting myself up here in the northerly part of Arizona, not to mention dodging the hostiles in these parts. Got to make up for my trouble somehow."

Though he couldn't find a lot to admire about a woman in her line of work, Matt did have to credit Peggy with a glib tongue and a good head for business. Pulling the plug and draining off even more of his personal bankroll, he said, "Since that's the case, I'm going to have to ask you to do something really special for me."

She backed away. "I don't cotton to beatings, if that's what you got in mind."

"Don't worry," he assured her. "I don't get any pleasure out of pain—mine or anyone else's. I am willing to offer you double what it cost you to get here for what I want. Interested?"

"You mean, figure up how much I spend twixt here and El Paso, and double that?"

"You got it right, sugar."

Peggy's eyes sparkled in the darkness and for a moment, Matt almost thought he heard her purring.

Then she sidled up to him, licked her lips, and said, "Why didn't you say you had special needs in the first place, honey? For that kind of money, I'll do pretty near anything you want, anytime."

"Then it's settled?"

Peggy hesitated a moment, not quite trusting him, but then smiled and ran her hand up and down his thigh. "It's a deal, honey, and believe me, I ain't gonna be disappointing you none."

Matt glanced around the inside of the saloon, a ramshackle building of plaster and planks, without a second floor. If the whoring was linked to the saloon, business was probably conducted out back in filthy little cribs. He needed to get her somewhere quiet, where they couldn't be overheard.

Looking back at Peggy he asked, "Where are you staying, sugar? I hope for the kind of money I'm spending, you at least have a decent room somewhere."

"You bet I do, handsome, and it's a regular room at a fine hotel." With a wink and a toss of her bright red curls, she said, "Come on, honey. I'll show you that and a whole lot more."

The view from the saloons of Whisky Row consisted of the courthouse and about half of the plaza, as well as a few of the more refined businesses Prescott had to offer—such as the hardware store, butcher shop, and the assortment of restaurants that lined Aubrey and Gurley Streets. Late at night, candles were rarely seen glowing in the dark from those establishments, with the exception of the apartment above the Squat and Gobble Cafe. Tonight, however, the entire block was dark, even though Maggie sat in her rocker by the window looking out on the streets below.

As often as not, she sat there with the candle blown out, lounging there in secret to watch the goings on along Montezuma Street. Not that Maggie longed to be a part of that crowd, but the music and gaiety drifting up with the breeze always made her feel as if she were missing something, as if life were passing her by.

Staring out her window, while cowboys, soldiers and loose women frolicked in the street couldn't exactly be thought of as meddlesome or prurient, but Maggie had to admit the activity gave her a certain amount of pleasure. Observing such things offered a tantalizing taste of sin in her otherwise austere life.

What she didn't like about the proceedings tonight was the fact that she'd seen Matt going from one saloon to another—just the way he'd done the night before. The man had the right to indulge a fondness for whisky or gambling, of course, but Maggie couldn't stop wondering if he might also be down there looking to satisfy his hunger for women as well.

Not that it was any of her business if he was busy indulging all three vices at the same time. In fact, she had no business in any man's life.

Now that she was nearly thirty, Maggie supposed that her life was about over in that regard. With the exception of Holly, she'd almost forgotten what it was to have anyone touch her, man or woman, with simple, uncomplicated love or with lust.

Until Matt.

She'd learned through the years to feel nothing of herself as a woman, not even when she watched her friends at the Gab and Jab Club with their men, Gus and Hattie included. She trained herself not to feel anything when she observed the soldiers from Fort Whipple as they wooed the young ladies in town, not even envy.

Until Matt.

Maggie had convinced herself that she was through with all that nonsense, that she was done with the business of love and romance. Through with giving any part of herself, and getting nothing in return.

So why was she sitting here in the darkness watching Matt? She hadn't seen the man for two days now, not since he'd run out of the cafe so mysteriously. Not since she'd thrown herself at him, then demanded that he sit down and talk to her about her lusty ideas. She'd driven him off all right, that much was as clear as a bowl of Gus's turkey stock. Everything else, questions like why him, why now, were like pebbles stuck at the bottom of a big kettle of mud.

It was a curious thing after all these years, Maggie wanting a man the way she wanted Matt Weston. She hadn't felt desire this strong since those long ago days in the barn when Rafe showed her the magic hiding within her own body. Now that he was back in her life, after a fashion, her desire should have returned for the only man who'd ever awakened her. But here she was instead, desperate for the touch of Matt Weston, and without a thought for the man who'd fathered her child. Maggie wasn't entirely sure what that made her, but she did know that such thoughts had surely doomed her to the fires of hell.

What disturbed her even more than sheer physical desire was this massive sense of confusion, the bewilderment of wanting one man so badly while loving another. And what of *love* in all those jumbled up feelings? She'd loved Rafe with all her heart those many years ago, and still did, yet all she could think about was Matt. She lived and breathed for their stolen moments together, filled up to overflowing whenever he was near, and still Maggie could not pinpoint her exact emotions where this stubborn, quietly irresistible lawman was concerned.

Not that her feelings mattered in any case. All that mattered here was Holly's happiness—and that was directly linked to her father, Rafe Hollister. Oh, how she wished, and not for the first time, that she could confide in her friends, or at least seek the counsel of a more experienced woman. There was no one Maggie could trust with the truth. Not even her family.

It occurred to her then that the next Gab and Jab session was coming up soon, a noisy sewing circle started by Prescott mothers and wives as a way of keeping in touch with one another. The idea was to discuss the news of the day, swap patterns, and even to gossip a little. All they ever seemed to want to talk about was the trouble they were having with men—a subject Maggie could finally identify with, if not share her troubles.

As she considered ways of querying the women about her concerns, without raising their suspicions, Maggie saw Matt stroll out of the Little Feather Inn. He was clearly accompanied by a woman of easy virtue, a soiled dove who was built like a sack of flour—short, squat and round. Not only was the strumpet the exact physical opposite of Maggie, but an enormous expanse of flesh shone brightly where the bodice of a decent dress should have been.

Her heartbeat accelerating, Maggie watched with morbid fascination as the couple made their way down the street, then headed up the staircase of the Prescott Valley Roadhouse. There wasn't a soul in town who didn't know that calling the place a roadhouse was just a sly way of hiding its true purpose. No inn for weary travelers, the hotel was a whorehouse, plain and simple.

Jumping out of her chair, Maggie pressed her face against the window, oblivious to the frigid glass beneath her skin. As she watched Matt and the woman disappear inside a room at the top of the stairs, something dark and venomous slithered into her thoughts, a shadowy hatred that made her feel as if she'd gone utterly and completely insane.

An even odder sensation came over her then, a sense that she was standing alongside herself watching someone else commit the acts of a madwoman.

Even that didn't stop Maggie.

Thirteen

Upstairs in Peggy's room, Matt made himself comfortable in a lumpy velvet chair the color of rancid pork while she tended to her personal business behind an elaborate hand-painted Chinese screen. Other than a bed covered with a surprisingly respectable chenille spread, Peggy had a dressing table, a small dining table, and even a brass hat rack so her customers wouldn't have to toss their articles of clothing onto the floor.

As he admired the way she conducted her less-than-admirable business, Peggy stuck her head around the corner of the screen and said, "What do you like best, sugar? Undressing me yourself or watching me do it?"

"Neither. In fact, please keep your clothes on."

She frowned, but then chuckled. "I think I see the trouble. It's the peg leg or just the thought of my stump—I expect it makes you a little squeamish, huh?"

"No, really, I don't mind about your leg at all." Talking about it was another matter. Matt quickly changed the subject. "Come on out here a minute, would you sweetheart?"

Eager to please, as long as money was involved, she popped around the screen and headed for her little dressing table. As she primped before a miniature oval mirror, Peggy said from over her shoulder, "Do you have any objections to using a French Secret, sugar pie?"

Matt did not want to get into a discussion about condoms or

preventatives anymore than he wanted to discuss her stump. He ignored the subject entirely. "Get over here and sit down a minute, Peggy. I want to talk to you."

Turning toward him, she shrugged and limped over to her bed. "I can just as easily use an alum douche if you don't cotton to having your cock wrapped up in—"

"Christ, Peggy," he said, bent on ending the discussion. "I am not interested in bedding you. I just want to talk. Now sit down and listen to me."

Clearly puzzled, she took a seat on the edge of the mattress just a couple of feet away from Matt's chair. Then she scratched the dark roots of her red hair and said, "I don't think I got hold of what it is you want from me. Exactly what is it I'm supposed to do to earn all that money you promised me back at the saloon?"

"Not much when you think about it, darling. All you have to do is pack up your things tonight, then get your overworked ass on the first stagecoach out of town."

"Leave Prescott?" She pushed away from the mattress, nearly toppling off of her peg leg in the process. "As long as Rafe Hollister's on that same stage, I'd be glad to oblige."

Matt slowly shook his head. "Rafe isn't part of this deal, and I think you know it. I also think you know why."

"I don't know nothing except you dragged him off against his will and left me to rot in El Paso." She set her jaw. "That and the fact that me and Rafe belong together."

Steady on her feet now, Peggy began *thumping* back and forth in front of Matt, her own peculiar style of pacing. In the process, she stirred up the air with the sour-sweat aroma of moldy buckskin and stale perfume.

"Rafe has a wife and child here in Prescott," said Matt softly. "He won't be needing you anymore."

"That ain't true!"

Peggy whirled on him, and this time when she stumbled, she

did fall. Matt tried to help her up off the floor, but she fought him off and used her own mattress to right herself again.

"Be honest," said Matt, sticking close by in case she fell again. "You didn't really expect to be Rafe's partner forever, did you?"

Until then, he hadn't realized the state she was in. Shoulders trembling, a sob in her throat, she said, "Darn tootin, I did. All's I ever wanted to do was get married and maybe even have a family."

"Married?"

Matt hadn't meant to be so vocal in his surprise, but it did have a favorable influence on Peggy. She turned on him with a fire that burned the tears from her eyes.

"I never planned to be no whore, you know," she said defiantly. "And I ain't figuring on being no whore for the rest of my life. It's the truth when I tell you that all I ever wanted was to get married. I just ain't had such good luck with men in the past, especially with the bastard who cost me my leg."

Reminded again of her disadvantage, Matt took Peggy by the elbow and steered her over to the chair he'd vacated. "Sit down and let's start over again. The truth from here on out, all right?"

She nodded as she sank onto the lumpy velvet. "I've been a lot a things to a lot of folks, Captain Weston, but I can guarantee you that I ain't never been much of a liar along the ways."

"Good. Neither have I." Checking the chenille to make sure it was clean—it was—Matt took a seat on the bed across from her. "How did you lose the leg, if you don't mind my asking?"

"I don't mind a'tall. I was running with Bob Younger at the time—"

"Younger? Of *the* Younger Brothers, Cole and Jim and—"

"And so on," she said, finishing for him. "Yep, one and the same. Bob was about the best-looking man I ever seen in my entire life when I fell in love with him. He asked me to marry

him and I said I would, but that was before I found out he had
a bit of a mean streak in him."

She picked at the leather fringe of her buckskin dress as she
spoke, head down in either shame or sorrow. Probably both.

"He turned that streak on me during the summer of seventy-
six," she continued. "That was right after the gang robbed the
train at Rocky Cut, Missouri. The law caught up with us long
enough to arrest Hobbs, who was one of the boys. Then the
dirty bastards went and took a few shots at the rest of us."

Peggy raised her chin, a mixture of pride and pain warring
in her cherubic features.

"I thought Bob loved me back then," she said, able to look
Matt right in the eye. "He said he did anyways, but when them
agents came at us, he quick grabbed me and used my body to
keep the bullets from hitting him. Laid that leg of mine to waste
in no time."

Matt supposed he could have said a lot of things in response;
I'm sorry, too bad. He might even have admonished her for
running with a gang of outlaws, implying that she got no worse
than she deserved. Instead he withheld all judgements and offered her the latest accounting of the Younger gang.

"In case you don't know, Bob and his brothers ran out of
luck a few months after that train job when they decided to rob
a bank in Minnesota. They were arrested and sent to prison,
where they still are today."

She nodded, unimpressed with the information. "I know all
that, but I don't care about Bob no more, haven't for a long,
long while neither. What I care about is Rafe. He treats me
better than Bob ever did, and I ain't gonna let him go without
putting up the biggest stink I can raise. You got to understand
that much, don't you?"

Matt tried to make sense of the kind of love Peggy was talking
about, if indeed she was referring to her attachment to the man
and not looking for vengeance over having lost something she

liked to think of as hers. Matt had never experienced such a love himself, nor could he recall observing that kind of devotion in others. Not even his own mother and father—until the union disintegrated, anyway, when Matt was just ten.

Again he tried the only thing he knew—logic, albeit this time with a gentler touch. "I can see that you're willing to fight for what you see as yours, Peggy, but what you don't see is that Rafe was never really yours in the first place. He married Maggie long before he met you. She's got first claim on him. That's the way she and everyone else is going to see it, too including the law."

"Then it's true?" Slow fat tears began to roll down her cheeks. "Rafe really is married?"

Left with nothing else to say on the matter—or maybe he wasn't up to addressing it further himself—Matt simply nodded.

Peggy closed her eyes, thinking things over, he supposed, then opened them to surprise him with a newfound sense of determination.

"I hear what you're saying, Captain Weston, and think that you're speaking the truth. Trouble is, I just cain't let myself believe a word of what you've told me until I hear that same tale straight off of Rafe's own tongue. Until that happens, I'm gonna be staying right here in Prescott."

"Dammit, Peggy, you're not listening to reason."

"Maybe I am, maybe I'm not. Mostly I'm just listening to my heart."

There was nothing more to say. Any man or woman fool enough to listen to the irrational, illogical, and always muddled musings set off by their emotions, were just asking for heartbreak and worse. That was merely one in the long list of reasons that Matt never listened to anything but his gut.

And right now, his gut told him to get his ass back to the cabin for a long overdue confrontation with Rafe.

* * *

The following day around noon after she'd cleaned up after the last of the breakfast crowd, Maggie walked a few doors down the street to The Bashford-Burmister Company. Thanks in large to Mary Bashford, in many ways the town's social leader, the socially prominent women of Prescott met at the large mercantile store on a bi-monthly basis for their Gab and Jab needlework sessions. At Mary's direction, her husband William cleared a corner of the store near the stove and provided chairs and refreshments for the ladies, an arrangement that left the townswomen feeling indebted and grateful toward the businessman's wife. Not so their sentiments towards Jessie Fremont, who was married to Arizona's Territorial Governor, John Fremont.

As Maggie came upon the group of twelve and slipped onto an empty chair, she listened in to pick up the thread of the conversation. Not surprisingly, the topic revolved around the abrupt resignation of Governor Fremont just days after Thanksgiving.

Emily Smith, the butcher's wife said, "In my opinion, there's a lot we don't know about the whole sordid affair. It's definitely fishy."

"No thank you, darling," said Hattie, who didn't bother to look up from her crocheting. "Trout gives me terrible gas."

A few of the women rolled their eyes Hattie's way, but most were used to her malapropos and ill-timed remarks, and generally ignored her.

Among the latter was Mary Bashford, who said, "Well I don't see the mystery, nor do I think we've lost anything. I say good riddance to that Governor-do-nothing-Fremont and his highfalutin wife."

"Amen," said Hattie, eliciting a few groans. "We've been needing a people's representative for a long time now, someone more interested in the welfare of Arizonians than in Scottish

Oak fireplaces and trips to New York. Good riddance to the whole blasted lot of them."

As one, the group and Maggie turned to stare at Hattie with awe. At best, conversing with the woman was like trying to hold court with a butterfly. Her mind flitted from random thoughts to fanciful musings, never quite landing on any subject long enough for intelligent discourse—unless, of course it had to do with her flock of turkeys. The women stared at her now because it was the first time in memory that Hattie had ever made a truly lucid or clever remark during their discussions.

Unnerved by the sudden attention and undoubtedly mistaking its basis, Hattie gave off a feckless smile along with her trademark cackle before adding, " 'Course being a big important political lady-in-waiting and all, I expect Jessie has to travel a lot to buy all those clothes. Why, do you know that woman owns a muff and a hat made out of genuine polo bear fur?"

"Who cares?" said Sarah Goldwater. She preferred to correct Hattie, then ignore her odd remarks. "For your information dear, Jessie is the first lady, not a lady-in-waiting, and it's polar bear, not polo."

As the wife of Morris Goldwater, who was the manager of the M. Goldwater & Bro., general merchandise store, in addition to being Prescott's Mayor, Sarah seemed to believe that her words were worth their weight in gold. She usually had, or at least tried to have the final say on any subject that had to do with the welfare of the town.

She did so now. "I think the rest of us are quite aware that Jessie travels so much simply because she hates it here and always has. I have it on good authority she once told a friend that Prescott was a good four days' travel from a lemon, as if we're so uncivilized, we exist on grubs and roots."

Some of the ladies gasped, but most of them nodded sagely, certain that Jessie Fremont either did or would say those exact same words. Maggie was among the nodders.

From the time of the Fremonts' arrival in Prescott just three years ago, the governor had spent far more time with his mining interests and political aspirations back East than he had in his office at the territorial capital. Jessie was no less obvious in her distaste for the "uncivilized" West, preferring instead to live in New York whenever possible, under the guise of "the governor's agent."

Those facts alone didn't bother Maggie too much since the Fremonts' only child, daughter Lily, assumed the role of official hostess during her mother's and father's frequent absences. The fact that Lily no longer lived in Prescott, however, bothered Maggie a great deal, and on more than one point. Not only was Lily glib and intelligent, probably the best friend Maggie had ever had, they were kindred spirits. With the exception of a couple of older widows and young soldiers' daughters of marriageable age at Fort Whipple, she and Lily were the only women in town who lacked husbands. The only real difference between them was the fact that Lily, at thirty-six, chose spinsterhood over marriage.

Because of that bond, Maggie jumped into the discussion with her own theories about the sudden turn of events. "Whatever we think of Jessie Fremont is immaterial. The fact is, I believe the governor was forced into resigning by territorial legislators—and I think I know why."

All heads turned, including the beautiful and impeccably coiffed head of Mary Bashford. Pleased to be taken so seriously, Maggie went on to say, "You all know that Lily Fremont was her father's assistant and hostess when her mother wasn't in town. Because of that, Lily knew as much or more about governing this territory than John Fremont ever did. She was, in essence, the governor of Arizona Territory."

A couple of the women snickered, but most of them simply looked at Maggie as if she'd lost her mind. Clarifying her point, she said, "You don't believe me? Think about it—whenever an official wanted something done or had to have a government document signed, who made sure the job was done and who signed the papers? Lily, that's who."

"So what if she did?" Mary dropped her needlework into her lap. "That hardly makes her the governor."

"John Fremont," said Hattie. "Now that I think on it, I believe he up and re-signed or something."

Although she normally indulged her aunt, this time even Maggie ignored her as she said to Mary, "Maybe it didn't exactly make Lily the governor, but knowing men and their ways, I think they couldn't stand the idea of having a female run the territory, and that's why they made her father resign."

After much buzzing among themselves, Mary Bashford turned a thoughtful expression on Maggie and said, "I suppose you could be right. I do recall reading an editorial not too long ago in Tucson's *Arizona Citizen* that said Governor Fremont was as ignorant of Arizona as the emir of Afghanistan. Lily on the other hand . . ."

Hattie, up to her elbows in the verdigris wool she was crocheting into a shawl, looked up to say, "Is that what happened to Lily? She took off for Afghanistan?"

"That's right, Hattie," said Sarah Goldwater, her tongue sharp and impatient. Addressing the rest of the group, she added, "All I know is that I gave up my favorite Turkish chair to help the Fremonts' furnish their house when they first moved here. I feel like I've been robbed."

"You're not alone on that score," said an indignant Mary. "I gave them a matching pair of exquisite crystal lamps, brand new."

This set off a round of complaints from the rest of the group, each lady eager to list the priceless items she'd donated to help furnish the new governor's home. In time, talk turned to Christmas and the gifts they were stitching or crocheting for family and friends. Maggie, who wasn't particularly fond of sewing in any form, had brought needle and thread to the Gab and Jab session, but only so she could string popcorn to use later on her Christmas tree.

Jabbing a piece of popcorn as she spoke, she asked Mary, "Is it true that you asked your husband to buy you a telephone, of all things?"

Mary's spine stiffened. "My home is some distance from town, as you know. I thought such an instrument might make me feel safer when I'm there without William."

"But who would you contact?"

Mary's eyes narrowed briefly, then she went back to her needlepoint sampler, a pattern of roses draped over a lattice arbor. "There's a telephone at Fort Whipple," she explained. "Theodore Otis has one at the Post Office and at his house. I could contact the fort or Otis if I needed help, and get it almost immediately."

Hattie stilled her butterfly wings long enough to make a relevant, if incendiary comment. "Maybe you can get William to install a second one of those contraptions here at the store. Think how easy it'd be to keep tabs on him!"

Hattie burst out laughing after that—cackling actually—and even though Maggie could see that a few of the others had to restrain themselves from joining in, the room suddenly grew dark with a gloomy silence.

"What are you saying, Hattie?" Mary dropped the sampler into her lap again. "That my husband can't be trusted out of my sight?"

Hattie's expression went blank, as if her mind had fluttered off again and she simply couldn't locate it.

Coming to her rescue, Maggie said, "Of course not, Mary. A beautiful woman like you doesn't have to worry about keeping tabs on her husband. I do think there's some cause for concern about others though, especially as long as we continue to allow the goings-on along Whisky Row."

The group of women groaned as a unit. Martha Rush, wife of District Attorney Charles Rush, gave a timid laugh as she said, "I don't mind the saloons and bawdy houses too much. As long as Charles is able to get his needs met elsewhere, he at least has the decency to leave me alone."

A few women vocally seconded that opinion, a few more with silent, furtive nods, but others, Flora Marion among them, took exception to the idea of sharing anything that belonged to them with others.

"If I had my way," said Flora. "I'd blast Montezuma Street and its notorious saloons right out of town and the territory."

"An entertaining idea, Flora," said Mary, "but if we did that, we'd quickly wind up in the city prison. I'm not at all concerned about my William, but the temptations along Whiskey Row are strong for a good many other husbands." She cast a knowing glance around the room. "Maybe we should talk to Marshal Dake about the problem."

The subject had turned to men, precisely where Maggie wanted it to go. She said, "We can't expect the marshal to do much about Montezuma Street, not as long as he's so busy with territorial laws anyway."

"I could ask my Ben to help out," suggested timid Pearl Sloan. "Maybe he could shut a couple of those saloons down."

Maggie and just about every woman in the room knew how effective Sheriff Sloan would be—about as helpful as a stray dog at butchering time. She suggested an alternate solution, one that had quite a lot of appeal to her.

"That's one idea, Pearl, or maybe we can get the city council to hire someone special to clean things up a little. Captain Weston would be a good man for the job. He's a Texas Ranger."

"Don't you just love those rangers?" Giggling under her breath, Hattie dropped the pile of wool into her lap and sighed. "That Matt's a real he-man and so is his partner, the El Paso Kid."

"Who is the El Paso Kid?" asked several ladies at once.

"Goodness me . . . I don't really know."

Hattie turned her vacant eyes Maggie's way. Even though the last person she wanted brought into the discussion was Rafe Hollister, she did the best she could to explain.

"The El Paso Kid is in town with Captain Weston on a special assignment, something they can't discuss."

"That's true," said Pearl. "They're friends of my Ben, at least Captain Weston is. I haven't had the opportunity to meet Mr. Kid, as yet."

Before Maggie could divert the subject away from Rafe, Flora Marion rejoined the conversation with even more enthusiasm than before. Although her husband John was co-owner and editor of the town newspaper, *The Arizona Miner,* no one concerned themselves that what they said here would wind up in the morning paper. There was an unwritten rule of conduct when it came to the Gab and Jab Club meetings—nothing left the sewing circle.

"I don't believe I've seen the El Paso Kid as yet," she said, "but I got quite an eyeful of that Captain Weston this morning. He's a real lady-killer all right."

Something in the way she talked, or maybe it was the look in Flora's eye, told Maggie there was a lot more to her story. Curiosity, she told herself, and nothing more, prompted her to ask, "Where did you meet Captain Weston?"

"I didn't exactly meet him, but I did see him and a woman at Cob's Boarding House."

Cob's was in a respectable part of town, nothing at all like the disreputable roadhouse on Montezuma Street. Who could Matt have been visiting? Maggie wondered.

Digging deeper, she said, "I, ah, was under the impression that Captain Weston didn't have a wife."

"I didn't say wife, Maggie." Flora, a beautiful young woman with a wild streak she wore like a feather boa, gave a little wink.

"I said woman. He was there setting her up, you know? Arranging for *and* paying for her room."

Wide-eyed Sarah Goldwater asked, "Are you sure about that, Flora?"

"Sure as I am about anything. I went by the boarding house to take Elizabeth Cob a pot of soup—she's been kind of sickly lately. Anyway, Weston and his tart came in about the same time."

Again the group gasped as one.

Hattie raised her head, looked at Maggie and said, "You brought tarts to the meeting, sweetie? Apple or pumpkin?"

"Apple," said Mary, eager to pursue the former topic even though she knew that Maggie had brought cinnamon donuts to the meeting. "What makes you think Weston's girl is, you know, loose?"

Flora threw back her head and hooted a lusty chuckle. "A lot of things, I guess, but the most important was the fact that her dress was positively indecent, cut so low, I swear I could see her navel."

The group ooh'd and ah'd about that. Then Mary said, "What else, Flora? Was she wearing lip rouge?"

Flora tapped the side of her head, dragging the agony out. "Yes, but even a respectable woman might take it in her head to paint and powder her face. I ask you, though, who else besides a saloon hostess would dye her hair the same color as a monkey's behind?"

"No one I know," said Maggie, sick to death of the topic.

Until that moment, she'd refused to face what her heart had been trying to tell her. Now it was painfully clear. Flora had just described the prostitute Maggie had seen with Matt the night before. The very woman who led him up to her room at the "female boarding house." She grew cold inside at the thought of them together, then hot at the idea of him setting her up in a respectable part of town. At a place where even little Holly could see their shameful comings and goings.

She told herself that it was none of her business, that the poor man had every right to chase as many women as he could catch. If either of them was in error, it was Maggie—she knew that now, even though she'd been torn when she joined the group, confused over her feelings for Matt Weston. Instead of following his escapades and finding him guilty, it was high time she settled her sights on the only man who should matter to her. Somehow she had to find a way to win Rafe Hollister back.

Feeling sorry for the idiot, Matt had purchased a second bottle of whisky the night before and taken it to Hollister before going in search of Peggy. When he came back to question the man later, he found Rafe so passed out that he couldn't be awakened. The next morning when Matt attempted to bring him around, Hollister was still about half-drunk and sick as a dog, to boot. Leaving him to sleep it off a while longer, Matt returned to Whisky Row to make sure that Peggy had done the one thing she promised—that she'd moved out of the roadhouse and into a room in a decent part of town.

Matt quickly discovered that Peggy was about as predictable as Rafe when it came to matters of common sense. She'd left the roadhouse all right, but she'd opted to move into a "female boarding house" on Granite Street, one discreetly located directly behind the offices of the Yavapai County Chamber of Commerce. Although the clientele were of a high caliber and the location wasn't quite as blatant as the Prescott Valley Roadhouse, the business conducted within each room was precisely the same.

With just a little gentle probing, Matt was able to figure out that Peggy was simply too ashamed of her livelihood to set foot in a more decent part of town. Taking pity on her, he escorted the unfortunate woman to a respectable place, away from the critical eyes of Prescott's more prominent citizens.

With that chore behind him, Matt wandered back to Montezuma Street for a taste of the roasted meat he'd been smelling all morning. Bob Brow of the Palace Bar had buried a whole pig in a pit of hot coals back of the saloon, and was offering free pork sandwiches to all his patrons as long as they were drinking, gambling, or both. Matt ordered a beer and sat down to his first meal of the day. After ordering a second beer and a sandwich for Hollister, he finally began the trek back to the cabin, where by now, he would surely get the answers he sought.

Matt hadn't gotten as far as the hardware store before he heard a squeaky voice calling to him from the Plaza courtyard.

"Captain Matt?" cried Holly, the frigid December wind whipping her words across the street. "Come help me, please."

About then a wagon loaded down with supplies passed between them and directly behind that came a team of oxen dragging a pile of lumber into town from a nearby mill. Afraid that Holly's state of mind might convince her that she could dodge between the two rigs, Matt shouted at her to stay put and took the risk himself.

When he reached the other side of the street and Holly, she was practically in hysterics. "What's wrong, sweetheart?" he asked, hunkering down beside her.

"It's Matilda, Captain Matt." Tears garbled her words. "I think she's dead!"

Assuming the worst—that the tortoise had been carried off by a dog or a wild critter, he said, "Did you leave her outside?"

Holly shook her head. "Never, never. But she's sick and won't be my friend anymore."

This didn't make a damn bit of sense to Matt, but it gave him an out. "This sounds like something your mother should be helping you with. Besides, I doubt she knows you're outside in this cold wind." He rose and gave her a friendly little pat on the back. "Now run along before you get us both in trouble again."

"You got to help me, Captain Matt. Mama's with her ladies sewing and I can't go there. Mama don't know nothing about Matilda anyway." She took his hand and tugged on it. "Come on. Maybe you can fix her."

Left with no rational excuse not to have a look at the tortoise, Matt let Holly drag him back toward Gurley Street and the Squat and Gobble Cafe. Except for Gus, who was so busy cleaning turkeys he barely looked their way, the restaurant was deserted. Feeling as if he were being led astray somehow, Matt reluctantly followed the child up the stairs to the apartment she shared with her mother. When Holly headed for a door leading her into a bedroom, he drew the line.

"I'll wait out here," he said. "You get Matilda and bring her to me."

With a hiccup and a nod, she scampered into the room. After just a couple of minutes, she cried out, "Captain Matt! Come quick!"

Against his better judgement, he went into a room clearly embellished with the trappings of a grown woman, not those of a child. Other than the usual pitcher and wash basin, the toilet table contained brushes, hairpins, and a few tortoise-shell combs for pinning a lady's heavy locks in place. He was definitely in forbidden territory—Maggie's bedroom. Matt's eyes immediately went to the bed and its fluffy white coverlet. He briefly imagined Maggie lying there, her honeyed tresses spread across the snow white pillow. Then Holly called out to him again.

"Matilda was right here when I left," she complained. Sprawled on the floor belly-side down, Holly was pointing to an area just under the foot of her mother's bed. "She's gone, Captain Matt."

He chuckled softly. "That right there makes it a pretty good bet that your little friend is still alive—wouldn't you say?"

Holly considered that a moment. "I guess so, but even if she didn't die, I know she's really sick."

"Why do you say that?"

"'Cause Matilda doesn't want to move or play with me anymore, and she hasn't ate her food good lately either, not even her favorite stuff."

"You mean prickly pear?"

"That and punkins, too, her best treat. Mama said the ones she was saving for pies fell off the window ledge on accident and broke, so I got to keep the big pieces for Matilda, but she wouldn't even eat them. All she wants to do is hide under my mama's bed. She won't even go in her box anymore."

Suddenly, Matt couldn't imagine why he hadn't figured this mystery out the minute he walked into the room. "I don't think Matilda is sick, sweetheart. I believe she's just going into hibernation. Do you know what that means?"

Holly shook her blond curls.

"Well, I may not have it completely right myself, but some animals, things like tortoises and bears, feed themselves up during the fall, then find a hole or a hiding spot, crawl into it, and sleep for the entire winter. It's perfectly normal and the way Nature set things up for them."

Holly seemed to accept the explanation, and still she fretted. "But where did she go? I want to look at her when she's hibb— when she's sleeping."

"Hibernating, and yes, you probably should know where she's chosen to bed down for the winter. It'll be safer for her that way."

Matt glanced around the room and came up with only two places the little reptile could have hidden herself away. Somewhere under the bed, or in the small closet, whose door was ajar.

Opting for the most likely of the two, he said, "Come on over here, Holly, and have a look inside your mama's closet. I'll bet you'll find Matilda buried under something in there."

Crawling on hands and knees, she made her way to the door and tugged it open. The darkness inside the small room swallowed up most of her except for her boots, and then suddenly, she began to fling articles of clothing and slippers over her back and out onto the floor at Matt's feet. When she'd finished clearing the closet of what had to have previously been Maggie's neatly folded garments, Holly backed out through the door, then faced him and turned her palms up.

"She's not in there, Captain Matt. She runned away and I'll never see her again."

Tears glistened through her lenses, threatening to spill. In a panic, Matt glanced at the coverlet again.

"Don't cry. Matilda is probably hiding under the bed someplace where you couldn't see her before. I'm too big to go in there after her, but you can crawl under there and take a better look around. I'll bet you find her up against the wall in the corner over there."

She sniffed a couple of times, but then disappeared under her mother's mattress.

While Holly searched for her pet, Matt looked around at the mess she'd made of Maggie's things. In the interests of saving time and getting himself out of the room as quickly as possible, he decided to help the kid out a little. Hunkering down in the midst of the clothing and shoes, Matt began to fold a few of the items, then realized that most of them were petticoats and shifts, undergarments he had no business looking at, much less touching. This was a chore Holly would have to take care of herself.

Before he climbed to his feet, however, Matt paused to indulge himself with the feel of Maggie's cambric chemise, rubbing the soft material between his thumb and forefinger. It was scented, as the other garments were, by a distant hint of orange blossoms mingled with what he could definitely identify as dried currents, an earthy scent that made him think of Maggie's hair and how much he liked the feel of it on his skin.

Without thinking beyond those thoughts, Matt brought the chemise to his nostrils, intent on savoring the aroma a moment, when the door to the bedroom suddenly opened wide and in stepped Maggie.

Her gasp was loud and horrified, prompted no doubt by the sheer surprise of finding anyone, much less a man, in her bedroom.

The look that followed when she saw that he was practically wallowing in her underthings, was nothing short of scathing, tinged with something akin to hatred.

Fourteen

"What do you think you are doing?"

Maggie stood in the doorway, hands on hips. Geronimo in full battle raiment would have seemed less daunting. Her eyes all but shot sparks and her nostrils were flared. For a minute Matt thought he saw smoke curling off the brim of her bonnet. And who could blame her? God knew what kind of perversion she thought he'd been up to with her underwear.

Warding her off with a raise of his hand, Matt cleared a path through her petticoats and climbed to his feet.

"I know this must look a little strange to you," he said, forcing a casual tone. "But it's all really very innocent."

"What it is," she said, swinging her voice like an Apache war club, "is criminal. If you think for one minute that your status as a captain in the Texas Rangers will keep me from going straight to Ben Sloan to let him know exactly what kind of man he hired, then you've got another think coming."

Maggie grabbed hold of her skirt and raised her hems then, preparing to head back out the door. Matt lunged forward and caught her by the elbow.

"Wait a minute, please?" He forced a small chuckle. "I swear to you, Maggie, it's not what—"

"Get your filthy hands off of me."

If Matt hadn't ducked in the next second, the palm of Maggie's hand would have met the side of his face with more force than he cared to think about. Unfortunately he was off balance at the time, leaning to the left. When he dodged the blow, the stress on his bad hip was too much for the damaged muscles there. Matt could feel his leg folding up beneath him, but he was powerless to stop the fall.

He hit the floor with all the grace of a hobbled plow horse. As he lay there groaning in pain, from under the bed came a squeaky voice to add to his problems.

"I think Mama's mad at you, Captain Matt."

He turned on one elbow to see Holly peering out at him from beneath the fluffy white coverlet. Her eyes sparkled through their lenses and she was grinning like a jack o' lantern. Thoroughly enjoying his moment of humiliation.

"Your mother isn't mad," he said, grumbling to himself. "She's downright pissed."

"That's a bad word, Captain Matt." But she giggled throughout the rebuke.

"Holly?" Maggie strolled deeper into the room. "Are you in here, too?"

Her evil grin still in place, the little imp stuck her head all the way out from under the coverlet and looked up at her mother.

"Here I am, Mama," she said brightly. "I thought Matilda was sick and Captain Matt came to fix her."

Before Maggie could jump to any worse conclusions than she already had, Matt turned to her and said, "That's the truth of it. We just came in here looking for that damn turtle, and Holly threw everything out of your closet thinking Matilda might be hiding in there. I was only trying to clean the mess up a little when you came in."

Maggie didn't so much as favor him with a glance. She addressed her daughter as if they were the only two people in the room. "Is that the truth, Holly?"

"Yes, ma'am, and look." She scampered out from under the bed, tortoise in hand. "I found Matilda! She's okay, not sick because Captain Matt said she's sleeping like a bear and Nature won't let her wake up yet."

Maggie lifted the reptile onto her palm. "She must be hibernating."

"That's right!" Holly clapped her hands. "You know about hibinating?"

"Yes, darling, I do."

At last Maggie chose to look at Matt. To his surprise and disappointment, there wasn't an ounce of understanding or kindness in her expression. If anything, she looked even madder.

"In fact," she said icily. "I know about a *lot* of things."

Matt couldn't imagine what she was talking about or why she continued to be so mad at him.

"Maggie," he said. "I swear—"

"Yes, I've heard you. So has Holly. In fact, I think we've both heard quite enough. If you're done examining the turtle?"

She pointed to the open door, effectively booting him out. No thank yous, no apologies for assuming the worst of him. Just goodbye without the frills. The pain in his hip no match for the ache in his heart, Matt climbed to his feet, grabbed his hat, and stalked out of the room without another word.

To say that his mood took a turn for the worse during the walk between the Squat and Gobble Cafe and his cabin, would be like saying that a stick of dynamite makes a little *bang* when it's detonated. Matt was up to his eyeballs and beyond with Maggie, her irksome daughter Holly, and that sweet little saloon angel, Peggy. Of course, all those irritants aside, he knew who was truly to blame for all of his troubles.

Everything that had happened to him since he left El Paso the first time had something to do with Rafe Hollister. In fact, just thinking about the damn fool who'd made this infuriating assignment necessary in the first place had Matt so crazy, he all but ran back to the cabin. By the time he unlocked the padlock and kicked open the door, even he wasn't sure what he might do next.

"You'd better be awake, Hollister," he warned as he headed for the man's cot. "Because if you're not, I think you're about to die in your sleep."

Rafe bolted upright on the thin mattress and rubbed his eyes. "What'd I do?"

"You need a list?"

Rafe scratched his head. "What fur?"

"Aw, Christ . . . never mind. Here's your supper."

Reaching into his jacket pocket, the one he'd landed on when he fell in Maggie's bedroom, Matt withdrew the squashed sandwich he'd bought for Rafe and flung it onto his blanket. He lit the lantern hanging between the two beds so he could see better and then he took a seat across from him on his own bed.

Again Rafe asked, "What's got yur gizzard in such an uproar?"

An oddly quiet rage settled over Matt then, a lull between storms. "I'm glad you asked, Hollister. For one thing, I bought not one but two bottles of whisky for relaxing with. Since you were hog enough to drink up the first one, I was stupid enough to think that maybe you and I might share the second one over the next week or so. What do you think happened instead?"

He scratched his head and then made the mistake of grinning. "I drank it all up, too?"

"Judging from the smell of your putrid breath, I'd say that's one hell of a fine guess."

There wasn't much quiet about Matt's anger anymore. For some insane reason, he wanted to leap off his bunk and beat the man within an inch of his life. Instead he went on with his tirade.

"You seem to have gotten so stinking drunk, in fact, you've completely missed the last day or so. I was wondering why a man would want to do a thing like that, and then I figured it out. Know why?"

Rafe let out a stuttery chuckle. "Cause I like whisky so dang much?"

Matt slowly shook his head. "No, I think it's because you've got me to do all your dirty work, which leaves you free to do damn near anything you want to do—like drink up all my liquor."

"That ain't why I drank it up, nuh, uh. It's them there wildcats screeching around the cabin all night long. Scairt me half to death. I had to get drunked-up if'n I was gonna get any sleep in this here hell hole."

"I can't say that I've been getting much sleep myself, *amigo.*" Matt smiled, showing way too many teeth for anyone, even someone as dumb as Rafe Hollister, to actually think he considered him a friend. "Want to know what I've been doing while you're here drinking my whisky?"

Rafe's eyes said no, but some surprisingly intelligent corner of his brain urged him to say, "Course, I do."

"I've been busy pimping for Peggy and letting Maggie use me as her whipping boy. Say thanks, Rafe. Say it now."

Fool that he continued to be, Hollister got to his wobbly feet instead. "Peggy's still out there whoring? Didn't I tell y'all that I didn't want that gal whoring no more?"

"Shut your goddamn mouth."

Fully aware of what he was doing this time, Matt drew his gun, cocked it, then leveled it on a pockmark between Rafe's eyes.

"Sit down," he said with a quiet rage. "Do it now."

Rafe collapsed rather than sat, but he did give Matt his full attention.

Holding the Colt steady, Matt said, "I am sick to death of this entire assignment and in no mood for any of your games. Do you *comprende* so far?"

Rafe nodded carefully, holding an aching head.

"Good." Matt did not feel the need to lower the pistol. "God knows I promised to stay until I see things through on Christmas morning. That's about three weeks from now. Three very *long* weeks. Are you still with me?"

"I know what you mean if'n yur talking about Holly's surprise and such. I still don't see why y'all think ya got cause to be so dang mad at me."

"It's your women that have me so riled up, Rafe. Trying to keep them straightened out is just about to wear me down. It's time you sobered up and helped me out a little. Think you can do that?"

Hollister thought on that a minute, then shrugged. "I ain't sure what all's going on, but I'd be glad to help out if'n y'all will just get that there gun out of my face. It's making me as edgy as a blind snake charmer."

Matt glanced at the pistol then looked back at Hollister. Seeing the man's point, but no less intent on hanging onto his attention, Matt laid the Colt across his lap. And left it cocked.

"How's that? Better?"

"I 'spect."

"Now then, as I was saying, I'm about done looking after your women for you. For now, Peggy is safe in her room at a respectable boarding house. I'll continue to check on her whereabouts once a day, but that's it. Fair enough?"

Rafe hung his head and his bottom lip. " 'Tain't the daylight I worry about when it comes to that gal's whereabouts."

"Fine," said Matt, losing his patience again. "I'll check up on her once a night. Now let's talk about Maggie."

"What about her?" Rafe looked up, startled. "She ain't been out whoring, too, has she?"

That oddly quiet anger suddenly exploded inside Matt's head. In one swift, impulsive movement, he raised the gun and fired, blowing a hole through Hollister's shirt just below his left armpit.

"Son of a bitch!"

Rafe leapt off the cot so fast, for a minute, Matt thought he might have done more than simply trim the hair in the man's underarm. Then Rafe held the shirt away from his body and stuck a finger into the bullet hole.

"You blowed a hole in my best shirt!" he complained. "Coulda been me just as easy. Y'all gone crazy, Captain?"

At that moment, Matt couldn't have disputed the charge. In fact, he hadn't felt this crazed since Chief Victorio and his vicious band of Apaches dropped off a hostage they'd tortured near Matt's ranger camp in Mexico's Candelaria Mountains. The man, a good friend as well as a fellow ranger, took three agonizing days to die thanks to an intentionally sloppy scalping job.

"Son of a bitch, Captain." Rafe hopped from one foot to another, apparently making a moving target of himself. "Would y'all please put that dang gun away?"

Again Matt had to concede that the man had a point. And again he laid the pistol in his lap. "All right. Let's move onto your future plans while I'm still in a fairly good mood. And Rafe?" He glanced down at the gun. "I told you to sit down once. I'm not accustomed to asking any man to do anything twice. *Comprende?*"

Hollister dropped to the cot as if he really had been shot.

"What do y'all want to know?" he asked, his tone and expression surly. "I ain't got no secrets no more."

Matt somehow doubted that, but he went ahead anyway. "I need to know exactly what you plan on doing after Christmas. Are you figuring on staying around here to be a father to your daughter?"

"Sure. I think I already done told y'all that much."

"And what about Maggie?" Matt asked quietly. "Are you

going to settle down and be a good husband, or is she going to have to hire someone to go looking for you again?"

Rafe held up both hands and shook his head. "I admit that I done her wrong in the past, but I aim to make up for all that. If'n you ever see fit to let me out of this here jailhouse, I figure on courting her but good, too."

Although he didn't find the subject any too humorous, Matt had to laugh over the idea of a man courting his own wife. Then again, Rafe hadn't been much of a husband and not for too long either. But he had brought up a valid point.

"You mean if I were to let you come and go as you please, you'd be courting Maggie instead of running around with Peggy down on Whisky Row?"

Hollister nodded decisively and without hesitation. "I done a lot wrong in my life, and whilst I do not reckon that Peggy is one of them wrong things, I know what I got to do now. I got to forgit about Peggy and make an honest woman outta my daughter's ma."

"An honest woman, *amigo?*" Matt laughed. "A man makes an honest woman out of a female he's ruined, not his own wife. Don't you mean to say that you plan to finally become the husband you promised you'd be all those years ago?"

Hollister sighed with more breath than Matt thought he could hold in his slender body. Then he said, "I do not know why I cannot git you to listen to me on that score."

"I'm listening now, Rafy boy. I'm listening good."

"The plain facts is that I ain't never—hear me?—*never* been married to nobody. I especially ain't never been married to that Maggie Thorne. She's a goddanged liar if she says I have."

Ten minutes ago that statement would have had the Colt back in Matt's hand before Rafe had a chance to duck. Somehow, he knew without asking for clarification that Hollister was telling the truth. His gut told him so and his gut never lied.

But he had to ask, "You're absolutely sure about you and

Maggie? What about Salt Lake City? Could you have been
drunk at your wedding and forgot about it?"

"Salt Lake City happened just like I told y'all, and I wasn't
much of a drinking man in them days." Rafe pounded his own
knee with his fist. "Maggie was a spinster when I put her on
that stagecoach for Arizonie, and a spinster she stayed, near as
I kin figure. Before ya think about shooting me agin, I want
y'all to know that I do reckon to marry her just as soon as I git
a chance to ask for her hand. That's why I need courting money."

Hollister droned on then, prattling about Gus and Hattie and
how well the restaurant seemed to be doing, the musings of a
man who figured he'd just struck gold in just about every way
imaginable. In many ways Matt supposed that he had, but at
the moment, he couldn't see past Maggie's duplicity. Or the fact
that her lies had dragged him into the entire and suddenly sordid
affair.

Matt got up from his bunk, drove his hand into his pocket
and pulled out his last few bills and coins. Flinging them onto
Rafe's blanket, he said, "Here. Take it. Take it all. Buy Maggie
the goddamn moon if you want to. Just keep me the hell out of
this mess from now on."

Then, without another word, he slammed out of the cabin,
locked Hollister inside it for what would probably be the last
time, and disappeared into the night.

Above the Squat and Gobble Cafe, Maggie had just stoked
the fire as she prepared to retire for the night. Strolling idly
over by the window where the candle still burned, she casually
took yet another peek at Whisky Row through the turkey's tail
feathers. The usual complement of soldiers were milling around
outside the various saloons, but she'd yet to catch sight of a big
white hat or the confounded ranger beneath it. Not that she
cared in the least what he did or didn't do with the tarts who

played fast and loose with their charms. Matt Weston could turn every last notorious woman in town into his mistress if that's what he wanted. It was his right. And absolutely none of Maggie's concern.

She did have to admit to a certain curiosity over Matt's destination after he left her apartment earlier in the day. At the least, she felt she owed him an apology for overreacting the way she had when she found him amongst her underpinnings. She'd thrown a conniption fit over the shock of finding him there, of course, not because news of his red-haired tart was so fresh on her mind. She didn't care beans about Matt's carryings-on with that woman. She simply didn't want him to think that she'd gone crazy.

As she leaned over to blow out the candle for the night, Maggie heard something at the window, a sound that reminded her of birds pecking against the glass. Her heart in her throat, she pinched out the light and opened the window. Peering out over the wooden tail feathers, she saw that Matt stood beneath the false front. His fist was cocked and raised, prepared to fire another salvo of pebbles.

"Is there something I can do for you?" she said, feeling a sudden rush of exhilaration.

"Yeah. Come down and open the damn door. I'll be waiting right here."

Puzzled and half-afraid, wondering why Matt sounded so angry and even more bewildering, why he insisted on meeting her so blatantly out front of the cafe, Maggie hurried downstairs and quickly let him into the restaurant.

"Evening," Matt said as he dropped his hat on a table and moved away from the window. "Is Holly asleep?"

"Yes. She has been for at least an hour."

"Good. We sure don't want her listening in on this conversation."

Matt sounded mean and ugly, completely unlike himself. "What's wrong with you? Are you drunk?"

He laughed, but there wasn't a pinch of amusement in his tone. "I wish the hell I was—maybe later."

Maggie searched his expression, trying to make sense of his sudden coldness. She could barely make out his features in the vague light from the gaslamp outside the cafe, but what she saw startled her. His mood was darker than the moonless night, as ugly as he sounded. Before she had a chance to question him further, Matt started for the back of the restaurant.

"Maybe we'd better talk over here," he suggested. "I no longer feel that my duties include safeguarding your reputation, mind you, but I guess I do have what's left of my own to think about."

"Matt?" she said, following after him like a lost puppy. "Why are you talking to me like this? What's happened? Is it to do with Rafe?"

"Don't worry about him." Again he laughed, and again, without humor. "Your darling *husband* is just fine. I'm the one with the problem, the fool who actually believed all your lies, then promised I'd take on this asinine job."

Some sixth sense told her exactly why Matt was so angry and what had made him so, but Maggie wasn't ready to own up to her own culpability so easily. Taking the coward's way out instead, she glanced at the kitchen door, gauging the distance, and decided to flee before things got more unpleasant between them.

Matt was one step ahead of her. He blocked the path before Maggie had gotten two steps toward the kitchen. "Going somewhere, Mrs. Hollister?"

"Get out of my way," she said with a toss of her head. "I don't have to stand here and listen to the ravings of a madman."

"But you do." Matt's voice was as soft as a bed of fresh-fallen snow. And just as icy. "Before I leave town, I have to know why you lied to me and took it upon yourself to make a mockery of everything I stand for. You owe me that much and a whole lot more."

"You're leaving town?" He couldn't. Not now that everything was going so well. "But you promised you'd stay."

"And you swore you'd tell the truth." He took her by the shoulders and hauled her up short. "I don't see where my broken promise is so much different than one of your lies."

Although deep inside Maggie didn't believe for one moment that he would actually harm her, she was more frightened than she'd ever been. And sick at heart.

"Matt, please . . . don't do this. Let me go and stop saying these things."

He immediately eased his grip, but didn't release her. "Not until you explain a few things to me, if you can. First off tell me why you lied, why you let me go on thinking that Rafe was your husband."

And just like that it was out, lying there between them like some stinking quagmire. Maggie had told the lie so often, even then she couldn't bring herself to admit the truth.

"I warned you about him," she said, boldly stepping into the bog with a feeble defense of herself. "Rafe's a liar. How could you believe him over me?"

"It wasn't easy, Maggie, not at first anyway. But then he asked me to pay for a few baubles he wants to use as gifts when he asks you to marry him."

Before she could stop herself, Maggie expressed her shock. "Rafe actually wants to get married—he said that?"

"That's right." He touched her cheek with careful regret, then snatched his fingers away, finally letting her go. "He said he wanted to make an honest woman of you at last. Isn't that thoughtful of him?"

Maggie didn't know whether to laugh or to cry, to scream or dissolve into sobs. This should have been cause for celebration and joy—after all, her dreams were finally coming true. If she and Rafe married, not only would little Holly get her Christmas wish, she'd also get the family she'd always wanted. And Maggie wouldn't have to spend her nights or the rest of her life alone. But she could find no joy in the news or gratitude for the man who brought it to her.

"All right," she finally admitted, sinking up to her neck in the quagmire. "I had perfectly acceptable reasons, reasons someone like you apparently cannot understand, but yes, I did lie about being Rafe's wife. I guess I thought you'd understand."

"I understand all right. At least, I think I know why you told everyone else you had a husband—to avoid the shame of being an unmarried mother."

"Shame?" It stung to have Matt, of all people, think this of her. "You think I lied on my own behalf?"

"What else?" He pulled her close, as if thinking of embracing her, but at the last moment, kept a respectable distance between their bodies. "I needed the truth from you, Maggie, and you swore that I had it. You lied."

"You and your stinking truth." Maggie curled her fists and nailed them to Matt's chest, not striking him, but wanting to. "Tell me—if I'd told you the truth, would you still have gone after Rafe? Would you have chained and dragged the man back to Prescott if you thought for one minute that he was not my legal husband?"

"Hell, no."

Now that he'd been sucked into the quicksand with her, Maggie was able to smile as she said, "That's why I lied. I knew that was the only way I'd ever get you or anyone else to bring him to me."

With a shake of his head, Matt gave off a bitter laugh. "Where I come from, saving yourself a little humiliation isn't reason enough to compromise your principles."

"Don't you know me better than that?" So angry she could

hardly speak, Maggie backed away, retreating to the corner of the room.

"The lies, my entire life," she went on to say. "Everything I do or care about revolves around the only good thing that ever happened to me—Holly. I don't care what anyone, not even you, thinks about me, but I would do anything, lie, cheat, steal or even do murder, to keep that child from harm."

"Maggie, I—"

"Shut up and listen to me. I will say this." Even Maggie was surprised by the force within. "I lied to make damn sure that my daughter never, ever heard herself referred to as a bastard. For that, I'll keep on lying no matter what you say about me or who you say it to."

"Christ, Maggie." Matt advanced on her, trapping her in the corner without so much as laying a finger on her. "I wouldn't have betrayed your trust in me on that score. You know that."

"I know nothing of the sort. I hardly knew you when I hired you for this job. For all I knew you'd slip up and tell Ben Sloan everything I confided in you. Until today, only Rafe and I knew the truth about Salt Lake City, and that's the way I wanted it to stay."

"I gave you my word. That should have been good enough."

"Rafe gave me his word, too," she tossed in cruelly. "And look how well he kept that."

"Don't compare me to him. Don't you ever so much as say my name in the same breath as his."

Maggie realized that she'd touched a raw spot. Even though that's what she'd wanted, she saw the naked truth in his eyes. She'd hurt him. And badly.

"I'm sorry," she said, meaning it. "I'm just tired of defending myself, I guess, tired of having to bear the whole burden when Rafe should be carrying at least half of it."

"To hell with Rafe." Matt took her back into his arms, but it was with that unrelenting anger, not the tenderness she needed. "And to hell with blame. I just came here to make sure you knew why I had to go."

"You're still planning to leave?"

"Hell, yes. Why would I stay?"

Confused and even a little frightened, Maggie struggled against his grip. "Let me go, Matt."

"The hell I will—not yet."

It was then she realized there was something else at stake here, something that went a lot deeper than his sense of outrage or a few necessary lies.

"Why are you still so angry?" she asked.

"I think you know."

"No, I don't." Again she tried to pull away, only to find herself tighter in his embrace. "All I know is that you're scaring me."

"Sometimes I scare myself," he whispered harshly. "And I'm angry, beautiful Maggie, because I thought you were married."

"But everyone thinks I'm married. Why should the fact that I'm not, trouble you so much?"

"Why?" His head fell back and he laughed. "You honestly don't know?"

When she didn't answer immediately, he showed her.

Fifteen

When Matt kissed her, branding her with both his anger and his lust, Maggie surprised herself with the sudden rush of passion in her own response. She didn't try to stop him or cry foul, not even after she felt his body hard against hers, so hot and so urgent. She couldn't have, even if she'd wanted to.

Maggie knew precisely what Matt was about when his big hands moved from her shoulders to her waist and below, realized without question where they were headed as they began to slide down the smooth, slick surface where the painted walls came together. She knew but did nothing to stop him, or herself.

Even after Matt pinned her beneath him on Gus's new floor, Maggie didn't try to resist—how could she, when she wanted this as much as he did? If the truth were known, Matt was the one with second thoughts, the one with the slight hesitation to his movements, especially once he realized they were sprawled partly under a dining table on the floor of her uncle's restaurant.

Of course Maggie didn't doubt for one minute the depths of Matt's need—he wanted her and with a desperation she could almost taste. He needed her all right, and not because he was trapped alone with her in some frozen little barn like Rafe had been; not because she was the only female in sight. Matt wanted her, Maggie, the woman. She even dared to believe that it was her he wanted when he dallied with that loose woman.

There was no question that she wanted him, too. Maggie

needed Matt the way the earth needs the sun. His touch, the very scent of him lured the neglected female inside her. She couldn't and wouldn't think of what this meant beyond that. Not now. Maybe never.

In a sudden frenzy, Maggie clawed at Matt's clothing, tore at the buckles and buttons, and urged him to do the same for her. When they were as naked as they would take the time to be, when the warmth of his thighs brushed against her bare legs, she tried to speak, to beg him to hurry, but all she could manage was something akin to a strangled meow.

"Maggie, sweetheart," Matt whispered, his face nestled against the curve of her throat, lips teasing the sensitive skin there. "God how I want you. I can't help feeling this way even though I know that it's wrong, can't seem to stop myself from touching you. I swear that I never, never—"

"Stop."

"Stop?" He rose up a little, his glorious dark hair lost in the pitch black of the night. *"Stop?"*

She laughed wickedly, loving the lusty sound of her own voice. "Stop making up excuses and trying to find reasons that we shouldn't be doing this. You might come up with one we can't ignore. Are you so willing to take that risk?"

"Oh, no. Hell, no."

He came to her again then, nuzzling the tender spot beneath her ear before filling her mouth with a river of kisses. After that, the heat didn't build up between them so much as it exploded into a sudden inferno, more heat than she'd ever known standing hours over a hot stove. An undeniable urgency, something as white hot and intense as their passion ignited in Maggie, driving her beyond the frustration and madness of simply wanting Matt, and sending her straight into pure, primitive lust. Into and beyond insanity.

With them both panting harshly like a pair of wild animals, Maggie writhed beneath Matt's expert touch, begging him to take her, for God's sake, and to take her now. Desperate to have all of him and more, when Matt teased, hesitating at the last moment, she saw the gesture for what it was—a final chance to turn him away. In defiance, in something that went beyond the mere physical, Maggie raised her hips in surrender, giving herself as she never had before.

She was no innocent. She'd known the touch of a man, knew what it was to feel desire and to have that desire slaked. Maggie had long ago lost her innocence, and knew—or thought she knew—precisely what to expect. What she hadn't known before was this delicious feeling of wildness, a perfectly feral and savage rush of desire that descended on her as Matt stretched and filled her to the limit. At first she cried out with shock at the size of him, and then with joy as at last he began to move within her.

Digging her fingers into Matt's back and calling his name over and over, all too soon the release Maggie had been expecting claimed her, coming in waves of pleasure that ebbed only slightly instead of fading away. Before she had a chance to understand her body's unusual response, Matt deepened the last of his powerful thrusts and she felt herself surging forward again, overtaken by an even more potent force that sent her crying and screaming to its crest. After that, Maggie went into the mindless beyond, reeling with a sense of gratification she'd never known.

It took a long while—or what seemed like a long while—for her to make sense of herself or the circumstances again. When Maggie's mind was clear enough for lucid thought, she realized that Matt had collapsed across her body—and that one of his hands was firmly clamped to her mouth. She could barely breathe, much less fill her lungs.

"M-a-w-w," she said, against his palm. "Cann breve."

Understanding the problem if not the words, he moved his

hand, then began to stroke her cheek. After a long, comforting kiss, he asked, "Are you all right?"

"I am now." After reaching up to help herself to another kiss, she said, "Why were you trying to smother me?"

Even in the vague light she could see Matt's adorable dimples taking shape. He almost looked embarrassed. "You were making so much noise, I was afraid you'd wake Holly. Hell, for a minute there, I thought you might even wake the dead."

Grateful for the lack of illumination as his meaning came clear—by then Maggie's cheeks had to be the color of holly berries—she said, "I sure don't remember making any noise. Are you certain I was as loud as all that?"

He glanced up, then back at her. "I don't want to have to figure out a way to explain to Gus why the paint peeled off the ceiling in here."

Despite the ribald nature of their conversation, Maggie couldn't help but burst into laughter. When she playfully slapped Matt's nude backside in the next minute, the sound and the way he started at the impulsive gesture shocked her into thinking about where they were and their present situation. The floor was cold, almost icy, but Maggie hadn't noticed that before. And had she really been so loud that she might have wakened her daughter? If Holly had come down the stairs to investigate the noise and opened the door to the dining room, would she even have heard her enter the room? Neither she nor Matt had taken the trouble to lock the front door after he came into the cafe. Maggie seriously doubted that either of them would have heard the bell go off if an intruder had stopped by. What kind of woman did that make her? she wondered. What kind of mother?

As she considered all this, Matt rolled away and sat up, his back to her as he began to dress.

"I don't know how to say this, Maggie," he began, "or even

how to say it right, but I want you to know that I did not come here tonight with ideas of seducing you."

She didn't think she could stand it if he took tonight away from them, if she allowed him to turn it into something ugly, a thing to be ashamed of and forgotten. Besides, if anyone was to blame, Maggie knew the fault belonged to her. She'd driven Matt to this as surely as she'd denied her own feelings for him. She had to let him know that no real harm had been done, and that neither of them needed to assign blame or to feel any. What happened here wouldn't change her plans—she couldn't let it— nor would it change the way she felt about Rafe. She still loved him a little and, crazy as it may have seemed, intended to accept his marriage proposal.

"Matt, please," she said, turning to see that his back was still to her. "Don't ruin what we had here tonight. Don't apologize and don't expect me to."

"What's done is done?" Matt said from over his shoulder. "Is that what you're trying to say?"

"Something like that, I guess."

He climbed to his feet and fumbled with his belt buckle in the darkness, leaving Maggie a little privacy to straighten her petticoats and smooth her skirt. When she stood up and moved to join him, Matt abruptly turned and started for the door.

"I'd better be going now," he said, sounding casual but somehow awkward. "We've taken enough chances with your otherwise spotless reputation tonight."

Maggie followed him to the door, relieved on the one hand by his cavalier attitude, but terribly disappointed by it on the other. She didn't expect declarations of undying love, but something was missing. Something terribly important. "Matt—wait, please?"

He turned to her, his features bathed in the soft glow of gas-light, illuminated enough anyway to show her the face of a man in a certain amount of pain. Had their moments of passion on the cold floor damaged his already injured hip? "Are you hurt?" she asked.

He hesitated, chuckling softly under his breath, then shook his dark head as he answered. "Don't worry about me," he said, touching her cheek. "I'll be fine. Just take good care of yourself and Holly. And Maggie? Be happy."

Again he started to turn away, and again she stopped him. "Wait a minute. That almost sounds like goodbye. You aren't still planning to leave town, are you?"

"Why not? My job is done and I don't see any reason to keep Rafe locked up anymore. He isn't going anywhere. He wants to marry you, remember? Just the way you planned."

There was something more, a deeper meaning to those words, but Maggie was just too dazed and confused to make sense of them. She was not, however, at all ready to let him go.

"My plans aside," she said. "I can't let you leave town, not now, and not like this."

"Why not, Maggie? What is there to keep me here?"

His expression began to darken then, reminding her of the man he'd been when he first showed up in the street. Then he went on, sounding like him, too.

"As much as being with you tonight has meant to me, I'm not the kind of man who can be happy settling for a few stolen thrills from time to time. I have to have all of you, Maggie, or nothing at all."

"That isn't possible," she said, frustrated by their circumstances, angry at him for pointing them out. "You knew that before you came here and before we . . ." She stumbled around in her mind, looking for a ladylike way to phrase their moments of passion.

Matt saved her the embarrassment. "You're right. I did know the rules, and still I couldn't keep my hands off of you. That's why I have to go."

"But what about your promise?" Wanting desperately to believe it herself, Maggie reminded him of the one person they'd forgotten for a short while. "You swore that you'd see this assignment through for Holly until Christmas morning. You're still a man of your word, aren't you?"

"I try to be." Matt smiled a little at that, not quite producing the dimples, and again reached for her, this time caressing the edge of her jaw with his thumb.

"Under the circumstances," he added softly. "Don't you think it would be better if you released me from that promise? I don't think my staying in Prescott is going to do either of us much good."

Maggie threw herself into his arms, as if she thought clinging to him might make him stay forever. "We aren't the ones that count in this, Matt. You have to stay on Holly's behalf. It would break her heart in more ways than one if you go before Christmas, especially if you're not here to see her wish fulfilled at last."

Remaining in his embrace, Maggie pushed back enough to look into his eyes. To satisfy herself that he did understand. "Remember the way Holly called you Daddy? As fanciful as that may be, she'll hang onto that illusion until her real father shows up."

Matt gave off a heavy sigh. "I hadn't thought of Holly's feelings for me. I guess she would think that I'm deserting her, at least until she and Rafe are properly introduced."

"I'm glad you understand, Matt. It means a lot to me. You mean a lot to me." She leaned forward and lightly kissed his lips. "Holly and I will never forget you, you know. Never."

His only response to that was a long, careful look. Then he released her. This time when Matt turned and started for the door, Maggie let him go.

The following morning brought the first snowfall of the season and a heightened sense of Christmas joy throughout the entire community of Prescott. Children traveled in small groups as they went about their chores, occasionally bursting into song in preparation for the big night of caroling to come. The streets were bustling with mule-drawn freight wagons hauling last minute merchandise before the roads got too bad. Most of the employees at the Capital building had gone back to their home towns to spend the holidays with the families they'd left behind, leaving the streets and the festivities to those who called Prescott home.

The scent of pine could always be detected in town, but never was it so sharp and crisp as it was during this time of year. In addition to the fresh-cut Christmas trees brought into town on a daily basis by its inhabitants, the ladies' group—all of them members of the Gab and Jab Sewing Club—had tied fragrant boughs of pine and cedar together with bright red ribbons then fastened them to the fence posts surrounding the courthouse plaza. Wreaths made of the same boughs and ribbons could be found in shop windows and in homes.

Homer Ludlow turned his barber pole into a Christmas tree by stringing garlands of holly berries from the globe at the top. Gus, God love him, tied several branches of mistletoe together and hung them above the door of the cafe, making sure there were enough berries in the clump to ensure him a kiss from every female in town. The first to receive a kiss and a berry from Gus had been Holly, who promptly buried her prize in her pumpkin patch in hopes of growing her very own mistletoe tree. Until Maggie's second year in Prescott, a community Christmas tree had graced the plaza, a symbol of unity to which gifts and ornaments were attached. Five years ago a prankster hung a joke gift on one of the branches, offending one of the town's more sensitive citizens. The man, who never identified himself, promptly chopped the Christmas tree down. So far, no one had thought to plant a new tree or even suggested reviving the tradition.

As Maggie cleaned up tables and took customer orders, she wondered how many of her own family traditions would fall by the wayside now that Rafe was about to become a part of the family. Did he think of Christmas Eve as the time for the biggest celebration, or Christmas Day? Was he the religious sort, a church-going man, or would she and Holly make the long walk up Gurley Street for Christmas services the same way they had in the past; alone?

Thoughts of Rafe had occupied Maggie's mind off and on for years now, sometimes with anger, sometimes as wistful dreams. Never before had she considered what it would be like to have him here with her and Holly, to actually share their lives and daily routines with another person. A near stranger. What would Rafe be like as a husband and father? Maggie suddenly wondered. Tender and caring or demanding and selfish?

She thought about all that and anything else that might help to keep her from thinking about Matt, an exercise in futility if ever there was one. She could still feel his hands on her, taste his passionate kisses, and hear the desperate murmurs of a man driven to the limits of his control. By morning's light, giving into their mutual desire no longer seemed to be a relatively harmless indulgence. It couldn't be healthy, thought Maggie, this business of loving one man while dreaming of another, of planning her future as Rafe's wife with thoughts of lying in Matt's arms never far from her mind. Those were the musings of a madwoman or a sexual degenerate. Either of which made Maggie wonder if perhaps she hadn't gone insane.

The bell above the door jingled as she finished dusting the crumbs from a tablecloth, but before she could turn to see who the new customer was, someone at the next table hissed, catching her attention.

"Psst!" It was Flora Marion, who was lingering over her tea with Sarah Goldwater. "Well I'll be horsewhipped—can you believe that the tart that handsome ranger is keeping down at

Cob's Boarding House is here? Where does she get the nerve
to come waltzing into this cafe?"

The last thing Maggie needed was a reminder of Matt's other
interests or to have to serve the woman, but Flora's horrified
features and just plain morbid curiosity got the better of her.
Feeling as stiff as the wooden statue outside the Little Feather
Inn, she turned and caught her first clear look at the woman
who could have Matt anytime she wanted him.

Although she hated to admit it, Maggie did concede that the
cheap little piece of dry goods was fairly attractive—or would
have been if she'd taken more care with her appearance. She
wore a modest costume in daylight that covered her enormous
bosoms, but her short pudgy little body looked as if it might
burst through the seams of the tightly fitted suit at any moment.
Her best feature, the cute round face of a child, almost made
up for her otherwise overblown figure. She had the kind of
features that probably made most anyone who looked upon her
want to smile, maybe to even think of tickling her a little or
chucking her under the chin. Maggie wanted to plant her fist
into that cute little nose.

"Well?" said Flora with a decided dare in her tone. "You're
not going to let her stay, are you?"

"I . . . I don't know, Flora. Why don't you finish your tea
and let me worry about it?"

With that she weaved her way through the customers and up
to the front of the cafe, where the woman was still standing and
looking annoyed.

"Good morning," Maggie said, unable to keep her eyes off
that mop of outrageously flame-red hair. "How may I help
you?"

"Depends, sugar." She stood there looking Maggie over as
if she were buying a head of livestock. "I'm trying to find
someone."

"Perhaps," said Maggie with undisguised sarcasm, "you

ought to try asking at the courthouse. We only serve breakfast here."

"The someone I'm looking for works at this here cafe, I'm told. A gal that calls herself Hollister. You know her?"

Instinct told her it could be a mistake, but she quickly identified herself anyway. "I'm Maggie Hollister. What can I do for you?"

"You're her?" The woman took a couple of awkward steps back, looked Maggie up and down, then said, "Damn. I wasn't expecting someone so dang big."

For the first time in her life, Maggie thought she finally understood what it was that prompted men to war. A kind of bloody haze clouded her vision and her entire body went taut as she said, "And I wasn't expecting *you* at all."

"I don't reckon that you were, sugar." Unfazed, Matt's paramour pushed out her breasts, straining the buttons on her jacket. "I still cannot get over the size of you."

"This is a cafe," said Maggie sharply, her patience at an end. "If you stopped by for a meal, then I suppose I can't keep you from taking a seat at an empty table. I can't promise how soon I'll get to you, however, as I do have other customers."

"I ain't hungry, sugar."

"In that case, I'll thank you to leave."

If Maggie had insulted or angered the woman, it sure didn't show. In fact the corner of her mouth tugged into a sly grin as she said, "Ain't you the spunky one, Miss High-and-Mighty."

Maggie stepped around her and opened the door to the cafe. "I think you'd better leave," she said, intending to throw her out if she didn't leave of her own volition.

The woman turned slowly, facing Maggie, but made no move to exit the cafe. "I ain't leaving," she said, "until I make sure you know that you cain't have just any ole man you get a hankering for. Keep your hands off'n mine, you hear?"

It dawned on Maggie then, and much too late, that Matt's

tawdry mistress had somehow gotten wind of what happened between them last night. That little indiscretion was hardly a subject to be discussed in public, much less within earshot of ladies from the Gab and Jab Club.

"I said," shouted the tart, "you hear me?"

"Yes, I hear." Maggie stepped back across the threshold. "And I think we'd better finish our discussion outside."

Then, without so much as giving the woman a chance to reply, she took hold of her elbow and half-escorted, half-pulled her out the front door.

"Hey—hey!" objected Matt's mistress, slapping at Maggie as she tugged her outside. "Take your hands off'n me."

When Maggie pulled the woman up even, she gave a final push to her back, shoving her out of the restaurant before any more harm could be done. Caught in mid-step, the tart tripped over the threshold and tumbled out onto the boardwalk.

Stunned, she lay there sprawled flat on her back with her skirt up around her waist. A wad of scarlet petticoats fluttered high in the breeze, revealing a pink satin garter holding a ratty stocking up above the woman's right knee, and a wooden peg where her left leg should have been.

Horrified by both the sight and the way she'd manhandled the unfortunate soul, Maggie quickly shut the door to the cafe, then went to the woman's aid.

"My Lord," she said, genuinely sorry. "I didn't mean to be so rough. I didn't know about your leg. Please, let me help you up."

"It'd please me if'n you'd just get away from me," she snarled back. "I can get up myself, thank you very much."

As the woman struggled to a sitting position, another voice reached Maggie's ear, one that sent a shiver down her spine.

"Mama?" said Holly. "Why did you push that lady down? She only gots one leg."

Maggie glanced down the boardwalk to the hotel next door

and saw a small group of children playing a game of checkers, a little gathering that apparently had contained her daughter until a moment ago.

"Everything's all right, Holly," she said, desperate to send her back to her friends. "Go ahead and finish playing your game. The lady just had a little accident."

"Accident, my big fat ass," said the tart, up on her elbows by now. "Ain't you woman enough to admit it? Y'all done that on purpose."

"No, I didn't—I swear it."

Since her first concern was for Holly, who couldn't tear her eyes off the scandalous petticoats or the peg leg, Maggie turned away from Matt's paramour and issued her daughter a direct order.

"Go back to your game of checkers this instant, young lady. I won't allow any argument."

Normally that tone of voice got Holly to moving, and fast. Not today.

"In a minute, Mama." Coming a few halting steps closer, Holly asked the fallen woman, "What happened to your other leg, ma'am? Did you cut it off with a knife like Uncle Gus did?"

Gus had severed the tip of his index finger while butchering turkeys, hardly an apt comparison, but that was the way Holly saw things.

"Young lady," said Maggie more sharply. "It's not polite to ask personal questions. Go back to your game this instant or I shall have to punish you."

"She ain't doing no harm," said the tart. "Besides, she ain't said nothing I ain't already heard before. Stick around, kid. Things could get real interesting."

To Maggie's horror, Holly giggled and sat down next to the woman.

About that time one of the soldiers up on Montezuma Street hollered, "Cat fight!"

Within moments a crowd began to gather.

Fuming inwardly, Maggie leaned over, bared her teeth, and said, "I suggest that you let me help you up—*now.*"

"Be my pleasure, sugar."

Showing a great deal more intelligence than Maggie would have credited her with, the tart reached out to accept the offer of help.

The moment their fingers locked, however, the woman gave a sudden jerk, catapulting Maggie up and over her prone body.

She flew through the air for a few amazingly weightless moments, then landed face down in the street with a *splat* that shot slush, mud, and God knew what else up her nose.

Coughing and sputtering as she raised her chin out of the muck, Maggie was just beginning to get her bearings when something heavy pounced on her from behind.

"I'll teach you to go messing with my man," said Matt's woman, her voice screeching into Maggie's ear.

"G-get off!"

Something cold, colder than the snow beneath Maggie's belly, suddenly slid alongside her throat. Then she heard something even colder—the click of a pistol's hammer.

Summoning all of her strength, Maggie twisted and rolled, grappling for possession of the gun as she struggled to free herself from the trap of the other woman's body.

Clawing and kicking, the two rolled deeper into the muck, hair, legs and skirts flying. In the midst of her struggles, Maggie heard cheers from the crowd, the incredulous sound of her neighbors and friends finding sport with the spectacle of this saloon dove grappling with one of their own in the street.

Renewed with a sense of outrage beyond anything she'd ever known, Maggie flipped herself and the tart over, then made a final lunge for the weapon.

One or both of them groaned.

Then someone screamed.

The next sound Maggie heard was the ear-shattering retort of a gun.

Sixteen

Throughout his life, Matt spent a whole lot more time thinking about women than he ever had in the actual company of the fairer sex. Life was easier that way for both Matt and the ladies he dreamed about.

As long as thoughts of love or a long-lasting romantic relationship remained only in his mind, never did he fret that he might say the wrong thing or make an awkward, unwelcome advance. Neither did he worry about riding off to an assignment only to return and find that the girl of his dreams was more sinner than saint. Never would he suffer as his father had, growing old before his time and embittered over a wife who'd run off with a traveling silhouette cutter. Adding insult to injury, Audrey Weston had fled her responsibilities in favor of a man who'd had the audacity to leave her unfinished portrait behind.

His mother's abandonment hit Matt hard even though he'd witnessed the loneliness of her life, the solitude of a woman whose husband was hers less than three days a month. His father, on the other hand, a formerly clever and vigilant captain of the Texas Rangers, was devastated by her deceit, ruined as a ranger and a man. After his wife's betrayal, Robert Weston turned reckless, always leading every charge with the abandon of a man who viewed each mission as the possible instrument of his own suicide. Matt's father finally found the peace he sought at the end of an Apache arrow some four years later, a time that still weighed heavily on Matt's mind, not to mention, kept his heart out of the line of fire.

Until now.

When he'd ridden into Prescott, Matt had held tight to the idea that the root of most desire was nothing more complex than a lust for the unobtainable. Once the obsession was acquired, be it a possession, a talent, or even a woman, the object was no longer a thing to covet or to crave. In his own experiences, this theory always held true.

Not so with Maggie Hollister—or whatever her name might be.

After one night with Maggie, Matt's lust for her was far from sated, had become in fact, the reason for his very existence. He couldn't wait to see her again, to hear her sweet voice or to touch her soft skin. She'd invaded him, burrowed under his skin and into his vitals as easily as a tick makes himself at home in a man's scalp. And Matt didn't mind the subsequent itch one damn bit.

Still he should have headed back to Texas despite Maggie's pleas for him to stay. Matt didn't belong here any more than he deserved to be Holly's pretend daddy; even less than he deserved to be Maggie's pretend lover. Yet here he was, heading toward the destruction of his own heart, and strangely enough, feeling pretty damn good about it.

"Maggie," he whispered to himself, as he'd done several times over since morning. To say her name was to start a song in Matt's heart, an aria proclaiming the sudden and abundant love he felt for her. Or whatever this feeling might be.

Such were Matt's thoughts as he made his way into town and headed toward the Squat and Gobble Cafe that afternoon. Skipping stones along the way and whistling to the tune still playing in his heart, he'd just crossed Goodwin on the plaza side of Montezuma Street when Matt saw a crowd gathered just up the road beyond the cafe. Pausing a moment to try and figure out

what drew them there, Matt heard the door to the courthouse
bang open. Glancing toward the pink brick building with only
casual interest, he was surprised to see Maggie descending the
bank of concrete steps.

He waited there on the grassy footpath, intending to escort
her to the restaurant, but as she drew near, then looked up to
see him standing in her path, Maggie's general dishevelment
and reaction to seeing him was not what Matt had been expecting. Something was terribly, terribly wrong.

Not only was her skirt mussed and caked with mud, the full
mutton-leg sleeve of her blouse was torn and clinging to the
bodice by only a slender thread. Her usually glossy hair hung
down around her shoulders in damp stringy clumps, the shine
and golden hue now dull with the same mud that fouled her
clothing. Her lovely face was streaked with both tears and dirt.

"Jesus, Maggie," he said, reaching out to her. "What in the
hell happened to you?"

"Don't talk to me," she said, blood in her eye. "Don't look
at me and don't ever say my name again. Most of all, stay the . . .
the *hell* away from me, you vile, vile man."

Never had Matt heard her swear like that, nor had he ever
been the recipient of such a venomous look, not even when he
brought in the son of Apache war chief Nana and had him
hanged as a horse thief.

"What happened, sweetheart?" he asked again, utterly confused.

He got no answer because by then, Matt was talking to Maggie's back. She'd whipped right on by him and was now stomp-
ing up the street toward the cafe.

"Maggie, please—what's wrong?"

At that she turned back long enough to wag a warning finger
at him, but didn't say another word. Growing irritated now, Matt
was just about to go after her and demand an explanation, de-

spite her open hostility, when Ben Sloan called to him from those same courthouse steps.

"Hold up there, Captain. You're just the person I was going to go looking for."

"Sorry, Ben, but it'll have to wait. Something's happened to Maggie."

"Sorry, nothing, son." Ben reached the bottom step, but didn't proceed any further. "I've got a woman in jail who's asking for you and another—Maggie, there—who says you're the one who's gonna pay the bill for all the damages."

That stopped him in his tracks. "What damages?"

"Then you really don't know," said Ben slowly.

"I told you, I don't know a damn thing."

"Right. Well, first off there's the matter of a new gaslamp, then some costly repairs to the Arizona Brewery's delivery wagon, and finally the price of six kegs of beer, seven if the crowd lays waste to the one that didn't bust when the wagon overturned."

Although thoughts of Maggie were strong on his mind, Matt was completely baffled. "What in the hell are you talking about? And what's wrong with Maggie?"

Sloan pressed a finger to his lips and urged Matt to join him. "We'd better take this discussion inside, son. I'm afraid the events of today have already given this town enough grist for the gossip mill to last all of Yavapai County for at least a month of Sundays."

Without waiting to make sure that Matt followed him, Sloan went back up the steps then opened the door and held it in that position until Matt joined him on the other side of the threshold. Once they were both inside the building, the lawman showed him into his office and closed the door.

Sloan pointed out a chair. "You might want to sit down for this, Captain. This story takes more wrong turns than a blind mule."

Taking him at his word, especially as he considered Maggie's odd behavior, Matt slid onto the spindle-backed chair across from the lawman's small pine desk. "I'll be all ears, Ben. What the hell is going on around here?"

"Well," said Sloan, resting his hip against the corner of his desk. "I'm pretty sure that I don't have even half the answers yet, but most of what I know is bound to have the Reverend Wilson preaching hell and damnation for a good long time. And by the way—in case you're wondering, Marshal Dake ain't in town, so for now, your involvement in this mess is gonna stay between you and me."

"My involvement?" Matt almost came out of his chair. "I don't even know what the hell happened—will you please tell me what this is all about?"

"Did you get a good look at Maggie?"

"I did. I've seen men dragged across the desert behind a Comanche pony who came out looking better than that, too. What happened to her?"

"She got into a knock-down drag-out with that gal I got locked up, is what happened, the very piece of goods who's asking for you."

"Maggie was in a fight?" Now he did come out of his chair. "That doesn't make a damn bit of sense, and what gal could possibly be asking for me?"

"Sense or not, it's all true. The other gal's name is Miss Peggy Dawson, new to town. She mentioned that you're kinda responsible for her." Sloan winked. "If you get my meaning."

He did. With a groan, Matt dropped back into the chair and tugged the brim of his hat down low over his eyes. This assignment, the kind no active ranger would even consider taking on, was rapidly becoming one of the most complicated of his long career.

"Shit," was all Matt could think to say about this newest mess.

"Yep, that's pretty much what Miss Dawson had to say about the matter, too. She told me I could just go stick my head in a barrel of shit, is what she said when I locked her up."

Thinking back to something Sloan had said earlier, Matt asked him to repeat the information. "You mentioned that Maggie's fight was with another woman—was it Peggy?"

"That's the gal, all right. Those two went at it tooth and nail right in the street out front of the cafe. Gathered themselves one hell of a crowd, too."

Matt couldn't fathom what could possibly have brought them together other than Rafe, a thought too disturbing to contemplate. "Did either of them happen to mention what the fight was all about?"

Sloan shrugged. "That there's the puzzle. Maggie ain't talking, even though I threatened to lock her up, and all I got from the other gal so far is a few cuss words and a face-full of spit."

Again Matt couldn't think what to say. "Shit."

"That's about the size of it." Sloan hopped down off his desk. "I'm mostly interested in who's gonna pay for them damages. Are you really responsible for that one-legged gal?"

"No," was Matt's automatic response, but then he drew in a deep breath and gave his answer a second thought. He hadn't handled the situation with Peggy very well in El Paso or she wouldn't have thought she could just breeze into Prescott and reclaim her man. To some extent, Matt supposed he was responsible for the chaos all around him.

Owning up to a small piece of the ugly affair, he said, "Well, now that I think of it, I suppose Peggy is my problem. What got damaged and how much do I owe?"

Sloan whistled long and low. "Like I said—them gals were tumbling around in the muddy street a while, but it wasn't until one of them drew a gun and commenced to firing that things got out of hand."

Again Matt leapt to his feet. "Why didn't you tell me there was a gun involved? Was Maggie hurt?"

"No, thank the Lord, nobody got shot. No person anyways. What did get shot out was one of them new gaslamps outside the plaza square. Cost a pretty penny, too."

The last thing of concern to Matt right then was a damn streetlight. "I'll take care of it. You're sure no one was hurt?"

"Only Maggie's pride, I expect. That and her coin purse, unless you feel like settling up with the Arizona Brewing Company while you got your money bags out."

"What the hell does the brewery have to do with this?"

Sloan grinned as he said, "A second bullet nicked the hind end of the lead horse hauling the brewery wagon. It and the rest of the horses bolted, then took off up Montezuma Street instead of down, the way the driver had the wagon turned. Snapped the axle clean in two and dumped the load—seven barrels of beer, six of which sprung immediate leaks."

It was then Matt had the fuzzy recollection of a crowd gathered just past the cafe. At the time he'd been so busy wondering what happened to Maggie and her clothing, he forgot all about the unusual number of townsfolk in the street.

"With all that free beer just spilling out for the taking," Sloan went on to say, "I figure most of the menfolks are going to be pie-eyed before sundown, which means I'm gonna have my hands full stopping a passel of fights. I was hoping you might do what that gal says you will and claim responsibility for her. I got enough to do tonight just riding herd on the beered-up citizens of Prescott without worrying about no female alone in my jail."

Left with little choice, Matt quickly agreed, even though he still wondered exactly what had prompted the fight between the two women.

"Don't worry, Ben. I'll see that Peggy stays out of trouble, at least for the rest of the night."

"You do that, son, and while you're at it, make sure she doesn't leave town until the bills for these damages are settled."

Matt nodded. "Done."

Visibly more relaxed, Sloan slapped Matt's shoulder. "I ain't never been with no one-legged woman. What's it like?"

Matt cast a weary eye on the man as he said, "I wouldn't know. Now why don't you go let that gal out of jail before I take it in my head to just pack up, ride on out of Prescott, and forget that I ever knew anyone in this town. That idea is sounding more attractive to me by the minute."

Sloan didn't waste his breath or so much as a minute of Matt's time after that. He just hurried out of his office and in an instant, returned with his captive in tow.

After the sheriff left them to their privacy, Peggy flopped her indignant behind in the chair and said, "Look at what that giant bitch-woman went and done to my best getup!"

With a dramatic sweep of her hands, she showed off her ruined gown. Then she pointed to three deep scratches that ran from the corner of her left eye to the tip of her nose.

"And looky here at this!" she said, wincing. "Ain't too many men have a hankering to waste their hard-earned cash on no scarred-up whore. Why ain't that bitch in jail where she belongs?"

Matt braced his hands on the arms of the chair to either side of Peggy, trapping her in her seat. "Mind your mouth, Miss Dawson," he said, grinding his teeth. "In fact, shut it until I can get you out of here and back to your room."

She grumbled a moment, but finally went along with his wishes. After that, a grim-faced and silent Matt escorted the thoroughly bedraggled saloon hostess back to her room at the boarding house, where he insisted that she stay until she received further instructions from him.

At first Peggy seemed eager to argue the point and even tried to offer her version of the events leading up to her arrest, but

Matt was in no mood to talk to anyone but Maggie. At least with her, he was reasonably certain he'd get the truth. Peggy must have seen something in his eyes or in his expression. She quickly reversed her course by agreeing to his terms and promising to remain in her room until otherwise notified.

After that Matt again headed back to town and the Squat and Gobble Cafe. He'd just started up Gurley Street from the east side of Cortez when he saw Holly coming toward him. Laughing and shrieking as she made her way along the boardwalk, at first he couldn't figure out why she was having such difficulty walking. Then as she drew near, he realized that she had a pair of roller skates clamped to her boots.

"Look at me, Captain Matt," she cried out, laughing and squealing at the same time. "I got skates on!"

She launched herself toward him before he could answer, but the skates and her feet remained behind as if glued to the boardwalk. Matt lunged forward and caught the girl just before she hit the deck.

"Take it easy with those," he cautioned, wondering what he was going to do with the pair he'd purchased for her. "You'll likely bust your skull if you're not more careful."

"I'm trying to do it good, Captain Matt, but I don't know how to make them go." She looked up at him, laughter still shining in her big brown eyes. "The El Paso Kid said I just need to practice to learn how to ride on rolly skates, but he didn't tell me what to practice."

"You've seen the El Paso Kid today?" Something twisted in Matt's gut. Something he had no business feeling.

"Yes, silly." She regarded him through her spectacles, looking at him as if he were the dumbest man on earth. Then she sighed with great impatience. "The El Paso Kid just gave me these rolly skates a little while ago because he said he likes me. I told him I don't know how to do skating, but he said I just have to practice. What do I practice, Captain Matt?"

Realizing what Rafe must have done, though he could hardly believe it, Matt took another, closer look at the skates. They were an exact match to the pair he'd bought in Phoenix.

Seething inside, Matt managed a smile for Holly as he said, "Since the El Paso Kid was kind enough to give you the skates, I really think he ought to be the one to teach you how to ride them, don't you?"

Holly shook her head resolutely. "He said he's too busy for such nonsense. Besides—I want you to teach me. Will you?"

Looking up the boardwalk to where it ended at the cafe, Matt's eyes narrowed. "Let's go ask your mother what she thinks, shall we?"

Again Holly shook her head. "Mama's in a bad mood. She and a pretty lady with only one leg fell down in the mud. Mama had to go away with the sheriff after that."

Until then, Matt hadn't realized that Holly had witnessed the altercation between her mother and Peggy. Doing his best to make light of the subject, he laughed as he said, "That lady thought your mama was someone else, sweetheart. She didn't mean to knock her down in the mud. Everything's all straightened out now."

Holly sighed with the exasperation of a full-grown adult. "The lady didn't do it—Mama knocked *her* down, and then they both fell in the mud."

Matt abruptly changed the subject. "Let's go ask your mother about these skates."

"I told you that we can't go talk to Mama, Captain Matt. The El Paso Kid told me to go play with my skates and not to come back to the cafe for a long time. He said he and Mama gots lots of things to talk about and that I shouldn't bother them."

Inside the Squat and Gobble Cafe, late afternoon shadows had begun to fall. Rafe, who'd been hemming and hawing, talking but not really saying anything for nearly an hour, glanced at Maggie and made yet another casual, unnecessary comment.

"Must be nigh on to about dinnertime. It's gettin' as dark as the inside of a cow's ass in here."

Maggie cringed a little at the expression. "Now that you mention it, it is getting late. I have to get busy in the kitchen before the customers start arriving, Rafe. Is there anything else on your mind before I get to work?"

His gaze fell to the floor and he stood there shuffling his feet. "There is one little thing, something I've been meaning to ask y'all."

"Well? Ask away."

Still staring at the floor, Rafe fidgeted as he finally said, "I was wondering, thinking that maybe it was about time for me and y'all to throw in together."

Was he proposing marriage or some kind of business arrangement? Maggie let him stew in his own juices a moment before saying, "I'm not sure I know what you mean, Rafe. What are you asking me to do?"

"Dang it all woman, don't y'all know it when a man's putting hisself on the table for y'all?"

After waiting for this moment for so many years, Maggie wasn't about to make it easy on him. "I guess not, Rafe. So you're putting yourself on the table for me? What, exactly, does that mean? Am I supposed to serve up one of your skinny hams for supper tonight?"

Though he'd been there for nearly an hour, Rafe had yet to show her the respect of removing his hat. He did so now by tearing it off his head and slamming it to the floor.

"It's no dang wonder you never caught yurself a man 'fore now," he said, his temper running his tongue. "Cain't y'all even recognize a offer to get hitched when it comes yur way? I'm asking y'all to marry me, woman. Yes or no?"

Maggie didn't know whether to laugh or to cry. Tears sprang

into her eyes when she thought of how long she'd waited—prayed—for those words, or something like them, to come to her from Rafe Hollister's lips. But she wasn't exactly crying. She'd also expected to feel euphoric at this moment, or at the least, joyful enough to dance in place. All Maggie could seem to muster by way of emotion was an attack of the giggles, incomprehensible and unseemly as that reaction may have been.

Perhaps she'd been waiting too long. A sweet dream might eventually spoil, she supposed, the way berries left too long on the vine tended to sour and rot. God knew the fruits of her love for Rafe had gone unharvested for much too long. It wasn't that Maggie didn't want to marry Rafe—that wish had been second only to bringing him home to Holly. It wasn't that she didn't love him either. How could she not love the man who'd fathered the child she worshiped above all? Of course she loved Rafe Hollister and would marry him, the sooner the better. She only wished she could be more excited by the idea, more eager to place the rest of her life—her very heart—in this man's hands.

Rafe bent over and took his hat from the floor, then fiddled with the brim as he said, "Well? Ain't y'all gonna answer me?"

Since any forbidden thoughts of a future with Matt had died out in the muddy street with his mistress, Maggie almost found it too easy to say, "Of course, Rafe. Yes, I will marry you."

He nodded sharply, as if he'd never been in doubt as to what her answer might be. "When?"

Although she hadn't consciously thought it out, the answer came easily. "Christmas Eve, after Holly's gone to bed for the night. That way we can all wake up in the same house as a family for the first time on her birthday."

Again he nodded. "It's done then. I hope y'all ain't expecting no fancy ring. That hound-dog ranger of yourn spirited me out of Texas so fast, I never got hold of my poke."

"I'm not expecting anything for myself, Rafe. All I want is your promise that you'll be a good father to Holly."

"I brung her a pair of rolly skates, didn't I?" Apparently insulted by the question, he raised up his chin and tugged at his coattails. "Don't be worrying about me, woman. You'd best be thinking about having a little more respect for the man who's about to become yur husband."

"Sorry, Rafe," she said, biting her lip against another, even more ill-timed urge to laugh. "I meant no offense."

"None taken."

Still fiddling with the brim of his hat, Rafe approached her, his gaze buzzing about the room like a horsefly, pausing here and there but never really landing on anything.

Then he steeled himself and said, "I don't got no ring, but I reckon I do know what comes next. This is about the time I ought to at least give y'all a little kiss. It ain't like we never done that—and more—before. Besides, we are fiancéed and all."

Maggie's impulsive response was to throw back her head and laugh. He even joined in, apparently thinking her reaction was one of joy. Allowing Rafe his illusion, she sighed breathlessly and said, "Oh, Rafe, you're so irresistible!"

"Dang tootin', I am, sugar. Now pucker up and brace yurself, woman. I mean to remind y'all just how irresistible I can be."

And so Maggie did as he asked, hoping to find the excitement she'd been missing in her life. Closing her eyes, she recalled the thrill Rafe's kisses had given her so long ago in her father's bleak barn. Depending on the girl she'd been then, hoping the past and the heat of Rafe's kiss today would be enough to burn the memory of Matt's embrace from her mind, Maggie gave herself up to the man she would soon marry.

Two doors down from the cafe, Matt tightened the screw at Holly's right toe, adjusting the skates for the umpteenth time so they'd fit her more comfortably and wouldn't leave blisters on her tender skin. Then she set off down the boardwalk again, blond curls streaming out behind her as she finally got the knack of roller skating.

Smiling to himself as he watched the youngster master the beechwood wheels beneath her, Matt rose off the boardwalk and turned toward the cafe. It seemed to him that Maggie and Rafe had had more than their share of privacy by then. He also figured that he'd waited more than long enough to find out what had caused the fight between Maggie and Peggy earlier in the day.

Courteous enough to peek into the window of the eatery before simply barging into the room, Matt was treated to the sight of the two of them standing together and laughing. Maggie's head was angled back as she took her delight, her throat vulnerable and exposed to Hollister's lascivious gaze.

Matt barely had time to recognize that his hands had curled into tight fists before Maggie fell into Rafe's arms and accepted his lusty kiss. Unable to watch their embrace beyond that, he rolled away from the window, his back flat against the gaily painted boards that made up the false front of the Squat and Gobble Cafe.

Like glass beneath his heel, for a moment, Matt thought he could hear his own heart breaking, a muffled implosion that crushed his ribs and caved in his chest. He closed his eyes against the sensations, his mind against the sounds, but knew that no matter how hard he tried to deny the destruction within, he'd never be the same man again. He was rent inside, scraped clean of his vital being. The only thing left was a great, dark crater, at its center, a pulsating lap of quiet pain.

For the first time in his life, Matt thought he finally understood how his father could have ridden directly into the path of a renegade's arrow.

Seventeen

Matt was still pressed flat against the bright yellow and white planks that made up the exterior of the Squat and Gobble Cafe, still feeling dead inside when suddenly he realized there were voices all around him.

Holly was shrieking and tugging on his pant leg, demanding that he make some comment over her mastery of roller skating; Maggie was there, too, thanking him for the help he'd given her daughter. Maggie didn't have the slightest notion that he was dying inside; and even better, Rafe stood right beside her, puffed up like a peacock at mating time. He went on and on about the surprises that might show up, come Christmas morning.

Matt didn't want to look at or talk to any damn one of them. Mostly he just wanted to collect Louie and ride the hell out of town.

Rafe, of all people, seemed to realize that something was wrong. Suddenly, he couldn't get rid of the females fast enough.

"Tell you what, gals," he said to Maggie and Holly. "Why don't the two of y'all run along inside now. Me and Matt got some ranger things to discuss that ain't fittin' for yur delicate ears."

"We have to get those tables set anyway," she said, gathering Holly close.

Then, with no more than a particularly vicious glare at

Matt—for reasons he still couldn't understand—Maggie shooed her daughter into the restaurant and then followed her inside.

Once they were out of earshot, Rafe did not inquire about Matt's troubles. Instead he puffed out his chest again and said, "Well, congratulate me. I went and done it."

"You've done lots of things, Rafe, most of which should have gotten you hanged by now." Matt's mood was more somber than the rapidly darkening skies. "What have you done this time, other than steal my property and give it to an innocent little girl as if it were actually yours to give?"

Scratching his forehead just beneath the brim of his hat, Rafe thought about that a minute. "Y'all talking about them rolly skates?"

"I am."

"Well, shoot, pardner, I figured y'all wouldn't mind too much if I borrowed them a while."

"First of all, I'm not your pardner, and secondly, just how do you see that you 'borrowed' those skates when Holly told me that you gave them to her?" Christ, but he was pissed. *"Gave* them, you fool."

Rafe took a couple of steps back. "I only meant to borrow them until I can buy y'all a pair to replace em. I noticed that yur little gal wasn't here in Prescott like my li'l Holly is, so's I reckoned it didn't matter."

"I don't have a little gal like Holly." Rafe looked like he was going to say something stupid, so Matt quickly added, "Or any other kids."

"Then why'd you buy them skates?"

Matt took a deep breath, calming himself. "They just were a gift I picked up for someone, but now you've gone and spoiled it for me."

"Well I surely didn't mean no harm." Rafe started for the cafe. "If'n them rolly skates are so danged important to y'all,

I'll just march myself on inside and rip them wheels right off'n Holly's little feet."

Matt blocked the way. "You'll do no such thing, you idiot. Just let it be. What else have you done I should know about?"

Rafe gave him a blank look, but then suddenly slapped his own forehead and laughed. "Oh, yeah, I almost plumb forgot. I done asked Maggie did she want to get hitched."

The great dark crater in Matt's gut rumbled, threatening to erupt. "Did you now. And what did Maggie have to say about that?"

"What do you think she said?" Rafe hooked his thumbs under his suspender straps and puffed out his chest even further. "That gal jumped on me like a roadrunner on a sidewinder."

Until that moment, Matt had assumed that he was beyond pain where Maggie was concerned, but something raw stabbed at him, opening old wounds, carving out a few fresh ones. With what he tried to present as an indifferent shrug, he turned away from the luckiest bastard on the face of the earth and stepped down off the boardwalk.

Like a calf that didn't quite take to the idea of being weaned, Rafe hopped into the street beside him, nudging his shoulder even as Matt tried to shy away from him.

"Ain't you got nuthin' to say about my news?" he said. "I thought the reason you dragged my ass outta Texas and clean through Arizonie Territory was so's I'd do the right thing by Maggie and our li'l one. The least y'all can do is congratulate me on my upcoming wedding."

Though it was one of the hardest things he'd ever had to do, Matt reached out and shook Rafe's hand. Maybe then he'd go away and leave him in peace. "Congratulations. I'm sure you'll be very happy together."

"Happy?" Rafe snorted his laughter. "I said I was getting hitched—show me a happily married man, and I'll show y'all a fella who's done been planted six feet under."

Rafe kept on laughing, looking at Matt as if expecting him to find some humor in the statement, but he couldn't even make himself crack a smile. At last Hollister grew bored with him.

"Well, I'd best get on with my business now," Rafe said, finally giving Matt reason to celebrate. "Just one more thing I want to ask y'all. Would ya do me the honor of standing up for me at the wedding?"

Without so much as a moment's hesitation, Matt said, "No Rafe, I would not. You'll just have to find someone else to do that little honor for you. I'm scared half to death of preachers and weddings." Not a total lie.

"Oh." If Rafe was disappointed, he got over it quick. "Well, in that case, I reckon Maggie will have to round up someone else to do the chore. Thought I'd give y'all first shot since yur expert tracking is what brought us together again, so to speak."

"Thanks for thinking of me, but no thanks."

"I reckon I'll be seeing you back at the cabin later, then."

With that, Rafe took off in a cloud of flapping coattails, gangly legs, and the puffs of powdery snow he kicked up as he dashed across the street.

Matt's first impulse after that conversation was to head on over to Whisky Row, where he would proceed to get himself so drunk he couldn't hit the ground with his hat. He probably should have done exactly that, too, but as he passed by the cafe and happened a glance through the window, he saw Maggie pushing her way into the kitchen. She seemed to be alone. Convincing himself that he could neither rest nor get drunk until he knew what had happened between her and Peggy, Matt swiveled on his heel and went straight through the front door and on back to the kitchen.

As he hoped, Maggie was alone. Her back was to him, but she tensed when he pushed open the door, clearly aware that someone was there, if not who.

"Afternoon," he said quietly, trying not to startle her. "I told

Ben Sloan I'd try to sort out the troubles between you and Miss Dawson so he can get this mess settled once and for all. Have you got a minute?"

When she turned to face him, Maggie pinned Matt with a pair of rattlesnake eyes, all but hissing as she said, "Sort things out? *You?* If it wasn't for you, none of this would have happened."

She turned her back to him again, then returned to the huge pile of dough she was kneading.

More confused than ever, Matt edged a little closer to her. "What did I do to get you so damn mad?"

She didn't answer him right away but made a low sound in her throat instead, something akin to a growl. Despite the warning, Matt inched close enough to reach out and touch her. He didn't though, not yet.

"Maggie," he said softly. "Sweetheart, I have no idea what you're talking about. Ben told me you and Peggy Dawson got into a fight in the middle of the street. He doesn't know what started the argument and neither do I. Would you please enlighten me a little?"

Furiously shaking the dough from her fingers, Maggie turned on Matt, splattering him in the process.

"I'll enlighten you all right," she said, eyes blazing. "How can you stand there and act so innocent? How can you stand there at all after that sleazy little tramp had the nerve to come after me at my place of business? Do you know that she actually pulled a gun and tried to shoot me?"

"Jesus, no . . ." That wasn't quite true. Matt shrugged and said, "Yes, actually, Ben did mention there were gunshots, but he didn't seem to know who fired them or why."

Without warning, more splatters of dough hit his face. Matt reached up to wipe them away, but only managed to smear a little of the sticky stuff onto his fingers.

"Dammit, Maggie, how was I to know that Peggy would come gunning for you?"

"You should have known—this is all your fault, Matt Weston." She shook a fist in his face, dusting him with the excess flour clinging to her hands. "What have you got to say for yourself?"

Christ, he'd never seen her so mad. She fairly glowed.

"All I can say is that I think you're about the most beautiful thing I've ever seen."

The comment came from his heart, but even if it hadn't Matt figured such a compliment would have eased Maggie's foul temper a little. It only seemed to make her madder. She was smoldering inside, desperately thinking of a way to lash out at him.

When her gaze flickered over to the counter where a small bowl filled with eggs sat, she stared at it a moment and looked back at him. Then an odd little light came on in her eyes.

"Maggie," he said, clearly warning her. "If you're thinking what I think you are, you'd best think again."

In one swift movement, she swept the bowl from the counter, flinging the contents at him. The crockery glanced off Matt's knee, but not before all three eggs exploded against his legs.

With yolks and slime dribbling down his clean denims and onto his newly polished boots, Matt stepped away from the mess, even though most of it insisted on clinging to his clothing.

He looked up at Maggie, his own temper rising, and said, "What the hell's wrong with you? I didn't ask Peggy to come here or send her after you. Why are you throwing food at me?"

"Liar."

She then grabbed up one of the neat little balls of dough she'd just formed and threw it squarely at Matt's head. He ducked and watched it splatter against the stove. Just as impulsively, he scooped up a handful of flour off the counter and tossed it at Maggie's apron. It exploded against her bosom, a blizzard of white that mushroomed above her head then rained down on her hair and face.

"Why you no-good . . ." Maggie scooped a load of flour off the counter and sent it flying directly into Matt's face. "Low-down, cheating son of a, a *whoremonger.*"

Matt didn't even bother to dust himself off after that illogical outburst. He stepped forward, took Maggie by the shoulders, and half-dragged her along with him to the back of the room. Then he raised her to her tiptoes and pressed her shoulders up against the wall.

"I've had enough of this," he said. "I'm sorry Peggy came after you and I'm sorry that Holly had to be a witness to her attack on you, but dammit, Maggie, I am not to blame for what happened."

Tears filled her eyes. "But you must be. Why else would she know about us and think that I'm trying to steal you away from her?"

"What?" In shock, Matt released her. "What did you say?"

"Shush! Holly's upstairs," she said quietly. "I beg you, please don't talk loud enough for her to hear any of this."

"You don't have to beg me to do that," he whispered back. "But would you mind telling me what you're talking about? I swear to God, if things get any more confusing around here, I'm riding out of town, no matter how many promises I have to break."

"Go then," she said irritably. "Just don't forget to take your lady friend with you, not that she's a lady in any sense of the word."

It was all beginning to make perfect, if ludicrous, sense to Matt. Almost afraid to hear Maggie's answer, he asked, "What exactly did Peggy say to you?"

"She said that I was a high and mighty bitch." Those rattle-snake eyes were hard on him again. "And that she was going to teach me a lesson for messing with her man."

"Oh, Jesus, I don't believe this."

"Well it's all true." Maggie was seething. "Your little darling said even more after that, but I can't remember all of it now. I only know that she tried to kill me."

"Oh, Maggie, sweetheart." Matt reached out to her, longing to hold her in his arms, but she stiffened against his touch.

"You've got to believe me," he said, feeling like a beggar. "I hardly even know that woman."

"Don't try to deny that she's your mistress," she said with furious sarcasm. "You think that I haven't noticed you prowling Whisky Row with her on your arm?"

"You have?" He couldn't deny the charge, but he was surprised to know that she'd been watching him.

"If that's not enough, your nightly visits to that tawdry woman are all the ladies of this town can talk about. You haven't been particularly discreet, you know. If Rafe finds out she came after me, and why, it could ruin everything—just everything!"

Until then Matt thought of the entire incident as one huge and incredible maze of misinformation, nothing particularly harmless, just irksome and downright inconvenient. Now he realized that he'd been swallowed whole by circumstances beyond his control, trapped in half-truths and out-and-out lies. This time when he looked at Maggie, he saw that she was studying Gus's collection of butcher knives and cleavers, deadly instruments hanging within her reach along the back wall.

"Shit," he muttered without realizing he'd actually vocalized the thought.

"I'll thank you to take that kind of language out in the street, if you don't mind."

Instead of reaching for the knives, Maggie peeled his sticky fingers off of her shoulders, ducked under his arm, and went back to her pile of dough. From behind her, Matt made an attempt to clear his name, an impossible task.

"Your friends are right," he said, slowly approaching her. "I do stop by to check on Peggy now and then, but only to make sure that she's all right. She's just a friend, nothing more."

"You don't owe me any explanation about what you do with your private life, Matt. I have no claims on you. I'm just trying to protect myself and my daughter."

If he didn't do another thing in his life, Matt had to set this right. He had to, but how? Make himself look good by telling Maggie the truth and slandering Holly's father? Even if she believed him, there was no way he could strip Rafe of his credibility, especially now that he and Maggie were betrothed. Besides, he couldn't live with himself if he did something so low. His only hope was that Rafe would do the right thing if he ever got wind of the situation. It was a feeble hope, of course, but the only real option.

Sliding his hands across Maggie's shoulders, sticky dough and all, Matt gently turned her in his arms until she was facing him again. Flour clung to her eyelashes and the sculptured ridge of her cheekbones, an area where her tears made tell-tale tracks down to the edge of her jaw. Her hair was mussed, too, disheveled and coated with flour.

Dusting as much as he could from her cheeks, Matt said, "I wish you could believe me, Maggie. I know how bad this must look, and I'm sorry for that, but I'm asking you again to trust me. Peggy Dawson means absolutely nothing to me."

She wanted to believe him. God how Maggie wanted to believe in Matt again. In some ways, maybe she did. She'd observed enough to realize that men who frequented Peggy's sort rarely did think of them as anything more than a few moments of fun—she probably didn't mean anything outside of physical relief. All the same, that didn't make Maggie feel better. If anything, she felt more hurt, betrayed somehow, even though she had no rights where he was concerned.

Finally looking up at him again, she was startled at first by Matt's ghostly appearance. His features were all but obliterated by the flour she'd thrown at him, all covered except for his mouth and his eyes—the stormy gray eyes of a man she knew she could never forget. If she hadn't been so hurt and upset, Maggie might have laughed at the mess she'd made of him.

Instead she had to fight the sudden urge to cry as she said, "It doesn't matter what I think or what I believe. Just promise that you'll keep that woman away from me in the future, all right?"

"I'll do whatever it takes." With a soft groan, he pulled her into his embrace, and this time, Maggie didn't fight it.

"Maybe," he went on to say, "it would be a good idea if you do the same for me with Rafe—it might be best if you keep him away from me now that I know you've agreed to marry him."

Maggie turned away, unable to look into Matt's eyes any longer. "That's what I've wanted for a long time now, and precisely what Holly needs. Of course I'm going to marry him."

"What about your needs? Don't they matter?"

Assuming he was referring to their moment of weakness, Maggie felt her anger surging again. "Of course they matter, but nothing is as important to me as my daughter. As for the rest, what happened between us last night, well, I know you must be thinking that I'm no better than Peggy, but—"

"You have no idea in hell what I'm thinking about you or any of this. None."

Matt's sudden anger and the rawness she heard in his voice, startled Maggie. She knew what he wanted to hear—that she still wanted him the way she had last night on the dining room floor. She did. God knew she did, but what point was there in telling him now? What purpose would it serve if Matt knew how little Rafe's kiss had affected her, if he realized as she did that only one man's kisses could set her aflame—his own? It wasn't as if he'd be offering her a ring in place of the one Rafe hadn't produced. It wasn't as if she could accept it, even if he ever went crazy enough to make such an offer.

The irony in all this wasn't lost on Maggie, although she didn't feel she could share the revelations with Matt. Her father and Gus—both so rigid in their religious devotion they made Reverend Wilson look like the devil incarnate—would definitely see the irony. They would be all too happy to point out that she was finally paying the wages for her time of sin, forfeiting her happiness now for her loss of purity during those reckless moments in the barn. Her body had betrayed her then—and it betrayed her now.

When Matt lowered his head and his lips drew near, Maggie didn't turn away as she should have. She met his passion head on, matching him thrust for thrust as their kiss deepened into something that spiraled quickly out of control. His hands were in her hair, sticking to a few strands, and her own hands were groping the counter behind her in an effort to clear it off. Matt tugged her up hard against his hips, making damn sure she knew how badly he still wanted her.

In answer, Maggie swung her hands around him to grasp his buttocks, locking him in place in spite of the fact that she still had a clump of biscuit dough in the palm of one hand. Insinuating himself between her legs, though they both remained fully clothed, Matt rotated his hips against the swell of her womanhood, prompting Maggie to cry out with pleasure. She clutched his backside even tighter then, with a desperation that brought her to the brink of orgasm.

Damp from head to toe, half-crazy from wanting him, Maggie didn't even consider stopping Matt as he suddenly jerked the hem of her skirt up and plunged his hands inside her drawers. When he slid his fingers between her legs, stroking her there where she wanted him so desperately, she jerked violently against him, caught by the intensity of a sudden, body-melting release. Shivering all over with pleasure, wanting even more of what only Matt could provide, she released his buttocks, vaguely aware that she no longer held the clump of dough, and reached for the buttons on his trousers.

That's when Maggie heard the door to her upstairs apartment creak open.

"Holly!" she whispered, frozen with horror. Jumping away from Matt, she quickly whirled around to stand between him and the bannister. In case her daughter was already halfway down the stairs, Maggie had no intention of letting her get a look at the condition Matt had to be in by now.

Gathering as much calm as she could muster, Maggie called up the stairs in a decidedly quivering voice. "Holly, darling? Is that you?"

"Yes, ma'am."

Her tiny boots sounded on each stair, little angel thumps that weighed heavily on Maggie's heart.

"I'm hungry, Mama. Can I have some cookies and milk?"

As she came into view and caught sight of her mother's visitor, Holly gave a little gasp.

"Captain Matt! I didn't know you were here." She giggled, a shy fist at the edge of her mouth. "You look funny. How come you gots food all over you?"

Until then, Maggie had forgotten about the flour, eggs, and biscuit dough she'd flung at him. Forgotten, too, until her daughter made mention of it, was her own dishevelment and dusting of flour.

"How come your hair is sticking out and you're all white, Mama?" asked Holly as she reached the landing.

"Captain Weston was trying to help me with my biscuits. Uncle Gus has a bad cough and can't come to the restaurant today."

Holly looked from her mother to Matt, then shrugged and strolled over to the cookie jar. As she lifted the lid she said,

"Captain Matt isn't a very good turkey rancher. He's messy and not a very good cook too, isn't he, Mama?"

Laughing under her breath, Maggie shrugged an apology Matt's way as she said, "Well, sweetheart, I have to agree that he is a little messy. I probably should have asked you to help me instead."

"Uh, humm," she mumbled, her mouth full of cookies. Swallowing, she looked at Matt and grinned. "I hope you're best at getting Christmas trees."

Maggie looked to Matt again. "Christmas trees?"

"Holly asked me to go with her tomorrow," he explained. "I said I'd help pick out and chop down your tree. Maybe it would be better if you find someone else to do it."

"But you promised, Captain Matt." The cookies forgotten, Holly raced across the kitchen and threw her arms around his waist. "You promised you'd cut down our tree and help decorate it—you promised."

He looked at Maggie with a shrug. "I did promise."

"Gus is sick and all," she reasoned. "We certainly could use some help." Rafe hadn't offered to get the tree, in fact, hadn't even mentioned Christmas or the preparations involved. The decision made, she said, "Why don't you bring Louie to the cafe around eleven tomorrow. We'll work out the details then."

"Until then." Matt nodded her way, his expression unreadable, then leaned down to bid Holly farewell for the day. About that time the spoon handles jingled. A few minutes later, Hattie burst into the room.

"There you are, girls—oh, and Captain Weston, too. Didn't any of you hear me out there?"

They glanced at one another and shrugged.

Out of breath, Hattie continued, puffing loudly. "Gus had me bring up a turkey he butchered in case anyone just had to have one of his fried sandwiches. I left it out front at the first table I came to. Must weigh near fifteen pounds."

Hattie waddled a little closer, then paused to look them over. "What's this all about?" she asked, wiping a smudge of flour off Maggie's nose. "You two are a sight for sore eyes."

"The captain was just helping me a little," said Maggie, losing the battle against her tendency to blush. "He's, ah—"

"Messy, is what he is," supplied Holly.

"Yes," Hattie agreed, a sly look in her eyes. "It seems that he is."

Matt looked distinctly uncomfortable. He set Holly aside and started for the door. "I've got to be going now. See you ladies tomorrow around eleven."

"Goodbye," said Maggie. "And, er, thanks for all your help."

As he walked on by her and Hattie, Maggie saw that the clump of dough she'd been holding was stuck to the back pocket of Matt's trousers. Not only that, it was flattened, spread out to the size of her hand, complete with the imprint of all five fingers.

"Matt?" she called after him. No way could she let him run around town like that. "Your, ah, pocket. You must have sat on some bread dough or something."

As he reached around to the back of his trousers, Hattie turned to Maggie and sighed, swinging her hands in front of her skirt like a schoolgirl.

"Isn't that the cutest thing," she said, a little giggle in her voice. "Gus and I used to play with our food, too, especially when we were newlyweds."

Still giggling to herself, Hattie followed Matt to the kitchen door and watched him all the way out the front door.

After he'd gone, she turned back to Maggie with a sigh, and said, "Course we didn't use flour much, now that I think on it. We had most of our fun on candy-making day. It was a mite tastier than bread dough, too."

* * *

Across town at Cob's boardinghouse, Peggy had just received word that a gentleman was waiting for her down in the parlor. She naturally assumed that Matt had come back to give her further instructions, even though most times he had the brass to just march right on up to her room and bang on her door. Because she was so sure of her visitor, Peggy didn't bother to fluff up her hair or pinch her cheeks. She just dragged herself down the stairs, then nearly toppled over with surprise when she saw that Rafe was waiting for her in the parlor. He was turned out in a fancy black suit with hat to match, no less!

"Rafe, sugar," she cried, throwing herself into his arms. "I've been missing you so much I thought I'd die."

"Turn loose of me woman." Rafe roughly pushed her away, then nodded toward the foyer where old man Cob tended the desk—right along with everyone's business. "This here's a respectable place. Y'all got to act like a lady."

"Sorry, Rafe, but I was just so dang happy to see you, I kinda forgot myself for a minute."

He kept his frown, but immediately forgave her. "That's all right this one time. Hey—what happened to yur face? Somebody go after you, sugar darlin'?"

Peggy's hand went to the scratches on her cheek, and for a moment, she thought about telling him exactly who'd ripped into her. Then she realized she'd have to explain why. Suddenly, any mention of Maggie didn't seem like such a good idea.

"I, ah, took me a little walk up by them big pine trees this morning and fell into some brambles. Am I messed up bad?"

"No, sugar. Y'all look just fine to me." He touched the scabs briefly, looking like the Rafe she'd fallen in love with, then suddenly turned to stone. "I come by to see y'all 'cause there's something mighty important we got to talk about."

Peggy froze up. Lord, what if that giant bitch had gone and told him that she'd gone after her with a gun! Why, even though he'd never hurt her before, no telling what Rafe might do if he knew all that. He might just take it in his head to beat the shit right out of her or even kill her, depending on how pissed he was over the idea of her putting a slug in the mother of his child. Whatever he had to say and whatever the subject, he looked downright serious, mean-serious. Peggy forced a big, innocent smile and set out to find a better subject to discuss.

"I got something I been wanting to talk to you about for a long while now, sugar," she said. "Trouble is, we can't hardly talk about what I got in mind here where that dirty-minded Cob can just sit there and watch us."

To make sure he knew precisely what she meant—and more importantly, that he got totally distracted from whatever was on his mind—she ran her hand down his leg and up again to his crotch. There she proceeded to fondle him in ways guaranteed to fog up his mind.

"It's pretty near dark outside," Peggy whispered throatily, thrilled to notice that her plan was working extremely well. "Why don't you button up your coat, say your goodbyes, then sneak on around out back. I'll be waiting for you at my window."

"I cain't, Peggy," he said, sucking up a tortured breath. "I'd surely like to, sugar plum, but I just cain't."

About that time, she lightly ran the nail of her index finger along the hard ridge of him up to the sensitive tip. Lingering there, she began to draw lazy little circles with that same fingernail.

Rafe's eyeballs rolled to the back of his head. Then he licked his lips and said, "Which window did y'all say was yours?"

Eighteen

Ten more days until Christmas.

Matt didn't know if he could keep his sanity for that long. The situation between Maggie, Rafe, and even Peggy had gotten completely out of control. Not that he believed for a moment that he'd ever had any control over anyone or this particular assignment in the first place.

For one thing, he'd made way too many rash promises—not the least of which involved swearing to Maggie that he'd stay on in Prescott until Holly got over her daddy fixation with him. That meant he was stuck here, like it or not, until Christmas morning when Holly met her real father, the lucky bastard. Matt only hoped that the blasted headache pounding against his skull would be gone by then, even if he wasn't.

Going straight to Whisky Row had seemed like a good idea last night once he'd dusted himself off and cleaned up a little. He couldn't face anyone sober—not after Hattie spotted the ball of dough stuck to his ass and came up with her own conclusions on how it had gotten there.

Berating himself yet again for losing control of himself and the situation so easily, Matt rolled off of his bunk and sat on the edge of the mattress. Cradling his face between his hands, he willed the pulsating headache to fade and his stomach to settle. Instead his head nearly exploded when Hollister's unwelcome voice startled him from across the room.

"Y'all was drunker than a rat in a barrel of whisky when ya come in last night. Ready for a little coffee?"

Hollister held up a steaming mug, offering it to Matt, but he gingerly shook his head. "Thanks, but I'm not quite up to it yet."

He hoped to hell that Rafe realized he wasn't up to much of anything else just yet either. As irritating and stupid as ever, the damn fool took the mug of coffee for himself and plopped down across from Matt on his own bunk. Then he started rattling on about his upcoming wedding.

"Maggie thinks she kin talk Reverend Wilson into promising that he'll keep his mouth shut after the wedding so folks'll think we done got married before Holly was born."

Rafe paused, apparently expecting Matt to comment there, but he didn't feel up to so much as looking up.

His lack of interest didn't stop Hollister, it just slowed him up a little. "Maggie's gonna set the time for ten at night so no one in town is likely to come by," he went on to say. "We're getting hitched right there in the cafe. Guess when?"

"Christmas Eve," Matt muttered, hoping that would shut Rafe the hell up.

The fool jumped to his feet. "How'd y'all know that? I just found out about it myself."

"Maggie told me when I stopped by the cafe yesterday."

Rafe was quiet a long moment before he asked, "And what business did y'all have with my fiancée, I'd like to know?"

Matt's senses returned enough for him to recognize a certain possessiveness in Rafe's tone. The concern of a man who'd picked up the scent of another man's interest in his woman. When he finally looked up, he saw it in Hollister's eyes, too.

Christ, Matt grumbled to himself, but he'd made one hell of a mess out of things. The entire assignment had gotten so far off track, Matt wasn't sure he could get it headed in the right direction again. Or that he even wanted to try.

"I'm a talking to y'all, Weston."

Rafe's tone had gotten even more suspicious. Since he didn't feel that he was mentally sharp enough at the moment to outwit a dead man, Matt played the fool.

"Sorry, Rafe, but I'm not up to much conversation this morning. Did you say you were going into business with someone?"

Another long pause was followed by a heavy sigh. "Not exactly, but I was kinda thinking about that cafe, now that you mention it. What kinda dumb name is Squat and Gobble for a place of eats? Don't Rafe's Grub Wagon sound better to you, or maybe even Rafe's Vittles?"

In spite of his thumping head and dark thoughts, Matt laughed. "When did Gus turn the cafe over to you?"

"He didn't yet, dunderhead. But the man is getting on—hell, Gus got to be at least fifty."

"What about Hattie?"

"That wife of his don't have enough sense to run her nose, much less a place of eats. I expect I'll be taking over soon enough."

Again Matt had to laugh. "I think you're forgetting someone else."

Rafe scratched his mussed head. "You mean, Maggie?"

"Yeah, Maggie. It seems to me that she pretty much runs the place. What can you do there that she can't do for herself?"

Nodding thoughtfully, Rafe conceded, "She's got a pretty good head on her shoulders all right, but once't we're hitched, Maggie will be seeing things my way quick enough. And gettin' rid of that there squatting turkey name is first on my list."

As Rafe droned on about all his big plans for the future, most of which revolved around his giving orders but doing little else, Matt let his mind wander to other, more important matters. Specifically, a couple of complications he hadn't thought of during his long night of overindulgence. When Rafe finally began to bore himself and went back to the stove to cook up a little breakfast, Matt begged off by claiming a touchy stomach, then excused himself and went out for some air.

The little walk around town cleared his head enough for Matt to know that he had to talk to Peggy Dawson before things got any worse. He headed straight for Cob's Boarding House. When he arrived at Peggy's door and she saw who her visitor was, especially at such an early hour, the saloon angel nearly fainted with surprise.

"Mind if I come in?" Matt asked after he'd already stepped into her room and closed the door behind him. "Seems we have another little problem to straighten out."

For a woman decently covered by a long cotton dressing gown, a female who plied her trade in the nude, no less, Peggy suddenly became extremely shy. She tugged the wrapper tighter to her bosoms and clutched the opening at her throat.

"Well, I ain't exactly dressed for receiving no visitors of the male persuasion. You'd best come back some other time."

Matt was halfway across the room by then. He paused long enough to regard her from over his shoulder, laughed a little, then grabbed the simple wooden chair out from beneath her small writing desk and straddled it.

Looking Peggy square in the eye, Matt offered her two options. "You can talk to me now, just the way you are, or you can get dressed while I'm at the courthouse having a warrant drawn up for your arrest."

"Arrest me? What for?"

She actually had the gall to try and look the innocent. "For the attempted murder of Maggie Hollister. I believe Deputy Sloan still has in his possession the gun you used."

"Oh . . . that."

"Yes, Peggy, that." Matt pointed to her mussed bed. "Have a seat over there. You and I have a few things to talk about."

After she made herself comfortable, he said, "There's no

point in going over what you did to Maggie yesterday—I heard all the details."

"Her details, maybe, but what about the things she done to me?" Peggy pointed out the scabby scratches on her cheek. "Since when is it against the law for a gal to defend herself against a woman who's as big as any man?"

Matt had to struggle with himself, but decided it would be best to let those remarks slide right on by. He wanted Peggy focused on Rafe and Maggie's future together, and nothing else.

"I didn't come here to judge you," he said. "I just want to be sure you understand how things are—and how they have to be from here on out."

Peggy gave him a disinterested shrug, then looked away from him. Matt asked a question guaranteed to snag her attention again. "When's the last time you talked to Rafe?"

"Huh?" Peggy turned to him, lashes aflutter. "How could I talk to him when you told me I couldn't even see my man till you said it was all right?"

"Don't make me threaten you again, darlin'. I'd just as soon pick up that warrant as not. *When?"*

"All right." She picked at her floral robe, muttering to herself a moment before she finally admitted, "Rafe was here last night, but not 'cause I invited him or anything. He just come by to see how I'm doing, s'all."

"What did he have to say about the fight between you and Maggie?"

"He knows about that?" She gasped and clutched her throat. "I was afraid he'd kill me if he knew."

Her honest display of fear made Matt about as certain as he could be that she was telling the truth. "Relax, darlin'. He doesn't know if you didn't tell him, but if word gets out, things will really start to go wrong for you. You know that, don't you?"

She nodded vigorously.

"Good, then. Here's what you have to do." Matt fixed her

with the hardest stare he could manage. "For starters, *do not* breathe a word of what happened between you and Maggie to Rafe or to anyone else, for that matter. Nothing, you hear?"

"Yessir."

"Next, you absolutely must stay completely away from the Squat and Gobble Cafe and anywhere else Maggie might turn up. Understand?"

A teardrop rolled down one cheek. "In other words," she said quietly. "I ain't allowed in the respectable part of town."

"Sorry, but that's the way it has to be."

Matt climbed off the chair and shoved it back under the desk. Then he strolled over to where Peggy sat and lifted her chin with his finger. Her cute little-girl face tugged at something inside of him, making Matt wonder where and how things had started going so wrong for her.

With a sudden and overwhelming sense of tenderness, he said, "Here's the hardest but most important thing you have to do, Peggy. Christmas Day, with me as your escort, you're going to ride out of Prescott and never look back."

"But-but, I cain't do that! Me and Rafe, we're—"

"You and Rafe are finished. For good."

She burst into sobs. "I don't see why that has to be."

Matt refused to think about why from his standpoint, even though it ran a dead parallel to Peggy's, and simply said, "Rafe and Maggie are going to start living as husband and wife on Christmas Eve and there isn't a damn thing either one of us can do about it."

With a more eloquent expression than anything she might have said in response, Peggy looked up at him, her right eye twitching with rage. "We'll just see about that."

"No, Peggy, we won't." He caught her by the shoulders and hauled her to her feet. "If you're thinking of going after Maggie again, you can just forget it. If you so much as touch her in any way or even look at her wrong, you'd better hope to God that the sheriff hauls you off to jail before I get my hands on you. Do I make myself clear?"

Peggy stared at him a moment, then she pushed out a bitter laugh. "Perfectly clear, Captain Weston. You're in love with that giant bitch and want her for yourself."

Matt increased his grip on her arms, squeezing until she cringed and cried out in pain. Surprised that he'd gotten so violent, especially with a woman, he abruptly released her.

Peggy fell back onto her bed. "It's true, ain't it?" she said, laughing hysterically. "You are in love with that bitch. Don't you have enough gumption to admit it?"

Love wasn't a word Matt analyzed or thought about much, and he sure as hell wasn't in the mood to examine it or his feelings with Peggy.

Turning his back to her so he wouldn't have to look her in the eye, he said, "You and I don't matter when it comes to such concerns, understand? We don't belong in Prescott or with the folks who live here, and that includes Rafe."

Then he started for the door, adding, "For the last time, you've got two choices—either you promise to abide by my rules or I'll have to go get that warrant. What's it going to be?"

Behind him, Matt heard what sounded like a muffled sob. Then Peggy said, "I guess I'll take them stinking rules. I don't have to like it though, do I?"

"No, you don't, but you did make the right choice." He opened the door and stepped out into the hallway, looking back long enough to say, "And by the way—even God can't help you if you break any of those rules. *Comprende?*"

Matt's youthful memories of Christmas were buried somewhere at the back of his mind, forgotten with most recollections of his mother. All he knew of the holiday and its celebrations he'd learned on the trail in the company of other rangers, occasionally, his own father among them.

If they weren't able to acknowledge the yuletide in any other way, the rangers always managed to commemorate the day with the best Christmas dinner they could whip up. That usually consisted of roast geese and mallard ducks along with wild turkeys when they were available, and venison steaks when they were not. The camp cook made pies, fruit or nut, depending on supplies, and sometimes filled them with nothing more than caramelized sugar. At least one or two rangers brought along a fruitcake to share that he'd carried from home in his saddlebags.

One of Matt's favorites, a ranger known only as "Spooky" used to make a damn fine eggnog laced with brandy that was potent enough to bring a full grown horse to its knees. Of course that was before Spooky and his own fumble-footed horse fell over the side of a cliff in Mexico during a heavy fog. Matt's favorite eggnog chef was also the one who usually led the command in a chorus of Christmas carols each evening as the holiday drew near.

Never in his memory could Matt recall searching through a forest for the perfect tree, or dragging that flawless specimen up a flight of stairs to grace the parlor of a lady's apartment. But here he was in Maggie's home on his hands and knees, head and upper body buried beneath a mound of pine boughs as he tried to figure a way to position the tree without having it topple over onto him the minute he let go of it.

"How's that?" he asked Holly, who was guiding him as best she could. "Is it right in the middle of the window yet?"

"I think so," she replied, an excited giggle in her voice.

Now all Matt had to do was make sure the little wooden cross he'd nailed onto the bottom of the trunk was sufficient enough to hold the tree in place.

Testing his handiwork, he said to Holly, "Push the broom up

against the tree where I showed you earlier, and hold it in place. I'm going to let go now."

Downstairs, Maggie had just finished popping a big bowl of corn to insure that her helpers didn't eat the decorations instead of draping them around the Christmas tree, as planned. Adding a platter of cookies, a pitcher of milk, and a couple of glasses to the tray, she followed the trail of loose pine needles up the steps leading to her apartment door, which was still opened. Easily able to hear the activities inside the room, Maggie decided to eavesdrop a moment before joining her crew of elves. Matt's muffled voice was the first to reach her ears.

"All right, Holly," he said. "I'm going to let go of the tree again. This time you've got to try a little harder to keep the broom against the trunk until I say it's okay to let go. Promise?"

She giggled. "Promise, Captain Matt."

"Okay—push hard now!"

A moment later there came a muted thump followed by Matt's rowdy, but playful howls along with Holly's hysterical giggles. As Maggie came fully into the room, she saw that her daughter was rolling around on the floor, laughing and clutching her tummy. Matt was digging himself out from under the fallen tree, still howling and complaining loudly.

"Is that the best you can do, you little devil?" His hands appeared through a couple of branches, but the rest of him remained buried beneath boughs of fragrant pine. "You swore you wouldn't let that tree fall on me again, but I think you let it go on purpose. Well, did you?"

The more he complained, the harder Holly giggled, until Maggie thought she might actually choke. Acting the referee, she finally let them know she was there.

"What's going on in here, you two?" asked Maggie, as if surprised by all the racket. "I thought the Christmas tree would be up and decorated by now."

Matt stuck his head out from under the branches. "We're

having a little trouble getting the damn thing to stand on its own two planks."

"You said a bad word, Captain Matt," chided Holly, who promptly burst out laughing again.

"Sorry about that." Apologies rendered, Matt gave Maggie a sheepish grin. "I think now would be a good time to tell you that I've never done anything like this before. I don't seem to be much good at it either."

Still rolling with laughter, Holly offered an explanation without accepting any of the blame. "The tree fell on him, Mama— two times!"

"In that case," said Maggie, setting the tray on a table. "I guess I'll have to take over in here for a while."

After helping Matt to right the tree and secure it, she left Holly to fasten little baskets filled with gumdrops to the branches, even though she occasionally pilfered a few candies for herself. Then Maggie showed Matt to the sofa and urged him to rest up a while.

"Thanks for all your help," she said, offering him popcorn and cookies. "Holly can be very tough to turn down once she gets her mind set on something. She didn't want anyone but you chopping down our tree or helping to set it up. I appreciate your indulging her the way you have."

He shrugged and helped himself to a star-shaped cookie. "I enjoyed helping out. I don't remember ever having a Christmas tree before."

"Oh, Matt," she said, genuinely touched. "How sad."

"Sad? Not really." She saw the sense of loss in his eyes, even if he did try to shrug it off. "And now that I've worked with one, I'm not sure I've missed anything if being crushed beneath a dead tree is something a man's expected to do year after year."

"Just the same," she said, taking Matt's final statement as a cue to drop the subject. "We appreciate your help. It won't be long before you won't have to put up with Holly's endless list of chores and plans where you're concerned. Then you can breathe easy again."

Matt didn't exactly looked relieved over the prospect. He stared down at the braided rug beneath the table, then spoke so low, Maggie could barely hear him.

"I hope Rafe is prepared for Holly and her endless plans," he said, sounding a little sad. "She'll wear him down in a week, if he's not up to the task."

"He'll do all right." But even as she said it, Maggie wasn't one hundred percent convinced that he would. "In fact, I'm counting on her keeping him so busy, he won't have time to be underfoot while I'm trying to get my work done around here."

"Speaking of the cafe." Matt turned to her, concern etched on his brow. Inching closer to her until their knees were practically touching, he kept one eye on Holly as he whispered, "I think it's only fair for you to know that Rafe has done some talking about working here at the cafe."

"He has?" Maggie had trouble believing that Rafe had plans to work at all. "I rather assumed that he'd do whatever it was he did in Texas."

Again Matt glanced Holly's way. She was too busy winding a long string of popcorn around the tree and singing the same verse to "Deck the Halls" over and over to be bothered with their conversation.

Still Matt leaned in toward Maggie until their shoulders brushed before he went on. "I doubt you want Rafe taking up his former occupation here in Prescott. He was a gambler back in El Paso, and a rather bad one at that."

"I didn't know." The idea of Holly's father earning a living in the saloons across the way didn't set well at all. But it wasn't a subject to be discussed or decided between her and Matt. Maggie laughed a little as she said, "Maybe I can find something for him to do at the restaurant, after all. I wonder how he'd be at peeling potatoes?"

"I don't think peeling potatoes is what he has in mind. He even talked about changing the name of the restaurant to something that suits him better."

"Really?"

Maggie understood Matt's concerns about Rafe, and certainly had to admit to having a few of her own, but the very idea of the man taking over the cafe was so utterly laughable, she couldn't make a serious conversation out of the possibility.

"Believe me, Matt," she whispered, unable to hide a little chuckle, "I do know what kind of man Rafe is. He runs around making noises like a rooster, but at the first sign of trouble, he'd be the first to run straight for the chicken coop and cluck like a setting hen."

Matt burst out laughing. "I do see your point. I was trying to get his attention the other day, but not having much luck, so I pulled my gun on him. Not only did I have his attention until I didn't want it anymore, he damn near watered his own boots."

Maggie didn't exactly laugh over the thought, but she did feel that they'd reached some kind of understanding. "Then you know what I mean. When faced down, the man is absolutely no threat to me or this cafe."

"I hope things stay that way after you're married." Matt glanced at the tree, where Holly was still singing and still stringing popcorn. "I sure don't want that man taking advantage of you or that little girl."

Deeply touched, Maggie gently laid her hand across Matt's forearm. Feeling his heat beneath the shirt, she said, "He'll behave himself. I promise."

"How can you be so sure?" Matt turned to her, covering her hand with his own. "If I thought for one minute that he'd harm you or Holly, that he would be anything other than a decent husband and father . . ."

"Shush."

Maggie put her finger against Matt's lips, stilling the words she couldn't bear to hear. That's when she realized that they were not alone. Even over the clamor of Holly's off-key singing, the sound of boots scuffing across the wooden floor behind the sofa could easily be heard.

Before she could turn around to see who was there, Rafe Hollister's angry voice seemed to fill every corner of the room.

"Well, ain't this a cozy sight."

Nineteen

"It's the El Paso Kid!" squealed Holly, saving them all from the awkward moment. "How did you get here?"

"Yeah, Kid," said Matt, getting to his feet. "How did you happen to turn up without an invitation or so much as a knock on Mrs. Hollister's door?"

Faced down, Rafe clucked just like Maggie said he would. "Well, I didn't exactly figure I needed an invite to go walking into the cafe. I called out, but when nobody answered me, I just moseyed on back to the kitchen. Weren't no one there neither, so I come on up the stairs. Hell, the door was opened, wasn't it?"

"That's a bad word," said Holly, slipping between Matt and Rafe. "But it's okay. Captain Matt sometimes has mouth accidents, too. Did you catch any bad men today, Ranger El Paso?"

The crowing cock again, Rafe hitched up his threadbare trousers. "Not yet, little gal, but I reckon I still got time."

"Come look at our Christmas tree first," she said, taking Rafe by the hand and dragging him across the room. "Captain Matt and me went to the forest and he cut down the tree. I get to decorate it."

With a scowl that Holly couldn't see, Rafe looked over his shoulder at Matt. "Wasn't that extra-special nice of the captain. I expect that might make him think maybe he's entitled to a little something extra for his trouble, maybe something real special from your mama."

"It wasn't any trouble, Kid," said Matt, none too sure what Rafe's next comment might have been. "I looked all over for you this morning when I found out Maggie and Holly needed some help getting their Christmas tree. We figured you might want to take part in the festivities. Where were you?"

As Matt suspected, wherever he'd been, Rafe had been up to no good. His cheeks went all splotchy and he couldn't seem to look anyone in the eye as he explained.

"I been around, doing this and that. Sorry I missed out on the tree."

"You didn't miss it, Ranger El Paso," said Holly. "See? You can look at it all you want to right now."

She then proceeded to point out each decoration, explaining in detail how she'd cut snowflakes and stars out of wrapping paper Gus got from the butcher shop, how her mother had made the miniature dolls out of corn husks, and how she herself had baked pie dough cookies out of Maggie's scraps, then decorated them with sugar sprinkles and brightly colored glazes.

While Rafe was being so thoroughly entertained, Matt took the opportunity to say to Maggie, "I'd best be going now."

The smile she returned was filled with gratitude and maybe just a touch of regret. "Thank you, Matt, for all your hard work in helping with the tree. Holly and I really do appreciate it. See you Sunday?"

Rafe, who apparently had the ears of a hound, perked up at that comment. "What's happening Sunday?" he called across the room. "Anything I should know about?"

"It's a great big Christmas party!" said Holly. "That's when we get to dance and eat lots of candy and cookies, and then Santy Claus comes."

"You're invited, er, Kid," said Maggie. "Everyone in town is expected to attend the Christmas sociable."

"That right?" He raised one eyebrow. "You going, Captain?"

Before Matt could answer, Holly did him the honor. "Captain Matt is going to have the first dance with me. He promised."

"Did he now?" Rafe turned suspicious eyes on him.

"Holly asked me to, Kid." Wheedled was more like it, grumbled Matt to himself, even though he'd done his damndest to convince her that he was no good at dancing. "It didn't seem right to turn down such a pretty little girl's request. See you at the party, Holly."

Matt turned back to Maggie and reached for his hat. "Thanks for the cookies and a very entertaining afternoon."

Then he shot down the stairs as fast as his legs would carry him.

For Maggie, the next two days went by in a blur of sugar, flour, and pots of stew bubbling on the stove, as Gus's cold lingered on. Since Hattie wasn't much help in the kitchen, Maggie was forced to do most of the cooking for the cafe as well as her preparations for the upcoming sociable. On Sunday morning, she officially closed the restaurant so that she and Holly could attend church services, then Maggie returned to the cafe to finish up with her baked goods.

To Maggie's surprise, when she and Holly stepped into the kitchen, Gus was stoking up the fire under a huge vat of lard. His round cheeks seemed unusually gaunt, and deep blue smudges lined the hollows beneath his eyes, but other than that, he seemed in good spirits.

"Uncle Gus," said Maggie. "What are you doing here? You're supposed to be home in bed."

Holly wagged an accusing finger at him. "Aunt Hattie went to church with us because she thinks you're sick."

"Well, I guess Aunt Hattie is about to find out different, then, isn't she?" Gus laughed, prompting a bout of coughing. "She's probably wondering why you aren't there helping her with her candy-making."

With a gasp, Holly said, "Can I go, Mama?"

"Yes, but make sure you wear the biggest apron Hattie can find. I don't want that dress ruined."

Holly was already out of the kitchen by the time the sentence left Maggie's lips. Shaking her head over her daughter's endless energy, she joined Gus at the stove.

"I thought Doc Martin told Hattie that you had to stay flat on your back for at least another week."

"Doc Martin's got to make a living just like everyone else." Gus turned to her with a wink. "If I'd a' been forced to stay in that bed for one more minute swallowing spoon after spoon of his fancy patented elixir, you might as well have hauled me straight to the cemetery, mattress and all, then kicked dirt over me. A man can only be stretched out on his sickbed for so long without up and dying—so sayeth the Lord. Besides, there isn't nothing a good dose of cod liver oil won't cure."

"Chapter and verse, please? I don't believe I'm familiar with that quotation."

Gus reached for the freshly butchered turkey he'd brought to the cafe. "I've been abed with a fever, dear girl. My memory escapes me. Perhaps it sounds more familiar this way. Let us eat and drink; for tomorrow we shall die."

Although Maggie had to chuckle, she still didn't care for the grayish cast beneath Gus's jovial expression. Colds had a funny way of turning into pneumonia if a body wasn't careful.

Giving one last effort, she said, "Is there nothing I can do to make you go on home where you belong?"

"Nothing, Maggie, my girl—how can Prescott possibly have a Christmas buffet without one of my fried turkeys as the centerpiece?"

With a sigh, Maggie tied on an apron. "What can I do to help?"

"Let's work on the oyster stuffing so we can get this bird cooking. That buffet can't even get started until we get there with this turkey."

"No sir, it definitely cannot."

After that, Gus put Maggie to work chopping up cubes of bread to which he added butter, salt, sage, a dash of pepper, and a pint of stinky, slimy oysters. After she'd mixed all the ingredients together and moistened the stuffing with a little milk, Gus crammed as much as he could get inside the bird and set to trussing it good and tight. When he'd finished his masterpiece, he slid the turkey into the vat of boiling lard and left it to cook for a couple of hours.

As Maggie began work on her mincemeat pies, Gus fell heavily onto a nearby chair. "You can go home and rest now," she said. "I'm quite capable of watching the turkey while I make my pies."

"I can rest just as well right here," he said, stubborn as ever. "Besides, by now Hattie's probably got the entire house all sticky with her marzipan candy-making."

As Maggie chopped up the venison, apples, and spiced raisins, Gus went on to say, "I expect that Holly's going to be asking for the same thing from Santa this year, don't you?"

"If you mean will she ask for her very own daddy again, I would say, yes." She added bits of candied orange peel and citron to the mixture, along with a scoop of butter and a measure of apple cider. "In fact, she's already talking about it."

"Well," said Gus. "Is she going to finally get her wish or didn't the captain have any luck?"

Maggie was so surprised by the comment, she almost dropped the pot filled with her mincemeat mixture before she got it to the stove. Puzzling over his remarks and in no way certain how to answer him, she reached for one of the liquor bottles on the shelves near the stove and turned to him with it in her hand.

"Is it all right with you if I put a little brandy in the pies? It really does give them a much better flavor."

"I'm not the temperance police, Maggie. Suit yourself." He coughed into his handkerchief, then went back to his original question. "I asked you if Holly's gonna get her wish or not. Isn't that why Captain Weston came to town?"

Maggie's spine froze as she stirred the simmering mixture. "Now why would you ask such a silly question?"

"Silly?" he said, his tone indignant. "I'll have you know, Margaret Mary, that I've been watching you and the captain, not to mention Ben Sloan, all of you discussing little secrets since the day that ranger first rode into town. I have a right to know what's going on, being's how I helped raise the girl and all—did Weston find your man or not?"

The absolutely necessary lie about being a married woman aside, there was no way that Maggie could offer Gus anything less than the truth. At this point, she supposed there was no harm in his knowing about Rafe anyway.

"Yes," she admitted, the word barely audible to her own ears. "He found him in Texas and brought him here to Prescott about a month ago."

Gus nodded sagely, thinking on the information for a while. Then he suddenly slapped his thighs and said, "Lord above, it's that El Paso Kid character, isn't it? Holly has his coloring."

Maggie bit her lip and turned back to the counter. She couldn't imagine why, but all of Gus's accusations—true as they were—made her ache inside, as if she were about to burst out in sobs any minute.

As she began cutting lard into the bowl of salted flour for her pie crusts, he repeated, "Well? No sense hiding anything now. It is him, isn't it?"

"Yes," she admitted, feeling dirty somehow.

"That's the man you ran off and married?" Gus came up out of his chair. *"He's* the reason you broke your mama and daddy's hearts? Why that fool isn't nothing but a slice of French-cooked potato—a whole lot of hot air and not much else."

Surprising herself, Maggie jumped to Rafe's defense. "He's a good enough man at heart once you get past his impudence. You'll see if you just give him a chance."

Gus fell back onto his chair. "Lord above," he said, dramatically clutching his chest. "I guess I don't have much choice but to give that boy a chance, now do I?"

Maggie hung her head and softly whispered, "None of us do."

Gus made no comment to that, and for the first time that she could remember, Maggie discovered that she wanted him to stick his nose into places it didn't belong. Suddenly, she really needed and wanted his council.

He was too busy berating Rafe to let her get a word in edgewise. "Why didn't that fella come to town like a man and announce himself as your husband right off? Why would he be going around hiding behind the name of an outlaw?"

"It's not an outlaw's name," Maggie said. "He's pretending to be a Texas Ranger."

"A ranger known as the El Paso Kid?" Gus laughed and coughed at the same time. "I've never heard of anything so stupid in my entire life."

Since Maggie pretty much agreed with her uncle's assessment, she didn't even try to defend Rafe's choice. Instead she explained the need for a sobriquet.

"He didn't have much chance to think up a name. We planned it so he wouldn't reveal himself to Holly or to anyone but me and Matt until Christmas Day."

She paused to look at her uncle, sure he above all, would understand why. "I want her to believe that anything is possible, to know that if she prays hard enough, sometimes those prayers are answered. I want her to believe in miracles."

"Amen to that," said Gus, bowing his head.

"There's another reason we waited before presenting him to the family," she had to admit. "Rafe wasn't quite ready to accept the responsibilities of fatherhood when Matt first brought him to Prescott."

Gus's head snapped up. "How could any man not accept a beautiful child like Holly!"

She hushed him, even though they were the only two people in the cafe. "Please be quiet about this. Don't ruin it for me now. It's hard enough to keep Rafe a secret with him popping up from time to time. Holly wasn't supposed to so much as lay eyes on him until Christmas morning. It was an accident they met at all."

"Ah, yes, and I believe I remember how and why that happened. It was the day Holly went missing, wasn't it?"

She nodded. "But now that we've managed to keep it a secret this long, and with Christmas only one week away, I'd hate to have the surprise ruined. Please promise you won't tell anyone, especially not Aunt Hattie."

Chuckling to himself, Gus admitted, "I love that woman dearly, but I wouldn't ask Hattie to patch up my winter woollies for fear that all of Yavapai County would soon know that I had holes in my underwear."

Laughing along with him, Maggie leaned over and hugged his neck. "Thanks for understanding, Uncle Gus. It's all going to be worth it when we see Holly's face on Christmas morning."

"What about yours, sweet niece? Do you think you'll be as happy to have that wandering husband of yours back home where he belongs?"

Maggie couldn't answer that question correctly or honestly, not yet. To deny Rafe as her husband would surely break her uncle's heart, not to mention tear the family apart, so she was in no position to do that. She couldn't out and out lie anymore than she already had. Maggie was left with little choice but to assure him that everything would be fine.

"Sure I will, Uncle Gus. It will be nice to have a man around the house for a change."

After that slight fib, the rest of the morning and early afternoon went smoothly. By three o'clock when Gus, Hattie, Holly and Maggie arrived at the assembly hall, better than half of the town was already there. Those that weren't, were on their way. As the rest of the townsfolk made their way to the gaily decorated building, the air was filled with the sound of children laughing, sleigh bells jingling, and boots and horse hooves crunching in the snow.

Inside the huge room, which had been cleared for dancing and mingling, the buffet was already full to overflowing. In addition to Gus's fried turkey, the main table boasted crocks of baked beans, smoked beef and pork, several roasted geese, and lots of cold sliced meats. Complementing the heavy fare were loaves of freshly baked bread, batches of Maggie's muffins and biscuits, jams, jellies and several dishes of freshly churned butter. Vegetables of every description ran the length of the table, some fresh, but most in jars, and both sour cucumber pickles and watermelon pickles made from the rinds of the courthouse melons were plentiful.

Maggie and Holly made their way to the dessert table with the mincemeat pies to find it practically full up already with nut and fruit cakes, sugar, ginger, and spiced cookies, butternut fudge, bowls of dark chocolate candy balls, and Hattie's odd little marzipan candies molded into shapes that sort of resembled miniature turkeys. In addition to Maggie's offerings, there was also a large assortment of cherry, pumpkin, and apple pies.

Everything was perfect, thought Maggie as she scanned the buffet tables, but even that worried her a touch. Was it possible for things to be a little *too* perfect?

* * *

Since they had just rounded the corner onto Montezuma Street at the other end of town, Matt and Rafe had yet to hear the laughter and gaiety pouring out of the assembly hall. The streets were more mud than snow by now, since countless wagons, horses, and townsfolk on foot had already passed this way. But that didn't bother Matt in the least. In fact, he rather hoped that he and Rafe were among the last to arrive at the buffet. It wouldn't hurt to go over the rules with the man one more time to make sure he didn't make a mess of things this late in the game.

"The more I think about you socializing at this affair, Rafe," he said, slowing his steps. "The more I'm convinced that it would be too chancy for you to go off dancing with anyone but Maggie."

"Why? We ain't hitched up yet, and besides, no one knows that me and Maggie are fiancéed."

"They'll know you're her husband in a week, you idiot, and they'll definitely remember the way you behaved at their Christmas party. Dancing's out. And so is drinking, in case anyone offers you anything but plain punch. Understand?"

He grumbled a little, but seemed to accept his fate. "Is it all right if I help myself to all the eats I want? Y'all pretty near starved me to death since we left Texas."

Matt thought he'd taken extraordinary care of the man, given the circumstances, but Rafe did have a point—for a scrawny fella, he could put away enough groceries for two men twice his size and still be looking around for more. Matt couldn't imagine what he did with all that food once he swallowed it, but not much managed to stick to his bones.

"I don't care if you stuff yourself until you explode," said Matt, imagining the sight and liking it. "Just try not to throw up in sight of Maggie or her friends."

"I kin promise you that, no problem," he said. "There's only one thing I hate more than tossing my vittles up, and that's sleeping in that cold, cold cabin. I reckon that's about to change, if'n you know what I mean."

Matt did, but Rafe's sleeping with Maggie was not a subject open to discussion. "Don't forget," he said, a sudden rage burning the back of his throat. "Holly's going to be there. You can't just ignore her, but try not to say anything stupid around her. We don't want her to get suspicious about your true identity."

"Y'all don't got to worry about that. I ain't dumb." Rafe stuck the nail of his index finger between his teeth and chewed on it a minute, looking dumb before he said, "Speaking of my true name, I know things gotta change after Holly finds out that I'm her real pa and I got to tell her that I'm really Rafe Hollister, but I was wonderin'—do y'all reckon it'd be okay, I mean, could I still be the El Paso Kid, ya think?"

Matt's eyes rolled right along with his gut. "Why in hell would you want to be known as the El Paso Kid? It makes you sound like some kind of outlaw."

"Maybe it does, but I got to tell y'all—folks have been a damn sight more respectful to me as the El Paso Kid than they ever was as Rafe Hollister. I kinda like it."

Although it still seemed as ridiculous as hell, at least Matt could understand Rafe's position on the matter. The man wasn't what most folks thought of as an upstanding citizen. He'd been even less worthy of gentle society when Matt first stumbled over him. If a notorious nickname made Rafe feel proud of himself, who was Matt to deny him the opportunity?

"Hell, Rafe," he said. "I don't care if you call yourself Billy the Kid. Now that he's dead, I doubt that Billy would care either."

Rafe gasped. "Billy the Kid is dead?"

Matt realized there were folks who, for one reason or another, didn't even know that President Garfield had died of his wounds in September, some two months after an assassin's bullet struck him. But everyone, absolutely everyone knew that Sheriff Pat

Garrett had ended the life of Billie the Kid in July, just two short weeks after the president was shot. Everyone, it seemed, except Rafe Hollister.

Looking at him sideways, Matt said, "Trust me. Billy the Kid is dead. As for your nickname, you can call yourself any damn thing you want to as long as you never, *ever,* refer to yourself as a Texas Ranger again—*comprende?"*

"Yessir, I do *comprende* that. And since y'all don't seem to mind, I think I'll just keep on being the El Paso Kid. Seems like I might be asking for someone else's trouble if'n I was to borry another man's name."

"A wise decision," said Matt, amazed to find himself making such a statement in regards to Rafe Hollister.

Alerted by the sound of fiddles and merriment, Matt looked up to see that they were just two doors away from the assembly hall.

With one final warning, he said to Rafe, "The woman who is about to become your wife is in that building and so is your daughter. See if you can't remember that."

Rafe paused, then turned to Matt with an uncharacteristically thoughtful expression. "Yur the one best remember that . . . *Amigo."*

Twenty

When Matt walked through the door and into the assembly hall, Maggie's heart skipped a beat. Although he wasn't dressed in a suit, the way Rafe was, he wore a new chambray shirt of soft blue, a buckskin vest, and freshly pressed trousers made of dark brown denim. Around his neck he wore a silk scarf in seasonal red. He flipped his hat onto the rack near the door, then ran both hands through his dark hair, blending the hatband ridges into the thick waves that topped his head.

To Maggie, he was easily the most handsome man in the room, a thought obviously shared by her aunt.

"There's that good-looking ranger," said Hattie. "Don't you think Captain Weston would be a nice catch, dear? Why, I'd set a trap for him myself if I didn't have my Gus."

"But you do have Gus," said Maggie, irritably. "So maybe you shouldn't talk like that."

Hattie looked up at her with a frown. "What's got you in such a mood, dear? Maybe you ought to go have one of my marzipans. That'll sweeten you up a little."

Although she adored most candies, Maggie absolutely loathed marzipan, Hattie's or anyone else's.

"Thanks," she said. "But I really don't need sweetening. I'm just anxious for Santa to get here so Holly and the other children can tell him what they want for Christmas."

"Santa? Oh, yes. Santa." Hattie leaned in close and stretched on her tiptoes to make sure no little ears could overhear. "Who is our Santa this year?"

"Ben Sloan," Maggie whispered back. "Just like every other year."

"Really? I have the worst memory for such things." She laughed at her own expense, then brightened and said, "Look, dear, there's that handsome ranger. Won't he be a catch for some lucky girl?"

Maggie thought of pointing out that they'd already been through that conversation, but by then Matt was upon them.

"Afternoon, ladies," he said, one hundred percent male, adorable dimples and all. "You're both looking even more lovely than usual."

"In this old thing?" said Hattie, blushing as she smoothed the skirts of her new Christmas dress, a deep crimson bombazine trimmed in black velvet.

"Why, Mrs. Townes," Matt said, playing the gallant. "If you were wearing a flour sack, you'd still be the prettiest girl in the room."

"Oh, oh." With one of her nervous cackles, Hattie lightly whacked Matt's shoulder with her fan. "You are such a kidder."

"I wouldn't kid you about a thing like that, ma'am."

He then brought her fingers to his mouth and lightly kissed the tips. It was all too much for Hattie, who promptly burst out giggling and sashayed off toward a group of her lady friends, no doubt intending to repeat Matt's flattery.

When she was out of earshot, Matt leaned in toward Maggie and said, "That's a real pretty dress you're wearing. It looks extra nice with your hair."

Though it was out of style by a couple of years, the gown, made of lacy white cotton with a linen underskirt, was her best. During yuletide festivities, Maggie fancied it up with red satin bows and added a swath of blood red velvet to the train. She knew she looked as good as she could, and to have Matt notice, made her feel saucy. And a little reckless.

She looked at him sideways and said, "Don't think all that masher talk will have any affect on me, Captain Weston. I'm not so gullible as my aunt."

"Oh?" Matt inched even closer, brushing against her shoulder. "What does affect you, my dear? A little flour in your face, perhaps? Or how about if I were to crack an egg on the top of your head? Would that do it, you think?"

Maggie tried to keep a straight face, but it was impossible, especially as she thought back to the mess she'd made of his clothing. With a laugh, she said, "As I recall, you're the one partial to eggs. Did you ever get that mess out of your trousers?"

"I didn't even try," he said without missing a beat. "I gave those pants to Rafe. Now all the skunks in town like him best."

They both had a chuckle over that, especially Maggie, as she visualized Rafe trying to hang onto a pair of pants that were at least three sizes too big for him.

Then she turned to a more serious topic. "Where is Rafe? I thought he was coming to the sociable with you."

"He did." Matt glanced around the room, then settled on one of the buffet tables. "He's over there stuffing his face."

Maggie followed his gaze and saw that Rafe stood plate in hand gobbling down a huge mound of ham and beans. "That ought to keep him busy for a while," she remarked, wondering why he hadn't at least stopped by to say hello.

"I hope so, because, ah, Maggie?" Matt paused, suddenly looking unsure of himself. "I've got a little problem and I was hoping you could help me with it."

"Is this for real? You're not still going on about eggs and flour, are you?"

"I wish I were." He certainly sounded serious enough. "This is real as it gets. If I don't get some help, and soon, I'll have to break my promise to Holly. That wouldn't set too well with me or her."

"It wouldn't make me any too happy either. What kind of help do you need?"

Matt sighed and gave her a look pitiful enough to melt the soles of her shoes. "Holly insisted that I dance with her at this affair, and fool that I am, I said I would."

"If you're looking for my sympathy," she said warily. "You've got a long way to go to get it."

"I don't want sympathy, Maggie. I need help." He glanced around, again seeking a little privacy, then leaned in and whispered, "You must keep this information to yourself at all costs, but I've never set foot on a dance floor in my entire life. I don't have the first idea what to do."

Maggie threw back her head laughed out loud.

Beside her, she heard Matt's sharp intake of breath. "Is this your idea of discretion? I'm glad you find the situation so amusing. I don't."

"But it's so funny," she said, still laughing. "I don't know why exactly, but you asking for dancing lessons is the most hilarious thing I've ever heard."

He raised his dark eyebrows, indignant as an English lord. "Maybe I ought to ask someone else to help."

This side of Matt reminded Maggie of a pouting Holly, somehow. Again she fell into helpless laughter.

"Hattie must know how to dance," he said, pretending to scan the room for her. "I'll bet she'd be glad to help a fellow out, and wouldn't bust her ribs laughing about it either."

At the thought of her aunt teaching Matt anything, much less the art of dancing, Maggie laughed until tears rolled down her cheeks. About that time Matt finally said something that sobered her up, just about the only thing that could have calmed her down at that point.

"Mind you," he said. "I think you're about as entertaining

as a boil on my sit down, but your neighbors are sure enjoying this side of you."

Wiping her eyes with the back of her hand, Maggie looked up in horror to see that a few ladies from the Gab and Jab Club were huddled together, whispering and occasionally looking her way. Just thinking about the things they might be saying was enough to wipe the smile off her mouth. She'd barely managed to convince them that Miss Dawson was a stranger and had to have been insane when she attacked her. Raising the ladies' curiosity after so shocking a display was just asking for trouble.

"I see what you mean," Maggie said, suddenly as prim and proper as a preacher's wife. Without so much as a glance in his direction, she said, "Thanks for letting me know I was being watched."

"No thanks necessary." Following her example, Matt spoke out the side of his mouth. "That was a bribe. Now you have to tell me how to dance—and you've got to do it before Holly spots me."

"Let's get to it then." Maggie looked around the room, wondering if it would be better to try and blend in with the other dancers or to take him to a quiet corner of the room.

"Well?" he said impatiently. "What do I do?"

"I can't tell you. I have to show you. I'm trying to figure out where we should go to practice."

"Just tell me how it's done. I'm sure I can figure it out."

Maggie turned to look at him again. There was an unusual amount of arrogance in both his tone and his expression, enough that Maggie thought her laughter had probably wounded his pride. Still she couldn't resist taking a sarcastic jab at this sudden display of ego.

"Have it your way, Matt. When the band is playing a waltz, it's in three-quarter time like this: three ONE two, three ONE two. If, on the other hand, they're playing a reel or a square dance—"

"All right, all right," he said in surrender. "Show me, then, if you must. Just be quick about it."

In no hurry to make another spectacle of herself, Maggie led Matt to a quiet corner, then positioned one of his hands at the small of her back and took hold of the other.

Looking up at him, she said, "Are you ready?"

"I feel like an idiot."

"I didn't ask you how you feel. Are you ready?"

With a short, stubborn nod, he said, "As I'll ever be."

And then the lesson began. Figuring that a waltz or something like one was the most popular music to dance to, she began humming Strauss's "Lorelei." Once she had the rhythm down correctly, Maggie began to move, urging Matt to follow along as she demonstrated the dance. At first he limped along, moving sluggishly when he had to step out with his left foot, and completely out of rhythm when he led with the right.

Then things took a turn for the worse.

For a man who seemed so self-assured and highly adept at most physical pursuits, Matt turned out to be an extremely clumsy dancing pupil. He not only stumbled over her feet, smashing her toes several times, but even managed to fall over his own. And the way he held her was even more awkward. Maggie knew those hands well, knew them to be sensuous and gentle, strong, yet supple. Positioned to dance, Matt's arms were like planks and his hands became, stiff, unwieldy paddles.

Thinking he might relax more if he were in the proper atmosphere, Maggie led him out onto the dance floor when the band finally struck up a waltz. There she urged him to join the others, who were already swaying to the music.

"I can't do this," he said, his jaw tight.

"Yes, you can."

"No, I can't. I need more lessons."

"You're getting a lesson now."

He grumbled to himself, then stumbled and tripped over her feet. "Maybe what I need is a new teacher."

Maggie was onto him. "If you think getting me mad is going to get you out of this lesson, you're wrong. Now dance, you fool, dance."

As she stepped out and whirled him around with a particularly vigorous turn, Matt's eyes grew huge with something she'd never seen in them before—fear. The sight of a Texas Ranger looking so mortified, this big strong man who wasn't afraid of anything or anyone, tickled her funnybone. Maggie couldn't help but burst out laughing again.

"What?" he said, stopping in mid-stride. "What am I doing wrong?"

"Nothing, I swear," she said, hoping that his well-honed instincts hadn't warned him that she lied. "You're doing just fine. Listen to the music, follow along with the rhythm, and stop watching your feet. I think that's what is making you so self-conscious."

That final bit of advice worked the hoped-for miracle with her student. Oh, Matt still stumbled over her feet from time to time, but his hands no longer felt like boards and his entire body seemed less tense. So relaxed was he, in fact, that the way he held her became more of an embrace, the music, a song of love instead of a simple melody. When Maggie raised her eyes to meet his, she remained locked in his gaze for the remainder of the dance, all too aware that each of them harbored thoughts that had no place in a public gathering. By the time the music ended, her breathing had become quick and uneven, and she was flushed from head to toe. Though he should have released her immediately, Matt kept her close in his embrace as the other dancers parted and drifted away.

It was Maggie whose senses returned first, Maggie who finally realized that they were slowly becoming the focus of attention.

Backing out of Matt's embrace, she fanned herself and said, "It's gotten awfully warm in here. Shall we head to the refreshment table for a cup of cider?"

He nodded. "I *am* a little hot now that you mention it. Lead the way."

They'd barely reached the wassail bowl before Holly came bounding out of nowhere, hollering at the top of her lungs. "Captain Matt! You're here."

"That I am," he said, sipping his hot cider.

"Come on then," she insisted, tugging on his pants leg. "It's way past our time for the first dance."

Over her head, he winked at Maggie and mouthed, "Wish me luck."

Then the two of them headed off for the dance floor, where much to Maggie's surprise, the band broke into a particularly rowdy Virginia reel. Since Matt was in no way prepared for anything but a slow waltz, Maggie could barely stand to watch him struggling with the new steps. As he was passed from partner to partner, she could see the confusion and panic in his expression, and even worried that perhaps he'd fallen when he wasn't in view.

Mercifully, the dance ended prematurely when one of the city council members alerted the band to the fact that Santa Claus and his reindeer had been spotted coming up the street. Moments after that, Holly dragged Matt to where Maggie waited at the window.

"Mama?" she said, tapping Maggie's arm. "Captain Matt isn't too good at dancing either, Mama. Can we find something new for him to be good at?"

Aware that Matt was looking at her, waiting for her reply, Maggie glanced up. Their eyes met, a mistake. Maggie knew something he was better than good at, and Matt's expression said that he knew it, too. With a rush of blood that thundered in her ears, she tore her gaze away from his.

"Hush, now," she said to Holly. "That's not a very nice thing to say about Captain Weston. I'm sure he's a fine dancer."

"Nuh, uh," she insisted. "He's so terrible at dancing he hurt my foot real bad and then he made Mrs. Gardner cry."

Maggie looked back at Matt in alarm.

He shrugged. "I zigged when everyone else zagged. I never even saw the woman."

"You broke her ankle, Captain Matt."

"No, I didn't. She just said that I did. The lady might have turned her ankle a little after I broke the heel on her shoe, but it couldn't have been worse than that."

"Oh, Matt," said Maggie, trying not to laugh. "You didn't."

With a sheepish grin, he admitted, "I'm afraid I did."

"Looky!" said Holly, catching their attention. "There's Santy Claus and his reindeers."

And, thank the Lord for perfect timing, Ben really had arrived out front of the assembly hall, bells jingling loudly on the rig's traces. His reindeer in actuality were mules that belonged to a rancher in the valley. They were made up to resemble Santa's team by attaching bare tree branches to their halters. Ben himself was wrapped in a huge buffalo robe and his bald pate was covered with a long stocking cap knitted in bright red wool. He was, as always, the perfect Santa Claus as he climbed down from his sleigh—a drugstore's supply wagon decked out with holly, mistletoe, and ribbons sporting bells.

After hoisting a hundred-pound flour sack filled with goodies, Ben made his way into the building where he was immediately swarmed by children. Making a noisy fuss over him, they led him to the great Santa chair they'd decorated with shiny red ribbons and sprigs of pine. Most of the adults gathered around, as one by one, each child went to Ben to make his or her wishes known. Afterwards Santa gifted them with an orange and a fistful of hard candy.

When Holly's turn finally came, Maggie searched the room

for Rafe, but even though he'd promised to be there when his daughter asked for a daddy, he was nowhere to be found. Matt, God love him, stood on the opposite side of the big chair, encouraging Holly when it came time for her to approach Santa.

After swearing that she'd been good all year, Holly made her requests. "I'd kinda like a new doll, but not a baby doll. Can I have one with big long hair to the floor and real shoes on her feet? Oh, and since it's my birthday, too, could I have one of those little round guitars?"

"You mean a banjo?" said Ben in an unusually deep voice.

"Uh-huh, one of them and maybe a new writing pen for my mama?" Holly leaned in close, whispering so loudly even Maggie could hear her. "I got Mama some fancy writing paper for Christmas that costed eight whole pennies! Can you get her a new pen to go with it?"

"I'll see what I can do, little one. Anything else on your list? It's mighty big already."

She adjusted her glasses, then put her finger to her cheek. "I only want one thing for sure, Santy, so if I can only get one thing, will you please make sure to bring me a daddy for Christmas?"

"I'll sure try, sweetheart," he replied, ruffling her blond curls. "Since you've been so good this year, I'll try extra hard to see that you get yourself that daddy."

Thinking about Matt and how much he'd done to make sure that Holly's wish would finally come true, Maggie glanced over his way and gave him a warm smile.

"I know you'll bring me a daddy this year, Santy," said Holly, giggling as some private thought raced through her mind. "I know it for sure."

Again Maggie looked at Matt, this time with deep concern.

He shook his head as if to say that Holly couldn't possibly know what they had planned for Christmas morning. And again, she wondered where Rafe could be. Glancing around the crowd for a glimpse of his slicked-back hair, she found Gus to her right, and saw that he was noticeably upset. He approached her then and singled her out of the crowd.

"Take a walk with me?" he asked.

"Sure," Maggie said, wondering what could be troubling him so on such a festive occasion. Once they were outside and strolling up the boardwalk, he let her know what was on his mind in no uncertain terms.

"When we talked earlier in the kitchen," Gus said slowly. "If you'll recall, I was concerned about someone who calls himself the El Paso Kid stepping into Holly's life."

Maggie's stomach tightened. What had Rafe said or done now? "I remember."

"Well, now that I've gotten an eyeful at the sociable, I have to say that it isn't Holly's father that has me so worried—it's her mother."

Maggie stopped walking. And breathing. "Whatever do you mean by that?"

He turned to her, grim-faced. "I saw the way you and Weston looked at each other as you danced. The two of you weren't terribly discreet while Holly was talking to Santa, either."

"Uncle Gus!" Maggie was horrified on so many levels, she could hardly think. "I don't understand why you're saying these things."

"You're not fooling anyone, Maggie, least of all your old Uncle Gus."

In some ways, Maggie was almost relieved that her feelings were so apparent to him. Maybe now she could get the advice she so desperately needed. Maybe now she could finally understand her feelings for Matt. And her doubts about Rafe.

She lowered her voice. "Maybe it would be a good idea to have a little talk with you. Shall we go to the cafe?"

"It isn't me you need to talk to, Margaret Mary." He took her by the hand. "Come along with me on up to the church.

What you need is to get down on your knees and pray for God's forgiveness."

"Forgiveness? But Uncle Gus—"

"There's nothing you can say that I want to hear. It's the Lord who needs to hear how sorry you are for making light of the vows you made to your husband. Or have you forgotten the words of the gospel?"

That said, he fixed her with a benevolent stare and reminded her the way he knew best. "What therefore God hath joined together, let not man put asunder. That goes for woman, too."

Aglow in the aftermath of their lovemaking, Peggy snuggled deeper into the crook of Rafe's arm, unintentionally disturbing his slumber.

"Dang it all, woman," he said with a yawn. "Why did y'all let me fall asleep like that? I got to get back to that there sociable before Santy gets there."

"Aw, who cares about Santy Claus?"

"I do, for one." Rafe rolled onto his side and kissed the tip of her nose. "I ain't never seen no Santy. Have y'all?"

"No, but I'm told he don't really exist, so what's the point?"

He shrugged, then rolled away from her and sat on the edge of the bed. "I just kinda want to have a look at him, s'all. Nuthin' wrong with that, is there?"

"No, course not, Rafe." Peggy got up on her good knee, wrapped her arms around his shoulders, and rubbed her nipples against his back. "Can't you just stay with me a little longer?"

"No, I cain't. I got to get back to the party. I'm s'pposed to be there when Holly goes asking Santy to bring her wants. Why don't y'all just come along? The rest of the whole damn town is already there, near as I can figure."

Of course Peggy knew that she couldn't just up and go to the dance, and on two separate counts. For one thing, a goodly number of those townsfolk had seen the way she'd jumped that giantess. Those that hadn't seen, had mostly likely heard. By now, all of them pretty much thought she belonged in an asylum, not at a town dance. Even if she could figure a way to ignore the scorn and ridicule of those folks, there was no way to get past that damned ranger and his stinking rules.

Feeling ornery and left out, especially since none of this was her fault, Peggy saw it as her right to let fly what she thought of the town party. "Why would you want to leave me just to go spend the day with that mean Matt Weston, some big fat Santy who never bothered to come see either one of us 'fore now, and that big ole ugly woman who says she had your child."

"Hey, now, woman—I ain't never said Maggie was ugly. She's plain and big, is what she is, like a big ole camel, but she ain't ugly."

Peggy didn't much care for him defending the woman either. "A camel's got humps. How many humps does that Maggie got? One or two?"

Rafe's shoulders rose, then fell beneath her hands as he sighed with exasperation. "Now I ask you—would I waste my time on a woman who had even one hump? Would I?"

Forcing her to back away from him, Rafe slipped on his shirt and vest, then set to buttoning them. "Come on to the party, honey pie. It ain't like anyone knows y'all was a whore—do they?"

Peggy shrugged. "A couple might, I reckon."

Rafe said nothing to that, but Peggy knew by the way his body tensed that he didn't much like the idea. She hung her head, even though he was too busy dressing himself to look at her.

"I don't like parties, anyways," she said with a pout. "Are you sure you have to go back? I can think of a lot more interesting things to do right here in this room."

She reached for him, but Rafe shrugged her off.

"I got to be there when Holly asks Santy will he set me under her tree on Christmas morning, and that's that."

She was not about to lose her man to a child. Again Peggy threw her arms around him. "Please, Rafe, forget all that and let's run off, now, today, just you and me. We could go some-wheres else, a new place like maybe Laredo, and make our own babies. What do you say, lover?"

He scooted around on the edge of the mattress until he faced her. With a surprising tenderness, Rafe touched her cheek as he said, "I wish I could run off with y'all, sugar face. You and me, we pretty much get along like two pups in a basket."

"Yes, Rafe, we surely do." Her heart soared with sudden hope. "We belong together, you and me."

"True as that might be, I cain't go off with y'all." Again he touched her cheek. "I ain't done much right in my life, Peggy, but now I got another chance to make up for all that."

"You done lots right, Rafe. You ain't never done me wrong, that I know of anyways."

A sudden light shone in his eyes, a sparkle that almost looked like a coat of tears. Next thing she knew he'd be bawling like a baby, and over what? A child. His child. That and a sudden sense of worth that she could never provide for him. Peggy knew then that she'd lost him for good.

"I reckon," he went on to say, ignorant of the fact that she was about to fall apart crying. "That this is my last chance to do something I kin be proud of. That's why I got to be with Maggie from now on, and that's my final last say on the subject."

Peggy sat back on her one good leg, unable and unwilling to stanch the sudden torrent of tears. Trying not to blubber all over Rafe, she said, "Then I guess I don't have no choice but to leave town with Captain Weston, come Sunday."

"Weston?" Rafe hopped off the bed, naked from his shirttail down. "Yur running off with the captain? When did all a' this come about?"

"Couple days ago. He just up and set down the rules, told me I was riding out of town with him on Christmas Day, and that was that. I guess he was right."

"Don't bet yur ass on it, sugar."

"What do you mean by that, honey pie?"

But he didn't answer her. Instead, Rafe marched over and snatched his fancy trousers off the dresser, then viciously drove his skinny legs into them. After jamming the tails of his no-longer fresh-pressed shirt into the waistband, he buckled his belt and slammed his feet into his boots, neglecting to don his socks.

Then he stomped over to the door and turned to her to say, "We'll just see who's making the rules around here from now on, woman. Oh, yes indeedy, we will."

Then he took off down the hallway without so much as a goodbye kiss.

Twenty-one

Matt had just polished off a slice of Maggie's mincemeat pie and was thinking of helping himself to another when Hattie tottered up to him. The mass of graying ringlets she'd pinned high to the back of her head were swaying like cattails in the wind, even after she stopped.

"You're such a nice tall man, Captain Weston." She looked up at him, all fluttering lashes and coquettish gestures. "May I trouble you to look around the room for my Gus? I've searched the assembly hall as best I can for him, but I'm just too short to see over anything but the head of a very small child."

"Being taller wouldn't help you at the moment, Mrs. Townes. I just saw Gus and Maggie head on out the door. Maybe they went back to the cafe to get some more food for the party."

She laughed in that odd little high-pitched cackle of hers. "I guess that would explain why I can't find Maggie either."

She got a blank look in her eyes then, usually the precursor to some outlandish remark. Next, Matt figured, she would be talking about Maggie's childhood or even drag him into her strange thoughts. God forbid, she might even bring up something like that glob of dough she'd seen stuck to his ass in Maggie's kitchen. Because he didn't want to be included in Hattie's next flight of fancy, Matt looked around for a distraction.

Too late for Matt to escape. She grabbed hold of his elbow

and went on with her prattle. "Don't you think our sweet Maggie looks particularly lovely today?" she said dreamily.

Lovely didn't do her justice, thought Matt. He'd never forget how she looked today, like an angel come to life in a flowing white gown with lots of slick satin ribbons. She'd fashioned a row of curls across her forehead, but pulled the rest of her hair back and tied it at the nape of her neck with a big red bow, leaving it to hang down the center of her back in a river of curlicues. Just the way he liked it. All afternoon Matt had been thinking about how much he wanted to tear that bow away and bury himself in Maggie's hair, to fill his senses with her fragrance, with orange blossoms and currants, and to have the right to stay there, if he wanted to, for the rest of his life.

"Come now, Captain Weston," said Hattie, lightly tapping his chest with her fan. "Don't try to pretend that you haven't noticed how nice Maggie looks today. I've seen the way you look at my niece."

Matt felt his face grow warm with embarrassment. "Of course, I've noticed her, Mrs. Townes. Maggie is a very beautiful woman."

"And she's frisky, too," said Hattie under her breath. "Don't think I didn't see that biscuit dough stuck to your back pocket—how do you suppose Maggie's hand print got there, too?"

By now Matt's face felt as if he'd stuck it in one of Gus's vats of boiling oil. "Mrs. Townes, I'm sure you thought you saw something on my pocket, but, I assure you that Maggie's hand print couldn't possibly have been there, too."

"I saw what I saw, Captain Weston. I didn't know Maggie could be so frisky." She giggled, then sighed. "Next you ought to try catching her on candy-making day—oh, wait. Maggie doesn't make candy. Maybe on cookie day. That would be fun."

Frantic for a distraction by then, anything at all, Matt took a wild glance around the room. Rafe Hollister, of all people, supplied the needed relief.

"Hey, Weston! I'm a-looking for y'all."

"Excuse me, ma'am," said Matt, planning to meet him half-way. "I'd better go see what he wants."

"Nonsense." Hattie clung even tighter to his elbow. "The heathen can just come to you, shouting that way. Tsk, tsk."

When Rafe reached them, he offered Hattie a sloppy greeting. "How do y'all do, ma'am." Rafe nodded slightly, but did not remove his hat. "Me and the captain here got some business to take care of, so if'n y'all don't mind, you might as well mosey on over where the rest of the women are flapping their jaws."

"But I do mind." Hattie took her fan and rapped him sharply across the back of his hand. "Kindly remove your hat, sir."

The color draining out of his face, Rafe did as he was told.

"That's better, young man. You've interrupted the very nice chat the captain and I were having about my niece." She turned to Matt to ask, "Has this insolent fellow met my Maggie?"

"Yes, ma'am, I have," said Rafe, saving Matt the trouble. "I guess y'all done forgot that I ate Thanksgiving supper with yur whole dang family. Me and Maggie's broke some bread a time or two since then, too. Don't y'all remember me?"

"Oh, yes, of course—now I recall. You're the El Paso Kid. Captain Weston and I were just talking about how lovely Maggie looks today. She and the captain are smitten with one another. Don't you think they would make a handsome couple?"

His face as white as his shirt now, Rafe's mouth fell open.

Matt scrambled with an excuse. "That's some pretty silly talk, Mrs. Townes. Have you forgotten that Maggie is a married woman?"

"I'm very aware of that, Captain Weston, and it really is a shame. You'd be free to ask for her hand if she hadn't run off as a sweet young girl and married that worthless Hollister fellow."

Rafe's color came back in a rush. "Now just a dang minute!"

"I'll handle this, Kid," said Matt, doing all he could to stop the conversation before it got even more out of control. Taking Hattie's hand from the crook of his elbow, he said, "Have you been nipping in the wassail bowl, Mrs. Townes? You're saying some awfully strange things."

She giggled, then opened her fan and covered the lower half of her face. "I do not indulge in the devil's brew, Captain Weston, but even if I did, I'd still know young love when I see it. How awful that Maggie isn't free to accept your attentions."

"Just a goddang minute here!" Rafe stomped his boots against the floor to make sure he got everyone's attention. He did.

Hattie's fan snapped shut and again she brought it down on Rafe, this time more sharply and right across his collarbone. He winced as she said, "I will not tolerate such language in my presence, sir. Now apologize."

His face was purple with rage, but again Rafe had enough sense to do as he was told. "Sorry for letting my tongue go on like that in a lady's presence, ma'am. This here uppity ranger has got my whole head in such an uproar, I cain't hardly think straight no more."

Now of all times, Hattie's flighty mind remained on the subject. Even worse, her memory returned.

"Is that true, Captain Weston?" she said, pointing her fan at him. "I understood that this man works with you, or is at the least, in your employ. Christmas is hardly the season to find fault with your peers, now is it?"

Peers? Now Rafe was to be thought of as his equal? Barely able to speak he was so angry, Matt said, "No ma'am, but I hardly think—"

She rapped Matt with her damn fan this time, catching him across the knuckles. "Enough excuses. Apologize to the man."

Thinking this was way above the call of duty, Matt gritted his teeth and said to Rafe, "Pardon me if I got your head in an uproar. I had no idea you were capable of such a variety of thoughts."

"Yeah, well," grumbled Rafe. "I am, and I come here to share a few of them with y'all. Maybe we'd best step outside so's I kin let y'all know exactly what I'm a-thinking."

"Outside, yes," said Hattie. "What a good idea. Fresh air for everyone. Did you know that my Gus has always wanted to go ballooning, up in all that air? Why, I'm terrified of standing on a chair and looking at the floor, let alone gazing down on Prescott Valley." She shuddered, then gave Matt a blank look. "Where do you suppose Gus got off to?"

"The cafe, ma'am. Why don't I go round him up for you?"

"Why thank you, Captain Weston. I would appreciate that very much."

"You're very welcome." Turning to Rafe, Matt grabbed hold of his arm. He was not taking any more chances. "Why don't you come with me? We can discuss that problem of yours on the way."

"Dang tootin', we will." He turned to Hattie. "Afternoon, ma'am." Then stuck his hat back on his head.

They hadn't gotten five feet out the door before Rafe lit into Matt. "Ain't it bad enough yur trying to take my Peggy away from me, do ya have to go after Maggie, too? I thought y'all was a decent sort!"

"Shut up, Rafe," he said, never slowing his stride. "Can't you wait until we get to the cabin before shooting off your mouth and showing the whole damn town that you don't have a brain?"

"I got a brain and I got eyes and ears, too. That's how I come to know what yur up to with my Peggy."

"Peggy?" Matt finally turned to look at the man. "What the hell are you talking about?"

"She done told me that yur planning to take her off with y'all on Christmas Day. Well I'm here to tell anyone who'll listen that she ain't going."

Christ, thought Matt. Couldn't anyone get anything straight? "We'll discuss Peggy back at the cabin if you just have to," he said irritably. "But no matter what you say, I guarantee you and your skewed eyeballs that she will be leaving with me on Sunday."

"The hell she will."

Rafe then made one of the boldest, if the dumbest move any man had ever made with Matt. He reached out, grabbed hold of his upper arm, then reared back and punched him in the mouth.

Momentarily stunned—for a skinny fella, Rafe packed one hell of a wallop—Matt just stood there and let the blood run over his bottom lip and onto his new shirt. As his temper heated up, he looked around to make sure they weren't being observed. Satisfied that he could kill the man if he wanted to with no one the wiser—and Matt sorely wanted to do just that—he wrestled both of Rafe's arms behind his back and began to drive him up the street toward the cabin, wheelbarrow-style.

"Turn me loose," Rafe insisted. "Git yur hands off'n me, ya no-good, lying, woman-stealing bastard."

"Shut up, Rafe," Matt replied calmly. "I'll be happy to discuss this in great *detail* when we get back to the cabin, but not before."

"That ain't good enough." He dug in his heels, making it difficult for Matt to push him any further. "I ain't gonna follow no more of yur rules and I ain't gonna shut up. How do y'all like them apples?"

Matt gave himself a moment to calm down and forget how much he wanted to end this fool's life, then made what he hoped was a rational decision. But first he looked around again to make sure they still couldn't be observed. The streets were deserted.

Turning back to Rafe with a big grin, split lip and all, Matt said, "I like those apples about as much as you're going to like these knuckles."

Then he landed a solid punch on Hollister's chin, a blow that folded Rafe over Matt's arm as if he were a load of laundry fresh from the line.

Once they were back at the cabin, it took Rafe another ten minutes to come around. After the fool woke up and found himself lying on his own bunk, in a matter of seconds he was spoiling for a fight again.

"Put em up," Rafe said, crawling off the mattress and staggering toward Matt. "No man messes with my woman and gits away with it."

"I'm not going to fight you, Rafe." Matt kept one step out of Hollister's reach, occasionally ducking one of his wild punches. "Exactly which woman are you talking about? It would seem that you have several."

"Peggy, for starters. I ain't gonna stand here and let the likes of y'all take her away from me."

Matt resisted the urge to laugh. "In that case I have a few starters for you, Rafe—you're less than a week away from being a married man, remember? How is it you're even seeing Peggy, much less concerned about who she takes up with from here on out?"

That gave him pause. Rafe quit stalking Matt long enough to say, "Well, I had to let her down easy, didn't I, maybe say goodbye? 'Sides, I don't see why she has to leave town, especially with the likes of y'all."

"Oh, she's leaving, Rafe, I guarantee it. Maybe that way she can carve out a new life for herself somewhere else while you're busy fitting in with your little family here in Prescott. Just to make sure there are no misunderstandings, rest assured that Peggy's new life will not include me. I'm merely her escort to wherever she wants to go."

"Humph," was the best Rafe could make by way of comment. Pacing now more than stalking, he hurled the accusation Matt had been dreading. "Even if that's true—and I ain't saying that I believe it—what about the goings on betwixt y'all and Maggie? I seen the way yur always looking sweet at her, and so has everyone else, including her very own aunt. Y'all been trying to court Maggie behind my back?"

There wasn't but one way to answer a question like that. With another question. "Now why would I do a damn fool thing like that?"

That might have been the end of it if Rafe hadn't come up with one of his more intelligent thoughts. He said, "Why does a man do anything when it comes to women?"

"Hell, I don't know. Why don't you tell me."

Gloating, Rafe said, "There ain't but one thing gets a man all crazy in the head over a woman. Take a look down inside yur drawers, Weston. What do y'all think? Got something in there causing a speck of trouble when my Maggie comes around?"

"Shut up, Rafe, or I swear to God, I'll shut your mouth permanently."

"That's it, ain't it?" he accused, and rightly so. "Y'all want Maggie for yurself."

"I'm warning you for the last time," Matt said, threats his only possible line of defense. "I don't want to have to make you any uglier than you already are, Rafe, but I will if you don't shut up now."

"Yeah, well, I don't want y'all to stand up fur me at my wedding, neither!"

"I said I wouldn't do it, remember?"

"I know, I know. I just want it known that I don't even *want* y'all to stand up for me now. I'm right sorry I ever asked."

Again Hollister began to stalk Matt, waving his fists. "Now

put em up, cause I mean to give y'all the walloping of yur life."

* * *

During Christmas week, Maggie's bedtime stories for Holly were always centered in some manner on yuletide and its true meaning. With Christmas Eve just three days away, tonight she was telling the story of the three wise men.

"Melchior, King of Arabia, brought a casket of gold; Caspar, King of Tarsus, brought myrrh; and Balthasar, King of Ethiopia, brought frankincense. Do you know why those gifts came to mean so much?"

Holly rubbed her tired eyes. "Because they costed lots of money?"

"Cost, darling, and no, that was not the reason."

Maggie stroked her daughter's brow, thinking how this little scrap of a child outweighed all the king's treasures combined.

"Why were they special, Mama?" asked Holly, bringing her back to the story.

"Because each gift was a special symbol of what Jesus was to become. Gold signifies a king; frankincense, a high priest; and myrrh designates a great healer." She went on to explain what each of those words meant, then said, "The wise men didn't appear to the Christ child until January 6th, the twelfth night. Do you remember what else that special time is sometimes called?"

Holly didn't struggle as she usually did with the word *Epiphany*. In fact, she said nothing at all.

Maggie glanced down and saw that she was sound asleep, her little head filled with the innocent dreams that could only belong to a young child. Suddenly feeling quite the opposite of her daughter—very old and very wicked—she kissed Holly's soft little forehead, then blew out the candle and tiptoed out of her room.

Maggie had done little but pray for divine guidance and forgiveness since the day of the social, when Gus had dragged her to church and left her there to make her peace with the Lord. Peace, it seemed, would be slow in coming; forgiveness, she suspected, impossible as long as she refused to acknowledge the sin in her feelings for Matt. Yet how could she look at their stolen moments together as anything but a gift? Especially now that he no longer stopped by to see her. He didn't even come to the cafe for coffee anymore.

In fact, her only source of information these days where Matt was concerned, was Holly, of all people. True to his word, he continued to visit her at Hattie's ranch each day, helping her with the turkeys and sometimes staying a while after that to enjoy a few cookies and milk and an occasional game of old maid. Matt was certainly doing the job he'd been paid to do, and more, but no longer did he seek Maggie's company. And, though it filled her with something that went beyond sadness, she supposed it was just as well that he didn't. Seeing him again would only prolong the agony of the inevitable.

Her mood sour, Maggie settled into her chair by the window and reached for yesterday's issue of the *Arizona Miner*. So far John Marion hadn't printed a word about the disgrace Maggie had made of herself by scuffling with that tart in the mud. This, despite the fact that by now, Flora had surely passed on the news. After a short prayer in which she begged God to let her good fortune continue, Maggie thought she heard a very familiar noise—something that sounded a lot like birds pecking at her window. Both memories and hope flooding her, she blew out the candle, leaped up from her chair, and peeked down through the wooden turkey feathers to the street below.

As she hoped, Matt was there, looking as if he were simply out for a casual evening stroll. As he walked by the restaurant, however, he fired one pebble after another at the carved turkey, a hunter intent on bagging the huge bird for his yuletide feast.

Dropping to her knees, Maggie fumbled with the window, but in her excitement it took a few minutes before she finally got it pushed up high enough for Matt to hear her.

"Come to the back door," she shouted in a whisper. "I'll be right down."

After he lowered the brim of his hat, acknowledging her, Matt continued on by the restaurant and disappeared into the dark shadows of the night. Maggie dallied upstairs just long enough to make sure that Holly was still sound asleep with her door closed tight. Then she donned a dressing gown over her chemise and flew down the stairs to the kitchen.

After letting Matt inside the room, she pushed the door shut behind him and breathlessly said, "I thought I'd never see you again, not like this anyway—alone."

"I meant to stay away, swore to myself that I would." He reached for her in the darkness and pulled her into his arms. "I just couldn't go without saying goodbye in my own way, privately. Christmas morning I won't even have the right to look at you, much less put my hands on you."

Without giving Maggie a chance to agree or even tell him that she thought the idea was perfectly wonderful, Matt took her mouth with his, hard at first, then more gingerly, wincing as he pulled away.

"What is it?" she asked, knowing instinctively that he'd been injured.

"Nothing. Get back over here. I need to kiss you again."

But by then Maggie had already ducked out of his reach and was busy lighting the candle in the wall sconce near the back door. When she faced him again, she could easily see that he had a bruised eye and that his bottom lip had recently been split.

"What happened to you?" she asked, brushing a gentle fingertip over his injuries.

"I ran into a door in the dark. I'm fine."

"Of course you did, and of course you are," she said sarcastically, knowing that he was lying. He'd been in a fight, but suddenly, neither that nor the fact that he'd lied about it, mattered. All Maggie cared about now was Matt—and somehow, she intended to let him know it.

"You're not fine," she whispered. "And neither am I."

"That's why I had to come tonight." He took her face between the palms of his hands. "Not for me, but for you. I have to know that you'll be all right, Maggie, that . . . that you'll be reasonably happy."

"Oh, God," she said in a strangled whisper. "How can you ask me to answer something like that?"

"Because I have to know—I have to, don't you understand?"

Falling into his arms again, Maggie breathed deeply, filling her nostrils, her lungs, every part of her with his scent. Then she told him what he wanted to hear. "I'll be all right. I'm always all right, but oh, how I wish that things could be different for us, that somehow we could—"

"Shush." Matt slid his fingers over her mouth, stilling her. "There's no sense even thinking that way tonight, not when we have so little time together."

"But what if we—"

"There are no what if's for us, Maggie. We both know that I can't give you anything close to what you already have here in Prescott."

"What? This apartment and the restaurant?"

Matt laughed, but the sound was bitter, filled with irony. "No, sweetheart. I'm talking about your family. You'd wind up hating me eventually if I forced you to choose between me and Gus and Hattie, especially after the way they took you in. And that doesn't even take Holly's happiness or her Christmas wish into account."

Matt was right, painfully so. They were doomed and Maggie knew it, but still she couldn't let her hopes die so easily. "I know what you're saying, I do, but there must be a way—there must be."

Shaking his head slowly, Matt closed his eyes for a moment. Then he said, "There's something I want you to know. One of the reasons I came by is to tell you that I . . ."

He paused, looking troubled, then began again. "I want to make sure that you know how much . . ."

Again he paused, sighing deeply this time. "I'm not doing a very good job of this. I just want you to know that you'll always have a very special place in my heart."

It was as close as any man had ever come to telling Maggie that he loved her—one that meant it anyway. Coming from Matt, the knowledge nearly broke her heart. She thought of responding in kind, but a sudden sob tore out of her throat instead, ripping thoughts and words right out of her mouth. She began kissing him again instead, telling him how much she loved him in the only way that she could.

Somewhere in the back of his mind, Matt supposed he should have stopped Maggie when she came to him, but he couldn't make himself do it. If her kisses were all he'd have to remember her by, then Matt intended to collect enough of them this night to see him through eternity. Reaching behind her, he pulled the ribbon from her hair to set it free, then wound his fists through it, tying her to him for these few moments the way he wished he could bind her to him for the rest of her life.

Her responses were all he could have hoped for and more as Maggie's kisses became bolder, inflaming him beyond anything he'd planned when he impulsively came by the cafe tonight. Matt hadn't meant to push himself or her this far, at least not consciously, but the next thing he knew, his hands were beneath the folds of Maggie's dressing gown and he was caressing her with only the thin cotton of her shift between him and her naked body. A sense of urgency and animal passion drove him now, igniting such a need in Matt, he knew that nothing so intangible as right or wrong could stop him from having her this one last time.

Holding her just far enough away to unbutton the bodice of her chemise, Matt slid one hand into the resulting gap and began to caress Maggie's breasts.

Surprising him, she pulled out of his arms. "Not here. Not so close to the door."

"Where then?" Matt asked, impatient to have her back in his arms.

She looked around, then took him by the hand and led him across the kitchen floor to a deep alcove beneath the stairs leading up to her apartment. After she guided him to the corner where the back walls met, Matt slipped off her robe, then reached for the hem of Maggie's shift and began to raise the gown over her head.

Again surprising him, she tore the material out of his grasp. "No, wait," she whispered, gasping for breath. "Let me go blow out the light first."

"I'm not letting go of you for any reason tonight." Matt held her in place, making damn good and sure that she didn't escape him again. "Unless you're expecting some fool to stop by and bake a load of bread, who's going to see us, anyway? Let it burn."

"I don't think anyone is going to disturb us," Maggie said with a hollow laugh. "I'd just feel better if the candle was out."

"I wouldn't. Without the light, I can't see you, Maggie." He caressed her cheek. "Tonight I intend to find every little mole and dimple on your body, and learn what each inch of you looks like. It's a memory I'm going to have to keep for a long, long time."

"Oh, Matt please, try to understand." She twisted her face out of his hands and averted her gaze. "I—I can't let you do that."

"And why not?"

"Because, well, it's just that I'm so, you know . . . so darn big."

"Big?"

It didn't make sense to Matt, not at first. Understanding only one thing, that he had to lavish himself with a look at the woman he loved, he took hold of Maggie's gown at the opening, then ripped it clean through to the hem in one swift movement. Even though the remnants of a fire still burned in the big cook stove, the night chill must have reached her naked skin. She trembled slightly, then tried to cover herself with her dressing gown.

"I'm begging you," she whispered in a small, small voice. "Please don't look at me."

Understanding now, but not understanding at all, Matt caught her by the wrists and pinned her against the wall. "You're afraid to have me see you naked? Is that what's wrong?"

Still looking away, she nodded. "I'm not exactly the ideal woman."

Matt hooted a laugh—he couldn't help himself, even though he knew that he had to be quiet for Holly's sake.

Dramatically lowering his voice, he whispered, "You really don't know how beautiful you are, do you?"

"Beautiful?" She laughed feebly. "Me? You must be blind. I'm big and ungainly."

Done with trying to convince her in words, Matt backed away from Maggie just far enough to get another eyeful of her charms. Then he reached out and cupped both of her breasts in his hands, and held them a moment, admiring their dusky peaks as he softly said, "Big? Yes, I would say they are. Ungainly? Maybe to you, sweetheart, but they sure as hell don't get in my way."

Maggie snickered under her breath. "I wasn't talking about . . . that."

"Then I don't see the problem." Matt paused to look her over again. "Not with you anyway. The trouble is, looking at you gives me a very big problem."

Making sure she understood, Matt unbuckled his belt and freed himself from his trousers. After he took Maggie back into his arms, he lifted her up on her tiptoes and slid between her thighs.

Rocking against the curls at her groin, he asked, "Still think you're too big for me, sweetheart?"

She gasped, then moaned with pleasure. "I don't know."

"Then let's find out," Matt suggested, afraid if they didn't couple soon, he'd embarrass himself and disappoint them both.

"Yes," she whispered throatily. "Oh, yes."

Releasing her just long enough to rid himself of his boots and trousers, again Matt raised Maggie to her tiptoes, and this time when he went to her, she was ready and more than eager to receive him—hot, but incredibly tight. He had to go easy at first, slowly inching and stretching his way inside her until at last they were as close as a man and woman could get. It was hard for Matt to believe that she'd ever been with anyone before, let alone given birth to a child. She had such an innocence about her, such a tentative way of touching and kissing him that he could easily have believed that he was the first. The thought tortured Matt as much as it pleased him, saddened him even as it aroused him beyond anything he'd ever known.

Maggie threw back her head as his thrusts deepened and quickened, then gasped and began to call out his name. When she coiled her fingers in his hair and pulled him tight against her bosom, Matt nearly shot over the edge. He clung to what was left of his control for as long as he could, driving Maggie to peak after shuddering peak of ecstasy until at last, he could no longer ignore the demands of his own body. When sweet release finally came, it thundered down on him in a rush as molten as any forger's iron, as lethal and consuming as a prairie fire.

Matt's knees buckled beneath him, especially the left, and he nearly collapsed altogether. Grasping to balance himself, he held tight to a corner beam with one hand, and kept a firm grip on Maggie's backside with the other. Later, when his heartbeat had stilled and his breathing slowed down enough for him to speak, he had to force himself to break their intimate embrace. He was so happy at that moment, so completely fulfilled, he actually thought he might break down and cry if he didn't do something to change the mood. Him—*cry*.

His knees still trembling from their exertions, Matt smiled and said, "Now what's all this about you being too big?"

She laughed easily, with no hint of her former embarrassment. "I'm so glad you got that straightened out for me."

"So am I." He winked, making sure she caught the unintended innuendo in her words, then lifted the torn edges of her chemise and said, "Are you planning to put this thing back together again?"

Maggie glanced down at the ruins of her chemise. "I suppose I at least ought to try. I only have one other nightgown."

"That'll have to be enough."

Suddenly Matt was deadly serious and he wanted to make sure that Maggie knew it. "If you put a needle to this one, you might as well stick it through my heart while you're at it. Promise me you won't mend it."

She looked up at him with a frown. "Why shouldn't I?"

"Because," he said, admitting to her what he couldn't even bear to think about. "I can't stand the idea of anyone else so much as seeing you in this, let alone touching you. Promise?"

"Oh, my God—Matt." A little sob cut off part of his name. "How can we possibly go on pretending none of this ever happened?"

"Because we have to," he said, steeling his heart against the emotions warring within. "Now promise."

"Oh, Matt, of course. I promise."

"Then you won't mind if part of your gown is missing?" At her puzzled expression, Matt took one of the edges between his hands and tore off a kerchief-sized square. As he stuffed the material into his shirt pocket, he said, "Now I'll always have a part of you with me—a small part since you set so much store on size."

Tears welled up in her eyes, a warning sign that Matt couldn't ignore, no matter how much he wanted to. If he didn't go now, next thing he knew they'd be blubbering all over each other, him crying right along with her, both of them saying things that should never be said, dreaming things better left undreamt.

After quickly dressing himself, he took Maggie back into his arms. "One other thing before I go."

She tried to interrupt him, but he hushed her with a well-placed finger. "The time for talking is done, except for this one little thing. Always remember how beautiful you are, especially to me, how utterly perfect."

Matt immediately took Maggie into his arms after that, preventing her denial or anything else she might have to say on the subject.

Then he kissed her as fiercely as he dared, turned and walked out the door.

Twenty-two

When Maggie first went to see Reverend Wilson about performing a marriage ceremony between her and Rafe, she had a hard time convincing him that what she was about to reveal had to remain a secret, even from the minister's wife, Clementine. After giving his word, one hand pressed firmly against the Bible, the preacher grudgingly agreed to unite them. He also recognized that, given the circumstances, he alone would suffice nicely as both witness and preacher.

Not that Reverend Wilson knew precisely all there was to know about Maggie's past. She didn't come right out and lie to the man—she couldn't have—but she did make sure that he left their meeting under the impression that she and Rafe were renewing their union because they'd been apart for so long, not getting married for the first time.

Maggie wasn't particularly proud of the fact that she'd misled the religious leader, but then after all—he was a man of God who also wore a wedding ring. Sooner or later, the husband side of Reverend Wilson would be tempted to let slip the details of Maggie's sordid past, at least to his wife. That would never do. In all of Yavapai County, only Clementine Wilson had a looser tongue than Hattie Townes.

Maggie supposed his readiness to agree to such a clandestine affair should have lifted her spirits, but she couldn't even get excited about that.

Even though it was Christmas Eve and she looked forward to Holly's excitement in the morning, she'd been dragging both mentally and physically since Matt left the cafe three nights ago. No matter how hard she tried to cheer herself up, Maggie couldn't seem to get into a holiday mood. All she could think about was Matt and the fact that tomorrow would be the last time she'd ever see him.

Burdened down with those thoughts along with a fresh pork roast, a small wheel of cheese, and a nice fat goose for Christmas dinner, she stepped out of Smith's meat market and ran straight into the Reverend Wilson. He groaned and clutched his chest. Maggie staggered backwards and nearly dropped her groceries.

"Good gracious," she said, shifting her bundles to keep them from falling. "Please excuse my clumsiness, Reverend. I hope I didn't hurt you."

He dusted himself off looking none the worse, then snared her in his usual squinty-eyed gaze. "Afternoon, Mrs. Hollister. You gave me a bit of a jolt, but I'm just fine. Too much on your mind these days to watch where you're going?"

He uttered a secretive laugh and Maggie laughed along with him, knowing exactly what the preacher meant and that he would expect her to see the humor in the situation.

"I guess I do have my head in the clouds," she said truthfully. "I hope your plans for this evening are still coming along as scheduled. Any delays or problems I should know about?"

Keeping true to his word, the reverend perused the boardwalk on either side of them before saying anything more in order to make sure they couldn't be overheard.

"The good Lord willing," he said quietly. "I see nothing to prevent me from arriving at the cafe at precisely ten o'clock, as planned."

"That's lovely, Reverend Wilson. I'll see you then."

He tipped his hat and she nodded in return. Then Maggie continued on to the cafe, where Gus met her at the front door.

"There, there," he said, reaching for the roast. "Let me help you with that."

After he relieved her of all but one package, Gus fell into a coughing fit and headed for the kitchen. Maggie was right on his heels.

"That's it, Uncle Gus. It sounds like you're about ten minutes from pneumonia."

She marched up behind him and stripped him of his apron. He didn't even put up a feeble protest.

Turning him back toward the door, she said, "This cafe is officially closed until Monday. You go home now and curl up in front of a warm fire. I'll finish carving the ham, and Holly and I will bring it with us when we come for supper tonight."

For a moment she thought he might put up an argument, but then he sighed and gave in. "You win, Maggie girl. Guess I'd better rest up for tomorrow."

"Good idea, Uncle Gus. As you know, tomorrow is going to be an awfully special Christmas. You and Hattie are going to have to be at my apartment by dawn if you don't want to miss Holly's face when she sees what Santa has left for her. Maybe you ought to go straight to bed now."

He didn't of course, but later, after supper was finished, Gus trudged off to bed, instead of giving out peppermint sticks and the other small gifts he'd purchased, a Christmas Eve tradition he decided to save for the following day when he felt better.

Holly was so excited by all the yuletide festivities she could hardly stand up by the time they came home from Gus and Hattie's. She was in bed and fast asleep by eight o'clock, which gave Maggie two whole hours to prepare for her upcoming wedding. And to think about what her life would be like without Matt Weston around to fill her, both body and soul.

After settling on her white Christmas dress with all the red bows as a bridal gown, Maggie made her way downstairs into the restaurant and closed the window shades against the eyes of anyone who might be passing by. Then she went to one of the tables in the back and lit a single candle to let Rafe and the reverend know that she was there and waiting. When Rafe showed up at the door a little past nine, she'd been sitting at that table, staring into the flame for nearly an hour. And all she'd been able to think about during that time was Matt.

The knock was tentative, almost too light for Maggie to hear it, and for a wild moment, she thought of ignoring the sound. Then she thought of Holly upstairs asleep in her bed, of wishes and Christmas morning, and slowly Maggie got out of the chair and made her way to the door.

"Hello, Rafe," she said as he crossed the threshold.

"Evening, Maggie."

He went directly to a table near the window and dropped his ratty valise onto her clean tablecloth. As polished and well-groomed as she'd ever seen him, he then removed his hat and hung it on the rack before turning to her.

Rafe smiled, looking a little younger, the way he had so many years ago. It made Maggie want to try harder, to see him in a more romantic way. She hadn't, after all, given him much of a chance to woo her. The smile broadened and he licked his lips, readying himself for her. Maggie mentally prepared herself to open her arms to Rafe, if not her heart.

Then he said, "Y'all got anything stronger than coffee round here? I could use me a good stiff drink."

Maggie had to bite her lip to keep her grin from running wild on her, and she somehow managed to say, "Coming right up," without laughing in Rafe's face.

In the kitchen, though, it was another matter. Maggie chuckled the entire time it took her to gather the bottle of cooking brandy and two glasses—one for him, and one for her. When she returned to the dining room, she noticed that Rafe had already made himself at home at the back table. He sat in one chair. The lower half of his legs and his boots sat in the other.

Borrowing a chair from another table, Maggie sat down across from him and poured the liqueurs. "Hope this is what you had in mind," she said. "I don't keep spirits around except for cooking."

Rafe snatched up one of the glasses and downed the drink in one gulp. After making a face, he said, "It'll do, woman."

Maggie, who didn't imbibe, and had only tasted a bit of alcohol on her fingertip once, took a tentative sip of hers. She shuddered, surprised by the decided kick it packed, then took another sip. Since she was going to marry Rafe Hollister tonight, romantic devil that he was, she figured it wouldn't hurt to be at least a little tipsy.

"When's that there preacher fella coming?" asked Rafe as he helped himself to another glass of brandy.

"Reverend Wilson ought to be here in about thirty minutes or so. Are you nervous?"

He shrugged then tossed back the shot of brandy. "I expect I might be just a touch on the jumpy side. What about y'all?"

She nodded. "Me too. It isn't every day I just up and get married."

"Me neither, woman." Rafe rolled his eyes, then poured more brandy into his glass. "And 'fore I go getting myself all roped and tied, I think I have a right to know what's going on betwixt y'all and that there ranger."

Maggie nearly fell off of her chair in shock. She knew Matt would never admit their indiscretions or even hint that anything had happened between them. With another taste of brandy for courage, she looked him square in the eye and called his bluff.

"Why, Rafe, whatever are you suggesting? That I'm some sort of loose woman?"

"I ain't saying y'all did nothing wrong. I just cain't stand the way that man is always gawking at yur hair and such, like he's gone and staked a claim on y'all."

She laughed. "Oh, Rafe. You must be mistaken. Even if Captain Weston does look at me from time to time, I'm sure he doesn't mean anything by it."

"He'd best not." With another swallow of brandy, he added, "Least ways he ought not bother y'all anymore. A few days ago I made dang sure he wouldn't, too."

Terrified that Matt had already left town, or worse, she said, "What did you do to him?"

He slipped his thumbs under his suspenders and puffed out his chest. "I told him I'd kill him if'n he ever looked cross-eyed at my woman again. Then I commenced to beating the tar right out of him. That'll teach him to think twice before he messes with any woman who belongs to the El Paso Kid."

Maggie might have been concerned, if not for two things; for one, she had no doubt that Matt could fend off any kind of attack Rafe might mount—if he wanted to. She also knew, more out of instinct than anything, that Rafe had been the cause of Matt's black eye and split lip. And she knew without a doubt that Matt had actually allowed the assault on his person—and even thought she knew why.

Trying hard not to let a sudden burst of hatred for Rafe show in her eyes or her voice, she looked across the table at her husband-to-be and said, "I wouldn't worry about Matt Weston. I understand he's leaving town tomorrow for good."

Maggie assumed that news would calm the man down, but instead, Rafe seemed even more agitated. He snarled as he said, "I know all that, woman. Doncha think I know all that?"

Again he reached for the bottle, and Maggie had a fleeting thought of wrestling it away from him, but then a loud knock sounded at the door, freezing them both in mid-movement.

"That the preacher?" asked Rafe in a whisper.

"I think so," she whispered back. "Put the bottle and glasses in the kitchen, would you please? I think we've both had enough brandy."

Assuming he'd do as she asked, Maggie smoothed her hair, then went to let the preacher in. "Good evening, Reverend Wilson," she said, quickly closing the door behind him. "Pleasant enough night for so late in December, isn't it?"

"Yes, Maggie." He removed his hat and coat, then straightened his sleeves. As she escorted him to the back of the room, he added, "It's a very pleasant Christmas Eve indeed. Where's your young man?"

About that time the door to the kitchen crashed open and out swaggered Rafe. He'd removed the glasses and the bottle, as she'd requested, but Maggie had an idea that he'd also removed the brandy from its container.

"Evening, preacher man. I'm Maggie's fella, Rafe Hollister. Most folks know me as the El Paso Kid."

The reverend looked at Maggie with worried eyes.

"Rafe is a former Texas Ranger," she said by way of explanation. "Apparently his last assignment lasted for nearly seven years."

"That's right, Preacher," said Rafe, missing the sarcasm in her tone. "Rangering does tend to keep a man away from home, but us rangers got to do our sworn duty, and all. The womenfolk just got to learn there's going to be spells when they got to get along without us lawmen. Wouldn't y'all agree?"

"Ah, well . . ." Reverend Wilson cleared his throat. "I suppose we'd better proceed. I have much to do in preparation for tomorrow's services."

With that he reached into his jacket pocket and withdrew a small Bible with some papers in it.

"Maggie," he said. "If you'll just stand to my right and direct Mr. Hollister to stand to the left, we can proceed."

As Maggie arranged herself and Rafe, she stole a couple of glimpses at him, searching for something in the man's eyes that might help to remind her of how and why she'd fallen in love with him so many years ago.

Before she could succeed, Reverend Wilson was saying, "We have gathered here tonight to join this man and this woman in holy matrimony. Under the watchful eye of the Lord . . ."

Matt's first thought on Christmas Eve had been to head straight for Whisky Row and get drunk enough to forget that the woman he loved was marrying another man. The forgetfulness would only be temporary, of course, and if he drank too much, he'd probably feel like a pile of horse manure in the morning. Given that, he'd most likely sleep past dawn in the bargain, which meant he'd miss out on Holly's surprise from Santa. In the face of all that, he wisely decided it would be best to stay right in his cabin for the night. For some damn fool reason, Matt wound up taking another walk around town instead, an insane journey that so far had led him around the courthouse square and past the Squat and Gobble Cafe no less than four times.

He'd left the cabin shortly after Rafe washed himself up, dressed in his best suit, and gathered his belongings to head out for his new life. It would have been so easy right then, as the son of a bitch ambled out the door, to just shoot him in the back and be done with it. Matt almost wished that he had it within himself to do such a thing, but he didn't. So, dammit all to hell, he couldn't.

Now here he was, still walking and torturing himself with the vague image of a single flicker of candlelight cavorting on the window shades at the little cafe. His own inner visions of what might be going on behind those shades were even worse, especially after a man dressed in the frock coat of a preacher stepped up to the door and began knocking on it. Shortly after that, Matt's stroll around town, not to mention his last hope, came to an abrupt end.

Slipping around behind a lamp pole, watching the scene before him like some kind of Peeping Tom, Matt saw the door to the Squat and Gobble Cafe open. With just the soft glow of a single candle to light her, he caught a tantalizing glimpse of Maggie as she invited the minister inside. She was wearing the white Christmas dress that looked so good against her honey-colored hair, and a wreath of tiny white flowers surrounded her head. Most devastating of all, Matt could easily see that she was smiling. Happy.

In all his days, through all the grisly sights and tortuous assignments, nothing before had ever had the power to reach into his guts and twist them so painfully as the picture he saw now, the image of a woman he didn't know. From this moment on, Matt had to convince himself that he and Maggie had never kissed, never clung to one another in an impassioned embrace, never dreamed of being together forevermore. Pretend, in fact, that they'd never met. That he'd never loved her.

Unwittingly, Maggie helped to make it easier for Matt to stop torturing himself and move on.

Still smiling, she closed the door behind the preacher and shut Matt out of her life forever.

Twenty-three

Bravery was easily the most recognized hallmark of any man sworn into the service of the Texas Rangers. There weren't many who surpassed Matt Weston when it came to that particular attribute, either.

All the accolades of his service record aside, Matt thought perhaps the bravest thing he'd ever done was to walk away on Christmas Eve after the cafe door closed—despite the fact that the woman he loved was just moments away from becoming Mrs. Rafe Hollister.

By early the next morning, that act of bravery also struck him as about the stupidest thing he'd ever done.

He'd hardly slept last night, and it showed. His eyes were those of a man who'd spent Christmas Eve on Whisky Row, even though Matt hadn't taken in so much as a drop of beer. He couldn't think straight either and had one hell of a time trying to get dressed. Because lighting a candle would remind him too much of that single flicker on Maggie's window shade, he put his clothes on in the dark. And washed up and combed his hair that way, too.

He set out for Maggie's place as the first light of dawn slipped over the horizon, but then had to hurry back to the cabin to collect the gifts he'd purchased earlier in the week; a deck of cards for Holly, and for her mother, a gilt and silver inkstand in the shape of a sleigh, complete with a fancy steel pen. If

Rafe Hollister didn't like the idea of Matt buying gifts for his family, he could just go stick his head into the well-used privy out back of the Little Feather Inn.

Matt didn't believe in giving much consideration to regrets. A man did what he did, and if it turned out wrong, he made damn sure that he didn't repeat the mistake. He did wish, however, that he could have stayed around Prescott long enough to find a puppy for Holly. Matilda was a nice, uncomplicated pet as pets went, but she wasn't particularly warm and cuddly, a quality any child would appreciate. Besides, there was the matter of that winter break the tortoise took from her little mistress and the world around her. Holly needed something to take up the slack. A big-eyed puppy would have filled that vacancy nicely. A young dog that Matt hand-picked especially for her.

By the time he neared Gurley Street and saw Gus and Hattie approaching from the east, the blood had begun to pound in Matt's temples. He was in no mood to face them, Rafe, and least of all, Maggie and Holly. It was sheer insanity to even try. What could he have been thinking when he promised Maggie that he'd come here today? He had no desire to see her on her first morning as Mrs. Rafe Hollister, her body soft and warm, fresh from her new husband's bed. Just thinking about it got Matt so upset, by the time he reached the cafe where Gus and Hattie were waiting for him, his fists were balled and his teeth were bared.

Hattie, who was grinning like a fool, didn't seem to notice his mood. She beamed as she said, "Merry Christmas, Captain Weston! Isn't it a lovely morning?"

Though he thought it the most dismal morning of his life, Matt said, "It sure is. Merry Christmas, Hattie."

Her husband was more observant. "Looks to me like you had a merrier Christmas Eve, Captain—the way of transgressors is hard."

Gus was mocking him, hurling biblical passages as if he

thought Matt deserved punishment of some kind. He couldn't figure out why the man had it in for him, and he supposed he should have set him straight, but Matt was just too damn tired and sick at heart to bother. If Gus wanted to believe that he'd been out drinking and whoring on Christmas Eve, then let him. Let the whole damn family think what they would.

Ignoring Gus, Matt cast a bloodshot eye at Hattie, who was humming away in that strange little world of hers. "Is Maggie up yet?" he asked. "I doubt she'd appreciate our barging in on her until she's good and ready for us."

"Maggie, still sleeping?" Gus grinned, spreading the tails of his mustache from ear to ear. "Not on this morning. With the grand surprise she has in store for us, she's probably been up for hours." He then opened the door to the cafe and gestured for Hattie and Matt to step inside. "Shall we?"

Although he entered the restaurant as directed, Matt hung to the rear of the little group as they trudged up the stairs to the tiny apartment. Gus beat on the door, but instead of waiting for Maggie to open it, he let himself in and urged the rest to follow. All Matt wanted to do was turn tail and run like hell.

"Anyone awake in here?" Gus called out as he stepped into the room.

"Yes!" Maggie's voice rang out, harmonizing with the church bells sounding all over town. "Come in, you two. Holly's awake and it's all I can do to keep her in her room."

Matt stood firm as Hattie followed her husband into the apartment, but then Gus glanced down and gestured for him to get his butt up the stairs. He'd rather have taken a beating, been drawn and quartered, or even skinned alive by Geronimo himself than set foot into the middle of the little family scene about to unfold, but there was no way out now.

As Matt inched his way into the room, Maggie glanced his way in surprise. "Oh, you're here, too. I was afraid you were going to miss all the excitement."

At the moment, the only sight Matt would have regretted missing was the luscious vision who stood before him. Maggie was wearing a lovely gown of emerald velvet, a color that looked even better on her than the white Christmas dress. Her hair was loosely tied at the nape of her neck with a simple red ribbon, leaving the bulk of it to wind down the back of that brilliant green velvet like a golden river of honey. Maggie's eyes, while shadowed with fatigue, were sparkling with excitement and her skin was more luminescent than it had ever been. Christ, but she was beautiful. So beautiful, in fact, Matt momentarily forgot that he and Maggie were not the only two people in the room.

"See what I mean, Maggie," said Rafe, who was sitting to the side of the Christmas tree. "He's a-gawking at y'all just like I said he does."

Matt sent a vicious look his way, but the fool just grinned in return. The new Lord of the Manor was wearing the broadcloth suit Matt had bought for his wedding and his hair was greased and slicked back. Polished as he may have appeared otherwise, he thrummed his bitten-down fingernails against his pant legs. He also bore the same dark shadows under his eyes that Maggie did, making it a sure bet that the two were worn out from their wedding night activities.

Just thinking about that made it impossible for Matt to acknowledge Rafe beyond a short nod. He quickly looked away from the fool and found himself caught in the very narrow gaze of Gus Townes. It was the kind of look Matt had seen often during his years as a ranger, a definite, deliberate challenge. If Gus wasn't known as such a God-fearing, Bible-spouting zealot, Matt would have dropped into an immediate crouch and drawn his weapon in self-defense.

"Is everyone ready for Holly's surprise?" said Maggie, breaking the deadlock between the two men. "I'm going to let her out of her room before she breaks down the door."

"I been ready for an hour," said Rafe.

"Where are we going?" asked Hattie.

Gus gently elbowed her ribs. "Hush up, darling. No one is going anywhere. We're waiting to see Holly get her present from Santa."

Matt didn't say anything, but no one seemed to care. Maggie glided off to her daughter's room, knocked lightly on the door and said, "Is anyone awake in there?"

"Yes, Mama!" came Holly's muted screech. "Can I come out now, please?"

"I guess so."

Maggie opened the door then, and out flew Holly, the hem of her nightgown and the tails of her robe flapping along behind her like wings as she raced across the room. Heading straight for the trio standing near the door instead of going to the Christmas tree where Rafe sat in wait, she bounded into Matt's arms.

"I *knew* you would come," she cried. "I knew it!"

Matt resisted the strong urge to kiss her and ruffle her pearly curls. "Merry Christmas," he said. "And happy birthday, you little devil."

Gus nudged him aside, even though Matt still held Holly in his arms, and kissed her round little cheek. "Merry Christmas, baby," he said to her.

"Happy birthday, sweetheart," said Hattie, pinching the spot her husband had just kissed.

By then Maggie had caught up to her daughter. "Holly, darling," she said. "Now that you've greeted everyone, are you ready to see what Santa brought you this year?"

"Yes, Mama." Her big eyes sparkled behind her spectacles, but they never left Matt's face.

"Well, sweetheart," Maggie went on to say, her hands twisted in knots. "You know how you've always wished that Santa would bring your daddy for Christmas?"

Still looking at Matt, Holly nodded even more rapidly.

"Santa searched and searched, and he finally found him."

Over Holly's head, Matt could see that Maggie's eyes were filling with tears. As she continued, her voice broke.

"Sweetheart—your very own daddy is here in this room."

"I knew it!" Holly cried, wrapping her arms around Matt's neck so tightly, she practically cut off his breathing. "I knew Captain Matt would be my daddy if I prayed hard enough! I knew it!"

Rafe, quiet in the corner by the tree until then, leapt out of his chair. "What the hell is that all about?"

Hattie, in her usual fog, looked at Maggie in bewilderment. "Why, how can Captain Weston be Holly's father, dear? I thought he just got into town."

"By all that's holy, wife," said Gus, his face suddenly as red as Santa's cap. "Can't you ever get anything straight? Weston isn't Holly's father—it's that fool over there."

"Now just a gol dang minute," said Rafe as he approached the group.

"I'll have none of that cussing," warned Hattie, waving the gaily wrapped package she'd been carrying. She then turned to Matt and said, "Didn't I once tell you that I thought you and Maggie made a nice couple? Why you should have mentioned that you two were already married, you rascal, you!"

Before Matt could straighten Hattie out, Holly slapped her little hands to both sides of his face, and squealed, "You and Mama gots married?"

"Dang it all, anyways," said Rafe, elbowing his way toward Matt. "Y'all turn loose of my girl this second, or I swear, I'm a-gonna beat the tar out a' ya right here and now."

"Good God, Hollister, get hold of yourself," Matt said. "I didn't start this damn mess, you did."

"I simply will not tolerate that language another minute!" Hattie punctuated that declaration by whopping Matt across the shoulders with her package, a gift shaped something like a banjo.

Holly pushed her away. "Don't be mad at my daddy, Aunt Hattie. He sometimes has mouth accidents and says bad words, but he doesn't mean them."

"He's not yur daddy," said Rafe, reaching out to her. "I am."

"Captain Matt is too my daddy," she insisted, refusing to even look at her father.

"Who's your daddy?" said Hattie, her eyeballs spinning.

"Goddang it to hell," said Rafe. "I am."

After that, all hell broke loose.

Hattie reached out with the same dented package she'd used on Matt and beat Rafe alongside the head with it, setting off a few dissonant chords from within the wrapping paper.

Rafe could have spouted every cuss word in the English language and Matt wouldn't have known it—he couldn't hear anything past Holly's screechy voice and Gus's blustery objections to everything anyone had to say.

Matt had just about decided to set Holly down so he could sneak out of the room and everyone's life for good, when Maggie finally restored some semblance of order to the group.

"That's enough!" she said, looking pale. After snatching Holly out of Matt's arms and into her own, she retreated over by the Christmas tree. "Please, everyone," she said. "Be quiet so I can clear up this mess once and for all."

It took a minute and several grumbles from the principals, but Maggie finally got the quiet she demanded. Catching Holly's little chin in one loving hand, she said, "Darling, please listen carefully. Captain Weston is not your daddy. Your real daddy is standing right next to him. Will you please come introduce yourself properly, Rafe?"

Without hesitation, he stepped forward. "The El Paso kid is just my nickname, little gal. I'm really Rafe Hollister, yur honest and real live daddy." He stretched out his arms. "Come give us a kiss."

For a heart-stopping moment, Holly looked back at Matt, disappointment clearly etched on her tiny features. Then she reached out to her father and allowed him to take her into his arms. Rafe moved away from the others, seeking a little privacy as he and his daughter murmured whatever it was they had to say to one another, and suddenly the formerly boisterous room was much too quiet.

Finally Hattie, who'd been unable to take her eyes off the reunion of Holly and her father, looked away long enough to say, "Are you sure about this, Maggie? I thought Mr. El Paso just came into town, too."

"Quite sure, Aunt Hattie." She laughed, easing the tension. "Rafe and I met years ago."

"But what about Captain Weston here?"

"He's a friend, a very good friend that Ben Sloan hired to track down Rafe." She turned to Matt and smiled. "We all owe the captain a very big thank-you now that my little secret is out in the open."

"Why, yes, I suppose we do. Thank you, Captain Weston, for making our little girl's wish come true." She sighed heavily. "I suppose this means that you and my Maggie will not be getting married after all?"

"Hattie!" said Gus. "By all that's holy, what in hell is it that makes you say such things?"

When the swearword fell from Gus's lips, his little dumpling of a wife staggered with horror and might even have toppled over had Matt not been there to catch her. When she regained her balance, Hattie swung her battered package at Gus and whopped him right smack on the top of his head.

Then she said, "Isn't it enough that everyone else seems to be cussing on Christmas Day—must you join in with them, you heathen, you?"

"I beg your forgiveness, darling wife," Gus said as he rubbed his head. "But sometimes the things that come out of that sweet mouth of yours, are enough to make a saint take the Lord's name in vain. Where do you get such ideas?"

As those two went on with their bickering, Matt saw that he and Maggie were alone—for the time being, anyway. Under his breath he said, "I guess I ought to be going now before Hattie decides that I'm your father or something equally as crazy."

"Please don't go. Not yet, anyway."

Maggie laid a gentle hand on his forearm and gave Matt a smile that made him weak in the knees.

"I really have to talk to you," she explained. "But first I have to know that everything will be all right between Holly and Rafe."

Together they glanced at the "new" father. He was sprawled on the floor with his daughter, playing with the doll she'd found beneath the Christmas tree.

"Thanks," said Matt, who'd seen enough. "I'd just as soon go now. It'll be easier that way."

He didn't feel the need to elaborate. Maggie, of all people, knew exactly what he meant and how much this scene must be hurting him. Again she gave him a smile worthy of taking his legs out from under him—this one a little secretive—and then Maggie turned toward her husband and daughter.

"Captain Weston is leaving for Texas now, Holly," she said. "Don't you want to say goodbye to him?"

Flinging her doll aside, she jumped up from the floor and raced across the room.

"How come you gotta go?" she asked, tears slipping under the rims of her glasses. "Can't you stay and be my daddy, too?"

Matt opened his mouth, but he didn't know what to say or how to say it. He wasn't even sure he could speak.

"Mama?" Holly tugged on Maggie's velvet gown. "Can I

please have two daddies, one for Christmas and one for my birthday?"

"I don't know if that's possible, darling."

"Anything's possible."

The voice sounded like Rafe's, but Matt could hardly believe that such a declaration could come from his mouth. Yet right after he said it, the luckiest bastard on the face of the earth climbed to his feet and swaggered across the room. Gus and Hattie were equally surprised, and hung on Rafe's every word as he continued his shocking statement.

"No one knows better than me that nothing's impossible," he went on to say. "And I got Captain Weston here to thank for it. If he hadn't dragged me outta Texas and brung me here, I might never have known any of y'all, much less my sweet little gal, Holly. Thanks, Captain. That there is one I owe y'all."

Since he couldn't bring himself to say "you're welcome," the best Matt could manage was, "Forget it. I was only doing my job."

"Well, *amigo,* it might surprise y'all to know that now I'm gonna do mine." That said, Rafe directed his comments to Gus and Hattie. "Since Maggie's kin is pretty much the closest thing I got to family, I want to be honest enough to tell y'all that there's some things I done in the past that I ain't too proud of. I reckon I made a mess of a few others here and there, too."

"Please, Mr. Hollister," said Gus. "Spare us the details of your sordid life."

"I wasn't gonna tell y'all the sorts a' things I done, just confess that I done a few of 'em. I done a lot of good, too," he boasted, puffing out his chest. "I'm about the best Indian fighter around, the fastest pony express rider this side of the Mississippi, and there ain't nobody faster on the draw—"

"Rafe," said Maggie, cutting his wild tales off before he proclaimed himself the next president of the United States. "Just tell them what you told me last night when Reverend Wilson stopped by."

"Right." Pausing a moment to work his way back to where he'd gotten sidetracked, Rafe said, "Since I always like to do the honorable thing, I asked Maggie would she marry up with me last night, all legal-like."

"What are you saying, young man?" said Gus. "That you and Maggie weren't legally married before?"

"Sure we was, legal as a ball and chain, but being the honorable fella that I am and all, I went and set her free a few years back."

"Set her free?" Gus scratched his head.

Hattie, still following the subject, came to a surprisingly reasonable conclusion. "You mean you divorced her?"

"That's right, ma'am. The minute I knew I was gonna be off fighting wars and such, I seen a judge to help me get shuck of that woman so's she could be free to wed again. I was kind enough to send Maggie a letter about the divorce and all, too, but she tells me she never got no letter. I reckon someone besides me was riding the pony express by then, or she'd a know'd we was divorced for sure. Yessireee."

"Divorce?" Gus bellowed, coughing a little. "What therefore God hath joined together, Margaret Mary—remember? There will be no divorce in this family!"

Standing beside Matt, Maggie didn't dare risk a glance in his direction to see what he thought of Rafe's "confession." She was having a hard enough time trying to control her own excitement as it was, despite Gus's reaction to Rafe's news. She'd known, of course, that her uncle wouldn't take kindly to the idea of divorce, but she'd agreed to the plan simply because it freed her from the obligation to marry Rafe—and it beat the devil out of telling Gus that Holly had been born out of wedlock. Divorce was a stigma Maggie could fight with her head held high, especially since Rafe had surprised her by being man enough to take the blame for the whole thing. Gus would probably never be happy about her status as a divorcée, but he wouldn't think less of her for it. And he would never look at Holly with the word "bastard" at the back of his mind.

Her heart going out to her uncle, Maggie did her best to calm him. "The divorce happened without my knowledge, but it did happen. No use arguing about it now. We didn't even plan on mentioning it since we were going to get married last night."

Hattie turned horrified eyes on Rafe. "You and Maggie were married last night? Without me as her matron of honor? How dare you, young man!"

For a moment Maggie thought she might go after Rafe again with what was left of her Christmas package, but again surprising her, he came to his own defense in the nick of time.

"There weren't no marriage, ma'am." This was the side of Rafe Maggie had first fallen in love with—the man who could, when pressed, think of others first. "I reckon since I left Maggie alone for so long, she went and got too set in her ways to put up with having a man underfoot. She couldn't go through with getting hitched to me again after all this time, and I cain't say that I blame her much."

From over her shoulder, Maggie heard Matt choke out the word, *"What?"*

She elbowed his ribs, tenderly, but pointedly. What they had to say to each other needed to be said in private.

Again addressing the group, Maggie said, "If we're all about out of surprises around here, I think I'll go downstairs and get busy with the coffee and our Christmas breakfast."

She started for the door, but turned back to add, "Matt? Would you mind giving me a hand?"

"I'd be *more* than happy to."

Before he took a step toward the door, Holly raced up and tugged on his pant leg. "But I don't want you to go, Captain Matt. Can't you stay here with us some more?"

"Damn right I can," he said gruffly.

"That's a bad word, you know."

"I know," he said, ruffling her blond curls. "I guess I'm going to have to work harder on not cussing."

"I can teach you how," she assured him. "You just got to say *thunderation* like Uncle Gus does when he can't catch the turkeys."

"Er, ah, Holly," said Gus, clearing his throat. "Get on over here and see what your Aunt Hattie brought you for Christmas—if there's anything left of it, that is."

Laughing to herself, Maggie continued on down the stairs. She was so tired and emotionally spent, she could barely see where she was going, but unless she'd misjudged the entire situation badly, she had a very good idea of where her future was heading. She also knew that soon she would finally have the chance to say the things she'd been longing to say to Matt for weeks. Things like how much she loved him—how much she'd always love him, no matter what happened now.

Moments later, he walked up behind her and slipped his arms around her waist. Pulling her tight against his body, he whispered into her hair, "Pinch me quick. If I'm dreaming, I want to know it now."

"It's no dream," Maggie said, feeling a little dreamy herself. "It's the best Christmas present I've ever had."

"Then you're not—he's not . . ."

"That's right." Turning in his arms, Maggie helped herself to a taste of Matt's lips before she went on. "Something in me wouldn't let me marry a man I don't really love—maybe it was the brandy."

"Brandy?"

"I'll explain that later. All I know is that when it came time for us to take our vows last night, I fainted dead away. Rafe revived me, of course, and that's when I convinced him to tell the preacher that I was too ill to continue. After Reverend Wilson left, the two of us had a very long talk."

"And that's it? Rafe agreed to the divorce just like that?"

"You may not want to, but you've got to give Rafe credit for this. It was all his doing, everything right down to his being a pony express rider."

Matt rolled his eyes and clutched his chest, which didn't surprise Maggie in the least. She'd expected this news might stun Matt a little—she herself had nearly fainted again when Rafe first came up with the idea.

"We were up half the night talking," Maggie said, determined to make sure he knew everything. "I couldn't think of a way to keep Holly's name from harm if we didn't marry as planned, so Rafe worked on the problem a while and came up with the idea of the divorce."

"Damn," Matt said, shaking his head. "I just can't believe this of him. Why would he do it? You didn't tell him about us, did you?"

"Oh, no." Not that she hadn't considered the idea. "I thought it would be better for our relationship to grow on him and everyone else slowly. Besides, I wasn't sure if you wanted to stay on in Prescott long enough for it to matter."

Matt's smile wasn't deeply dimpled, but lopsided and sexy as all get out. He kissed the tip of her nose and said, "We'll get around to that in a minute. First tell me about Rafe—Jesus, I never thought I'd say something like that to you."

Maggie laughed, but quickly grew serious as she said, "I know you haven't seen much good about him since you met, but Rafe did what he did today because he wanted to do something right, for a change. He wants to be a good man, Matt, but he's never had an honest chance before. I really believe that of him."

"Yeah, right," he said, grumbling under his breath. "I'll believe that when I see it."

"I think you just did. There's something else you ought to know while we're on the subject of Rafe Hollister."

Matt arched a skeptical eyebrow. "Let's see—you don't love him and you didn't marry him. I don't think that I give a damn about anything else where he's concerned."

"You might give a damn about this." Playing the innocent, Maggie lowered her chin, and peered up at him through her lashes. "In return for the story he made up about our divorce, I promised to go along with all his lies, you know, the grand stories he told Gus upstairs and even the, ah, one about being a Texas Ranger."

"You didn't." Matt fell back a couple of steps, clutching his chest again. "You wouldn't."

"I would," she admitted, "and I did, but only because backing his lies seemed like a really cheap price to pay for my freedom."

"Cheap, huh?" Matt didn't come to her or even smile. He folded his arms across his chest, then set his jaw in a frown. "This assignment was supposed to earn me a little money. So far it has cost me every last dime I earned, not to mention, eaten into my savings. Am I now expected to claim Rafe Hollister as one of my peers?"

She nodded. "If you don't mind too much."

"I mind all right, but it doesn't look like I have much choice—unless, of course, I'm not happy with your answer to my next question."

Hope soared in her, swelling her throat so much she could hardly say, "And that is?"

"I want to know how much more this job is going to cost me before it's over."

"I—I don't understand. The job is over. It won't cost you another cent."

He laughed. "I doubt that. Surely your newfound freedom comes with a very high price tag."

Maggie closed her eyes tightly as if thinking the idea over, but the gesture was just her way of stemming the tide rising up in her eyes. Did he mean what she hoped he did, dreamed he did?

Surprising her, Matt came to Maggie in the next moment and swept her into his arms. He began to kiss her, starting with her tightly closed eyes, then working his way across her cheeks and down to her mouth.

When he finally let her up for air, Matt's voice was husky as again he said, "How much more will this cost me, beautiful?"

This time, Maggie was ready with an answer. "The rest of your life, Captain Weston. My freedom will cost you every day of the rest of your life."

Epilogue

Much to Peggy's relief and supreme joy, Rafe married her on New Year's Day, 1882, one week after Christmas and one lousy day after Captain Weston went and married that giantess who'd tricked Rafe into fathering her daughter.

When Ben Sloan heard that Captain Weston had married and intended to stay on in Prescott, he tore off his tin star and slapped it on the captain's chest so fast, he darn near run the man through with the business end of the badge.

Peggy supposed she liked the captain well enough, but now that he was the law in Prescott, she steered clear of him whenever possible. After all, the man knew pretty much all there was to know about her—and she suspected that Captain Weston was the kind of man who didn't forget much. The only thing that had her confused about him was his choice in women.

What would any man with two good eyes see in a big ole gal like that Maggie, anyway? The captain was too good-looking and too much man to just up and settle. Peggy figured the big ranger must have somehow fallen in love with the consarned woman, but damned if she could understand how such a thing could have happened. The only thing she knew for sure regarding those two was that the captain didn't marry Maggie because she tricked him the same way she'd tricked Rafe.

Oh, Captain Weston's wife was in a family way all right, as big as a bass fiddle around the belly, in fact, but she had a few weeks to go yet. Enough anyway to fit into the acceptable time frame between a wedding and a firstborn child.

It was on account of Maggie's expected baby that Peggy was a little jealous of those two. She and Rafe had been trying to start a family, but she hadn't caught just yet. Maybe her body just needed a little more time to get over all the abuse she'd suffered at the hands of her customers during her years of whoring. In the meantime Peggy was content to make a decent home for her man, and keep his clothes cleaned and pressed.

Because Rafe's work took him into the more heavily forested areas, their cabin was located several miles north of Prescott. Going to town to visit his daughter and pick up supplies wasn't much trouble for Rafe, but it was a good long journey for Peggy, who had to ride in a borrowed wagon or buggy on the rare occasions she ventured into Prescott. Of course, that was just fine with her. For now, anyway, keeping her distance from the townsfolk was in her best interests, especially if she ever hoped to have a child of hers attend school with the other children.

More than just a couple of men in town had intimate knowledge of Peggy's former occupation. It wasn't a bad idea to give them plenty of time to forget about her before she went strutting down the street like any other high-born lady. Even if there wasn't a soul in Prescott who'd let on about her whoring days, plenty of them knew that she'd tried to kill Maggie, a silly little mistake that wouldn't soon be forgotten by the more uppity types in town.

All that considered, Peggy figured that living so far outside of town wasn't such a bad thing. And it did keep Rafe fairly close to her while he was at work. She was so proud of him and the clever way he got himself such an important job. After introducing himself as The El Paso Kid to the man who was in charge of the sawmill, all he had to do was mention the name Virgil Earp—who happened to be the mill's former owner. After that it was just a matter of convincing the man that he was an old friend of Earp's, and that Virgil thought Rafe would make a fine boss for a crew of loggers.

After that, Rafe explained, he just stood there fingering the handle of his gun while the man thought about hiring him, and the next thing he knew, he was a foreman in charge of the biggest work crew! It probably didn't hurt that word from Tombstone had recently reached Prescott about the bloodbath between the Earps and the Clantons a couple of months back. Whatever the reason for Rafe's success, Peggy was feeling mighty grateful. She thought, in fact, that she'd never been more content in her entire life. Only one thing was missing that would make her joy complete—a tiny little bundle from heaven.

A sudden thought struck Peggy right between the eyes. Maybe all she had to do to make sure that her wish came true was to follow the same path Rafe's daughter had chosen.

Yes! by God—if she didn't have a baby coming by next Christmas, all she had to do was march right on up to Santy Claus and tell him to bring her one. In fact, she might even tell him to go ahead and bring two.

Author's Note

Prescott, Arizona, has long been a favorite travel destination of mine. When I discovered that this charming little town also billed itself as Arizona's official "Christmas Town," I knew I had to set *Maggie's Wish* there.

In addition to the towns I explore in the name of research, the particular era is also very important to me. I chose the year 1881 for this novel because so much was happening in the burgeoning states and territories at the time. Not only was our President James A. Garfield assassinated, leaving Chester A. Arthur to fill in as president, but Billy the Kid was gunned down by Sheriff Pat Garrett, and the Earps took on the Clantons at the O.K. Corral. On a lighter note, Barnum & Bailey's Greatest Show on Earth opened in March, the American Red Cross was founded in May, and Pablo Picasso was born in October. All in all, a very interesting year.

For me half the fun of researching a town and its history comes with the on-site research. In this case since Prescott is only a day's drive from my home in California, my husband and springer spaniel Murphy joined me in the motor home to make the trip. We camped in an area known in 1881 as Point of Rocks (now called Granite Dells), then together we roamed the courthouse square you read about in the story. I for one could easily imagine Matt's frustration as he lapped that square the night of Maggie's wedding. Since I'm a stickler for detail, we also studied Whisky Row at length, in the name of research of course, and wondered what Maggie would think if she could see us threading our way through the establishments there.

I hope I was able to bring the town and its inhabitants as alive for you in the pages of *Maggie's Wish* as they were for me. I'd love to hear your thoughts about the book and its setting. I can be reached at P.O. Box 1176, El Cajon, CA 92019; by e-mail at: s.ihle@poboxes.com; or on the internet at:
http://romance-central.com/SharonIhle.

About the Author

Sharon Ihle is the best-selling author of eleven historical romances set in the American West. In addition to traveling, research as well as pleasure trips, she enjoys hanging out at the beaches near her Southern California home, fishing in nearby mountain lakes, and making a nuisance of herself at her daughter's home in London, England.

ROMANCE FROM JO BEVERLY

DANGEROUS JOY   (0-8217-5129-8, $5.99)

FORBIDDEN   (0-8217-4488-7, $4.99)

THE SHATTERED ROSE   (0-8217-5310-X, $5.99)

TEMPTING FORTUNE   (0-8217-4858-0, $4.99)

Available wherever paperbacks are sold, or order direct from the Publisher. Send cover price plus 50¢ per copy for mailing and handling to Kensington Publishing Corp., Consumer Orders, or call (toll free) 888-345-BOOK, to place your order using Mastercard or Visa. Residents of New York and Tennessee must include sales tax. DO NOT SEND CASH.

ROMANCE FROM JANELLE TAYLOR

ANYTHING FOR LOVE   (0-8217-4992-7, $5.99)

DESTINY MINE   (0-8217-5185-9, $5.99)

CHASE THE WIND   (0-8217-4740-1, $5.99)

MIDNIGHT SECRETS   (0-8217-5280-4, $5.99)

MOONBEAMS AND MAGIC   (0-8217-0184-4, $5.99)

SWEET SAVAGE HEART   (0-8217-5276-6, $5.99)

Available wherever paperbacks are sold, or order direct from the Publisher. Send cover price plus 50¢ per copy for mailing and handling to Kensington Publishing Corp., Consumer Orders, or call (toll free) 888-345-BOOK, to place your order using Mastercard or Visa. Residents of New York and Tennessee must include sales tax. DO NOT SEND CASH.

ROMANCE FROM FERN MICHAELS

DEAR EMILY   (0-8217-4952-8, $5.99)

WISH LIST   (0-8217-5228-6, $6.99)

AND IN HARDCOVER:

VEGAS RICH   (1-57566-057-1, $25.00)

Available wherever paperbacks are sold, or order direct from the Publisher. Send cover price plus 50¢ per copy for mailing and handling to Kensington Publishing Corp., Consumer Orders, or call (toll free) 888-345-BOOK, to place your order using Mastercard or Visa. Residents of New York and Tennessee must include sales tax. DO NOT SEND CASH.